MY ONLY

A MY FIRST, MY LAST SPINOFF

BROOKELYN MOSLEY

85 MEDIA LLC

ISBN (eBook): 978-1-965507-40-7

ISBN (Paperback): 978-1-965507-52-0

First Edition, 2025

Published by 85 Media LLC

85 Media LLC

6614 Avenue U # 575

Brooklyn, NY 11234-6021

www.BrookelynMosley.com

Home is where the heart is.

— UNKNOWN

BYBK EXCLUSIVES

Bed Bully
Stuck
LHR Rewind Series
Home Before Midnight
Maybe This Time Will Be Different
Lovekilla
Incoming Call
Rough
WYD
Drinks on Me
Cali & Lee
Ray & Jay
Living Out a Love Song
Glimpses
One Mic
With Love, Ayanna & Dallas
Just Friends
Lena's Ex-File
Dream Boss
Chateau Luxure

MORE BY BROOKELYN MOSLEY

Links to the below stories can be found here (https://brookelynmosley.com/ebooks-paperbacks/)

Novels/Novellas/Novelettes/Series

- No Fraternizing, Pt. 1
- No Fraternizing, Pt. 2
- No Fraternizing, Pt. 3
- First Came Love: The Love, Hate & Revenge Prequel
- Love, Hate & Revenge, Pt. 1
- Love, Hate & Revenge, Pt. 2
- Love, Hate & Revenge, Pt. 3
- Girl Code
- Mr. & Mrs. Jones
- Forbidden: An Anthology
- They Call Me Mello
- A Love Deferred
- Indecent Arrangement
- Last Comes Love
- Ebb & Flow
- PRIDE
- Meant To Be
- LUST
- Loveless
- GREED
- Rekindled
- My First, My Last

• ENVY

• Ready or Not

• So This is Love

• Home Before Midnight

• GLUTTONY

• When Luke Met Juliette

• When Life Gives You Sunsets

• In Love, I Trust

• Wrath

• Sloth

• Raising Love

Short Stories

• Unsilent Knight

• Twice In Love

• Home For Christmas

MESSAGE FROM THE AUTHOR

Thank you for purchasing *My Only*, the spinoff of *My First, My Last*. This story has been years in the making—living rent-free in my mind since I finished the friends-to-lovers tale it follows.

While I highly recommend reading *My First, My Last* for full context, *My Only* stands on its own, so feel free to dive in now and start your journey.

There are no major trigger warnings, aside from moments of grief as Ayla processes her father's loss during 9/11 in New York.

This book marks both an ending and a beginning: it concludes the love story of two of my favorite characters and introduces Greene Gardens, a new setting in my world. I hope you enjoy this next chapter in Ayla and Hassani's love journey as much as I loved writing it.

Thank you again. Enjoy!

Love,

BK

P.S. There are some character cameos in My Only. You can find links to those characters' original stories in the Character Cameos section of this book.

PROLOGUE

NOW – EARLY SUMMER 2023... PRESENT DAY

yla

I SIGHED, TRYING TO STOP MY STOMACH MUSCLES FROM TWISTING. When that didn't work, I rolled my tongue around in my mouth, immediately tasting the bitter aftertaste of the coffee, I'd had two hours prior.

I'd been sitting in the same spot since 10 p.m.

It was now 2 a.m.

And Hassani was still not home.

I shook my head and attempted to loosen the tension in my jaw, but it clenched right back.

The kitchen was dimly lit, with only the stovetop light on. The soft orange glow cast faint shadows around the room. It seemed like the shadows grew darker the longer I sat there.

My eyes drifted to the plate of food still sitting on the kitchen table across from me. I rubbed my lips together at the sight of it.

I'd peeked at it too many times since I placed it there hours ago—

before I'd woken up, after turning in at nine, only to realize my husband still wasn't home.

My eyes burned like hell. Beyond the exhaustion from lack of sleep, my mind had been working on overdrive, creating scenarios to fill in the blanks reality had left.

I was alone in this big-ass house… again.

I rolled my eyes and turned toward the fresh cup of coffee I'd brewed. My second cup. The first was at midnight. I made both just to stay awake—because I couldn't bring myself to fall asleep in our bed again, only to wake up wondering how late he got home this time.

His absence was because of the Greene Gardens Project.

Hassani becoming the principal architect responsible for the commercial and residential properties in the new upstate development had been a thorn in my ass I couldn't pull out. Sure, his involvement had changed our lives in great ways, but it also had him staying out late, spending time with a particular person he had no business spending time with, and pissing me off every fucking day.

I should've said something sooner. When his late nights started happening too frequently, I should have spoken up instead of worrying about sounding like the proverbial nagging wife.

Because this was ridiculous.

My focus snapped to the clock on the stove just as the time changed to 2:05. My attention kept bouncing between the plate of food and the time… constant reminders that he wasn't here.

I inhaled a deep breath and stood. Padding my way to the kitchen window, I leaned over the sink, trying to get a glimpse of the front of the house.

I didn't know what I expected to find. Maybe a part of me half-expected to see Hassani's car in the driveway. Or to see him stepping out of it just as I went to look.

And would that have made shit any better? Would it have been any less fucked up to see him arriving home at two in the morning?

I pressed my lips together and bit the inside of my cheek as I ruminated on that question.

The thought of calling him had crossed my mind at least five times. First, when I got out of bed. Then, when I checked our home office, thinking I'd find him sketching in that sketchbook of his, like always. If he had been in there, I would have teased him about it like I always do, saying that sketchbook was his Bible.

Twice, I thought about calling him as I sat at the kitchen table for the past four hours.

And now, the thought returned.

Because something had to have happened for him to still be out this late.

Despite my concern, my thoughts kept drifting to deceit and betrayal.

I returned to my seat at our kitchen table, slid my coffee closer, and took a sip. A few minutes later, the lock on the front door clicked, breaking the silence in the house.

I turned my head in that direction, setting my mug down. Hassani's footsteps were heavy as he made his way down the corridor from the front door to the kitchen. I picked up on the faint sigh and suppressed groan that escaped him.

His silhouette made me straighten in my chair. Even in the dimly lit kitchen, I could tell his appearance was disheveled. When he flicked on the kitchen light, my heart sank the moment our eyes met.

"Oh, shit!" He slapped a hand to his chest. "Baby?" He chuckled nervously. "Damn. I ain't even know you were in here."

I said nothing. Still too busy analyzing his appearance.

His tie was loosened, the top buttons of his dress shirt undone and slightly wrinkled. His sleeves were rolled all the way up to his fore-arms—something he only did when he was home and trying to relax before getting undressed.

I squinted as I continued assessing him. And the longer I observed, the angrier I got.

He froze in front of me, the forced smile on his lips disappearing. His eyes darted along my face.

The guilt in his hazel-green eyes was so evident I could touch it.

"Baby," he started, his tone soft, almost apologetic. "Why you just sitting there all quiet?"

I said nothing.

I couldn't move my tongue from the roof of my mouth long enough to speak. The disheveled clothing, the late arrival home, his tone, his body language… I felt myself short-circuiting.

For the past year, there were so many nights I'd stayed up waiting for him—watching the clock, listening for the door—before finally giving up and just going to bed.

It started with him coming home late once. Then it became twice a week. Eventually, it was an every-night thing. Sometimes, I only knew he had returned when he caressed my skin in the middle of the night, waking me from sleep. If not for that, I would've thought he never made it home at all.

And I always gave Hassani the benefit of the doubt. Always assumed he was just working late. The Greene Gardens Project was massive, so I figured work was keeping him away.

Tonight, though?

Shit just felt… *different.*

"Ayla," he said. "Why are you still up—"

"Where were you?" I interjected. My voice was hoarse and heavy. I almost didn't recognize it.

He opened his mouth to say something but then closed it. All I got from him was a hard swallow.

I scoffed, a bitter laugh escaping me. I exhaled every ounce of air in my lungs, not wanting to ask my next question but knowing I had to.

"Were you out with Harper, Hassani?"

He shut his eyes and sighed. "Ayla—"

"Yes or no," I spoke over him, my chest rising and falling so fast the influx of air made me lightheaded.

"I *was,*" he admitted. "But then my—"

"God." I exhaled sharply. After a brief pause, I said, "Hassani, I *can't* do this shit anymore."

I shook my head slowly. The moment the words left my lips, I felt the sting in my nose, the welling of tears in my eyes.

"I can't do this, and I don't want to."

"Ayla—"

"Every fucking night since you started this project, Hassani, has been hell for me."

He closed his eyes and dropped his head forward.

"This woman you're working with… *hmph*." I laughed bitterly once more but inhaled a deep breath after, one that ached in my chest. "She is up to something, and I'm *tired* of telling you about her. Tired of you making excuses. Tired of you making me feel like I'm acting crazy. And yet, here you are, walking into this house at this hour, telling me you were out with her."

"Nah, man," he tried. "You didn't let me finish—"

"Were you or were you not out with her, Hassani?" I exhaled.

"I… I was, but, baby, not for—"

"I want…" The words were right there, caught in my throat, suffocating me as I tried to hold them back. I shook my head, squeezed my eyes shut, feeling the tears well behind them. The words burned as I tried to swallow them down.

"A," Hassani started, "Baby, I—"

"I want a divorce."

Hassani staggered back as if I had physically struck him. His hand fisted at his chest, right over his heart.

If the house had been silent before, the silence doubled now. My words carried weight, crashing to the floor between us, cracking the stone beneath our feet, breaking something between us, too.

"Ayla," he said, stepping toward me. I held up a hand, stopping him.

I had thought about it before but never actually said the words out loud. Never thought I'd ever have to.

But I'd had enough.

My resolve was clear, and for the first time, I didn't feel like I was carrying a heavy anvil on my heart.

I wanted out of this… out of these feelings, away from these doubts.

And I wanted out now.

I stood from my seat.

"A. Boogie," Hassani whispered, his voice breaking.

That almost made me falter. Almost.

But I kept moving, my steps quick, determined.

He reached for me as I passed, but I slapped his hand away.

"Fuck, Ayla, come on, *don't do* this right now."

I turned back, my lips trembling as I fought like hell to hold in the cry threatening to burst through.

"I've been losing you for months, Hassani." I inhaled shakily. "But tonight?" I met his gaze, my voice barely above a whisper. "You lost *me*."

The pressure in my throat made it impossible to breathe as I walked toward the guest bedroom.

"Ayla, please—"

His voice shattered behind me as I stepped inside and slammed the door shut.

PART I
THE BLUEPRINT

The original plan. The beginning... when the vision is first imagined...

CHAPTER 1

THEN – MID-SPRING 2017... SIX YEARS EARLIER

*A*yla

THE MOMENT MY MOTHER AND I STEPPED ONTO THE AISLE, IT FELT LIKE stepping into a dream. The ocean waves rolled in soft harmony beneath a steel drum band playing a reggae rendition of *Endless Love*.

And when Hassani and I locked eyes, I had to inhale a deep breath to keep it together.

My mother sniffled beside me, and I swear it only took one glance from me for her to start crying the cry she'd been holding in all over again.

I couldn't help but snort a laugh at her. "Mama, please."

"I'm sorry, beloved." She dabbed at her eyes while looking away.

She'd been crying all morning. If I'm being honest, she'd been crying since we landed in Montego Bay, Jamaica.

My mother designed and sewed wedding dresses for a living, so you'd think she'd be used to the emotional weight of weddings. But I guess because this one was her daughter's, it just hit differently.

I never imagined my wedding would happen like this—spontaneous, breathtaking, and so completely us. But when Hassani looked at me one night and said, "Let's just do it," I knew there was no other way.

"What?" I asked, rolling over to face him in bed.

It had been four years since we made things official. Two years since he proposed—right after I stepped out of the shower, fresh from our visit to the National September 11 Memorial & Museum. But between Hassani's grueling architecture projects and the clients who kept recommending him to other entrepreneurs, his work schedule was rarely free.

We'd agreed that once his latest project wrapped up, we would start planning our wedding. Our parents had grown tired of waiting and brought it up every chance they got.

"Let's just get married in May," he said.

"That's in two months."

He smiled. "I know."

I giggled. "I remember the last time you said 'let's just do it' and proposed we get married in a month. That was two years ago."

And part of me was grateful we hadn't rushed it. But saying yes to that leap, even back then, had built a deeper trust between us—one that only grew stronger over time.

"That's why I'm saying let's just do it now... but this time, for real." His smile grew wider. "Look, work's always going to be work. And while I'm grateful for the projects coming in, I'm tired of waiting to say 'I do.'"

I smiled back, shaking my head. "Where the hell are we going to get married in two months?"

Jamaica.

I had never been to the island, but both of Hassani's parents were born and raised there.

He promised it would be the perfect setting for our nuptials—stunning, intimate, and something we could pull off in little time.

"You two are like a getaway, Favorite Girl," my Aunt Laurie had said when I told her where we'd be having the wedding. "So, it makes total sense to have a destination wedding."

She was the first person I spotted as my mother and I stepped onto the aisle. Aunt Laurie dabbed at her eyes with a tissue, her smile so grand it made me stutter a breath.

I had never imagined my wedding. Never saw myself in a big, puffy dress. A traditional church wedding didn't feel right for me. So a destination wedding?

That made sense.

"You've been patient for way too long," Hassani had told me once we agreed to say our vows in Jamaica. *"And I'm ready to make you Mrs. Franklin like yesterday."*

"Like yesterday" was today.

On a serene beach at sunset, on an aisle lined with colorful tropical flowers—hibiscus, orchids—lit by soft lanterns glowing all around us as the sun dipped below the horizon, I walked toward my future. Toward a waiting Hassani and our officiant, my arm looped through my mother's.

What no one knew was that this morning, I cried like I hadn't cried in a while.

Before I faced the world and got swept into the whirlwind of my wedding day, I let myself bawl.

I may have never dreamed of my wedding, but I knew that when the time came, my father would walk me down the aisle.

I wished he could see me like this—happy, in love, on the arm of the woman who raised me.

I imagined him cracking a joke under his breath, probably making some remark about Hassani's nerves. The thought made me smile, even as the ache of his absence pressed against my ribs.

I blinked, pushing away the sting of tears.

This was a day for love.

And love, I knew, had a way of carrying us through loss.

Yet and still, it hurt me deep in a place I couldn't reach to soothe— that my dad wasn't here. There wasn't a day I didn't miss him, no matter how much time had passed.

My mother tightened her grip on my biceps as we moved farther down the aisle.

Expecting to see fresh tears in her eyes, I glanced at her again, only to be met with a huge smile.

"You look beautiful, Ayla," she whispered. "So very beautiful."

I smiled.

"And I know I've said that a lot today, but you truly do."

"Well, I had the best seamstress in the world to make my dress."

She giggled. "I don't just mean *the dress*, Ayla." My mother leaned in, hugging my arm a little tighter. "There's not enough lace in the world to compete with the natural glow you have today, beloved."

We were only steps away when she added, "Your father would have been so proud. *I'm* very proud of you."

The tears I thought I had under control threatened to fall. I had to fight like hell to keep them back.

I focused ahead, finding Hassani watching me as I approached. He must've swallowed at least twenty times as I got closer, visibly emotional. His hazel-green eyes glistened, his lids slightly red-rimmed as he fought back tears of his own.

I could not believe us.

Over here being so damn emotional.

He looked amazing in a tailored linen suit, a boutonnière of tropical flowers pinned to his chest.

We were *finally* doing it.

And as much as I was overjoyed, a small part of me was nervous too. These past four years, after reconnecting, had been nothing but bliss. I wondered if we could maintain that as husband and wife.

The moment my mother and I reached the end of the aisle, Hassani's smile was so wide I could count every one of his teeth. That just made my smile even bigger.

Our officiant, Reverend Malachi Harte, smiled brightly at us. Hassani's parents, Joslyn and Percy Franklin, had known Reverend Harte their whole lives—they'd all grown up together. Mr. and Mrs. Franklin had promised he would be the best person to officiate our wedding, explaining how he was known in the community for his deeply personal and meaningful messages for couples.

"Good evening, family and friends," Reverend Harte began. "We are gathered here today, under the setting sun and the watchful eye of the Creator, to celebrate a love that is pure, steadfast, and inspiring."

My mother nodded softly.

"Ayla and Hassani," he continued, glancing between us, "you have chosen this beautiful place, surrounded by the sea and sky, as the setting for the vows you are about to make." He gestured with a hand. "A place as vast and enduring as the love you share. Today, we honor not just the union of two hearts but the bond of two souls who have chosen to walk through life together, side by side."

Then, Reverend Harte turned to my mother.

"So now, I ask: Who gives this woman to be married to this man?"

I glanced at my mother just as she turned to me, pride and love shining in her brown eyes.

"With all my love," she said, her voice steady. "*I do.*"

I had to press my lips together to keep from completely losing it. It had always been hard for me not to cry when I saw my mother crying, and today was no different.

She leaned in and kissed my cheek, then gently placed my hand in Hassani's, smiling at him even bigger than she had at me before stepping aside. She moved toward her seat in the front row, settling in beside Mrs. Franklin, with Aunt Laurie to her right.

Our guest list was small. Intimate.

We'd only invited those we loved and who could fly out of the country on short notice. One of those people we loved included my best friend, Sunni, and her husband, Josiah, who sat just behind my mother.

The soft caress of Hassani's thumb over the back of my hand had me turning my head to focus on him. The second our eyes met, I smiled so big my cheeks ached.

"You look so beautiful, my God," he whispered as we faced forward. "Like… damn, A."

My dress was one my mother had closed all her bookings to create. She worked morning, noon, and night to make it perfect.

I told her I didn't know exactly what I wanted—just that it had to be white and that it couldn't make me hot.

She came up with a plunging neckline, floral, flowy lace design. Spaghetti straps. Delicate patterns of subtle palm leaves. Very boho and beachy, with the most stunning train—just enough, not over the top.

My mama was a genius.

And I knew I could trust her to make a dress that would do me justice.

She had insisted I pair it with a floral crown. Had insisted I pull my hair back into a bun, too. The final result?

Hassani only saw me at the altar.

"Marriage is not just a partnership," Reverend Harte said, his gaze sweeping over us. "It is a covenant. A sacred promise to love, honor, and cherish each other in *all* seasons of life."

"Amen," Mrs. Franklin said from her seat.

"There will be sunny days like today, filled with laughter and light," he continued. "But there may also be stormy ones." He lifted a finger. "On those stormy days, when the clouds gather and the waters rise, it will be your love, Ayla and Hassani, and your *commitment* that see you through."

I nodded.

"Marriage is not built in a single day." Reverend Harte smiled. "It is like the finest of homes. It takes patience, care, and a strong foundation to stand the test of time. And when the cracks appear, as they sometimes will, it is up to you both to repair them, to rebuild together, and to *never* stop adding new layers of love."

He paused.

"Because, as they say, home is where the heart truly is."

Reverend Harte held his hand out toward our small gathering of guests.

"To all who are gathered here," he began, "you are not just witnesses, *yuh* know?! You are part of this union. Ayla and Hassani have invited you here because you are their family, their friends, their village. Your love and support will surround them as they build their life together."

His eyes scanned the faces of our friends and family.

"So, as they exchange their vows, I ask you to hold them in your hearts, to lift them up in your prayers, and to remind them, in moments of doubt and uncertainty, of the beauty we have all seen here today."

Hassani had not let go of my hand once, and I couldn't help but blush at that.

In every conversation leading up to this trip, he had told anyone who would listen that he was getting married. It always made me laugh.

At Reverend Harte's direction, we turned to face each other to exchange our vows.

We had written them separately, promising to have them ready in time for our big day. And while the words had come straight from my heart, speaking them now—here, surrounded by the sea and sky, standing in front of him—made them feel even more charged.

"Hassani," I began, "from the moment we met, you've been the light that brings laughter and ease to my days. You are the dreamer when I'm the realist."

Reverend Harte chuckled softly.

"And the optimist when I'm afraid to hope." I nodded. "In you, I've found a partner, a friend, and a love that reminds me every day that life is better when shared."

Hassani closed his eyes and nodded at my words.

"I vow to stand beside you, even when life gets messy, to celebrate your wins as if they're my own, and to build a life with you that reflects all the joy and love we share. Today, I choose you. Forever."

"Damn," he whispered before a bright smile pulled at his beautiful lips.

"Beautiful," Reverend Harte commented. "And now, Hassani."

Hassani folded his bottom lip into his mouth and bit down as a smile pulled at the corners. "A. Boogie."

I tossed my head back in laughter as the crowd echoed with their own.

"Ayla, you are my foundation, baby," he continued, his voice steady, filled with emotion. "The steady ground beneath me when life feels unsteady. The spark that inspires me to dream bigger than I ever thought possible."

He licked his lips, shaking his head slightly. "Man, when I look at you... *hmph*."

I squeezed his hand, inhaling deeply to hold back my tears.

"I see a woman who challenges me, believes in me, and *loves* me."

I felt the weight of his words in my chest.

"You've taught me that love isn't just about the big moments, but the quiet ones. Those mornings over coffee, those nights spent dreaming together over red wine."

I stared into Hassani's eyes, feeling something stir deep inside me.

We had been together for four years, and while our love had always been strong, on this day, in this moment, it felt richer—stronger—something potent and undeniable.

"I vow to honor the woman you are, to never stop learning how to love you better, and to always come back to you, no matter how far life takes us." His grip on my hand tightened. "Today, I promise to build not just a home, but a life worthy of you."

Afterward, Hassani held my gaze for a moment longer before giving a small nod toward Reverend Harte, silently signaling that he was done.

"My God," Reverend Harte murmured, drawing our attention back to him. "*Dem* vows deep, man—*woi!*"

Laughter and applause broke out behind us, voices calling out their approval.

"Okay, all right," Reverend Harte said, grinning. "Let us dry our eyes here..."

More chuckles from the crowd.

"...and proceed." He gestured. "May I have the rings?"

Hassani and I had chosen not to have a maid of honor or best man, so we were responsible for our rings.

I had kept his on my thumb during the ceremony, and he carried mine in his pocket. We handed them to Reverend Harte, who held them in his hands for a brief prayer before passing them back to us.

"Ayla and Hassani," Reverend Harte said, his voice warm, "these rings are more than simple bands of white gold and diamonds." He looked between us. "They are a circle with no beginning and no end… just as your love has no limits."

I blinked back my tears.

"When you look at these rings in the years to come, may they remind you of this day, this moment, and the promises you have made to each other."

Reverend Harte gestured for Hassani to place the ring on my finger.

Hassani took my hand, biting his bottom lip as he smiled, then repeated the words the Reverend told him.

"With this ring," Hassani began, holding my gaze, "I give you my heart, my soul, and my unwavering commitment." He nodded, as if sealing his own words. "Let it be a symbol of my love for you, today and always."

Reverend Harte then turned to me.

"Ayla, repeat after me."

I took a steady breath and followed his words, holding Hassani's ring just before slipping it onto his finger.

"With this ring, I give you my heart, my soul, and my unwavering commitment. Let it be a symbol of my love for you, today and always."

And with that, I slid the ring onto Hassani's finger.

Reverend Harte smiled.

"Now, by the authority vested in me by the great island of Jamaica and the love of God," he declared, "it is my great joy and privilege to pronounce you husband and wife."

Mr. Franklin's booming voice rang out behind us, his cheers and applause making both Hassani and me laugh.

"Hassani," Reverend Harte said, his grin wide. "You may now kiss your bride!"

Hassani and I turned to each other, exchanging a mischievous grin.

But instead of going straight for the kiss, as Reverend Harte suggested, we stepped apart and extended our hands, clapping them together twice—our palms meeting with a soft smack that echoed lightly in the air.

Reverend Harte's chuckle turned into a full-blown laugh.

Hassani and I smirked as we raised our right fists, tapped our knuckles together, followed with a quick high five, then spun around, back to back, and slapped our hands together again in sync.

Our secret handshake, one we'd been practicing long before this day, ended with us facing each other again, our pinkies linking as we held eye contact.

Hassani whispered, "No take-backs."

I winked. "Forever us."

Laughter erupted behind us just as Hassani pulled me toward him, still linked by our pinkies.

He pressed a soft kiss to where our fingers joined before pulling me even closer—his other arm wrapping around me, his lips meeting mine in a deep, lingering kiss.

The crowd behind us cheered, laughed, clapped.

"As they walk down this aisle together for the first time as husband and wife," Reverend Harte announced over the noise, "let us all rise in celebration of Ayla and Hassani, whose love reminds us of what is possible when people come together with open hearts and open hands. Ladies and gentlemen, please put your hands together…"

Hassani pressed one last soft peck to my lips.

"…for Mr. and Mrs. Franklin!"

OUR FIRST DANCE WAS TO CASE'S "HAPPILY EVER AFTER," PLAYED BY the steel drum band that had been performing R&B renditions throughout the night.

I had experienced a whirlwind of emotions that evening, but nothing compared to the moment we gathered around the very large circular table for the speeches.

My mother started them off… and sent us all into tears.

She lifted her glass, her warm smile shining as she brought the mic to her lips, her eyes glistening with emotion.

"Ayla, I knew you were destined for something beautiful the moment you came into this world."

Hearing her say only that, almost made me burst into tears.

"Standing here today, seeing the woman you've become and the man you've chosen to be your husband, I couldn't be prouder. Your father *loved* Hassani from the moment he met him and told me that night when we were alone, 'Sonia, I just met my son-in-law.'"

I dropped my head, and Hassani pulled me in close, letting me lean against his chest.

"I know without a doubt that your father is smiling down on you right now, so very proud of his baby girl. I can feel his presence here all around us."

Hassani pressed a soft kiss to my forehead as I lifted my head to sniff back my tears.

"I want you two to know that marriage is about love, yes." My mother nodded. "But it's also about patience, understanding, and choosing each other every single day. Hold onto that, and you will be fine for all the rest of your days."

She raised her glass, her voice steady despite the emotion in her eyes.

"Hassani, take care of my daughter. And Ayla, take care of my son."

Hassani and I glanced at each other and leaned in for a quick kiss.

"To love, to laughter, and to forever," my mother finished. "Cheers."

The soft clinking of glasses filled the air, mingling with sniffles and quiet laughter.

A tear trickled down my face, but before it could fall all the way, Hassani was quick to catch it with his thumb.

"Hassani and Ayla," Mr. Franklin said, standing up in front of his seat.

Mrs. Franklin rose beside him, the evening breeze combing through her soft hair.

"Ayla, your mother has moved us all to tears," Mr. Franklin said. "So now it fall on me to make you laugh from *yuh* belly."

Laughter rippled through the gathering.

I wiped at my eyes, still grinning.

"Just like your mother said," Mr. Franklin added, gesturing to my mom beside Aunt Laurie, "your father's presence is here with us. Very much so."

I nodded, and Hassani wrapped his arm around my waist, pulling me close. He leaned in and pressed a lingering kiss to my cheek, his warmth making the air feel a little easier to breathe.

"And just like him and your mother, Hassani's mother and I are overjoyed that you two have finally set everything exactly the way it's supposed to be."

"Yes, yes!" Aunt Laurie called out beside my mom.

Mr. Franklin turned back to me, his eyes soft.

"Ayla, your father spoke about you like you hung the stars."

I swallowed thickly.

"So, when Hassani come to me, talkin' 'bout askin' you out, *mi* say, 'Wait now *bwoy… jus'* wait.'"

Laughter erupted again.

"My hesitation wasn't because Hassani was a bad guy." Mr. Franklin held up a finger. "I just knew he'd have to grow into the kind of man he needed to be — to love the woman you were becoming."

"*Mmm-hmm.*" Hassani nodded. "True, true."

"Today only makes things official on paper," Mr. Franklin continued. "But Ayla, from the moment your father left this earthly plane — and again, when Hassani told us you were together — you became my daughter too."

I smiled, feeling Hassani's arm tighten around me.

"It's set in stone now, my love," Mr. Franklin affirmed. "You two are married. And like Reverend Harte said, we are your village. Everyone here tonight is part of your support system. And as you both know, *I* take *my* responsibilities *very* seriously."

Hassani and I laughed.

"Hassani." Mr. Franklin turned to his son. "A good husband knows when to speak, when to listen, and when to act. Don't wait too long to fix what's broken—whether it's your wife's heart, a promise you made, or even the leaky faucet in the kitchen."

Laughter erupted from our guests.

"Show up—and always make it right. Always." He exhaled, emotion thick in his voice. "I love you both *so* much," he said, his eyes misting. "And I love you even more… *together.*"

He pointed at us next.

"This just feels so complete right now. I pray nothing but blessings and joy over what you've allowed the Most High to fuse together. You've made me the happiest man in this world. God bless this union, and cheers to you both."

Mr. Franklin lifted his glass of champagne high, then passed the microphone to Mrs. Franklin.

"Ayla and Hassani, *woi!*" She brimmed with pride. "*Mi* heart full, man. Everything just feel *right* today."

Laughter, claps, and cheers erupted from our guests.

"I still can't believe I'm not dreaming," Mrs. Franklin said, dabbing at her eyes. "But now, time *fi di* baby, *eh?*"

"Whoa, whoa," Hassani said, making me giggle. "Ma, easy now."

Children hadn't been a serious topic of conversation just yet, though we knew they would be part of our future. But for now? Mama Franklin really needed to slow down.

Mrs. Franklin smiled. "My sweet boy, Hassani, and my beautiful girl, Ayla." She turned to me with a warm smile. "Ayla, I knew from the moment I met you in your parents' kitchen, you and Hassani were gonna be more than friends. You know that, right?!"

I snickered as laughter broke out around us.

I glanced over at Hassani, and he leaned in, pressing a kiss to my lips before whispering, "I knew it, too."

I blushed, staring into his eyes.

"Ayla," Mrs. Franklin continued, drawing my attention back to her. "I want to share something my own mother told me on the day I got married."

She softened, voice warm as she spoke.

"She said, 'Love is not about never falling… it's about always reaching for each other, even when the ground feels unsteady.'"

I pressed my hand to my chest, feeling those words settle deep in a place I knew they'd never leave.

Mrs. Franklin held up a finger. "Marriage will bring you moments of joy so bright they'll take your breath away, but it will also test you like no other."

Her gaze bounced between Hassani and me.

"And in those times, remember this, you two: You are stronger together than you could *ever* be alone. Keep reaching for each other, no matter what. That's how you'll build a love that lasts a lifetime."

Then, with a knowing smile, she turned to Hassani.

"And Hassani, don't forget… sometimes reaching means doing the dishes without being asked, *bwoy*."

Laughter erupted once more as Mrs. Franklin raised her champagne glass higher. We all followed suit.

"Ayla and Hassani, I want you to do three things," she said, glass still lifted. "One, soak up today, the honeymoon, and all the good times you create together—because *those* are the moments you'll hold onto when storms pass through. Two, make me a grandbaby on your honeymoon in Saint Lucia…"

"Ma, come on with this!" Hassani groaned, running a hand down his face, which only made me—and everyone else—laugh even harder.

"And three," she added through her own laughter, "*never* go to bed angry at each other."

Hassani pulled me closer in response, his arm firm around my waist.

"To Ayla and Hassani, may your love always find its way home."

Another hour passed with speeches, eating, cutting cake, and taking pictures before the dance floor—or the stretch of beach we had cleared for dancing—was finally open.

"Favorite Girl," Aunt Laurie called as soon as the music started.

She pulled me into a tight hug, one so full of warmth I closed my eyes to soak it in.

Then she stepped back, cupping my face with both hands.

"Best wedding on the planet for the best girl on earth," she whispered.

I smiled, emotion heavy in my throat.

Aunt Laurie took my hand in hers. "And now that the mushy stuff is over…"

I laughed.

"Let's go dance!" she shouted, dragging me toward the dance floor.

The resort had provided us with a live wedding singer and a steel drum band. They performed reggae renditions of everything—from Jagged Edge's *Let's Get Married* to other R&B classics.

But when the band transitioned into reggae staples like Bob Marley and the Wailers' "Turn Your Lights Down Low" and Dennis Brown's "Here I Come," Hassani unapologetically stole me away from Aunt Laurie.

"I'ma be needing my wife now," he said, spinning me around before pulling me into his arms.

"*Aht!*" Aunt Laurie hollered, laughing. "I know that's right!"

Beneath a bright moon and an open sky, with the warm ocean breeze on our skin, Hassani rolled his waist to the rhythm of the steel drums—effortless, fluid, completely intoxicating.

He danced to reggae so damn well.

His waist moved, slow and controlled. His body swayed, pulling me in, making it impossible to focus on anything else but him.

The heat of the night had nothing on this.

He was such a great dancer, and I couldn't keep up.

I leaned back, laughter spilling out of me as he ground his hips against me. His arms wrapped tight around my waist, reminding me that he was just as skilled on the dance floor as he was in bed.

"You better stop," I whispered against his ear, wrapping my arms around the back of his neck. "I am not above starting on that baby, your mother wants, in front of everybody."

Hassani's eyebrows lifted. "Oh word?!"

Before I could react, he grabbed me by my thighs and lifted me off the ground.

I screamed, clinging to him as I instinctively wrapped my legs around his waist, breathless with laughter.

I pressed a kiss to his lips.

"I mean…" My best friend Sunni's voice rang out behind me. "Should *we* leave now? Should we go?!"

Hassani and I laughed against each other's lips.

"Right?!" One of Hassani's friends, Raphael, chimed in. "Save that for Saint Lucia."

Hassani smirked. "I can't wait to get you alone."

"Neither can I." I winked. "So, let's go."

I LAY ON MY STOMACH, CAMERA IN HAND, THE LCD SCREEN RAISED TO eye level as I focused my lens on the villa in front of me.

I clicked the shutter button, listening to the soft whirr of the shutter curtain opening and closing—allowing light to hit the sensor, capturing yet another breathtaking piece of this paradise.

It was the last day of our honeymoon in Saint Lucia.

And a week on this island wasn't enough.

Our private villa sat tucked away on the lush, tropical island, spaced out from the neighboring villas and facing the ocean. Turquoise water stretched as far as the eye could see, while palm trees and thick greenery framed the horizon.

The sun shined differently out here. Not harsh, not overbearing, but warm and golden. The kind of sunlight that kissed your skin rather than burned it.

I loved the way my skin glowed after spending my days under the open sky, the sun's rays blessing me at every angle.

According to Hassani, the villa's open space I immediately fell in love with was an open-concept design.

To me?

It was simply a luxurious, temporary paradise—floor-to-ceiling windows, a private infinity pool that seemed to spill effortlessly into the ocean, and the kind of view that made you want to stay lost in the moment forever.

I turned onto my back on the chaise lounge, shifting my gaze toward the ocean, only to catch Hassani watching me.

His golden eyes flickered between me and his sketchbook, pencil moving effortlessly along the white page.

Him and that sketchbook.

They were as inseparable as umbrellas and tropical drinks.

No matter where we were, Hassani was sketching something. His mind was always at work, bombarded with architectural inspiration—even here, on our honeymoon.

"Why am I not surprised that the little black book is here with us?" I teased, pulling another bikini from my suitcase. "I swear that sketchbook's cover never gets cold the way you always have it in your grip."

"Ha, ha," he said in a deadpan tone, pulling open the drawer of a bedside table in our villa's bedroom. "Always with the jokes."

We had just arrived in the villa, still unpacking before heading out to explore.

I was still riding high from the wedding—the only thing that could possibly compete with it was our wedding night. And now, a day later, we were on our honeymoon, hoping to keep the high going.

I lifted my gaze to the ceiling, mesmerized by how stunning every detail of the villa was.

"Yeah, you see it," Hassani noted quietly.

I glanced at him, catching the smirk tugging at his lips.

"This place is inspiring," he added, eyes sweeping across the space. He nodded. "And I'm gonna soak it all in... my way."

That's exactly what he had done and so had I.

Our days had been filled with snorkeling in crystal-clear water, lounging on the beach, exploring the island. Our nights were spent skinny-dipping in the infinity pool beneath a blanket of stars.

And the lovemaking.

God.

Lots and *lots* of lovemaking.

Sitting here now, on this chaise lounge, had been the longest we'd gone without putting our hands on each other.

Saint Lucia had been a dream.

And I wasn't looking forward to waking up outside of it.

I peeked over at Hassani again, catching the way he smiled at me, pencil still moving across the page.

He had shown me some of his sketches, and as always, I marveled at how effortlessly his hands translated what he saw into something tangible.

His sketches weren't just of the villa.

Some of them were of me.

Doing simple things—like right now, lounging on this chaise.

I aimed my camera at him, focusing on the way his fingers gripped the pencil, the slight crease in his brow, the way the sunlight high-lighted his profile.

And then… *click*.

Hassani smirked, his gaze lifting.

I said, "I'm going to start charging you for all these sketches you make of me."

Hassani smiled but said nothing in response.

I lay back against the chaise, eyes squinting against the sun. "I'll never forget this place."

"Same," he said softly, closing his sketchbook and setting it on the side table. "We need to start getting ready for the surprise I have for you, though."

Excitement made my heart flutter in my chest.

It was our final activity on the island—one Hassani had saved for our last full day in Saint Lucia.

We had done everything else the island had to offer… except for this.

And whatever it was, Hassani had been keeping it a secret.

Hassani walked over to me, the sunlight catching on his defined arms, abs, and chest, casting a shadow on the floor as he moved.

Even though he no longer ran track competitively, running was still part of his daily routine—even here, on the island.

He had kissed me out of bed every morning to join him, and I had never refused him. Not when I was always rewarded with a return to that bed and good sex until noon.

So, of course, I never complained.

My camera was in my hands again as he sank onto the edge of my chaise, my lens aimed at his handsome face.

He leaned around the camera, making me giggle.

His lips brushed against my neck.

"And how much should I charge for all these photos you've got of me on this thing?" he asked, his deep voice rumbling in my chest.

I closed my eyes as he sucked lightly on my skin, heat pooling low in my stomach.

Hassani trailed soft kisses from my neck to my cheek, then toward my lips.

I blindly reached for the side table, setting my camera down to free my hands, so I could take his face between them.

And when he pressed his lips to mine, we both moaned.

Didn't waste a second parting our lips, our tongues caressing as our kiss deepened.

Hassani settled between my thighs, his body heavy, his heat melting me from the inside out.

I didn't know if it was the island, the high of being newly married. But whatever it was, it was *new*.

And I liked it.

It was as if another layer of our relationship had peeled back, revealing fresh, untouched skin.

Because the way Hassani kissed me as a husband was different.

The way his hands moved over my body, the way he massaged my skin, taking our kiss deeper, drove me the kind of wild that felt like sin.

"*Mmm*," he groaned, lips moving against mine. "We gotta stop, or we're gonna miss the surprise I have for you."

I nodded but didn't let go.

Didn't stop kissing him.

Hassani chuckled, successfully breaking our kiss, but I pulled him right back in.

He pecked my lips once—twice—then finally pulled away.

A second later, he was on his feet, his swim trunks visibly tenting in front.

That was all I saw. All I wanted to see.

Hassani slid a finger beneath my chin, tilting my head back so I'd meet his gaze.

"Not right now. Later." He smirked, holding out his hand for me to take. "We gotta go."

I giggled, nodding as I took his hand and let him pull me to my feet.

The surprise was a sunset cruise around the island.

My jaw dropped when we arrived at the marina and Hassani revealed he had rented a private yacht for us to sail at sunset.

When we boarded, we had dinner on the upper deck, just before setting sail.

And once we were on the crystal blue water, I wanted to see everything.

I stood at the edge of the upper deck, one arm draped over the railing, one hand nursing a glass of champagne. My eyes locked on the sun, dipping below the horizon, painting the sky in fiery shades of orange and soft hues of pink.

I had brought my camera, but for the first time, I didn't want to capture anything.

I wanted this moment to exist only in my memories.

I lifted my champagne glass to my lips for a sip just as Hassani approached me from behind.

His hand slid along my stomach as he pressed his body close to mine.

I smiled from my heart before it even reached my lips.

"I feel like I'm living out a fantasy I never even knew I had," I whispered to myself, totally fine with him hearing it.

We had been together for four years, though it didn't feel that long.

Not when life had kept us so busy. Me with my work at the school, Hassani with his private architecture firm.

Our days had been filled with deadlines and due dates, making those four years feel more like one.

We didn't talk much about the wedding that never happened—the one he was supposed to have with someone else.

But sometimes, it found its way into conversation.

And yet, standing here, on this yacht, in his arms, with an island sunset before us, those four years felt more like one month.

Because getting married made everything feel new again.

Hassani turned me to face him, his arms locking firmly around my waist.

His eyes searched mine, his skin drinking in the fiery colors of the sunset.

"You're a fantasy I've lived out in my imagination way too many times to count," he remarked low. "A. Boogie."

I bit my bottom lip, lifting my arms to wrap around his neck, balancing on the arches of my feet.

Hassani walked me backward—stopping only when my body pressed against the ship's railing.

We shared a kiss, like always.

Hassani's hand found a home on my ass, squeezing firmly as his tongue moved against mine.

I pecked his lips before leaning back, my gaze locking with his.

"Planning this sunset cruise seems like it took a lot of effort."

"Nothing is too much effort when it comes to you." He tightened his hold around my waist. "You know that."

"*Mm-hmm.*" I smiled. "Don't go designing me a yacht, though."

He arched a brow. "You want me to design you a yacht?" His smirk deepened. "I *can* design you a yacht."

I leaned my head back in laughter, and when I leveled my gaze, he was watching me, smiling.

"You're not sleeping tonight, Mrs. Franklin," he promised the second our eyes met. "Not on my watch."

"Oh, I hope not," I replied, holding him tighter.

～

Eventually, sleep found us.

But as the seagulls cried overhead and morning light painted soft gold across our villa the next morning, I blinked awake to find Hassani asleep beside me.

Like most nights in the villa, we had fallen asleep on the outdoor daybed, just inches from the pool.

Waking up to the sound of waves, the scent of salt and sun, the endless stretch of ocean before us, had become a norm I would miss.

We were leaving today.

A part of me was sad, but another part of me was excited. Because when we left, I would be leaving as Mrs. Ayla Franklin.

I sat up slowly, shifting my gaze toward Hassani.

Last night, after returning from the sunset cruise, we hadn't wasted a single second getting our hands on each other.

The candles we lit flickered in the breeze, casting soft shadows against the walls, their glow blending seamlessly with the rhythm of the ocean ahead of us.

For our final night, we had slept outside in the nude, letting the warmth of the island wrap around us.

We wanted the sun to wake us.

Before we had drifted off, we had massaged each other. Our hands were slicked with the chocolate-coconut-flavored oil we had discovered in our honeymoon suite's gift basket, courtesy of the resort.

Hassani had been the first to use it.

Our first morning in Saint Lucia, he had drizzled it onto my skin while I slept—then woken me with his tongue buried between my thighs.

He had cleaned every drop of oil from my skin, stroking my clit in slow, tight circles until my back arched so high I couldn't breathe.

That man had wrecked me before I had even opened my eyes.

By the time my release had ripped through me, I was boneless, slipping back into sleep not long after waking.

I had vowed to get him back for that.

And now... I saw my opportunity.

I slipped from the bed, tiptoeing into the villa and toward the bathroom.

After freshening up and brushing my teeth, I returned just as quietly.

Hassani was still asleep.

I smiled, knowing he was about to wake up the same way I had.

I watched him for a moment, the daybed's light summer bedding barely covering him—his torso bare, the sheets pooled at his waist.

The massage oil from last night still gleamed against his golden-brown skin.

He looked like a well-chiseled statue, the slow rise and fall of his chest the only movement against the stillness of the morning.

With the bottle of edible massage oil in hand, I slipped onto the daybed's mattress, careful not to wake him.

Slowly, I lifted the covers.

Drizzling the warm oil onto his abs, his dick, I wrapped my fingers around him, my touch light. Focused.

Then, I took him into my mouth.

"*Mmm*," he groaned in his sleep, his body stirring.

His lashes fluttered, brows tensing, breath hitching.

Then, his eyes blinked open.

"Good morning," I mumbled, my lips still wrapped around him.

"Gah—" He growled, his jaw going slack, his abs clenching as I bobbed deeper.

His fist gripped the pillow I had slept on, pressing it to his face, his muffled groans spilling into the fabric.

I moaned, hollowing my cheeks, my tongue stroking where I knew he liked it most.

His free hand found my curls, fisting them, his grip tightening with every flick of my tongue.

His grunts deepened, roughened, his chest rising and falling in quick succession.

He tugged at my hair, the silent plea clear and not missed on me.

He was close.

Too close.

"*Fuck*, Ayla, fuck!" he groaned, yanking the pillow from his face. "I'm about to come, baby. I'm about to come."

I didn't stop.

Didn't pull away.

His entire body went still, every muscle locked tight, his abs rippling, his fists clenched, his jaw tensed in a silent cry.

And then, he let go.

A long, guttural groan tore from his lips, his body shuddering beneath me as I took everything he gave.

Only when he lay completely boneless against the bed, his breaths ragged, his limbs heavy, did I slowly release him.

For a moment, he didn't move.

Couldn't.

His chest rose and fell, his lips parted, struggling to pull in air.

I smirked.

Then, I drizzled more of the oil into my palm, wrapping my fingers around his softening shaft.

And stroked.

His body jerked beneath my touch, his breath catching.

"Shit," he exhaled as I climbed over him, straddling his waist.

His hands immediately gripped my hips, his fingers digging in as I dragged my slick heat over him, teasing. "*Damnnn*, baby. Damn."

Our wedding night and honeymoon were the first times we'd made love without a condom.

And while I was still on the pill, a part of me looked forward to the day when this—*us*, together, like *this*—would lead to something more.

To something we created.

I sank down slow, my body molding around him, my walls stretching to fit him perfectly.

His pupils dilated, his jaw slacked.

I smirked. "I told you I'd get you back, right?"

Hassani laughed lazily, then groaned, his hands tightening on my waist.

I rolled my hips, shuddering each time his erection grazed my most sensitive places.

His heat, his slick skin against mine, the way he rubbed against my clit with every motion.

It sent rolling pleasure shooting up my spine.

Hassani's grip tightened, his fingers digging in as he met my rhythm, thrusting up into me with well-timed strokes.

"Damn," he drawled, baring his teeth as I picked up speed. "I don't ever wanna wake up from this shit, baby."

As his hands roamed over me, as the waves whispered against the shore, I thought…

This is how it should always be.

Effortless. Whole. Weightless.

But a hum of doubt curled at the edges of my mind, too. A voice I wasn't ready to listen to…

Could it always feel this easy?

I let the warmth of his touch drown it out.

I lost myself in him.

In us.

In now.

I closed my eyes, surrendering to the pull of my release, my body tightening, my breaths coming quick and shallow.

And I whispered,

"I don't ever want to wake up from this either, baby."

But somehow…

We did.

CHAPTER 2

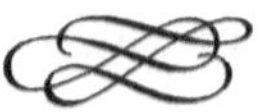

NOW – EARLY SUMMER 2023... PRESENT DAY

*H*assani

I INHALED DEEPLY AS I PUSHED OPEN MY GLASS OFFICE DOOR, MY STEPS heavy, the tension in my back even heavier.

Calling this morning difficult would be an understatement.

I grunted as I set my laptop bag on the desk.

Spread across it were scale models of Greene Gardens, blueprints covered in red-marked adjustments. Sketches I had barely touched.

This project was supposed to be the crown jewel of my career—the kind of work that solidified legacies.

But right now... it felt like a weight I couldn't carry.

I dropped into my office chair, rolling my eyes closed at the mess in front of me. A second later, I pinched the inner corners of my eyes.

The buzz of work surrounded me, conversations overlapping, the clatter of keyboard strokes, the click of heels and hard-bottom shoes as people moved through the office.

Though I had a private office near Park Avenue, I worked out of

Bryant Greene's 16-story high-rise—the headquarters for the Greene Gardens Project.

I could have easily stayed at my own office, only coming here for meetings.

But I had thought it would be easier to work alongside the teams I managed.

At least, I *thought* that.

But after last night?

After the conversation with Ayla?

I wasn't sure what the fuck was right anymore.

I leaned my forehead into my palm, my fingers scratching my fresh lineup. I was feeling a headache coming on.

It was too damn early for this.

Then again, last night had bled into this morning, and last night was the worst night of my life.

Through the glass walls of my office, I could see everything—architects hunched over sketches, project managers on their office phones, people moving in and out of meetings.

The Greene Gardens Project was the largest project of my career.

Since graduating college, every job I took on had felt big, until a bigger one came along.

The project before this one had been the biggest yet—a renovation of a restaurant in a Black-owned luxury hotel in Tribeca: The St. James.

It was that work—the one that challenged me the most—that got me the recommendation I needed to land Greene Gardens.

I thought this project was the best thing to ever happen to me.

The best thing to ever happen for me and my wife.

But lately?

Shit... I didn't know anymore.

My eyes burned, and I was sure they were red—not just from lack of sleep, but from the weight of last night.

From the weight of her words.

Ayla told me she wanted a divorce.

I grunted, pressing my head against the back of my chair.

Every time I replayed her words, my chest tightened, my heart twisting in a vice-like grip.

She didn't say it just because she was angry about me coming home late.

She meant that shit.

Every single word.

And that nasty fucking word…

Divorce.

The headache that had been threatening me all morning finally settled in, an uninvited guest sitting with me in my office, in my chair.

I rubbed my temples, trying to force myself into work mode.

Then, I heard the sound of my door pushing open.

"Good morning."

My body went rigid as soon as I heard her voice.

My eyes dropped first to her hips as they swayed in perfect rhythm, her navy-blue pencil skirt hugging her curves as she strode toward me.

The higher my gaze traveled, the more my teeth clenched.

By the time I reached the plunging neckline of her blouse, I had to force my jaw to unclench.

Then, finally, our eyes met.

Her red-painted lips curved into a soft frown.

"Oh." She tilted her head, her wavy brown hair slipping off her shoulder. "You look tired."

A slow pause.

"Late night?"

Yup.

Because of *her*.

Harper Royce.

The first time I met her, I had known she was attracted to me.

She never made it a secret.

And at first, I hadn't thought it was a big deal.

She was harmless.

I wasn't blind.

She was a beautiful woman. Five-foot-nine. Flawless, warm brown skin. A body built for lingerie catalogs.

Every man in this office could see that.

And she never shied away from showing it.

With her tailored skirts, her blouses that hugged just enough, her heels that elongated her long legs.

Harper Royce was a woman who understood her feminine charm. And that charm was starting to get my ass in trouble.

"Yeah," I replied, clearing my throat when my voice came out rougher than expected. "Definitely a late night."

"*Aww*, so sad." She pouted as she sank into the chair across from me. "I'm sorry to hear that."

Her eyes bored into me, like always.

Sharp. Calculating.

Almond-shaped, dark brown, forever enhanced with subtle makeup and quiet seduction.

Harper was charming and *very* smart.

And not just book smart.

She had a calculated intelligence, the kind that could be dangerous.

I was learning that the hard way.

She was the interior designer for the Greene Gardens Project, specializing in modern, sustainable luxury interiors.

At thirty-four, Harper was a force to be reckoned with.

Highly educated. Graduated from Parsons School of Design. Well-traveled. Studied abroad in Milan.

She was good on the eyes and on paper.

But she was *no* Ayla.

Not by a mile.

No one was, in my eyes.

I still loved my wife. Still couldn't keep my eyes—or hands—off her after all these years.

Before I took on this project, everything between us had been great.

Now though? Everything was not.

Harper smirked. "I would've thought that after you ditched me last night..." She dragged out the last few words like an invitation. "You would have gone home to get some rest."

I scoffed a quiet laugh.

"I was a little bummed about that, Hassani," she added, voice soft, sweet.

I forced a polite smile.

That dinner—if you could even call it that—was nothing like what I imagined. But looking back, joining Harper was probably not my brightest idea.

Just us two.

And at that hour.

Especially when I knew that by the time I got home, long after leaving dinner, I would be returning to an angry wife.

A part of me had hoped Ayla would be asleep when I got in.

She often was.

Usually, I'd find her in bed, waiting for me—our bodies molding together in the dark, my hands tracing familiar paths, my lips waking her before the sun did.

But last night... she was awake.

Waiting.

And what she said?

That shit hit different.

But what hurt even more?

Waking up alone.

I rolled onto my back, eyes still closed, body moving on autopilot, the way it always did in the morning.

Reaching over, I lifted my arm, expecting warmth. Expecting her.

Instead, I felt cold sheets.

The second my fingers met empty space, it all came back to me in a rush.

I didn't have to open my eyes to remember. To know that Ayla hadn't come back to bed, choosing to spend the night in the guest bedroom.

Still, I opened them anyway.

Looked, just to be sure.

And when I saw it—when I saw that she hadn't returned to our bed after I came home, something inside me twisted.

I got up.

Didn't hesitate.

Padded across the room.

Took the stairs down to the ground floor where the guest bedroom was.

I turned the knob, pushed the door open and stopped cold.

The bed was neatly made. The room empty.

I jerked my head back.

Glanced over my shoulder, scanning the lower level of the house.

The house I designed as a teenager and redesigned with her in mind.

The sunlight poured in through one of the many skylights she loved.

And yet, she was nowhere.

What the fuck?

I moved through the house.

Kitchen? Empty.

Backyard? Nothing.

Laundry room? Vacant.

"Where the hell is she?"

Had this been any other morning, I would've known.

She'd be in Manhattan, setting up her classroom for her preschoolers.

But school was out.

Summer recess had started last week.

And this wasn't even a day she left the house.

She had always used today as a rest day after a long school year.

So where the fuck was my wife?

I reached for my phone.

Then stopped.

No.

The first time we talked couldn't be over the phone.

Not after how things were left last night.

"You look so tense."

Harper's voice snapped me back to the now.

I exhaled sharply, blinking.

She scooted to the edge of her seat, smoothing her hands down the barely-there wrinkles in her pencil skirt.

Then, before I could register her next move, she stood. Rounded my desk. Approaching me.

My lips parted to say something, but then she touched me.

Hands on my shoulders.

I stiffened, instantly. Because on impact, it wasn't just a touch. Not the casual, neutral lay of hands on a co-worker's shoulder.

It was a caress.

Soft. Slow. Intimate.

I barely registered her fingers trailing along my shoulder blades, because my eyes shot past her to my team.

The people moving through the office.

Too caught up in their work, their conversations to notice.

Harper's touch lingered.

Heat radiated where her fingertips brushed against me.

And it was impossible to ignore how inappropriate this was.

How invasive.

How fucking bold.

Too bold.

I grabbed her wrists, stopping her.

"I'm good."

My voice came out clipped.

Firm.

I turned my head slightly, just enough to look at her over my shoulder.

"Thanks, Harper."

Just then, my glass office door swung open, drawing my attention that way.

Our landscape architect, Levi Weston, stood at the threshold.

His eyes bounced between me and Harper.

Between her standing over me. Between my hands still holding hers.

A beat of silence passed.

Then, he cleared his throat.

I instantly released Harper's hands.

"I apologize if I'm interrupting *anything.*"

"Don't apologize," I said quickly, sitting up straight. "You're not interrupting anything *at all*. What's up?"

Levi's gaze shifted to Harper again before forcing a tight smile her way.

Then, he refocused on me.

"Here's the final site plan for the community park layout," he said, stepping forward and placing a folder on my desk. "I wanted you to review it before we finalize it with Bryant."

"Cool." I nodded stiffly, reaching for the folder and lifting my attention to him. "I got you. I'll have this back to you within the hour."

This looked so bad.

I knew it looked bad.

Even if I couldn't quite tell how Levi had interpreted what he had just walked in on.

"Cool," Levi said, giving me a casual salute before shooting a glance behind me. "Harper."

"Levi," she replied, sharp and short.

Levi exhaled a scoffing laugh before exiting my office.

Behind me, Harper finally stepped away from my chair.

"Definitely get some rest when you make it home, tonight." She smirked, gesturing toward the door. "I should get back to work. The designs aren't going to design themselves, right?"

My tongue felt heavy in my mouth as I watched her move toward my office door.

Then she paused, turned, and smiled.

"Plus," she added, her voice light, almost playful, "I don't want anyone getting the wrong idea. You know how our people like to talk."

She said it so sweetly, so innocently, that someone unaware wouldn't have picked up on the subtext.

Wouldn't have picked up on the subtle amusement in her tone. Like she was playing some kind of game.

Before stepping out, she added, "If you need anything, you know where to find me."

I tracked her with my eyes through the glass walls of my office as she exited, heading toward her own.

My heart was hammering at that point.

My pulse sped up as unease settled over me.

I'd dealt with women throwing themselves at me before.

Had many conversations with my father about being careful, because not all attention was good attention.

Over the years, those talks had evolved. Became more direct.

Especially before I exchanged vows with Ayla in Jamaica six years ago.

His words echoed in the corners of my mind in that moment, numbing me.

Making it impossible to focus on anything else.

"Any woman who would want to ruin your marriage is a woman who wants to ruin your peace."

Harper had always been flirtatious.

I used to brush it off.

Office banter.

Nothing serious.

But lately?

I was starting to wonder if I had been willfully blind.

I had assumed Harper's flirting was innocent, like every other woman in my past. But now, I wasn't so sure.

This felt deliberate.

And with Levi walking in, seeing what happened… I hoped it wouldn't become office gossip.

Levi wasn't the type to stir shit up, but still, I was concerned.

I shook my head, inhaling a deep breath, then forcing the thoughts away on my exhale.

Then, I flipped open the folder Levi had brought me and forced myself into work.

But deep down, I knew.

This?

What just happened?

It couldn't happen again.

Not after last night.

Not if I wanted to fix what was already breaking.

CHAPTER 3

THEN – EARLY SUMMER 2017... SIX YEARS EARLIER

$\mathcal{H}$assani

"Hassani, would you get up?"

Ayla's voice was soft, but I could hear the smile behind it.

I glanced up from my sketchbook, watching her at the kitchen counter, reaching for ingredients, and got distracted.

By her.

By the way those soft, round hips moved as she stretched just a little too far.

"Got me over here doing all the work."

"Lies," I teased, my attention split between her and the lines I was drafting on the page.

It was our first night in the house I had designed… and I was still sketching.

We were supposed to move in right after I proposed years ago. That had been the plan—get engaged, set a date, and start our life here.

But my business had taken off faster than expected.

One project had turned into three.

Deadlines had dictated our lives, and the house we had dreamed of living in had sat empty.

Until now.

Our first night under its roof, and I already knew… we belonged here

I skimmed my pencil lightly along the page, leaving behind the faintest ghost of a line. A guideline, just enough to map out the structure before I added detail.

I was sketching a built-in spice rack next to the stove.

Watching Ayla set up to cook, straining just a little to reach the high shelves, had given me the idea.

It would be a useful addition.

Plus, any excuse to draw, I was taking it.

The world always went silent when I sat with my sketchbook.

There was something grounding about putting pencil to paper, shaping the world exactly how I envisioned it.

Ayla peeked over her shoulder and giggled.

"What are you drawing anyway?"

"A built-in spice rack," I told her. "It would look good by the stove."

She sighed, shaking her head. "Baby, you already designed the house." She moved toward the fridge, her slippers sweeping across the stone floors. "Are we adding to it already? This is literally our first night. We just got here."

I grinned, my pencil gliding effortlessly along the page. "A masterpiece is never truly finished, A. Boogie."

She rolled her eyes playfully before making her way back to the counter.

Boxes were everywhere, evidence of a life half-unpacked, a home just beginning to be lived in.

I had some time off between projects at my firm, so I had agreed to spend the next two days helping Ayla unpack. Starting tonight, after dinner.

"Can you get me the dried basil from this shelf up here?"

I glanced up.

"I put it up there earlier and didn't realize the recipe called for it."

I smirked, pointing my pencil at her. "See? That's why we need a built-in spice rack…" I arched a brow. "And a step stool, shorty."

She turned, her smirk matching mine. "No, we don't." She tapped the counter next. "Because I got a tall husband for that."

I snorted a laugh.

"Plus, I don't need a step stool." She gestured at one of the kitchen chairs. "I could just use that… like I did earlier. Like I *always* did when I lived alone."

My smile vanished. "Hell nah." I stood from my seat, rounding the island to get to her. "If I had seen you standing on that chair, I would've stopped you. I'm not having my woman climbing on furniture to reach shelves."

Ayla watched me approach, her lips twitching like she wanted to argue, but didn't.

I stopped in front of her, reaching up easily and grabbing the dried basil off the shelf.

I handed it to her.

"Baby, I swear," I warned, "I better not see you standing on things to reach for stuff."

"Or what?" She grinned. "What are you going to do?"

"What am I—" I closed the space between us, backing her up against the counter. "You wanna fuck around and find out?"

She dropped her head back laughing while playfully pushing me back.

I joined her at the counter a moment later, chopping vegetables while she stirred the sweet Thai chili sauce.

Together, we moved in rhythm, a quiet dance in our brand-new kitchen.

"Can you pass the peas?" Ayla asked, standing over the stove.

I grinned. "Like we used to do?"

She turned, instantly bursting into laughter.

Her laugh was infectious, and I couldn't help joining in.

I handed her the peas, and we kept working in easy silence—until she started humming.

I knew the tune right away.

It was the song from that Thanksgiving episode on *Martin*—the same one I'd just brought up. A play on that J.B.'s joint, "Pass the Peas."

Her humming turned into singing, and before I knew it, we were both singing out loud, voices bouncing off the bare walls.

We were loud, off-key, and laughing so hard we could barely breathe.

We probably sounded ridiculous to the neighbors.

But I didn't care.

Because this? *This* was home.

And I was there in that moment, but also somewhere else.

Watching Ayla, my wife, in the home that had once been nothing more than a sketch.

A dream from architecture camp decades ago.

Back then, my instructor had asked us to design houses for the future.

And on a whim, I had said, "I want to design a house for my future wife."

It had been just an idea.

A fantasy.

Some rough blueprints in an old sketchbook.

Nothing more.

I never actually thought it would become something real.

But now, here we were.

Standing inside a place that had only ever existed in my head, now brought to life in stone, wood, and glass.

Our home.

Overhead, in the kitchen—just like in the other rooms of the house —was a skylight, this one wider than the others.

A view of the night sky stretched above us.

The stars Ayla always wanted to see were hidden tonight, but even still, the sky was a sight to behold.

She shot a glance over her shoulder as she moved toward the fridge.

Ayla smiled then winked. And just like that, my heart stuttered.

A wave of completion washed over me.

Like everything in my life had finally clicked into place.

Like nothing else mattered.

And I wondered… Did Ayla feel it too?

This weightless, perfect moment?

Because the shit felt too good to be mine alone.

After filling our bellies, we sprawled out in the living room, talking about everything. From furniture shopping to where we would take our first vacation as husband and wife.

Then, we decided to spend just an hour unpacking a couple of boxes.

We figured we could spread it out over the week to keep it from feeling overwhelming.

Ayla cupped her phone, scrolling through a playlist she'd put together.

"Make sure it's loud," I told her. "'Cause how else do you listen to '90s R&B?"

"See? That's why you're my hubby-lover-friend." She giggled. "Because that's the *only* way to listen to it."

Soon, the melody of a familiar hit filled our sound space.

"Yo, A," I said, lifting my head. "You know you got the most stuff here, right?"

She kissed her teeth and waved me off.

"You do," I insisted, standing to my feet. "I'm on the third box, and most of it is *your* stuff."

"*Mm-hmm…*"

"Three full boxes of books," I said, crouching down to keep unpacking. "I'm swimming in memoirs, romance novels, biographies, and self-help books over here."

"Hassani, I know you are *not* talking."

I looked up just as Ayla held up a pair of my Jordans.

"These are the fifteenth Jordan sneakers I've pulled from a box. Fif*teenth*."

I did a double take when I realized she was holding up my Concord 11s.

"Aye, aye." I jumped to my feet. "Don't hold them like that. Got the soles too close to the white upper, baby."

She pursed her lips, eyes amused.

I gently took them from her. "These are considered the most beautiful Jordans ever made." I marveled at them, taking in the sleek black patent leather, the crisp white upper. "You gotta hold them with respect, you know? Talk nice to 'em."

Ayla snorted a laugh as I set them down beside her. "Well, then, talk nice to my books because the same love you got for your sneakers is the same love I have for my books. But double. Got it?"

I grinned, hands raised in surrender. "Aight. I got it."

Just then, the playlist restarted.

A new song.

A familiar song.

The opening melody hit the air, and we froze.

Case's "Happily Ever After."

Our song.

The song we had danced to during our first dance as husband and wife.

The one our steel drum band had played flawlessly at our wedding.

Slowly, we turned to each other.

The melody moved toward the first verse.

Neither of us spoke. We didn't have to.

I just held out my hand and she took it without hesitation.

I pulled her into me, her body molding perfectly against mine as I slid an arm around her waist.

She melted into me, the way she always did, as we swayed to the song.

We danced in the middle of our oversized living room, surrounded by unopened boxes.

None of it mattered.

Not with the woman of my dreams pressed against me.

Not with our hearts beating in sync.

If perfection were a moment, it would be this.

Because in that wordless time, I heard everything. And I felt even more.

Our laughter faded into something deeper.

Something so damn beautiful.

A reminder that Ayla wasn't just my best friend anymore. She was my partner for life.

I lowered my head, pressing a kiss to her curls, inhaling her scent.

I told her, "I wanna build you something as beautiful as this house one day."

She smiled, her arms tightening around my neck. "That's nice, but baby, I'm not trying to be married to a workaholic. How long would something *as beautiful as this* take to build?"

"Doesn't matter how long."

I ran a hand through her coils and curls, my touch lingering.

"It can take however long. I'll always have time for you—and if I ever run out, I'll make more."

So many nights I had prayed for this moment.

Prayed for another chance with her.

For a way to make up for the years we lost after we stopped speaking post-college graduation.

Once I had moved to Washington, D.C., I had thought that was it. That we were done. But we weren't. And I was so grateful for how things had turned out.

Ayla pulled back, lifting her head as the song came to an end.

Our eyes met, and I kissed her.

Deeply.

She sighed softly against my lips, her body pressing closer.

Her soft moans did it for me.

The way they always did.

Evident by the firming happening in my jeans.

Ayla giggled against my lips as the song faded into another R&B classic. "You are so damn easy."

I tipped my head back in a laugh, making her laugh too. Before she could say anything else, I scooped her up into my arms.

She squealed in response. "Hassani!"

"It's time for bed."

She pointed around us. "Aren't we unpacking?"

"Nah, we're done," I replied with a smirk. "As I'm sure you felt."

Her eyes darkened for a second before she licked her lips and nodded. "Yeah, you're right. Let's go to bed."

We stripped down and got ready for bed, me in just boxers, Ayla in a cami and panties.

Standing at our his-and-her sinks, we brushed our teeth, sneaking quick glances at each other in the mirror.

Every time our eyes met, we smiled around our toothbrushes.

When I wasn't focusing on her, my gaze moved around the master bathroom. Everything—the shower stall, the freestanding tub, the matching sinks—had been designed with intention.

I had wanted us to have our own space but still be together, like we were now.

I looked at Ayla again, and she looked back at me.

I started brushing faster.

She squinted her eyes, instantly catching on, and picked up speed.

"Oh, you're accepting the challenge?" I mumbled.

"Accepting?" she teased. "Baby, I'm already winning."

At that point, we were flying through our routine, both of us laughing—until she had to hunch over the sink to spit out her tooth-paste before she swallowed it by accident.

"I won," she declared, spitting once more.

"No, you didn't." I laughed. "The only reason you spit was because you were about to choke."

She grabbed one of the towels folded on the vanity, giggling. "A win is a win."

Minutes later, we settled into bed.

Ayla adjusted herself under the covers, reclining against her pillow, and I just watched her.

Studied her.

For so many nights, I had wanted to be in her bed full-time.

From the time we started dating to when I proposed, we had maintained separate apartments.

I had moved from D.C. and gotten my own place in Manhattan, always holding onto the dream of us being here, in this house, in this bed, together.

Now, it was real.

Her hair was wrapped in a silk floral headscarf, her beautiful legs tucked under the covers, her breathing steady as she settled in.

She looked comfortable. At peace. At home.

Something about that warmed me in a way nothing else could.

I was living my dream.

For so long, I had imagined what life with her would have been like if she had said yes when I asked her to give us a chance on our college graduation day.

Now, here we were.

This was it.

I hadn't just imagined it anymore.

I was *in* my dream.

Ayla turned her head and smiled at me. "What?"

I almost brushed it off but decided not to.

"I dreamed this," I said, a slow smile pulling at my lips.

Her brows furrowed slightly as she turned more toward me. "Dreamed what?"

"You, here. In this bed beside me, under the skylight above us." I glanced up, then back at her. "I dreamed this."

Ayla's hand moved to my chest, her fingertips brushing over my skin. "And what exactly did we do in this dream?"

I grinned, sliding my arm around her waist. My palm smoothed over her round ass, my grip tightening as I pulled her closer.

"I pulled you close, just like this."

She giggled, lifting her leg to drape over my hip. "*Mm-hmm...?*"

I ran my fingers along the smooth brown curve of her calf.

"Then I kissed you..." I leaned in, brushing my lips against hers. "Like this."

Ayla moaned against me, the sound shooting straight through me, making my dick twitch in response.

She parted her lips, her breath mingling with mine. "What else?"

I groaned, rolling her beneath me, her thighs parting instantly to make room for me.

Our lips stayed locked as our tongues tangled.

I reached between us, pulling my erection through the slit in my boxers, then moved the seat of her panties aside.

"Then I slid in slow," I sighed as I sank into her warmth, feeling her walls mold around me. "*Just* like this."

She gasped, her fingers flying to the back of my head as she rolled her hips, meeting my first thrust at just the right moment.

"I *love* your dream, baby," she sighed, arching under me.

"I love you."

I sank deeper, losing myself in her heat, in her softness, in the way her body responded to mine.

Losing myself in the certainty that this—us—would always be enough.

That this moment was forever. But forever has a way of slipping through your fingers when you least expect it.

CHAPTER 4

THEN – LATE SUMMER 2021... FOUR YEARS
LATER

yla

"*Mmm.*" The second I stepped into the kitchen, I inhaled deeply. "Smelling good."

Hassani chuckled as he stood over the stove, flipping a pancake.

Overhead, I stole a glance through the skylight. It was just past six in the morning, and the sky was beginning to brighten. Soft morning light filtering in.

I had watched seventeen seasons pass while living in this house. Witnessed how the morning light stretched longer in the summer and retreated in the winter.

We were a few weeks away from autumn, still in the final days of summer, which meant I had time to enjoy these sunrises before driving to Manhattan with Hassani for work.

Mingling with the scent of sweet pancakes and savory scrambled eggs was the rich aroma of fresh coffee, and I went straight for it. I needed it. My eyes were burning.

Musiq Soulchild's "Betterman" played low from our small Bluetooth stereo as Hassani moved between flipping pancakes and sketching in his sketchbook.

I snickered while reaching for a mug. The man was always sketching something. Doodling everything from a built-in bookshelf for my ever-growing collection of nonfiction books to a cozy nook beneath the staircase, perfect for reading or for him to sketch.

I teased him about it all the time.

But I loved it.

"Good to see you finally made it down here, Mrs. Franklin." Hassani turned off the stove, moving the final pancake to a plate. "I thought you were gonna oversleep today."

"Well, if someone didn't keep me up last night, I would've reported for duty on my day to make breakfast." I poured my coffee and leaned back against the counter. "I could barely get out of bed this morning."

His grin was smug as he plated the food. "Oh, so now it's *my* fault?"

"*You* wouldn't let me sleep." I took a slow sip of coffee. "You know my bedtime is ten."

"We were in bed by ten."

"Yeah, and making love on and off like rabbits until two in the morning."

He feigned confusion. "Was it until two?"

"Yes, Energizer Bunny."

He snorted a laugh before closing the space between us, stopping just long enough to press a kiss to my lips. "Good morning."

"Good morning," I murmured against his lips before pecking him twice more.

When I opened my eyes, his hazel-greens were locked on mine.

He winked.

I smiled.

"Come on." Hassani nodded toward the kitchen table. "Let's eat."

This had been our routine for the past four years.

Breakfast together before heading to work—me at my school with my preschoolers, him at his private office a short walk away. Lunch together in his office. A drive home in the evening. Cooking dinner together. Rinse and repeat.

We alternated breakfast duties, but that morning, my husband had worn me out, so he took one for the team.

Our lives were predictable, and I had come to love that predictability. I had my own car, could have lunch with the teachers at school who felt like my extended family, but nothing beat my routine with Hassani.

It was comfort. The kind I had always wanted.

"What are you getting into after school today?" he asked, forking some eggs into his mouth.

I sliced into my pancake. "I want to start planning next year's end-of-summer trip. Get a head start this year so I have more time to find a nice hotel."

Every year, right before the school year started, Hassani and I took a trip somewhere new.

He knew traveling was something I had always dreamed about as a kid. And he knew how much I admired Aunt Laurie for her solo adventures across the world.

I had tried traveling alone once I was old enough, but it always felt like something was missing.

Then I started traveling with Hassani.

And I realized what was missing was him.

It had become a part of our life together, something I treasured just as much as the home we built.

"How about you?" I asked. "What are you getting into when we get back home?"

He tapped his sketchbook with his pencil, smiling. "Got something I'm working on for the basement—"

The sudden ring of his phone cut him off.

We both turned toward it as it vibrated on the table near his plate.

I glanced at the stove clock. 6:15 a.m.

My brows pulled together. "Who could that be?"

"No idea." Hassani picked up his phone, flipping it over to check the screen. His brows furrowed even deeper. "I don't know this number."

It was a little early for the phone to be ringing.

I thought it but didn't say it, too curious to find out what it was about.

By the third ring, Hassani answered, putting the call on speaker. "Hello?"

"Good morning."

The voice was bright and chipper, as if it were six in the evening, not six in the morning.

"I'm Chelsea Foster, the assistant to Bryant Greene. Am I speaking with Mr. Hassani Franklin?"

Hassani immediately straightened in his seat—so did I.

"Yes."

Our eyes met, my hand flying to my chest.

"Is now a good time to speak, Mr. Franklin?"

"Yeah," Hassani replied quickly, clearing his throat. "I mean, yes. Now is good."

"Perfect." She giggled. "I apologize for calling so early, but Mr. Greene requested I make contact to confirm if you're available to meet with him today."

Hassani blinked hard at that.

"He was able to review your proposal and go over your community sketch. He'd like to discuss your plans further with you in person."

"Oh! Okay… *umm*…yeah, cool." Hassani shook his head. "I mean… good. Great."

I slapped a hand to my mouth, my eyes wide in shock. I removed my hand long enough to mouth, *Oh my God.*

Earlier that summer, Hassani had told me about a major project he had written a proposal for.

One of his former clients from 2018 to 2019, Arielle St. James— owner of several luxury hotels, including the largest one in Tribeca— had recommended Hassani to an acquaintance. Hassani thanked her and left it at that, not thinking much of it

That acquaintance turned out to be Bryant Greene—something Hassani only discovered when the multi-billionaire personally reached out, inviting him to create a proposal and sketch based on his vision.

Hassani had jumped on it, completing everything in just a week.

We hadn't heard anything back. Not a word.

So Hassani moved on, focusing on life and work, believing he wouldn't get a second meeting.

Until now.

"Mr. Greene only has a small window of three hours before he flies out of the country," Chelsea continued. "He needs to meet with you this morning. Would you be able to make it to his office in Manhattan within the next hour and a half?"

Hassani shot straight up, his chair clattering to the floor behind him.

I snorted a laugh.

"Absolutely," he told her. "Yes, I'll start heading there right now."

"Fantastic! I'll let security know. Just give them your name and ID when you arrive."

The moment the call ended, Hassani ran a hand over the top of his head, his wide eyes snapping to mine.

He whispered, "Oh, shit."

"Oh, shit." My smile was so big, it ached my cheeks. "Baby!"

"I know." He dragged his hand down his face before glancing at me again. "Damn. We gotta drive in together. You're not done eating—"

"It's okay."

I said it because I felt like I had to.

Because honestly?

It stung a little.

Our morning routine had never been broken.

And now, he was barely touching his breakfast, and I wasn't even ready to leave yet.

"You sure?"

I nodded quickly, forcing a smile. "Of course, Hassani. This is *huge*. Are you kidding me?"

He nodded, chest rising and falling quickly as his eyes scanned the room.

"Go," I told him, smiling genuinely this time. "Go to that meeting and shine like the star you are, baby. You got this."

He stared at me for a long beat.

"Baby, go. Now!"

Hassani exhaled deeply, puffing out his cheeks as he let the breath go. "Aight, aight. Cool."

I stayed at the kitchen table, finishing my breakfast.

Every so often, my eyes drifted to his untouched plate.

It was small, I told myself. Just one breakfast missed.

But as I sat there alone, the silence felt different.

A break in the rhythm.

It was probably nothing.

Probably.

Less than ten minutes later, Hassani was back in the kitchen, adjusting his tie over his slim-fit dress shirt and slacks, looking like a billionaire himself.

"You sure you're good to drive into the city?" he asked, scanning the counter for his keys. "You got gas in your car?"

"I'm all set."

"Aight, cool."

He turned to leave, then cursed under his breath and doubled back.

Before I could blink, he was in front of me, crouching down and pressing a long, deep kiss to my lips.

I cupped his face, my thumbs stroking his jaw.

"I love you, A," he whispered against my lips.

"I love you."

Then he was gone, leaving me alone for breakfast—one of the rarest times that had ever happened.

DURING THE SUMMER, MY CAR GOT MORE ACTION, BUT EVEN THEN, I mostly used my days to catch up on the rest I never got during the school year.

I couldn't remember the last time I had driven to work.

The drive was smooth. Parking, however, was a nightmare.

It felt weird sitting in the car alone.

Without Hassani beside me, the ride felt quiet.

Lonely.

When he drove, my mind could wander as I ran my mouth in the passenger seat, while he leaned forward in his seat, checking his mirrors or cussing under his breath at whoever he swore had no business in the left lane.

I missed that already.

Still, I got to my destination safely, and hopefully, Hassani and I could still meet for lunch.

Then he could tell me everything about his meeting.

From what he had explained, Bryant Greene's project was major.

Hassani hadn't been given much detail for confidentiality reasons, but he knew the job would have him as the principal architect overseeing several projects.

I wondered if this meeting would finally give him more insight—whether today was the day he found out exactly what he was being asked to design.

I parked a few blocks north of my school, as usual.

As I crossed the street, I noticed a few teachers gathered outside near the entrance.

Unusual.

At this hour—half an hour before our students arrived—we were usually setting up our classrooms or catching up in the breakroom over coffee.

Seeing some of the ladies outside the doors made me quicken my steps.

Something was wrong.

"Hey, good morning, y'all." I greeted them as I walked up, scanning their faces. "What's going on?"

Valerie pressed a hand to my shoulder.

"Girl."

She shook her head, her locs swaying side to side. "You just missed a whole *Jerry Springer* segment."

My brows shot up. "What?"

Just then, loud commotion echoed from inside the school.

I turned toward the door. "Is it safe to go in there?"

Another teacher, Charlese, giggled. "It's safe *now*. Come on."

"Some woman showed up here less than an hour ago," Valerie started as we stepped inside, "claiming to be Janae's husband's girlfriend."

I stopped dead in my tracks. "Excuse me?"

As soon as we stepped in, the air felt different.

Hushed whispers. Tension.

Hysterical crying echoed down the hallway.

It was like I had walked into an alternate universe—like someone had ripped the heart out of Park Avenue Prep.

Janae and her husband had been married for over a decade.

Their love was the kind we all admired.

She always came to work glowing and smiling, talking about him like he hung the damn moon.

She spoke highly of him—about everything he did for her and their three children.

They even had a social media presence, celebrating their marriage online.

Just last month, we all double-tapped her anniversary post, her husband, beaming, holding her hand over a candlelit dinner.

The caption?

"Still my best friend. Still my forever."

And now?

This.

Janae's husband regularly sent her flowers, each with tiny love notes attached.

Whenever we saw a delivery, we didn't even have to ask who they were for.

They were always for Janae.

Always from him.

But now, as I looked up the hall, I saw her collapsed into a chair, surrounded by teachers, her shoulders trembling. Her makeup smudged. Her hair slightly disheveled. She looked shattered.

I walked over, not to ask what happened.

Just to be there for her.

Because Janae was always there for everyone else.

She was everyone's happy place.

She shared inspirational quotes in our group chat.

Lifted us up on our bad days.

And now, seeing her like this?

It hurt.

"Hey," I said softly, resting a hand on her shoulder, lowering myself so our eyes met. "Are you okay?"

She patted her red, puffy eyes, sniffing back the tears that hadn't fallen yet. "I can't believe what the hell just happened."

"*What* happened?"

Her breath shuddered as she dropped her arms.

Her eyes darkened.

"This *bitch* came here…"

I jerked my head back. "Damn."

"Approached me as soon as I got out of my car—talking about how she's been sleeping with my husband for over a year."

My stomach dropped.

"Just like that." Her lip curled in disgust. "Showing me pictures. Text messages…"

My heart started pounding.

"Telling me she's tired of hiding it. That he's been telling her he's gonna leave me for her." She inhaled sharply, her chest rising and falling. Her eyes flicked around the hallway, the weight of everyone's stares pressing in on her.

Then, as if making a decision in real time, she exhaled sharply.

"I can't stay here."

She jumped to her feet and turned on her shoes, storming toward her classroom.

I turned to the other teachers. "Should we call a sub or something? Like... what do we do right now?"

We all stood there, looking just as stunned as the next person.

It wasn't just about *what* had happened.

It was about what it *meant*.

Because the kind of love we thought Janae had?

The kind we all looked up to?

The kind of love *I* hoped *I* would always have with Hassani?

It had been a lie.

Once Janae was gone, the rest of our staff held a quick meeting, deciding to secure a substitute teacher for her class.

With only ten minutes left before I had to greet my kids in the yard, I sat at my desk, trying to collect myself.

The entire morning had gone nothing like I planned.

Breakfast with Hassani. The unexpected call from Bryant Greene's office.

Then showing up at school only to walk into the aftermath of a marriage crumbling.

It shook me.

Not just because it was Janae.

Not just because of how publicly it happened.

But because of how fast it happened.

One woman. One visit. One set of claims.

And a marriage fell apart.

I exhaled sharply.

Would Hassani ever put me in that position?

At work. Preparing to start my day.

Only to be approached by a woman claiming she had been seeing my husband behind my back.

"*Uh-uh,*" I mumbled, shaking my head. "Nah."

Hassani would never do some shit like that.

He loved me.

I trusted him.

But Janae trusted her husband too, right?

I shook my head again, forcing the thought away.

That wasn't my reality.

And it never would be.

Hassani would *never* put himself—or me—in a situation like that.

He wasn't that kind of man.

I inhaled deeply, then stood.

Rolled my neck. Loosened my shoulders.

Shook off the weight of everything before stepping toward my classroom door.

Because in the eight years Hassani and I had been together—four years married—I trusted him.

I knew he had my best interests at heart.

Always.

I pushed open the door and stepped out, pushing the thought aside.

My life wasn't Janae's.

I reminded myself of that as I walked toward the yard, forcing a smile, preparing to greet my kids.

But no matter how much I tried to push it away; I couldn't shake the feeling.

That something had already taken root.

Small.

Invisible.

But growing.

CHAPTER 5

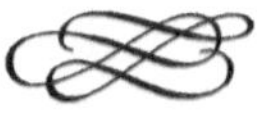

NOW – EARLY SUMMER 2023… PRESENT DAY

$\mathcal{H}$assani

I swaggered into the employee lounge, greeting a few colleagues as I made my way to the coffee bar.

The break room inside Bryant's office building, on the Greene Gardens Project floor, wasn't just a place to grab coffee.

It was an experience.

It was one of the reasons I accepted the office Bryant offered instead of primarily working out of my private office a mile away.

Though I still paid rent for that space, I made enough to do so comfortably—but working out of the Greene Gardens floor actually saved me money.

The space was designed with the same high level of innovation as Greene Gardens itself, reflecting the company's culture of luxury, comfort, and community.

I was steps away from the coffee bar when I noticed Levi, our landscape architect, standing by one of the machines, stirring his drink.

I approached, clapping a hand to his shoulder.

He looked up and nodded, holding out his hand for a dap. "What's good, what's good?"

I smiled, accepting his hand, then reached for a paper cup. "Need fuel, man. I need all the fuel."

He chuckled. "I'm surprised it took you this long to get here. You've been locked in your office all morning."

"Yeah, man." I shook my head, focusing on my coffee. "Finally needed liquid energy."

The break room was massive, almost like a high-end café.

Floor-to-ceiling windows flooded the space with natural light, offering a panoramic view of Manhattan's skyline.

It was both relaxing and invigorating. The perfect place to recharge while working on such a massive project.

Some days, I felt like I'd bit off more than I could chew.

Other days, I felt like I could conquer the world.

But today, I just felt like shit.

Usually, I had home to look forward to.

But after last night?

I had no idea what I was going home to.

Would Ayla even be there?

I hadn't wanted our first conversation to happen over the phone—but I'd changed my mind, called her all morning, and she still hadn't answered once.

Hadn't called me back either.

Levi handed me the folder I had one of the project managers take back to him after he dropped it off at my office earlier.

"He finalized it," Levi informed.

I flipped open the folder, leafing through the pages, nodding as I reviewed the designs. "Like I knew he would."

Levi was a landscape architect I brought in from North Carolina, recommended to me by a former client.

Before Greene Gardens, he worked freelance, but his work spoke for itself.

His attention to detail? Impeccable.

His vision? Next level.

His layout featured green spaces, fountains, walking trails, playgrounds, and community seating areas.

The rainwater garden feature wasn't just for aesthetics. It also functioned as a natural drainage solution.

We were making Greene Gardens look so damn good, even *I* wanted to live there.

"This is solid," I commented, still reviewing the designs. "The placement of the rainwater garden is smart. It minimizes runoff without wasting space." I nodded. "And the seating areas along the trails? Makes it inviting, not just functional."

Flipping to another page, I grinned.

"You did good work. I'm sure Bryant was happy."

"Ecstatic," Levi confirmed with a short laugh. "He was in a good mood today."

I laughed, knowing exactly what he meant.

This project was huge.

The pressure immense.

We weren't just designing houses and buildings.

We were creating a village.

The weight of that responsibility was heavy as hell.

I sighed, feeling that weight pressing on me.

And not just from work.

From home too.

I just hoped this project wasn't about to wreck my marriage.

Levi stood quietly beside me.

Too quiet.

I peeked over to see him leaning against the counter, his eyes still on me.

"What's up?" I asked.

Levi inhaled deeply, then exhaled. "Look, I gotta say something."

I frowned, my grip tightening on my coffee cup.

"About what happened earlier in your office with Harper?"

I swallowed hard. Tensed up immediately. "What about it?"

Levi pressed a hand to his chest. "I know it's none of my business but… be careful with her."

I placed my paper cup on the counter, my stomach twisting.

For the longest time, I thought Harper's flirting was just harmless fun.

The kind of attention that meant nothing.

But if I was being honest?

I never told Ayla about any of it.

Not when Harper started standing a little too close after meetings.

Not when she made those slick comments about my smile or my eyes.

Not when she first started calling me "Hass" like we had history.

I never mentioned it.

Because I knew—deep down—it wasn't as innocent as I pretended it was.

Levi straightened his back, his eyes scanning the room before refocusing on me.

"I don't know if you know this," he started, "but she tried the same thing she's trying with you, with me."

I arched a brow.

"Pushed up on me at an after-work function last year." He shook his head. "I had to remind her I was married."

He held up his left hand, the diamond wedding band glinting under the bright lounge lights. "I mean, hello."

I snorted a laugh.

"Can't miss or forget this shit." Levi chuckled. "My wife saw to it *no one* could miss it."

"So, you reminding Harper that you're married…" I started. "That didn't stop her?"

"Not even a little," Levi replied, his expression darkening. "I had to start talking about my wife every time I saw her. Anytime she paid me too much attention, I'd bring up Calese—constantly. And honestly? I was doing it more for Harper's safety than mine."

I chuckled.

"Y'all pay me well, and I love what we're doing—building this community in a major way."

I nodded, understanding.

"I've done the whole getting-involved-with-a-woman-I-shouldn't-be-involved-with thing at work before, and I'm never doing that again." He blew out a breath. "That shit almost ruined my life *and* career—had me freelancing just to survive. Believe me, I learned my lesson."

I set my paper cup down.

"Plus, like I said, constantly reminding Harper I was married," he continued, "was more about protecting her than it was about protecting me. Because, well, Calese be Calesing."

I laughed, shaking my head. "Knowing your wife? I believe you."

Levi took a sip of his coffee, then added, "Look, you're a good dude, Hassani. And I know you love your wife."

"With every breath in me," I affirmed.

"Exactly." Levi nodded. "I met Ayla. She's real. Solid. Things I know you already know. But Harper? That woman don't care nothing about that, man."

He glanced behind us, then lowered his voice. "She likes to see how far she can push things. It's like she gets a thrill out of crossing boundaries. I don't really know what her deal is."

I blinked twice. "*Hmph.*"

"That's why she don't like me anymore." Levi snickered. "She doesn't take rejection well. After so many failed attempts—and me always bringing up my wife—now all Harper gives me is attitude. And often."

He shook his head. "I just make sure to keep my distance, 'cause women like her can be dangerous. For real."

I nodded, playing it cool.

Levi had handled things the right way with Harper.

Harper had an undeniable presence.

She was a beautiful woman, and she knew it.

She was fully aware of her feminine charm and wielded it with precision.

It was nice to be around, I won't lie. But I wasn't stupid, nor would I ever consider exploring anything beyond work with her. Ever.

I was used to women throwing themselves at me.

But this?

This felt different.

Maybe because I was older now? Maybe because I was married?

Whatever it was, this situation wasn't like the others.

Especially after last night.

Ayla said she wanted a divorce.

Even now, the words felt unreal.

"I hear you, man," I finally told Levi. "I got this, though. I know better than to let some office crush mess up my life."

Levi nodded. "Word."

Because what the hell would that look like?

Me—principal architect on one of the biggest projects of my career—caught up in some mess over Harper?

Hell no.

"Still," Levi added, tossing his empty cup in the trash. "Just watch your back with her. Women like her got a hard time hearing no. Feel me?"

"I feel you."

"Aight, boss." Levi gave me a firm pat on the back, making me chuckle.

"Let me get back to work," he announced. "'Cause you're a cool boss, but I know you don't play that either."

"Let me know if you need anything for the next phase of the project," I told him as he walked out.

As Levi disappeared down the hall, movement in my periphery caught my eye.

Harper.

Stepping out of her office.

Her eyes darted from Levi's retreating form to me, lingering just a second too long.

Then she smirked—slow and knowing—before slipping back inside.

I stared in that direction for a breath, before blinking myself out of it.

Levi's words played in my mind as I refocused on my drink.

I stayed in the break room for a bit, drinking my coffee at the bar. Closed my eyes, letting the caffeine do nothing to energize me.

I was tired—beyond fatigued.

And there was no telling if I'd even get the rest I needed tonight.

Because, it's like I said, I had no idea what I was returning home to.

I stared down at my coffee, my stomach tightening.

An uneasy feeling settled in my gut.

I needed to take the Levi approach with Harper and shut whatever she was up to down.

I'd viewed it as innocent for too long.

But after what Ayla told me last night…

I prayed I wasn't too late.

PART II
THE FRAMEWORK

The structure that holds everything together. The trust and connection that gives love its shape...

CHAPTER 6

THEN – EARLY AUTUMN 2021… TWO YEARS EARLIER

yla

"I'm not used to not seeing you for this long," I whined into the phone, my house slippers sweeping against the floor.

"Well, Favorite Girl," my Aunt Laurie teased, "that's your fault for never visiting me in Mexico."

I snickered, shaking my head as I turned the corner.

I laughed, but her words lingered.

When I was younger, I used to dream of traveling the world like she did—hopping from country to country, collecting stories instead of things.

But now?

My life with Hassani was my adventure. Steady, secure, and exactly what I'd always wanted.

I'd called Aunt Laurie at the perfect time… just before she boarded a flight to the Mediterranean.

"I haven't seen you since last summer," I said, heading toward the kitchen. "We're in October now. That's over a year. And you know how I get when I don't see my Aunt for a while."

She giggled.

"You laugh, but I'm serious, Aunt Laurie."

"Then come to Mexico."

I rolled my eyes. "Aunt Laurie."

"What?" she teased.

"The last two times I made plans to visit, you said you were traveling." I shook my head. "You're not even home long enough for me to come. You're not even home now! So *please*, stop inviting me."

She laughed. "Okay, touché. You got me there."

"At this rate, the only way I'll see you is if I grow wings and fly alongside the planes you insist on hopping on every other week."

Her laughter deepened.

Aunt Laurie was officially retired—or semi-retired, as she liked to put it. She still picked up gigs as an Independent Fashion Buyer if the price was right.

After her divorce, she realized she loved her freedom more than any man. She packed her things, traveled the world, and eventually settled in Puerto Vallarta, Mexico.

…Whenever she *could* sit still long enough.

I'd tried solo traveling before, but it always felt lonely.

Now I just lived vicariously through Aunt Laurie.

"What can I say?" she sighed. "I don't like to sit and wait. Life's too short for that—even waiting for you to come visit me in Mex-i-co."

I snorted a laugh.

In the background, I heard an airport announcement over the speakers.

"Are you at your gate?" I asked, stepping into the kitchen.

And that's when I saw something that made me jerk my head back.

"I am," she confirmed. "I'm about to board my flight. I'll call you next week."

"Okay." I blinked; my eyes locked on something new in the kitchen. Something that wasn't there that morning. "I love you. Have a safe flight."

"Thank you, Favorite Girl. I love you too."

The call ended, but my confusion didn't.

"What in the hell?"

I took slow steps forward, closing the distance between myself and this… *thing*.

Leaning in closer, I examined it, squinting. *"Ew."*

At first glance, it looked like an alien spaceship had crash-landed between my coffee maker and the coffee carousel.

But no…

I tilted my head.

Was it a… melting coffee cup?

An oversized, ceramic, melting coffee cup, painted metallic silver with splashes of red and blue.

The design was all over the place.

It was too much.

And it had Hassani written all over it.

"Oh, *uh-uh.*" I shook my head and immediately turned to leave the kitchen, forgetting all about the coffee I had come to brew.

We'd been in our house for four years now.

Hassani had made a few improvements—a built-in spice rack, a reading nook beneath the staircase, little details that made our home even better.

And while his building projects always hit, his decor choices were a continuous miss.

We'd already discussed and agreed that he would check in with me before buying any new decor for the house.

And yet…

That chaotic mess of ceramic was sitting in my kitchen.

I stormed through the house, heading straight for the home office.

Hassani had been glued to his computer all morning, emailing back and forth for the Greene Gardens Project he was still in negotiations to join.

The moment I reached the open doorway, I spotted him, seated in his leather chair, eyes locked on one of the two computer monitors in front of him.

The office had a sleek, masculine feel, with warm wooden tones.

I told Hassani to design it however he wanted since he used it far more than I did.

My only contribution? Storing the books that didn't fit on my many bookshelves throughout the house on his wall-mounted bookshelf.

He was kind enough to give me a shelf—just one—while the others were reserved for his architecture books.

Beside his long, fast-moving fingers typing on the keyboard was his infamous sketchbook, laid open with an unfinished sketch on the page.

In front of him, one computer screen glowed with a blueprint, the other with an email he was typing.

I leaned against the doorframe, watching the muscles in his forearm flex as he typed.

Clearing my throat, I tapped the wooden frame before crossing my arms over my chest.

"What's up, baby?" Hassani asked, eyes still glued to the screen, fingers still typing.

"Oh, nothing," I started. "Just horrified so early in the afternoon."

He glanced at me, his hazel-green eyes scanning me briefly before refocusing on the screen. "Oh yeah? That sounds fun."

"Baby?"

"Yeah?"

"What the hell is that monstrosity by the coffee bar?"

He snorted a laugh, still not looking away from the screen. "It's art."

"It's ugly."

I caught his side grin just before he turned his head.

"Jaleel Gordon has one just like it in his house."

I rolled my eyes. "Oh my God."

"I read about it in Architectural Digest."

"*Mm-hmm…?*"

"It's a D-Slam original."

I squinted. "A D-Slam original?" I rubbed my lips together before continuing. "You mean that expensive, controversial stuff that retired basketball player makes and calls art?"

"He's an artist now, A."

"Oh, he's *definitely* something." I pointed behind me. "And *that* thing in there is something *else*. It doesn't go with the aesthetic at all. I thought we talked about this."

"It looked too good not to get it, though," he said, finally abandoning the keyboard to swivel his office chair and face me.

"How much was it?"

He gestured casually with his hands. "Not that much, you know... Just a little 15K."

My eyes ballooned. "Fifteen *thousand*—"

"It was a limited-edition piece," he said, leaning toward me. "Only a few were made."

"*None* of *that* should have been made, if we're keeping it real." I stepped closer. "Fifteen thousand dollars is insane, Hassani."

"You can't really *price* art."

"I'm sorry... is the art in the house with us?" I folded my arms. "Because I'm not sure we're looking at the same thing."

Hassani shrugged. "I think it's beautiful."

"Shit." I released a scoffing laugh. "You call me beautiful all the time. Should *I* be worried?"

He barked a laugh, and I tightened my lips to keep from laughing with him.

Hassani grabbed my hand, pulled me onto his lap, and pressed his lips to my shoulder.

"Why didn't you talk to me before getting it? Like we discussed?"

"I wanted it to be a surprise."

I sighed. "Well... goal unlocked."

His lips trailed against my skin, his hand caressing my thigh, sending that familiar stir through me.

I shook my head at myself.

"You know what's interesting?" I asked.

"What?" he whispered against the back of my neck.

I turned to look at him over my shoulder. "You've been *too busy* to go furniture shopping with me, but you had time to pick out that ugly piece of art."

"Baby, it's not ugly."

"You're right, my bad." I smirked. "It would have to look ten times better to qualify as ugly."

He dropped his jaw, and I couldn't help but laugh.

That's when it hit me.

This was our first real disagreement.

I inhaled a deep breath, then stood, turning to face him.

"This is our first 'fight,'" I said with finger quotes.

He smiled, then licked his lips. "Wanna go fuck it out? You know… as a resolution?"

I laughed, moving closer to shove his shoulder. "I have a better idea."

"What?"

"We're going to buy the furniture you keep telling me you have no time to get."

He turned to his computer screen again. "Fine. We'll just order it online as soon as I wrap this—"

"Nope." I shook my head. "It's still early. We're going to the furniture store."

"Huh?"

"Huh?" I mocked, matching his deep voice. "We are going to a showroom so I can see it in person. I need to *see it* and *feel it*, and since you like to drop money on *ugly things*, we're going to redirect that energy."

I pointed toward the hallway. "I'm gonna go put my sneakers on—"

"Oh, you mean *right now?*" he questioned.

"*Mm-hmm.*"

He pointed at the screen. "Baby, I'm doing something right now."

"Yeah, I know." I smiled. "You're about to get ready so we can go to the furniture store."

Hassani stared at me, his light eyes unblinking.

I held his gaze, not blinking either, letting a sweet smile pull at my lips.

He inhaled deeply, then exhaled through his nose. "I'll start the car."

I smiled wider.

He licked his lips, then shook his head. "Damn." He kissed his teeth and stood next. "That smile will do it every time, I swear."

Hassani swaggered up to me, looping an arm around my head, pulling me into a gentle headlock.

His fingers dug into my waist, tickling me until I laughed uncontrollably.

"Come on." He kissed my forehead as we walked toward the front door.

HASSANI WALKED AHEAD OF ME, PULLING THE SHOWROOM DOOR OPEN.

As soon as he got in front of it, he turned with a smirk.

"After you, Queen Ayla." He did an exaggerated bow.

"Oh, don't be passive-aggressive," I teased as I stepped through.

He chuckled behind me.

Hassani insisted that if we were going furniture shopping, he would pick the showroom.

And it was *just* like him to choose an expensive one.

Verana Interiors, in the Flatiron District of Manhattan, was nothing short of luxury.

When I said I wanted to go to a showroom, I meant one in our town upstate.

Not in the heart of the city.

But I let it slide.

I just wanted new furniture.

We had been in our house for four years, and the furniture inside was a mix of what we'd brought from our old Manhattan apartments.

I'd had my furniture forever.

I wanted our house—the one Hassani designed—to have a cohesive aesthetic, not feel like random pieces thrown together.

Over the years, we'd transformed it into a home.

Now, the missing piece?

Furniture that fit.

As soon as I walked in, I knew it would be a challenge to find something within a reasonable budget.

For Hassani, though?

There was no budget.

Money, in his mind, was printed to be spent.

And he had brought us to a place where we could probably spend it all.

Various living room setups were arranged ahead of us.

The soft overhead lighting, elegant displays, and plush seating created a cozy, upscale ambiance.

It was beautiful—but expensive as hell.

I had barely stepped a few feet inside when I heard a voice.

"Oh, hello! Welcome, welcome."

I turned toward the sound, spotting a young, stylish woman approaching.

She wore a tight gray dress and a bright white smile.

But her eyes?

They looked past me.

Did a double take on Hassani and hadn't lost focus.

When I turned, I saw *him* focused on his phone, typing as he walked up behind me.

I inhaled sharply.

I already knew how this was going to go.

"Welcome to Verana Interiors." Her tone was bright, sugary, but her eyes were still locked on my husband. "I'm Mia, a sales associate here." Her voice practically purred. "And *you* are?"

I fought the urge to roll my eyes.

Here we go.

Some women flirted subtly.

Mia?

She might as well have thrown her phone number at Hassani's feet and waited for him to pick it up.

She hadn't even looked at me yet.

I released a soft scoffing laugh. "Hi, Mia. I'm Ayla."

My voice was firm, patient.

I waited until she finally met my eyes, before adding, "Nice to meet you, Mia."

She smiled sweetly.

Her attention flicked back to Hassani before snapping back to me.

"Pleasure." She cleared her throat. "What can I help you with today?"

I inhaled slowly, forcing myself to stay calm.

Between Hassani being distracted by his phone. Mia being too distracted by my husband… I was being tested.

Still, I answered smoothly. "My husband and I are here to browse furniture for our living room."

I took a slight step back, my elbow discreetly nudging Hassani's ribs.

His head jerked up from his phone.

"*Uh*, yeah," he said, blinking. "Furniture for the living room."

Mia's smile widened instantly.

The moment Hassani made eye contact with her, she practically glowed.

"Excellent." She giggled.

God.

This again.

"Do you have a specific style in mind?" Mia twirled a strand of her blonde hair, combing her fingers through it. "We at Verana specialize in exclusive, curated collections." Her voice was syrupy sweet. "I'm sure we can find something that fits your aesthetic."

I tilted my head slightly. "We're looking for something modern— but within budget."

Before Mia could answer, Hassani stepped closer behind me.

His arms wrapped around my waist, his chin resting on my shoulder.

"But you know," he added smoothly, "feel free to show us everything."

He pressed a slow kiss to my temple. "Budget's not very important, right, baby?"

I bit my tongue, feeling myself ready to protest.

Mia blinked out of her stare, her eyes falling to Hassani's arms around my waist. "Well…" She focused on Hassani again. "You've come to the right place. Let me show you around."

"Cool," Hassani replied, his hand moving to mine where he interlocked our fingers.

As Mia showed Hassani and me around the showroom, pointing out furniture that was both loud and wrong and beautiful but way too pricey, Hassani divided his attention between her and his phone.

On the car ride over, he explained that he and representatives for Bryant Greene had been going back and forth through emails regarding the Greene Gardens Project. They were negotiating terms that would determine if Hassani would join their team as a principal architect. He'd been in talks with them for a month now, ever since Bryant Greene's assistant called at six in the morning, asking Hassani to drop everything and drive into the city for an impromptu meeting.

If he landed this project, Hassani would officially be a millionaire. The starting salary alone was $1.2 million. His largest yet.

I would be married to a millionaire. The thought had me smiling.

Mia stopped in front of a modern-looking furniture set, sleek and dramatic, like it belonged on the set of *Miami Vice* and not in our home.

"Oh, I like this one," Hassani voiced.

"You have excellent taste," Mia said with another one of her little giggles.

Hassani took a seat on the loveseat, running his hand along the cushion.

"A little stiff," he commented, patting the cushion. "But it's more for style anyway, right?"

I arched a brow.

"Exactly," Mia concurred. "This is more of a statement piece, and you look fantastic on it."

"*Hmph*," I huffed, scanning the room for something else. "I was thinking something a little more… comfortable and *less* of a statement piece. It would be nice to actually relax on it sometimes. You know?"

Hassani was back on his phone again, eyes glued to the screen, typing, when Mia took a seat a little too close to him on the loveseat.

She lightly touched his arm. "This set, though pricey, suits a man like you, so this one is obviously the better option."

Hassani slid his eyes from his screen and glanced at where she touched him, realizing she'd taken a seat beside him.

His eyes snapped to mine.

I arched both brows and folded my arms.

He chuckled as he moved to the edge of the loveseat, quickly standing up.

"I'll check availability in our warehouse," Mia said, scooting to the edge of her seat to stand up after him. "And I'll be right back to let you know if we have this set ready to ship."

I followed her with my eyes as she walked off, scoffing to myself.

To say this was unusual would be a lie. From the time Hassani and I were only friends as teenagers, I'd watched women literally throw themselves at him. It was ridiculous. Pathetic, even. Always funny to watch, though—even as his wife.

It's crazy how even with a giant diamond ring circling his left finger, women still flirted with him. Often right in front of me.

I glanced over at Hassani, now standing beside me.

"You know, between you being distracted by your phone and Mia gearing herself up to get her ass beat down at her job," I started, "I'm not sure who's pissing me off more."

Hassani lifted his eyes off his phone to focus on me.

"Actually." I turned to face him. "*I* feel like *you're* pissing me off more."

"*Aww*, baby, baby," he said, sliding his phone into his back pocket.

"Then again…" I turned to look where Mia had walked off before shifting my attention back to Hassani. "I feel like you should take off your shirt, flex a pec, and see if you can get us a discount off ol' girl.

Turn on the charm a little. Show her some skin and attention so we can get this stiff-ass, expensive furniture for cheap."

Hassani hollered a laugh, making me laugh too.

He walked up to me and circled his arms around my waist, pulling me closer. "I told you I was working today. I'm sending emails back and forth—"

"Coffee bar, coffee bar," I cut in. "All I can see as you tell me this is that *ugly* sculpture on our coffee bar."

He snatched me closer and brought his fingers to my stomach, tickling me until I hunched forward, laughing louder, trying to escape.

Hassani wrapped his arms around me again and lowered his mouth to mine, pressing a long, deep kiss against my lips, parting them to slide his tongue in.

I moaned, pressing my hands to either side of his face as he held me even tighter.

After a short while, he gently broke our kiss and pressed his forehead to mine. "My first, my last, and my only," he said. "That's you. Always remember that. I don't see no one else. You hear me?"

I closed my eyes and smiled as he pressed another kiss to my lips.

Someone clearing their throat behind us had both Hassani and me looking that way.

It was Mia, her smile less bright as she closed the distance between Hassani and I.

"Okay," Mia started. "So, I was able to check availability on this set—"

"Mia, right?" Hassani quizzed, pulling me in front of him to hold me from behind.

She offered a small smile. "That's right."

"Let's not focus on this one right here," he said, gesturing to the furniture set he was originally interested in. "Whatever my wife wants, that's what we're getting."

Mia's brows shot up. "Oh... *umm*... yeah, of course." She moved her eyes to me, then swallowed hard. "What was the... *uhh*, style you said you were interested in?"

I forced a smile. "Modern, comfortable... *not* white."

"Right." She nodded. "Okay. Follow me, and I'll show you something you'll love."

I smirked. "Perfect. Please, lead the way."

For the next hour, Mia proved why she worked at a high-end furniture store. She walked us through pieces that matched the budget *I* had in mind while also satisfying the aesthetic I wanted. I had to admit, she was good at her job—*and* she wasn't so bad once she stopped flirting with my husband.

"You have great taste, Ayla," Mia said with a genuine smile after I settled on a furniture set that Hassani also loved. "I'll go ahead and place the order, set up the delivery time, and be back with all the details."

I nodded. "Thank you so much, Mia."

"Yeah, thanks, Mia," Hassani added, pulling out his phone the second it buzzed in his pocket.

"My pleasure, you two." She nodded before walking off.

I turned to Hassani, smiling, excited that we'd *finally* have a living room that felt like *ours*.

But when I looked at him, I noticed something was off.

He stood frozen behind me, his eyes locked on his phone's screen.

The smile fell from my lips. "Everything okay, baby?"

He lifted his gaze, his jaw dropping slightly.

"What?" I stepped closer. "What's the matter?"

His voice was low, almost disbelieving. "I got it."

"Got what?" I blinked. "The Greene Gardens Project?"

He nodded, slowly at first, then faster. "Yeah."

I smiled big. "They agreed to 1.2 million?!"

"Nah." He shook his head.

My smile melted.

"It's for 2.5."

I blinked. Hard.

This was the same man who, just a few months ago, wasn't even sure he'd get a second meeting. The same man who doubted whether he was *big enough* to be in the same room as someone like Bryant Greene. And now? He wasn't just in the room. *He owned it.*

"Wh-what?" I asked.

"I asked for more at our second meeting," he explained, still staring at the phone screen. "Told them that after reviewing the plans and realizing the enormity of the project, my compensation would have to be higher for it to be fair. I... I negotiated for more—I *never* thought they'd approve it."

"Wait." I held up a trembling hand between us. "2.5 million... *dollars?!*"

"A year. And for the duration of the project," he exhaled. "It's unheard of. And way above the average for an architect salary. But... yeah."

The excited scream burst out of me before I could stop it. I slapped a hand over my mouth. *"Baby!"*

I threw my arms around him, and Hassani lifted me off the ground in a spin.

"I'm so proud of you." I hugged him tighter. "Congratulations!"

"Thank you, baby. Thank you," he said, setting me down on my feet.

His grin stretched wide, lighting up his entire face, and it melted my heart.

Hassani had worked *so* hard for this. I'd watched him pour countless hours into proposals, take so many calls, stress over every detail. And now? It all paid off.

I glanced around the store and raised a hand when I noticed we had everyone's attention.

I laughed. "I'm so sorry, y'all..." I called out.

Then I turned back to Hassani, wrapping my arms around his waist. Low and just for him, I whispered, "But my man is a multi-millionaire."

He laughed, circling his arms around my waist and pressing a kiss to my lips.

I tightened my arms around him, sinking into the moment, into *him*, into *us*. I wanted to stay here forever, in this high, in this happiness.

But the thing about moments like these?

They don't last forever.

Not when the very thing that brings you joy... is the same thing that pulls you apart.

CHAPTER 7

THEN – MID-SUMMER 2022... NINE MONTHS LATER

*A*yla

Hassani turned off the car the moment he pulled into the reserved space inside the parking garage.

"I didn't even know this place had a garage," I said, scanning the cars parked around us. "I've been here for so many class trips in elementary school. How did I not know The Met had a parking garage?"

Hassani chuckled as he reached behind him, grabbing his sketchbook from the backseat.

"Do me a favor," he said, handing it to me. "Put this in the glove compartment."

I took the sketchbook and arched a brow. "We're at one of the most famous museums in the world, and you're worried someone's gonna steal your sketchbook, Hassani?"

He smirked. "That sketchbook is my life, baby. I don't take any chances."

"You have a reserved parking pass—" I pointed at the rearview mirror where Bryant Greene's signature was stamped on the permit— "and you really think someone's gonna break into the car just to take your book?"

"You said it yourself." Hassani grinned. "We're at a well-known spot. Anything can happen. Now close them pretty lips and put my book in the glove compartment so we can go."

I giggled, shaking my head as I did what he asked, then stole another glance out the passenger window.

"You ready?" he asked.

It was a loaded question.

Tonight was *The Greene Gardens Visionary Night*—an exclusive work event, and judging by the all-white, embossed invitation Hassani had brought home, it was a big deal. He had officially started working on the Greene Gardens Project last December. Since then, it had been all meetings, with the real work set to begin that coming Monday. But so far, everything seemed to be going well. He made it home at the same time every night for dinner, and we spent time together before heading to bed, just like always.

With school out for the summer, I had extra time on my hands. I'd considered teaching summer school. Park Avenue Prep gave teachers the flexibility to work with other grades. But in the end, I decided to focus on planning our annual trip instead. I still didn't have a solid date from Hassani, though. I didn't push him on it, figuring he needed time to settle into his new role first. If worst came to worst, we could stay local.

He was starting a huge project. I wasn't about to make him focus on anything else that wasn't as important.

"Am I ready?" I scoffed. "We're only in the garage, and I already feel underdressed."

He snickered. "You look great. Amazing. Like always."

"Maybe I should've worn a gown," I noted quietly, glancing into the rearview mirror to check my makeup. "I feel too casual."

I'd gone with a slim-fitting button-down tucked into a green denim pencil skirt, paired with silver sandals that sparkled under the car's lights. I was dressed for brunch, and the setting made me feel like I should've done more.

"Baby, I'm wearing a Henley tee, slacks, and Jordans," Hassani reasoned.

"Yeah, but everything you wear is designer, so even your *casual* outfit looks upscale."

He chuckled. "Bryant told us to come as we are. Nothing fancy. He literally said, '*This will be nothing fancy.*'"

"So much for that," I muttered. "Hosting an event at The Metropolitan Museum of Art but claiming it's *nothing fancy*? That's ironic."

Hassani pulled me into his arms and pressed a kiss to my forehead —then another. "Let's go, scaredy cat."

The first time he mentioned the event, I'd been floored.

"*I didn't know people could rent out museums for private events,*" I'd said over coffee.

"*Me neither,*" Hassani replied, sipping his. "*But this is Bryant Greene, so…*"

"*How much does something like that even cost?*"

Hassani shrugged. "I don't know exactly, but I overheard the interns whispering about it. Apparently, Bryant dropped over $50K just to rent the space for the night."

Now, standing here, I understood why.

To reach the event space, we had to take an elevator from the parking garage to the museum's ground floor. The moment we stepped inside, I was hit with awe.

I'd been to The Met countless times, but tonight, with only a handful of guests present, it felt completely different—like we'd been swallowed whole by the vastness of the museum, the art pieces looming over us like silent spectators.

At the direction of an event organizer, Hassani and I walked through several galleries, following signs for *The Greene Gardens Visionary Night.*

And then, I gasped.

We had stepped inside *The Temple of Dendur* in the Sackler Wing.

"Oh my God," I whispered, glancing up at Hassani to see if he was as taken by the space as I was.

It was breathtaking. Ancient Egyptian architecture, floor-to-ceiling glass windows, and a massive reflecting pool that made the space feel even more expansive.

"Okay." I swallowed hard. "*This* is next level."

Hassani chuckled, his deep voice echoing softly around us.

On the invitation Hassani brought home, there had been a printed explanation of why Bryant had chosen to host the event here. The artistic nature of the project aligned with the museum's setting, subtly reinforcing Bryant's belief that everyone involved in the Greene Gardens Project was contributing to something historic.

I already knew Hassani's role in the project was major. He was helping build a community—a place where people would live, work, and raise families—so I understood it was a big deal.

But that night, in *The Temple of Dendur*, I realized just how enormous of a deal it truly was.

Well-dressed servers moved gracefully through the space, offering champagne and hors d'oeuvres at every turn. My nerves had me reaching for a glass, hoping at least half of it would take the edge off.

I took a sip and immediately cringed, rolling my tongue around my mouth in search of any hint of sweetness. Missing entirely.

"It's not Moscato," Hassani teased, smirking. "So take it easy, baby."

"*Ha, ha,*" I said flatly, my eyes still scanning the room.

The soft lighting reflected off the water, giving everything an ethereal glow. The air buzzed with conversation, expensive perfumes mingling with the faint sound of classical music playing from unseen speakers.

We'd only been in the gallery for two minutes before people started coming up to Hassani, pulling him into conversations. Each time, he introduced me as, "*My wife, Mrs. Ayla Franklin,*" and without fail, they responded, "*It's nice to meet you, Mrs. Franklin.*"

And every single time, my heart swelled.

Watching Hassani work the room, seeing him in his element, was both awe-inspiring and terrifying. The man I'd known since I was a teenager had transformed before my eyes—still himself, but different. A polished professional. No slang, no casual banter. Just easy confidence, sharp intelligence, and an undeniable presence.

It was so sexy.

I stayed back when he was deep in conversation. I couldn't contribute to most of them—listening to architects discuss frameworks and fault lines went in one ear and out the other—but seeing so many Black professionals brimming with passion, talking about *making history*, that part?

That was inspiring.

Still, every time Hassani noticed I'd gone quiet for too long, he'd slide his fingers down my hand to interlock with mine, or wrap an arm around my waist, pulling me into the moment. It was those small gestures that mattered.

I was so damn proud of him, I could barely breathe evenly.

He had wanted this for so long. Since we were teenagers, he'd dreamed of being an architect. He had worked his ass off to get here, and now? He was *doing it*—doing it in a *big* way.

And yet…

I couldn't shake the feeling that, somehow, I was standing *outside* of it all.

Clink, clink, clink.

The sound of glass chiming rang through the gallery, drawing everyone's attention to the steps leading up to one of the Egyptian structures. Heels clicked against the stone floor as the crowd shifted toward the source, and before I could react, Hassani had already taken my hand, guiding me forward.

"Welcome, welcome," a deep voice boomed, effortlessly commanding the room. "I'm grateful I didn't insist on having a microphone—my voice is carrying just fine, isn't it?"

Laughter rippled through the crowd.

When we got close enough to see who was speaking, I inhaled sharply, my breath catching.

It was Bryant Greene.

The Bryant Greene.

A man I'd only ever heard about by name, whose face I'd seen on magazine covers. And now? He was standing just feet in front of me.

And my husband was working for him.

Bryant's suit was perfectly tailored, fitting him like it had been painted onto his body. In one hand, he held a sparkling glass of champagne, exuding effortless confidence. His beard was immaculate, his skin flawless, and his posture imposing. The same stacked, powerful build as my husband.

The hype around the multi-billionaire was definitely justified. Respectfully.

"Tonight," Bryant began, his smooth baritone settling over the room, "we are not just celebrating the beginning of a project." He paused, letting his gaze sweep over the gathered crowd. "We are celebrating the beginning of a legacy."

A murmur of agreement cascaded through the space.

"Greene Gardens is not just about infrastructure," he continued. "It's about *culture*. It's about creating something that will outlive us. Something our children and grandchildren... *and their grandchildren* will look at and feel *proud* of."

The room erupted into light applause.

"That is why I chose *The Met* as our venue tonight." He smiled, flashing a perfect set of white teeth. "This museum is filled with masterpieces that have stood the test of time. *That* is what we are building with Greene Gardens." He raised his glass. "And every single one of you in this room... you are the *artists*, the *visionaries*, the *creators*. This isn't just *work*—this is *history* in the making. Here's to you."

The room erupted in applause again, even livelier this time.

Hassani clapped so hard, his smile so wide, that I could *feel* him soaking in the weight of Bryant's words. And I felt it too—an energy humming in the air, charging everyone in the room, making me feel honored to witness it.

I had always known that Hassani's role as principal architect was *huge*, but tonight, I realized it was *monumental*. And with that realization came a weight I couldn't quite put into words.

"Whoa," I breathed, turning to him once the applause died down. "This is beyond incredible, baby."

"I know, right?" He let out a deep breath, puffing his cheeks as he exhaled. "My heart is pounding mad hard right now."

I pressed my hand to his chest and felt it—his heartbeat racing beneath my palm. I traced slow circles against his shirt, then lifted my hands to his face, cupping either side as I stared into his eyes.

"I am *so* proud of you," I told him, my voice thick with emotion. "You've worked so hard for this. You *deserve* this. *All* of it. And you're about to *kill it*. I can feel it in my bones."

Hassani inhaled another deep breath, nodding along with me.

"Hassani."

We both turned toward the familiar voice calling his name.

Approaching us was Bryant Greene, one arm wrapped protectively around a stunning, pregnant woman who walked beside him. Her belly was round but not *too* big, just enough to steal the show. She was radiant, with her long, perfectly rolled locs, glowing in that effortless way that made people stop and look.

My smile grew the closer they got, my eyes drawn instinctively to the small swell of her stomach.

"Mr. Greene," Hassani greeted, reaching out to shake his hand.

"Bryant," Bryant corrected, gripping Hassani's hand firmly. "I keep telling you, everyone else can call me *Mr. Greene*, but you?" He pointed at Hassani. "*Just* Bryant."

Then his gaze shifted to me, his smile widening.

He pointed toward me before looking back at Hassani. "Mrs. Franklin?"

"Yes." Hassani gave a proud smile, slipping an arm around my waist. "This is my wife, Mrs. Ayla Franklin."

Bryant took my hand with an easy confidence, his grip gentle but firm. "Pleasure to meet you, Mrs. Franklin."

"Likewise," I replied, charmed by his presence.

"And this…" Bryant said, his voice warm, "is *my* wife, Mrs. Zoe Greene."

"It's so good to meet you two," Zoe said, shaking my hand, then Hassani's. "Hassani, your quick doodle set the foundation for all of this. I hope you know that."

"Oh, God." Hassani chuckled, shaking his head. "From what Bryant told us; *we* wouldn't even be here if it wasn't for *you*."

"And *that* is a *fact*," Bryant agreed, grinning. "I married a *genius*."

"Well, we got that in common," Hassani joked, holding out a fist to Bryant, who bumped it with his own.

Zoe and I giggled.

"Well," I said, tilting my head, "who do I thank for inviting us to such an amazing place for a work event?"

"Isn't it stunning?" Bryant asked, his eyes sweeping the space again.

"It's *beyond* breathtaking," I admitted.

"That would be Mrs. Greene and her genius mind *again*," he said proudly, resting a hand over Zoe's belly. "It was her idea to host it here."

I warmed at the sight of how affectionate he was toward her, how he couldn't seem to keep his hands too far from her growing belly.

"A genius, indeed." I smiled. "Do you know what you two are having?"

"A *boy*." Zoe grinned, playfully rolling her eyes. "And I *haven't* been able to hear straight since we found out—this guy's been talking my ear off about it—"

"Hey, Mrs. Greene!" Bryant cut in, pulling her close to press a kiss against her temple. "You've better watch it."

I giggled at the way they bickered like a couple deeply in love.

"How about you two?" Zoe asked next. "Any children?"

I felt Hassani's gaze shift toward me, and instinctively, I glanced at him before refocusing on Bryant and Zoe.

"Not yet," I answered, my voice steady. "But soon."

"Yeah," Hassani echoed, just a beat behind me.

I don't know why I said that. Why *we* said that.

Especially standing *here*, at the start of the biggest project Hassani had ever taken on.

We had never sat down and had a *real* conversation about children. Not once in all the years we'd been together. Sure, we'd made casual jokes about what traits we hoped our future kids would inherit—his height, my curls, his hazel-green eyes—but that was it. It had always been hypothetical. Wishful.

And yet, those words—*but soon*—had just left my mouth so easily. *Why?*

"Well," Bryant said, clapping Hassani on the shoulder. "When the time is right, I'm sure it'll happen. And when it does..." He smirked. "They'll say their father helped build the village that it takes to raise our future's brightest minds."

"Amen." Hassani nodded.

The Greenes excused themselves shortly after, moving on to mingle with other guests. But their words? They stayed with me.

Children.

Why hadn't Hassani and I ever seriously talked about children?

We'd been *enjoying* our marriage, that much was true.

And every time my doctor asked me if I wanted to renew my birth control prescription, I had answered *yes* without hesitation.

But... why hadn't I *hesitated*?

"You okay?" Hassani's voice pulled me from my thoughts.

I blinked and turned to him as we stood by the makeshift bar, waiting for our glasses of champagne.

"Yeah," I lied, forcing a small smile. "I'm good. Just really getting high off the energy in here."

"Word." He nodded, accepting our glasses from the bartender. "Thank you."

Hassani handed me my glass and I took a slow sip of champagne, my thoughts still swirling.

I had *never* thought it before.

Not like *this*.

And now that I had… I wasn't sure I was ready for the answer.

Throughout the night, as Hassani introduced me to yet another one of his colleagues with his formal, *"This is my wife, Mrs. Ayla Franklin,"* my eyes kept drifting to the Greenes. I was so impressed by how protective and attentive Bryant was with his wife. A man who was both a leader and a devoted husband. At times, I almost forgot he was a multi-billionaire because of how visibly affectionate he was toward her.

I couldn't help but want that.

Not the marriage—I had that. Not the devoted husband—I definitely had that too.

I wanted the baby.

But damn, what a time to want that, right? My husband was about to be involved in the biggest project of his career. The timing couldn't be worse.

Bryant had said that when the time was right, we'd know. And now wasn't the right time.

For the next hour, Hassani and I moved through the gallery, stopping to admire the architecture in between his introductions. Amongst his team, I met Jordan Brock, his project manager, whose engagement ring was blinding, and his landscape architect, Levi Weston, along with Levi's wife, Calese.

"This event is insane," Calese said, tossing back the rest of her champagne before placing the empty glass on a passing server's tray. "Thank you," she added before turning back to me. "I have never in my life. Like, who does this? Bryant Greene, that's who."

Calese was so animated, not shy in the slightest. It was refreshing to see someone so down-to-earth in an environment that made me feel out of place.

"You smell so good, Ayla," she said, her bright eyes moving through my cloud of coily curls next. "And your hair! I'm obsessed."

"I'm obsessed with *yours*," I replied, smiling up at her perfectly shaped blowout. "It is *sparkling* under these lights."

"But your shape?" she said, gesturing at my head. "It's the perfect heart and frames your face beautifully. Has anyone ever told you that you look like a young Lauryn Hill? Lighter, of course. But *just* like her."

"It was the first thing I noticed when we met as teenagers," Hassani said, walking up behind me and wrapping his arms around my waist. "That's why I call her A. Boogie."

Calese pressed a hand to her chest. "That is too cute." She wrapped an arm around Levi's biceps when he came to stand closer. "Levi calls me Cali." Her deep brown skin glowed, as if she were blushing as she looked up at him. "I *love* it. It's always the cutesy nicknames for me."

I giggled.

"Anyway," Levi said, chuckling. "We're about to head out." He extended his hand to Hassani for a dap, and Hassani obliged. "Monday morning is when all the fun begins, huh?"

"That's right," Hassani confirmed. "The planning and design phase starts to ensure the first phase of homes and businesses is ready."

"Aight, aight." Levi rubbed his hands together. "Can't wait."

Calese turned to me and stepped closer. "Girl, I don't know what they're talking about, but it was *so* good to meet you."

I laughed as she took my hand, and I squeezed hers gently.

"It was *great* meeting you too, Calese," I replied. "I hope to see you again."

"And you *will*." She winked. "Nice meeting you, Hassani."

"Likewise," Hassani replied with a smile.

"Great meeting you too, Levi," I added.

"An absolute pleasure meeting you, Ayla." He smiled at me before focusing on Hassani. "Behind every great man, right?"

"Oh, you already know." Hassani chuckled. "Y'all get home safely."

The Westons were making their way to the exit when I turned to Hassani.

"Should we be getting ready to go too, or—"

"There you are," a light and airy voice said behind us.

I turned just in time to see a slim, statuesque woman strutting toward us, her bright, sparkling smile visible from across the gallery.

"I don't know why we keep missing each other, Hass."

I peeked up at my husband, catching the small smile he sent her way before wrapping an arm around me.

I locked eyes with him. "You know her?"

"*Uh*, yeah," he replied. "This is—"

"Harper Royce," she said, extending her hand toward me.

She was… stunning.

Warm brown skin, shoulder-length wavy hair—thick, full-bodied, not quite curly but not straight either. Sharp, dark brown eyes. Tall. Almost *too* close in height to Hassani.

I forced my hand up to take hers. "Nice to meet you."

She was dressed the way I *thought* I should have been tonight. A high-end designer suit, tailored to fit her slim waist and hips like a glove. Gold hoop earrings and bangles sparkled under the overhead lights.

No need to be fancy, my ass.

"This is my wife," Hassani said. "Mrs. Ayla Franklin."

"*Aww*, nice to meet you, *Ayla.*"

Ayla.

Not *Mrs. Franklin.*

Every other person had called me Mrs. Franklin after Hassani introduced me that way.

Even Calese had called me Mrs. Franklin before I told her to just call me Ayla. Calese was cool, and we clicked instantly. So, of course she could call me by my first name.

I did *not* give Harper that same permission.

And as petty as it sounded, I didn't like that she helped herself to that privilege.

"This place is gorgeous, isn't it?" she said to Hassani. "But nothing compares to how laid-back but *good* you look."

I jerked my head back so fast I almost gave myself whiplash.

Hassani glanced at me, then let out a nervous chuckle. "*Aw*, you know."

She giggled. "Oh, Hassani! Guess what I just got my pretty hands on the other day?"

"What?"

She winked. "Another D-Slam original."

Hassani's brows arched high. "Oh, word?"

"Sure did." She nodded, grinning ear to ear. "Special edition, of course. Only a few made."

"Damn." He chuckled. "That's dope."

Her eyes flicked to mine. "Hassani told me how much you *hated* the one he got for your kitchen?" She exhaled another one of her annoying little giggles. "I couldn't believe it. A *D-Slam original* is one of the most *coveted* art pieces in the art world right now."

I had to unclench my teeth before responding. "Is it now?"

"Oh, *yeah*." She pressed a hand to Hassani's chest, and my eyes followed every inch of that movement. "You're so lucky to have a man with such a good eye for art."

I stared at her hand—still *on* my husband's chest—before rolling my eyes up at him.

Hassani, always quick on the hint, stepped out of her touch and wrapped an arm around my waist.

In that moment, I *did not* want him touching me.

Who *was* this woman?

I know she introduced herself as Harper Royce, but *who* was she? And why did she seem so damn comfortable with Hassani already?

I had *never* heard of this woman before tonight, but somehow, she knew what was in *our* home. She knew enough to call him *Hass*.

And he *let* her.

"What do you do on the project, Harper?" I asked.

It was a question I hadn't needed to ask anyone else. Everyone else had been forthcoming about their roles in Greene Gardens.

Not *Ms. Thang* over here.

Too busy being a damn flirt, I guess.

"I'm the interior designer on the project," she supplied, smiling. "I work *very* closely with Hassani since I specialize in modern, sustainable luxury interiors. I'm designing all of the interiors in the commercial and business properties."

She tilted her head, faux curiosity lighting her features. "Has he not mentioned me to you?"

"Not a word," I said, holding her gaze.

"*Hmph.*" She feigned shock. "Strange."

She turned to Hassani, her smile widening. "I'm shocked, *Hass.*"

He chuckled nervously.

And I was at my wits' end with his damn chuckling.

"And," Harper continued, casually combing her fingers through her hair, "since Hassani and I work so closely together and *will* be working closely together through the *entire* project, I guess you could say he's kind of like my work husband."

I blinked as hard as I jerked my head back. "Excuse *me*?!"

"She's joking," Hassani said quickly, tightening his hold around my waist. "She's *just* joking."

I stared at her, my face *completely* blank while she grinned at me like she hadn't *just* disrespected me to my face.

See, I was used to women throwing themselves at Hassani.

They saw the light eyes, the handsome smile, the tall physique, the charm. It made sense. It was *easy* for them to want to be *seen* by him. I'd dealt with it for years, even before we started dating.

As teens, it was the girls who wanted his attention—who just needed him to *look* at them long enough for them to get lost in his eyes.

As adults? Same setup. The girls had just grown up.

But *this one?*

Harper Royce?

Nah.

She was *different*.

We had been speaking for five minutes, and I already saw how skilled she was at appealing to his interests.

It was deliberate.

Intentional.

But still discreet.

Like a scorpion hiding in a stiletto heel.

That D-Slam sculpture in my kitchen was hideous. Every piece of art that retired basketball player, Darren Slammons, made was ugly as hell. His work was widely critiqued for being overpriced nonsense. But here Harper was, acting like he was the next Michaelangelo. Like my husband was a genius for recognizing Darren's so-called artistry.

She was leaning into this shared interest between them.

Except, I *knew* better.

I saw right through her shit.

The entire time she spoke to us, she only engaged with me when it helped craft the image she was trying to sell to Hassani.

And *that* was a big problem.

I didn't like that.

Not one damn bit.

"Anyway," Hassani said, his voice light but firm, "we were just about to head home—"

"*Aw*, no! Why so soon?"

Harper did a playful little dance, swiveling her slim hips from side to side before resting her hand on Hassani's arm.

"The night is young. Why are you guys leaving *so* early?"

I could feel my pressure rising the longer I stood in this woman's presence.

Her audacity was suffocating me.

I couldn't take another minute of it.

"Harper," I said, forcing a polite smile. "It was nice meeting you." I peeked up at Hassani before refocusing on her. "You have a good night."

She blinked, her smile faltering just a little before she quickly fixed it.

"The pleasure was all mine... *Ayla*."

The sound of my name on her lips left a bad taste in my mouth.

Her focus slid back to Hassani, her dark eyes brightening under his gaze. "So, Monday?"

Hassani nodded. "Monday."

I ran my fingers over my coils, inhaling a slow, deep breath.

"Okay." She smiled again. "Until then."

Hassani lowered his hand to mine, threading his fingers between my own as we turned for the exit.

Only when we said our goodbyes to Bryant and Zoe did I speak again.

And those goodbyes were the *only* words I said from the museum gallery to his car in the parking garage.

The *only* words I said while we merged onto the highway and left the city behind.

For half an hour, silence sat heavy between us, lightened only by the quiet hum of R&B playing through the speakers.

Then finally, I broke it.

"I do *not* like Harper."

Hassani said nothing at first.

His fingers stroked through his beard as his other hand tensed around the steering wheel before he slowly released the pressure.

"She was *so* inappropriate, Hassani."

"She's harmless, baby."

I whipped my head in his direction.

"Are you *kidding* me?" I let out a scoffing laugh. "That woman *lit up* in front of me with her eyes *locked* on you. I could *feel* her manipulative ass before I even saw her."

"A. Boogie—"

"And you're supposed to be working *closely* with her?" I cut in. "Something she just *had* to make a point of?"

I stopped to take a slow breath, my heart hammering now.

"I'm used to women flirting with you. I don't like it, but I'm *used* to it. It's what comes with being with…" I exhaled, shaking my head. "*You.*"

He glanced at me.

"But I'm *not* okay with being disrespected the way Harper disrespected me, tonight." I shook my head, staring out the windshield. "I'm *not.*"

Hassani sighed. "Do you trust me?"

I turned to him, brows furrowed. "What?"

His eyes were still on the road, but his voice was low. Steady. "Do you *trust* me?"

"What kind of *fucking* question is that?"

"An important one." He licked his lips, shifting his grip on the wheel. "A, I know where home is. Aight?"

I sucked my teeth and looked away.

"People are gonna be *people*," he continued. "Women are gonna flirt, and… whatever. I don't care about *none* of that." His voice softened. "The *only* thing I care about is *you* trusting *me*."

"You *know* I trust you," I muttered. "But this isn't about that."

"Ayla, you know I don't entertain that bullshit. Come on, now."

"And yet," I said, turning my head to him, "this woman walked right up to a married man and greeted him like she was meeting her date at a bar." My jaw clenched. "I *trust* you. That goes without saying. But while trust is important?" My voice hardened. "Being *heard* by you? Is *just* as important to *me*."

I turned in my seat, facing him fully now.

"Feeling like what I say is *heard* and *matters* is important to me. You know I don't trip over this kind of shit. You, of all people, *know* that."

"I know."

"So *know* that if I'm saying something to you?" I reached out and pressed a hand to his biceps.

Only then did he glance at me.

"I want to be heard," I said. "I *need* to be heard."

I held his gaze until he broke it to focus on the road.

"And what I say needs to matter to you."

His throat bobbed. "It does matter."

"Then hear me when I say I *don't* like her. And I *really* need you to be careful with her because this thing she's doing?" I shook my head. "The thing you are calling harmless?" I squeezed his arm. "It's anything *but* harmless."

His lips pressed together, but he nodded.

"And that's me speaking to you not just as your wife, but as your *friend*, baby."

With that, I turned back in my seat, letting the silence settle between us.

I tried to shake it off.

Tried to let the night go.

Tried to brush off the interaction with Harper.

But the shit wouldn't leave me.

It clung to me.

Sat in my spirit.

That woman wasn't just flirty. She wasn't just bold.

She was determined.

And worse than that?

She felt like a valid threat.

When we arrived home, Hassani opened the front door, holding it for me.

I walked through the door, kicked off my sandals, and stormed toward our bedroom.

But before I could take another step, he caught my hand, locking his pinky around mine.

I closed my eyes and sighed, stopping in place.

He always did this.

With his pinky still hooked around mine, he moved in close behind me, his warmth reaching me before his touch.

In my ear, he whispered, "You mad at me?"

I licked my lips, keeping my eyes shut, not wanting to say yes.

But not willing to lie either.

I didn't even know what I expected from him tonight.

It was a work event. It's not like he could've been rude to Harper or checked her, no matter how blatantly she disrespected me. That wouldn't have looked right, especially with their project starting Monday.

But still…

Why hadn't he told me about her?

Why was I just now hearing her name for the first time, yet she knew enough about us to mention the sculpture in our home? Enough to call him by a nickname?

I felt blindsided.

Out of the loop.

And I hated that most of all.

I thought Hassani told me everything.

His pinky loosened from mine as he stepped in front of me.

Then, with those golden eyes locked on mine, he lifted our hands to his lips, pressing a soft kiss to my pinky.

Then another.

I swallowed, my pulse kicking up when he gave me that look. The one that always turned something hot and weak inside me.

"No take-backs, right?" he said softly, reciting the promise we made to each other at the altar.

And as always, I answered, "Forever us."

Then he dropped our hands and crashed his mouth into mine.

I sighed against his lips, my body betraying me as he backed me into the wall closest to our front door.

He parted my lips, slid his tongue inside, and I melted.

One strong hand gripped my ass, the other lifting me effortlessly, holding me against him as he moaned into my mouth.

I always unraveled when he touched me.

Always softened under the weight of his body.

The sound of his belt unbuckling made my stomach tighten.

I giggled against his lips. "Don't you wanna go upstairs and do this?"

Hassani hiked my pencil skirt up over my hips and eased my panties to the side.

"I can't wait that long," he admitted, voice thick with need.

Slowly, he let me slide down the wall, guiding me onto him.

I exhaled all the air out of me, clinging to his back as he filled me.

His thrusts were slow, intentional—each one long, deep. Balanced. Controlled.

He owned every inch of my body, moving inside me with a kind of patience that made me ache for more.

I let my weight fall into his arms, trusting that he had me.

"You're the only woman I got eyes for, A. Boogie," he said between groans, rolling his hips deeper. "The only woman I'll ever come home to."

His breath was hot on my lips as he rocked into me, slow and devastating.

"'Cause you've *been* the *only* woman who's ever felt like home to me. Ever." His hands gripped me tighter, his next thrust hitting right there. "And you always will."

I moaned against his mouth, wanting so badly for his words to be enough.

And for a moment…

They were.

I let them sink into my skin, deep inside me, just like him.

I let them warm me the way they always had.

But love alone isn't always enough.

And I learned that the hard way.

CHAPTER 8

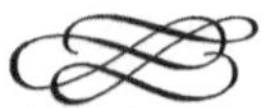

THEN – LATE SUMMER 2022... TWO MONTHS LATER

yla

As soon as I stepped into the faculty lounge, I inhaled a deep breath and fixed a smile onto my lips.

It was our annual work mixer at Park Avenue Prep, a tradition we held shortly after the school year began. A time to catch up, unwind, and bring our spouses—though that part was unwritten. It was the only event where we could truly mix and mingle.

For years, Hassani and I had arrived together, our little tradition locked in place. I'd stay late after school, change into my outfit in my classroom, then meet him for dinner before the party. We'd walk in at the same time, our bellies full, ready to be social.

This year was different.

This summer was *different*.

He'd started working on the Greene Gardens Project late last December, and by July of this year, I'd met his team. Because he was deep into the project, we hadn't taken our usual summer trip. Instead, we settled for a weekend staycation in Manhattan and called it a day.

And now, for the first time ever, he was late to my event.

I waited in my classroom as long as I could, checking my phone every few minutes for an update. But nothing.

So, I finally decided to go to the party without him.

"Ayla!"

I looked up from my phone and lifted a hand when I saw who was calling me. Aisha Townsend, one of the teachers whose classroom was right next to mine.

I took another deep breath as I closed the space between myself and the group of teachers I spent most of my time with at Park Avenue Prep.

None of them had spouses—happily single and always attending the event solo—so I decided to join them until Hassani arrived.

"Hey, y'all." I injected as much energy into my voice as I could muster. "What are we getting drunk off tonight?"

They all snickered, instantly catching the inside joke.

Park Avenue Prep kept things dry. The idea of teachers enjoying even a sip of alcohol under this roof—even at a work mixer—was practically a cardinal sin.

"Oh, you know," Aisha started. "Grape juice and apple juice. Getting high off this central air too."

I giggled.

"As always, the hair is poppin', Mrs. Franklin," another teacher, Celeste Ramirez, commented. "I love."

"*Aww*, well, you know." I patted my coils and curls and smiled. "Thank you, as always."

"Speaking of *Mrs. Franklin*..." Aisha turned to me with a teasing grin. "Where's the mister?"

"He's working late," I said, exaggerating a pout. "He should be here in the next hour, though."

At least, I hoped so.

"*Hmph.*"

The sound came from Janae, quiet but sharp enough to catch.

She hadn't been the same since late last summer, when her ex-husband's mistress showed up at school to tell her about the affair. I wasn't there when it happened, but the recap alone was enough for me to picture it.

Ever since that day, Janae had changed. She smiled less, spoke in sharp, biting remarks that we often let slide, knowing she was still processing everything. She moved into a smaller home with her kids, left her husband, and filed for divorce. She was going through it, and we all did our best to be supportive.

But she kept us at arm's length.

She ate lunch alone, avoided too much small talk, and never really let anyone in.

And none of us blamed her for that.

So, we gave her grace—because that was all she allowed us to give.

Sliding into the chair next to her, I wrapped an arm around her shoulder and gave her a quick hug. "How you doin', girl?"

She shrugged. "Breathing, which should count for something, right?"

I rubbed my hand against her back. "How are the kids?" I asked, knowing exactly what to say to make her light up. "Corey's gotta be taller than me by now, huh? I know he shot up like a bamboo tree this summer."

And just like that, her whole face changed.

Her eyes brightened, her lips curved into a genuine smile.

She *loved* her kids.

And talking about them was the one thing that always brought her joy.

Janae talked my ear off about every and anything involving her children, which led to a conversation about everyone else's children. From there, we moved on to TV, the news, and finally, our plans for the school year.

That was what Park Avenue Prep's work mixer was all about— catching up, laughing, and running our mouths about everything and nothing. It was one of the best parts of working here.

The faculty at Park Avenue Prep was like a second family to me. We spent so much time together, supporting one another in ways that extended beyond the classroom. Not much ever happened here, but every now and then, there'd be something worth bringing home to share with Hassani.

It wasn't the Greene Gardens Project, but it was a special part of my world.

Every so often, I checked my phone, hoping for an update. A text. A call. Something.

But an hour had gone by and still… nothing.

"Is Hassani still coming?" Vivian asked from across the table.

Vivian Carmichael had been at Park Avenue Prep before I was even born. She swore every year would be her last, promising to retire for real this time. But she always showed up every August for teacher orientation, and honestly? We loved her for it.

"You know I gotta see them stunning light eyes and that smile to kick off my school year the right way," she teased.

I giggled. "Watch yourself, Mrs. Carmichael, talking about my husband's eyes. Relax."

She threw her head back and laughed out loud, setting off everyone else at the table.

I laughed too, but inside, the question sat with me.

Where the hell *is* Hassani?

"I'm sure he's doing his best to finish up whatever's keeping him from winking and smiling at you," I told her with a grin. "Work has been nonstop since he started the Greene Gardens Project."

Monica Ellison, another teacher at our table, perked up. "Wait, is that the village upstate? The one started by that billionaire?"

I nodded. "Yup, Bryant Greene."

Gasps and wide eyes circled the table.

"I didn't *know Hassani* was working on that!" Vivian scooted to the edge of her seat. "What exactly is he doing?"

"He's the principal architect." My cheeks ached from smiling so hard. No matter how many times I said it, I marveled at how huge this job was. "He's in charge of designing and overseeing the building of all the commercial and residential properties."

"The *whole* village, Ayla?!" Vivian's eyes nearly popped out of her head.

I nodded. "The whole thing."

"Now, baby." She pointed at me. "You were supposed to lead with that. That's *huge*."

"Enormous," I agreed, scoffing with a laugh. "Bryant Greene even hosted an event for the project over the summer at The Metropolitan Museum of Art."

Jaws dropped.

"It was…" I sighed, shaking my head at the memory. "Beyond *anything* I've *ever* been to. That's when I really understood how big of a deal this was."

"Well then,…" Vivian said, waving a dismissive hand, "him being late makes sense, child. That's amazing, Ayla. Absolutely amazing."

Everyone nodded and murmured in agreement.

Vivian laid a hand over mine. "When you see him, you let him know I am very, *very* proud of him. *So* proud. Wow."

My heart swelled. "Well, when he gets here—if he gets here on time—you can tell him yourself."

Vivian smirked. "That man is busy literally building a village. He don't need to be here tonight."

I playfully rolled my eyes.

"What he *needs* to do," she continued, "is tell me how *I* can get a house over there, 'cause Lord knows I'm about sick and tired of this city."

"You say that every year, Viv," another teacher passing by chimed in.

"And I mean it *every* year," Vivian shot back. "Things are getting so damn ridiculous and expensive in this city. Do you know how much money I had to drop on…"

And just like that, she was off, pulled into another conversation.

I took the opportunity to check my phone again.

Still nothing.

I tapped on my messages, ready to text Hassani, when I heard a quiet *hmph* from beside me.

"First, they start missing little things like this," Janae spoke under her breath, her head propped in her hand. "Then, suddenly, they're too busy for everything."

It was like she had pulled a thought straight from my head and spoken it into existence.

My gut reacted before I could.

I turned to her, forcing a smile as I bumped her shoulder. "Now, Janae," I said, trying to keep things light. "Don't get back in the mood I just pulled you out of. Come on now."

She chuckled, shaking her head, but her expression didn't fully lift.

"All I'm saying is…" She popped a saltine cracker into her mouth, her voice quieter this time. "*Watch* the patterns, boo."

I stared at her for a moment, realizing too late that I'd been holding my breath.

Her words stung. More than I wanted to admit.

Because ever since the start of the year, everything *had* shifted.

Hassani and I had our routines. We had our life before the Greene Gardens Project. And the second he signed on as their principal architect, everything changed—fast. So fast my head was still spinning, trying to keep up.

I couldn't wait for the school year to start again, just so I could have something—*anything*—to ground me.

Then, my phone buzzed in my hand.

My heart leaped before I could stop it.

Maybe he was outside. Maybe he was on his way. Maybe…

> Hassani: I'm so sorry, baby, but I can't make it tonight. I'll make it up to you, though. I promise. I love you.

The air in my lungs just… stopped.

My fingers hovered over the screen, but my mind went blank.

I reread the text. Then reread it again. And again. Looking for something more. Some reason. Some explanation. Some proof that I wasn't slowly losing him to something bigger than me.

I started typing—*What's the hold up?*—then deleted it.

Typed again—*I told you about this, weeks in advance. Why are you canceling?*—deleted that too.

My chest felt tight; my fingers numb.

What was the point?

I settled on a simple reply.

Me: Ok.

That one little word felt like surrender.

"You all right?" Janae asked beside me.

I looked up, met her gaze.

Her eyes softened. Then, she kissed her teeth. "Girl, forget what I said. Please don't mind me. You know how *I* can be."

And I did *know* how Janae could be. But in that moment, I couldn't help wondering if she was right.

I shook my head. No. This isn't that. It can't be.

This was just work. Just one night. Just… *just…*

I swallowed hard, but Janae's words slithered back in anyway.

"Watch the patterns, boo."

I inhaled a slow, deep breath and flipped my phone over, pressing it face down against the table.

Then, I fixed a smile on my lips, draped an arm over Janae's shoulder, and forced myself to ask, "How was your summer?"

Because I needed to focus on anything else.

Anything but the fact that, even if it wasn't a big deal, Hassani had still just canceled on me.

And I had no idea why.

HASSANI
Three Hours Later

"Shit," I hissed under my breath. "Dammit."

I sat at my desk, staring down at the model home layout on my tablet, frustration bubbling in my chest. This was one of the five model homes for Greene Gardens—designed to showcase the range of styles, sizes, and layouts we offered.

Family homes. Luxury homes. Modern townhouses. Live-work hybrids. Accessible homes.

And it was *that last one* keeping me here late.

I set the tablet down, picked up my pencil, and started sketching adjustments on paper.

Harper sat perched at the edge of my desk, watching me work.

I exhaled sharply, fighting my rising irritation—losing the battle.

This issue should've been flagged *weeks* ago.

"Hey, Hassani," Levi's voice cut in as he stepped into my office, holding a folder. "I was just dropping off the updated community park design." He hesitated. "Didn't think you'd still be here."

"Neither did I," I muttered, not looking up.

Levi glanced between me and Harper before setting the folder on my desk. "What's got you stuck here?"

"Widening the accessibility pathways in the kitchen in the accessible homes." I shook my head. "We need at least 42 inches of clearance, and the original model didn't account for that. Especially in the kitchen and living area."

Levi frowned. "That's… a pretty big miss."

"Yeah." I threw a quick look at him, then Harper. My attention was back on my sketch when I added, "So now, we're shifting the island placement and reducing cabinetry depth to compensate."

"That's doable," Levi agreed. "Might need some custom millwork, but nothing we can't adjust before finalizing."

Harper crossed her legs, tapping a manicured nail against her knee. "Would've been easier if we'd planned this earlier…"

I glanced up just in time to catch something flicker across her face —satisfaction? Nah. I had to be trippin'.

Why the hell would she be pleased about this screw-up?

"Yeah," I exhaled sharply. "It *would've*."

She looked away, but not before I caught the ghost of a smirk.

This was a minor fix. A simple adjustment. But the timing of it?

It meant I had to cancel on Ayla.

I *never* missed her work mixer.

It wasn't fancy or high-profile, but it was *hers*. The one night a year I got to see her in her world. Her element. It killed me to text her that I wasn't coming.

My fingers tightened around my pencil as I swiveled toward my computer.

I clicked into my email and started typing.

"Bryant," I said as I worked. "Quick update on the model home. Adjusting the layout to improve accessibility: widening walkways to…"

"42 inches," Harper supplied smoothly.

I nodded. "42 inches. Lowering a section of the kitchen island for wheelchair users. Integrating flooring transitions for visibility. No delay expected. Will send finalized specs by morning."

I hit send, then leaned back in my chair, rubbing my temples.

Framing it as an *update* instead of an *oversight* was strategic. No need to shake confidence in the project over something we could fix overnight. But why the hell was I only hearing about this now?

A rustling sound pulled me from my thoughts.

"Oh, y'all ordered food?" Levi asked, picking up a white carton of takeout from the takeout bag on my desk.

Before I could answer, Harper reached out, smoothly plucking it from his hand.

"*I* ordered for Hassani and me," she said lightly.

Levi's brows lifted slightly before he glanced at me.

I mouthed, *nah*, and discreetly shook my head, subtly letting him know that wasn't true.

Harper had asked if she should order food earlier. I told her not to bother. I wasn't planning to stay late. I was already late for Ayla's work mixer, and I had no intention of hanging around eating Chinese takeout.

"Guys," I said, glancing between Levi and Harper. "I'll send over the final adjustments in the morning. Implementation needs to be immediate on this."

"Got you," Levi confirmed. "I'm heading out."

"Get home safe," I told him.

Levi nodded and walked off. The second he was gone, Harper leaned in, her voice dipping into something almost too familiar.

"Look at you," she mused. "Always solving problems. Always under pressure." She gestured at the takeout cartons. "Sure you don't want to take a breather? Celebrate another crisis averted?"

I reached for my phone, clicking the side button. The screen lit up with Ayla's reply to my earlier text.

Ayla: Ok.

Just that. No more.

I sucked my teeth and shook my head. "Nah, I'm heading out."

Harper's frown was quick, barely there before she fixed it into a sweet smile. "Bummer."

I stood, grabbing my laptop bag. "Have a good night, Harper. See you in the morning."

As I made my way toward the elevators, passing the floor-to-ceiling windows that framed the city's glow, I couldn't shake my irritation.

This shouldn't have kept me late. The problem could have been caught earlier—should have been caught earlier—but Harper conveniently brought it to my attention just as I was heading out.

And the timing? Yeah, that was suspect.

The moment she flagged it as urgent, I had no choice but to stay.

"Should we order something?" she asked as the night stretched on.

I barely glanced up from my tablet.

"I can order something," she added. "I'll order something."

I waved her off, too focused on fixing the flawed layout to think about food. The project was on a tight timeline. Bryant wanted residents moving in by a set date, and a problem as small as a flawed floor plan could slow everything down.

Harper didn't have to stay, but she insisted. She kept talking, filling the silence, while I barely engaged. I was too locked in, too determined to make things right.

Because this was the biggest project of my career.

I couldn't afford to be bad at this. Not even once.

So I canceled on my wife when I really didn't want to.

At some point, I took a short break and picked up my phone.

Ayla's text was waiting.

> Ayla: Are you still coming?

My stomach knotted.

I squeezed my eyes shut, exhaling slow and deep before unlocking my phone. I hated this. Hated that she even had to ask.

I started typing.

Me: Baby, I swear I'm trying

No. Deleted it.

Me: I promise I'll make it up to you.

Didn't feel right either.

Finally, I settled on the truth.

> Me: I'm so sorry, baby, but I can't make it tonight. I'll make it up to you, though. I promise. I love you.

"Everything okay?" Harper's voice cut through the quiet.

I barely looked up. "My wife has an event tonight. I had to cancel on her."

"You can just call her Ayla."

I furrowed my brows.

"You say your wife like we haven't all met her."

I studied her for a second before looking away.

The guilt sat heavy on my chest as I hit send.

"Ayla will understand," Harper said, tone light. "She has to. She's married to one of the best architects in the game. I'm sure she knows late nights and canceled plans come with the territory. I know I'd understand."

I just stared at her for a second.

Then shook my head and looked back at my work.

The drive home was quick. Light traffic meant I made it back in under half an hour.

From the driveway, I could see that all the lights were off.

It was after 10 p.m. Ayla had work in the morning, so she was probably already in bed.

I exhaled hard as I stepped inside, kicking off my loafers at the door. Undoing my tie as I climbed the stairs.

When I reached our bedroom, she was curled up under the covers, still and quiet.

Guilt gnawed at me.

I set my bag down, grabbed a quick shower, and brushed my teeth. On the way home, I'd stopped at the 24-hour deli, not far from the office, for a sandwich. Normally, we'd eat before her work mixers—grab dinner together, then head to the event.

Tonight should've been no different.

But it was.

I hoped she'd eaten something before coming home.

After my shower, I climbed into bed and immediately draped an arm over Ayla's waist.

But the second I did, she pushed my arm off.

I smirked. "I thought you were sleeping."

"You thought wrong," she rasped.

"You're up past your bedtime."

"And you missed my event. *And* you're *late* coming home."

There was no humor in her voice. She wasn't raising her voice, but I could hear the weight of her disappointment.

"I'm sorry, baby," I spoke lovingly, moving in close again. "Something came up at work that I had to fix, or the project would've been delayed."

"*Mm-hmm.*"

Dismissive.

I licked my lips and closed the space between us again. "I told you I'd make it up to you."

Ayla shifted further away from me. "Just leave me alone right now, Hassani."

I exhaled slowly, my eyes adjusting to the dim room. Then a slow smile tugged at my lips as I reached for my phone. Unlocking it, I tapped into my music app, typed in the title of a specific song, and pressed play.

The opening piano notes filled the air.

Our wedding song.

Case's "Happily Ever After."

This song had always been *ours*. It wasn't just the first song we danced to as husband and wife, it was a reminder of everything we were. I thought about our wedding and our honeymoon in the Caribbean at least once a month. One of the happiest times of my life. Of *our* lives. And every time Ayla was upset with me, I played this song to remind her of that.

I rolled out of bed and made my way to her side, extending my hand toward her.

Ayla stared at it for a breath before looking up at me. Then she rolled her eyes.

"You gonna leave me hanging, Mrs. Franklin?"

She kissed her teeth. "You left *me* hanging tonight."

But I didn't drop my hand. I just waited.

With an exaggerated sigh, she finally placed her palm in mine.

I pulled her into my arms, swaying with her in the dark once I got her in my embrace, the glow from the streetlamp outside casting a soft light over us.

At first, she avoided my eyes.

But the longer we moved together, the more her body softened. Slowly, her arms lifted, coiling around my neck.

I grinned down at her.

She rolled her eyes again, but this time, smiled back. "I'm *so* mad at you."

I tightened my arms around her. "I know. Tell me what I can do for you to forgive me."

She pursed her lips, looking away.

The song ended, then started over. I'd put it on repeat. Planned to keep holding her, keep swaying, even if we stayed up all night. I just couldn't let her go to bed mad at me.

So I leaned in and kissed her.

It started as a simple peck. That was the plan.

But the second our lips touched, it was over.

Ayla moaned, and I did too, our mouths parting, tongues meeting in a slow, deep kiss.

Soft caresses turned into something more, like they always did.

I guided her back toward the bed, keeping my lips on hers as she fell onto the mattress with a breathy giggle. But then she was moaning again—me on top of her, her fingers dragging along my shoulders as I kissed a path from her jaw to her neck.

She arched slightly, letting me pull her cami over her head, and I immediately took her nipple into my mouth.

"Hassani," she sighed, her voice melting into the music.

I groaned against her skin, flicking my tongue over her soft nipple before giving the other the same attention.

Rising slightly, I yanked my white tee over my head, tossing it aside, then trailed kisses down her stomach as I hooked my fingers into the waistband of her shorts, sliding them off.

She lifted her hips to help me.

Then I spread her thighs, pushed them back, and buried my mouth between them.

Ayla gasped, her back arching against the mattress as her fingers grabbed the back of my head.

"Happily Ever After" played softly in the background, her moans mixing with the song's melody.

I groaned at the taste of her on my tongue—sweet, warm, already slick for me.

She lifted her head, watching as I twirled my tongue over the soft pink bundle of nerves that made her body tremble.

"*Mmm-hmm*," she whispered, her lips parting, her dark eyes half-lidded as she held my stare. "That feels so good, baby."

That look alone made my dick throb.

Her head fell back, her body shifting against my mouth, chasing pleasure, rolling her hips as I licked her, sucked her, made her come on my tongue.

I groaned at the feel of her pulsing against my lips.

My hands pressed into her thighs, holding her open, keeping her exactly where I wanted her.

Her moans turned breathless, and she shuddered, legs tightening around my head as she let go.

And I wasn't close to done.

The moment she collapsed against her pillow, chest rising and falling, body spent, I climbed on top of her—sinking into her wet heat, hands-free.

"*Mmm,*" I exhaled, shuddering as her velvet soft walls stretched to take me in then wrapped tight around me. "Damn."

Ayla's body came alive again beneath me, her mouth parting, her eyes locking onto mine.

"I love you so much," I whispered, drinking her in. "You know that right, baby?"

She nodded, breath hitching as I rolled my hips in slow, desperate strokes, not caring about the time or that we had places to be in just a few hours.

By the way she pulled me down, pressing her lips to mine, moaning at the taste of herself on my tongue, I knew my wife didn't care about the time either.

"I'm sorry," I groaned against her lips, my hand searching for hers, interlocking our fingers. I slid deeper, listening to her whimper in time with my thrusts. "Forgive me, baby." Another slow stroke, deeper this time. "Forgive me, aight?"

Ayla moaned, nodding, gripping and releasing me between her thighs, her body stilling as pleasure stole through her.

Our wedding song played on repeat, wrapping around us like a promise.

Our bodies moved together. Lips tangled. More words whispered between kisses.

But then, something shifted.

Subtle. Tiny enough it could've been missed. But I felt *it*.

She moaned my name like always, held onto me like always, but when I locked eyes with her, there *it* was. A distance that hadn't been there before that night.

She was forgiving me.

But she *wasn't* forgetting.

I'd never canceled on her for anything. But things were different now. Since construction on the project started over the summer, everything had changed—no matter how much I wanted to deny it.

Deep down, I knew what Ayla and I were doing wasn't enough to fix the shift happening between us.

But for tonight, though… it would have to be.

So I loved on my wife that night, hoping, praying, that this would be one of the few times I'd *ever* have to tell her I'm sorry.

CHAPTER 9

THEN – LATE SUMMER 2022… ONE NIGHT LATER

yla

"After you, Mrs. Franklin," Hassani said, holding the restaurant door open for me.

I shot him a sidelong glance, and he chuckled, pressing a warm hand to my lower back as I stepped inside.

"Ayla, Hassani," the hostess, Miranda, greeted the moment she saw us. "Good evening, and welcome back!"

"Thank you, Miranda," I said, flashing her a bright smile. "Is our favorite table ready?"

"You know it is." Miranda winked at me. "And if it wasn't, you know I'd make sure it was."

I giggled. "My girl."

She laughed. "You two follow me."

"Thanks, Miranda," Hassani added, his hands settling at my waist as he gently guided me forward to follow our hostess.

Tonight wasn't just any dinner. It was a makeup dinner. The night before, he'd missed my work mixer, something he had never done before. And while I'd forgiven him, I was still feeling some type of way about it.

"Here you are," Miranda said, placing our menus on the table. "Your server will be with you in a moment. I hope you two enjoy, as always."

"I'm sure we will," I replied, settling into my seat. "Thank you, Miranda."

"Yeah, thanks, Miranda," Hassani echoed, following suit.

"Always my pleasure." She gave us a knowing smile before walking away.

Hassani gripped the back of my chair, pulling it out a little more as if adjusting my position. "Your throne awaits, Mrs. Franklin."

I rolled my eyes playfully. "Laying it on thick tonight, huh?"

He chuckled, pulling out his own chair. "Oh, I haven't even started. I'm saving that for when we get home."

"Yeah, yeah." I shook my head, fighting back a smile.

We were at Vernon's Prime & Seafood, an upscale yet cozy steakhouse in Manhattan, just a short distance from the Freedom Tower. The ambiance, as always, was perfect for date nights—intimate, warm, effortlessly romantic.

This place was a staple in the Franklin household. Hassani's parents, Percy and Joslyn, had been coming here for years before introducing us to it. After one dinner with them, Hassani and I were hooked. It became our go-to for special occasions or nights when we just wanted to indulge in good food and each other's company.

The decor had a timeless elegance—rich mahogany interiors, plush dark green leather booths, and gold-accented details that whispered luxury. Freestanding tables were spread throughout the dining area, offering the perfect view of the open kitchen, where fresh seafood swam in live tanks, waiting to be selected.

But what I loved most? The desserts.

One dessert in particular.

Which is why I pulled out my phone and said, "I gotta give Mrs. Franklin a quick phone call."

"Of course you do." Hassani smirked as he placed his phone on the table. "Y'all do this every time."

I grinned, navigating to my contacts. It was tradition—whenever either of us dined here, we had to call the other to ask if they wanted dessert. The answer was always yes.

The moment she answered, Joslyn's voice rang through the phone's earpiece, warm and teasing. "Good evening, Mrs. Franklin."

I giggled. "Hey, Mrs. Franklin."

She laughed, the sound as rich as the coconut-rum sauce drizzled on the dessert I was about to order for her.

"Hassani brought me to Vernon's," I said, peeking up at him and blushing. "So you *know* I *had* to call and ask if you wanted us to bring you the guava & cream cheese bread pudding."

"Oh, Ayla, you know the answer will always be yes, my love."

I grinned. "We'll stop by after dinner then."

"Can't wait!"

The guava & cream cheese bread pudding was one of Vernon's best-kept secrets. Joslyn adored it, always saying it reminded her of her Caribbean roots. The warm, buttery bread pudding infused with sweet guava puree, the mascarpone cheese pockets, the coconut-rum sauce that added just the right amount of kick. It was nostalgia on a plate for her.

For me? It was the caramelized sugar crust and the toasted coconut flakes that did it. Not to mention the scoop of vanilla bean ice cream melting on top, sealing the deal every time.

"Thank you, love," Joslyn said. "I can already taste it."

I laughed.

"And tell Hassani I said thank you in advance."

I placed the phone on speaker and said, "She said thank you."

"No problem, Ma," Hassani called out, leaning in just a little so she could hear him.

Joslyn let out a pleasant sigh. "I just *love* how you two still act like newlyweds."

Across the table, Hassani and I locked eyes. He smirked, and I smiled despite myself.

"I love to see that," she said with a smile. "Five years in, and you're still going to all your favorite places together. That's beautiful."

I nodded, offering an easy, "Yeah."

But the truth was, doubt flickered beneath that agreement. The only reason we were here tonight was because he'd missed my work mixer. This wasn't impromptu. This wasn't just because. This was a stop on his sorry tour.

"Anyway," I said, sitting up straighter. "We'll see you in a few hours."

"Looking forward to it," Joslyn said warmly. "Enjoy yourselves."

The moment I ended the call, Hassani asked, "Getting your usual?"

"Surf and turf," I confirmed with a nod. "As always. You?"

"*Aw*, baby." He winked. "You know I gotta be twins with you."

I laughed, shaking my head.

I wanted to stay mad. He'd stood me up the night before. And even though I understood the reason, even though he'd explained every-thing, it still stung.

But I was doing my best to let it go. Because that's what a mature, understanding wife would do.

I was lost in my thoughts when Hassani reached across the table, taking my hand in his.

I blinked down at our fingers before lifting my gaze to his.

The restaurant's golden light reflected in his hazel-green eyes, making them glow. And just like that, I felt my frustration slipping through my fingers. I could never look this man in the eyes and stay upset.

He smirked, running his thumb over the back of my hand. "Am I doing good so far?"

I pressed my lips together, fighting back my own smile. "*Mm-hmm.*"

He was doing great.

Last night, I'd planned to give him the silent treatment for days. When I got home from the work mixer, I made myself something to eat, showered, and got into bed. But I didn't sleep. I waited. For the sound of his car pulling into the driveway. For the soft thud of his footsteps climbing the stairs.

I'd been waiting up to vent. To ignore him. To be petty.

But Hassani wasn't having it. And as much as I hated him missing my event, I couldn't deny that I appreciated how deeply sorry he was.

And now, here we were—out to dinner on a school night. He *was* doing great.

Our server arrived, took our drink and food orders, and disappeared toward the kitchen.

"I'm gonna run to the bathroom and wash my hands," Hassani said, pushing his chair back.

"Okay, I'll go after you."

As he disappeared down the hall, I turned toward the large windows, my gaze naturally drawn to the Freedom Tower. There was always something comforting about it—even though I never had the chance to visit the Twin Towers when they still stood, and while my father worked in the North Tower. Maybe that's why this part of the city didn't trigger me. Maybe it grounded me instead.

A sudden buzz rattled against the table.

I glanced down, fully prepared to ignore it—until I saw the name on the screen.

Harper.

I jerked my head back.

Checked my phone for the time. 8:07 p.m.

Why the hell was she texting my husband after hours?

A prickle of unease skated down my spine.

Since meeting Harper at Hassani's work event, I hadn't given her much thought. Hassani never brought her up. He mostly talked about Jordan, Levi, and other members of the team.

But for someone he never mentioned, it was strange that she felt comfortable texting him at this hour.

I folded my lips into my mouth, dragging my gaze away from the screen.

It wasn't my business.

I wasn't that kind of woman. I never felt the need to check my man's phone. I always believed if you had to, then you probably shouldn't be with him in the first place.

But Hassani wasn't *just* my man.

He was my husband.

And why was this woman texting my husband after work hours?

Before I could stop myself, I picked up Hassani's phone, eyes locked onto the screen.

The notification only showed her name and the word "message."

I hesitated.

Then, before I could talk myself out of it, I quickly typed in his code and unlocked the device.

The phone opened straight to his messages.

There was no need to scroll, because there she was.

Harper Royce.

A string of texts dating back to December 2021—right when the Greene Gardens Project began.

And in every exchange, the same pattern: paragraph after paragraph, most of them sent by her.

> Harper: It was great meeting you today, Hassani. I'm looking forward to working with you.

> Harper: You are SUCH a visionary. I hope you know that.

I scrolled.

Hassani had responded... but barely.

> Hassani: Thanks, Harper.

> Hassani: I appreciate that, Harper.

That should have been enough to ease me. He wasn't entertaining her. He wasn't encouraging this.

And yet...

She texted a lot.

At first, her messages were strictly about work. But over time—especially in recent weeks—her texts had started to shift.

> Harper: Late nights at the office are way more fun when you're around. I swear. I'd lose my mind dealing with these design delays if I didn't have you to keep me sane. Hope you got home safe.

That one was from last night.

I inhaled slowly, letting the air fill my lungs. Exhaled through my nose.

But the calm I was searching for never came.

Hassani hadn't responded to that message.

That was good. That was something.

But it did nothing to soothe my frustration when I saw the message she'd sent him tonight.

> Harper: Saw this today and thought of you.
> Would look great in your office.

Attached was a photo of a D-Slam sculpture. Another ugly, over-priced mess, just like the one sitting on our coffee bar.

I stared at the screen, my stomach tightening.

Thought of you?

What the hell did that even mean?

My fingers hovered over the phone, tempted to scroll up further, to see what other shit she had to say in past weeks.

But I hesitated.

Did I really want to know?

I squeezed my lips together, my pulse humming in my ears.

This isn't me.

I don't check Hassani's phone. I don't dig. I don't snoop.

But why did I feel like I should?

A sudden movement in my peripheral made my heart jump.

I looked up.

Hassani was only a few feet away.

I swallowed hard, a flicker of guilt making my hands shake as I closed out of his phone and set it back on the table.

I didn't do anything wrong... right?

Pushing my chair back, I stood quickly. "I'll be back."

I walked past him, but he caught me by the hand, stopping me.

His eyes—golden, warm, always seeing right through me—searched my face. "You good, baby?"

My heart kicked up, but I forced an easy smile. "Yeah." I squeezed his hand, then gently pulled free. "I'll be right back."

I made my way toward the restroom, willing my pulse to settle.

But the moment I stepped inside, I went straight to the vanity, pressing my palms against the cool surface.

What the hell is this woman's problem?

She had to know what she was doing was inappropriate.

Lifting my gaze to the mirror, I caught my reflection. And what I saw made me pause.

Tears.

They were building in my eyes, and I hadn't even realized it.

I blinked, and one slid down my cheek. Then another.

Damn it.

Ripping a napkin from the dispenser, I quickly blotted my face dry.

Why am I crying?

I wasn't that upset. I wasn't that insecure.

But the questions kept swarming.

Why was Harper texting my husband?

Why was she thinking about his office decor?

And then...

Wait... what does his office even look like?

The realization settled like a weight in my chest.

I didn't know what Hassani's new office looked like.

Why didn't I know?

It wasn't important, I guess. It was *just* an office.

But something about *her* knowing—and me not—bothered the hell out of me.

When he worked out of his private space—only seven minutes from Park Avenue Prep—I used to stop by for lunch. We'd eat together, catch up, spend little moments in each other's world.

But now he was over ten minutes away.

And I hadn't bothered to stop by.

And he hadn't invited me.

I stood there for a few minutes longer, only leaving when another woman walked in and headed for a stall.

On the way back to our table, I debated.

Should I say something?

About the text? About not being invited to his office?

It all sounded so petty in my head.

I'd always hated how Hassani's ex-girlfriends treated me when we were just friends. They *hated* me. Always convinced I wanted him, that I was some kind of threat.

I never wanted to be that kind of woman to them.

And as his wife, I never wanted to make him feel like I was doubting him.

But as I walked back toward our table, all I could hear was one thing.

Harper's text, looping in my mind like a song I didn't want to hear. *"Saw this today and thought of you."*

God, I wished Harper had shown me the same fucking grace I gave to Hassani's girlfriends back when I was just his friend.

She clearly didn't see me as his wife, though. Just an obstacle. A footnote.

By the time I made it back to our table, Hassani spun in his chair, standing the second he saw me.

Always the gentleman.

If I hadn't just read those texts, I would have been smiling for real.

"Everything all right?" he asked, taking my hand.

I nodded, forcing a smile. "I'm great."

A lie.

Inside, I couldn't shake the feeling that something wasn't right to save my life.

Hassani stepped closer, pressing a warm kiss to my forehead before leading me back to my seat. He pulled out my chair, waited for me to settle before sliding it under the table.

So smooth. So effortless.

Like a man with nothing to hide.

So then… why hadn't he told me that woman was texting him?

The question sat heavy in my chest.

Through the rest of dinner, it was there. Hovering.

Hassani did most of the talking, and I nodded in all the right places. Laughed where I was supposed to. Chimed in when necessary.

I put on my best act.

And it was pure torture.

But what was I supposed to say?

Hey baby… ummm… I checked your phone and saw Harper texting you at weird-ass hours… thoughts?

It sounded so childish. So petty.

So insecure.

So… I let it sit.

The war raged on in my head while we ate, while we drank, even while I picked at my favorite dessert and barely tasted a bite.

By the time we left the restaurant, heading to drop off Mrs. Franklin's dessert before going home, I felt exhausted.

Outside, as we made our way to the car, Hassani took my hand, interlocking his fingers with mine.

"So, we cool again?" His smile was so bright. So damn genuine.

I looked over at him, wanting to feel the warmth of it. Wanting to let it all go.

I smiled back. "We're cool."

But we weren't.

I held his hand tighter than usual that night, my heart full of concern and my mind tangled in doubt.

And as we got into the car, one question played over and over in my mind.

Should I be worried about Harper?

CHAPTER 10

NOW – EARLY SUMMER 2023... PRESENT DAY

H assani

THE WOOD CREAKED BENEATH MY FEET AS I MADE MY WAY DOWNSTAIRS. Sleep had been shit—two nights of reaching for my wife only to find nothing but cold sheets. She hadn't come back to our bed since the night she told me she wanted a divorce. And I still couldn't accept that she meant it.

Despite my many attempts to talk to her yesterday via phone calls, we hadn't spoken since she hit me with those four words...

I want a divorce.

Every time I replayed them, it felt like a knife to the chest. My heart clenched, aching at the thought of her really meaning it.

No. There was no way.

We literally agreed... this was it.

No take-backs.

Forever us.

It was a running inside joke between us, but I meant it. At the altar, in every fight, every disagreement. I'd never wavered.

But two nights in a row of sleeping apart? I didn't know what to think.

The smell of breakfast drifted through the air, reassuring me that she was at least still here. That I'd get to see her before heading into the city for work. And I *needed* to see her.

Last night was another hard one for me.

The aroma of dinner had still lingered when I got home, which let me know she'd been here. But the house had been dark. She hadn't been waiting for me.

Knowing she was in the guest bedroom, I'd gone straight there after my shower. The door was closed, no light spilling from underneath, but I knew she was inside. I turned the knob.

Locked.

A pang shot through my chest.

"Ayla." My voice was calm, low, as I spoke to the door's surface.

No answer.

I tried again. "Baby, you in there?"

"I am."

I paused, inhaling slowly, afraid to ask my next question. "Can you open the door for me, please?"

A beat of silence. Then...

"I can," she said. "But I won't."

I stood there, staring at the door, her words settling into my bones.

I could've pushed. I wanted to push. I could've begged—wanted to do that too. But instead, I exhaled sharply and turned away, deciding to give her space.

This thing, whatever was happening between us right now... it would pass.

Just like always.

That morning, when I stepped into the kitchen, I wasn't sure if I'd actually see her.

But there she was.

And the sight of her made me falter in my step.

She stood at the coffee bar, stirring honey into her coffee, her head slightly bowed, deep in thought. When she lifted her gaze just enough to glance at me, she did a double take, like she hadn't expected to see me either.

The morning sun filtered in through the skylight, casting golden light over her. My Langston U track team tee hung off her frame, oversized, paired with her patterned sleep shorts that peeked out from beneath the hem. Even in all her quiet, even in all this distance between us, my wife was so damn beautiful.

She dropped her gaze to her mug.

"Morning," I said as I set my laptop bag on the counter.

No response.

Not even a glance my way.

Her delicate fingers reached for the milk carton, tilting it just enough to pour a splash into her coffee.

Something about the way she moved—intentional, distant—made me wonder if she was still mad at me from two nights ago... or if she was simply being dramatic.

I almost shook the thought away. No, this wasn't our first fight. Wasn't our first time dealing with the silent treatment. But this? *This* was different.

We'd had one other fight worse than this, not long ago. One I'll never forget. But even then, she didn't stay away for two nights straight.

The only other time she'd slept in the guest bedroom, it hadn't lasted long. I couldn't take it. Knowing she was just downstairs, under the same roof but feeling like miles away?

I told myself never again.

And yet... here we were.

This time, she wasn't just distant. She was shutting me out.

Ayla had *never* done that before.

"You're not gonna say *good morning* back?" I asked, closing the space between us.

Silence.

She just kept stirring her coffee, eyes trained on the dark liquid swirling in her mug.

The tension in the kitchen was thick enough to choke on. Our space, once filled with warmth and laughter, now sat heavy with unspoken words.

Ayla turned, moving around me with ease, opening the fridge to return the milk. I let out a scoffing laugh, shaking my head.

"A," I called out as she closed the door.

Nothing.

"Ayla."

Still nothing. She moved past me again, making her way back toward the counter—until I caught her wrist.

She gasped at the contact, body stiffening for just a second before she let herself be pulled into me. No resistance, just the tension humming between us.

Her brown eyes locked onto mine, searching. And I held her gaze, steady, unwavering.

I leaned in, brushing my lips against hers, testing, waiting. Her lashes fluttered, and for a moment, she stayed still. Then, slowly, her eyes drifted shut.

That was all I needed.

I took her mouth in a deep, claiming kiss, swallowing the moan that slipped free. She lost her footing for a second, but I was there, hands gripping her waist, keeping her steady. Without breaking contact, I lifted her into my arms and carried her to the kitchen counter.

There was nothing soft about the way we moved after that. The frustration between us bled into every touch, every gasp, every desperate moan. By the time I was yanking my belt free and she was slipping out of her shorts, we were frantic.

I hooked my hands beneath her thighs, pushing her legs back as I settled her against me, her knee hooking over my elbow.

Our mouths crashed together again, teeth and tongues clashing in an unspoken battle.

Her hands fisted my shirt as I guided myself between her soft, slick folds. Even through the urgency, I forced myself to take it slow, to feel every inch as I slid into her heat.

Ayla's head dropped back, lips parting in a sharp exhale.

"Shit," I groaned against her mouth, feeling her tighten around me.

Two nights without her was two nights too damn long.

She whimpered as I pushed deeper, her body arching into mine. Her lips found mine again, her tongue sliding against mine, desperate and wanting.

My movements were slow but deliberate, each thrust deep and controlled, dragging pleasure out of both of us. Our bodies moved in sync, a rhythm we knew too well.

Ayla leaned her head back against the cabinet, her grip tightening on my shirt. Her lips parted on a silent cry, her brows knitting together as I rolled my hips, stroking into her just right.

For a moment, we lost control—moans mixing with growls, teeth grazing, hands gripping. Her gaze met mine, dark and hazy, pupils blown.

It was too much. The way she gripped and released me in the same breath. The way her body trembled beneath my touch. The way she whispered my name like it was the only thing holding her together.

"Damn, Hassani... *mmm*," she moaned, voice breathless, body shuddering as her release slammed into her.

I felt her come undone around me, her walls tightening, pulling me over the edge with her. My grip on her thighs turned bruising as I fought to hold on, but it was useless.

A deep groan tore from my throat as pleasure crashed through me, so intense it had my vision blacking out for a second.

I collapsed against her, chest heaving. Ayla's legs locked around me, holding me close as we caught our breath.

And for a moment, *just* a moment, everything felt right again. Like we'd found our way back.

Like we were okay.

Until my phone chimed with a message.

Still breathless, I ignored it, pressing my forehead against Ayla's. This was what we did. This was how we fixed things—falling back into each other until the anger faded. Until we remembered what *we* were.

But Ayla had stiffened beneath me.

Her gaze dropped to my phone.

And then, in an instant, everything changed.

I followed her line of sight, my stomach twisting as I saw the name on the screen.

Harper Royce.

Just a name. Just a message alert.

But to Ayla, it was so much more.

Her fingers curled into tight fists. Her jaw tensed like she'd been struck.

I could feel the shift, the way her body went cold beneath my touch.

The warmth, the closeness, the moment we'd just shared… it was gone.

And in its place was something I couldn't name.

But I knew one thing for sure.

This time… sex wouldn't fix it.

Like I said, the text only said "message" and Harper's name, so I had no idea what she was texting me about. But the unknown was enough to make Ayla's entire body go rigid, her expression shifting right before my eyes, from sated to something else entirely.

She locked eyes with me, her lips pressing into a tight line before she kissed her teeth, loud and sharp. A second later, her palm met my chest, pushing me back with enough force to send me sliding out from her warmth.

I exhaled harshly at the loss.

But it wasn't just the way she pulled away. It was *how* she did it. The way she untangled herself from me like I was something she needed to be free of. Like I wasn't her husband. Like I wasn't the man who'd just been buried deep inside her, whispering how much I loved her.

And that? *That* had my pulse kicking up again, this time in panic.

Because sex always worked. Always. No matter how bad the fight, how tense the air between us, we always found our way back.

But now? She was still mad.

And the second my phone chimed with a message… she was gone.

I barely glanced at my phone, but Ayla did. And suddenly, every-thing changed.

Harper.

A cold knot formed in my stomach as realization sank in. This isn't just about an argument. It's not even about the late nights.

It's about *her*.

Ayla stalked toward the counter where she'd left her coffee.

"Baby?" I whispered, still breathless, reaching for her.

She stopped when I placed a hand on her hip, and I expected her to ease up, to exhale the tension sitting heavy in her shoulders. I expected her to let the moment carry us back to where we belonged.

Forever us.

But she didn't.

Instead, her body went cold. Not just physically. Cold in a way I could feel in my chest.

My phone chimed again.

Ayla grunted, snatching up her mug so fast that coffee sloshed over the rim, spilling onto the counter.

I jerked my head back, stunned.

"Have a good day," she spat, turning on her bare feet and storming out of the kitchen.

Not even bothering to sip her coffee.

Not even looking back.

Leaving me standing there with my dick out, slacks bunched around my ankles, and confusion hitting me like a punch to the gut.

It only took a few minutes of replaying everything in my head—every touch, every kiss, every whispered moan—for it to finally hit me.

Because sex always worked. Always.

But not after my phone chimed with a message from Harper.

That was when she shut down. That was when she closed herself off.

And the second I realized it, my stomach sank.

I yanked up my pants in haste, my mind racing.

I knew Ayla had been irritated by Harper since meeting her at The

Met, but I thought it was just that. Annoyance. I figured she didn't like her, but I *never once* considered that Ayla actually saw Harper as a problem that could break us.

But now?

Now, I wasn't so sure.

I took a step toward the hallway, ready to go after her, ready to fix whatever this was—only to hear the sharp slam of the guest bedroom door.

I froze.

"Damn."

She's mad mad.

Fuck.

I ran my fingers over the top of my head, frustration burning through me in waves.

Was it really Harper? Did she really consider Harper a threat?

Nah. There's no way Ayla would think I would…

I exhaled sharply, rolling my shoulders back as the weight of the last few months crashed into me.

Had I been blind?

Had I really convinced myself Ayla was just being dramatic about me coming home late all the time, when all this time… Ayla considered Harper to be a real problem?

And if so…

"How the hell am I supposed to fix that now?"

I had no clue. But I knew exactly who would. A man who I felt knew how to fix everything… and I prayed like hell that I was right.

PART III
THE FAULT LINE

A fracture beneath the surface. The breaking point... the test of what's built...

CHAPTER 11

THEN – EARLY WINTER 2022... SIX MONTHS
EARLIER

yla

I APPROACHED THE PINBOARD BY MY CLASSROOM'S READING NOOK, smiling as I pinned up a new class photo.

It was half an hour before my students arrived, and I was getting things ready for their day when I heard a voice at my door.

"Ayla," Rachel DeLeon—one of Park Avenue Prep's teachers—called out, poking her head into my classroom. "There's something waiting for you at the front desk."

The smile on her face was so big I could count all her teeth from across the room.

I arched a brow. "Could you smile any harder?" I set down the remaining photos on a nearby table. "What is it?"

"Just come and see." She giggled.

I couldn't help but giggle, too.

Peeking at my watch, I checked if I had time to spare.

It was a quiet morning at Park Avenue Prep. A freezing one, too.

Getting out of bed had been a struggle, and I wasn't quite over the effort it took to pull on my chunky brown sweater, jeans, and boots before heading out. The upcoming Christmas break couldn't come fast enough.

As soon as I stepped out of my classroom and into the hallway, my eyes landed on the front desk—and the massive, stunning bouquet waiting there.

A few teachers stood around it, all of them grinning at me.

"Girl," one of them said, smirking, "these are gorgeous."

"He did good," another commented with a knowing nod.

I smiled as I approached the flowers.

It was a mixed bouquet—soft pink peonies, white orchids, yellow roses, lilies, and baby's breath adding a delicate touch to it all.

I leaned in and inhaled deeply, closing my eyes at the sweet scent.

Our security guard, Kaedee, teased, "Are these from your man, or do I need to call him and let him know someone else is doing his job?"

I laughed. "Not you threatening to snitch, Kaedee. Damn."

She cackled.

"At ease, soldier," I assured her. "They're from him."

Reaching for the envelope tucked into the arrangement, I peeled it open and pulled out the tiny white card inside.

The message read:

> *I love you, A. Plus, you know… no take-backs, right? Forever us.*

A scoffing laugh left me instantly.

I knew *exactly* what this was. What he meant.

They were beautiful. Thoughtful. But was this a *just because* kind of gift, or was Hassani trying to fix something I hadn't even confronted him about yet?

I exhaled deeply, running my fingers along the edge of the note. And for a moment, I allowed myself to smile. But I couldn't shake the feeling that this had everything to do with last night.

"Damn. Where's the black pepper?" Hassani muttered, peering into the built-in spice rack beside the stove. "I can't find it anywhere."

I shook the excess water from my hands and made my way over to him. One glance at the spice rack was all it took before I grabbed the tiny bottle and handed it to him.

"Thanks, baby."

I smiled up at him. "You're welcome."

Returning to the shrimp I was prepping, I went back to deveining them while the familiar sounds of '90s R&B played from our tiny portable speaker.

"Is the paprika still on the rack or in the cabinet now?" Hassani asked next.

I shook my head, smiling to myself. "The paprika is still in the same spot, baby."

He sighed, leaning in closer to the spice rack, hunching his tall frame slightly. "I don't see it."

Snorting a laugh, I abandoned the shrimp and returned to his side, reaching for the glass paprika shaker—right where I said it was.

I looked up at him, and he met my gaze.

"Thank you again," he said.

"My pleasure."

He chuckled before leaning down to press a soft kiss to my lips.

It was one of the rare times he was home early from work. Most of the year had been a blur of late nights and early mornings, with him leaving before I even woke up for the day. The Greene Gardens Project consumed so much of his time that, at this point, I was used to seeing more of his absence than his presence.

But after I mentioned that it had been way too long since we cooked dinner together, he told me he'd make it happen. And tonight, he was making good on that promise.

It felt good to have him home before the sun dipped past the horizon.

We were vibing—cooking, cracking jokes, just enjoying each other like we used to in our newlywed days.

I had just finished seasoning the shrimp when I heard him grunt under his breath.

"What are you looking for now?" I asked.

"The grapeseed oil."

I pointed above his head. "In the cabinet, first shelf."

He nodded, turning to open the cabinet door. "Damn, why don't I know where anything is?"

"Because it's been a minute since you've cooked in here, principal architect."

He tossed a glance over his shoulder, narrowing his eyes in mock annoyance.

I burst out laughing.

"Yeah, aight," he mumbled, shaking his head.

Drying my hands on a paper towel, I walked up behind him, wrapping my arms around his waist and resting my cheek against his broad back.

"I'm just playing with you," I murmured, turning my face and rising onto the arches of my feet to press a kiss between his shoulder blades. "I am so proud of you."

He took my hand, lifted it to his lips, and kissed the back of my wrist.

"You're doing great," I whispered, placing another kiss against his shirt before returning to the shrimp. "I knew you would."

With dinner done and plated, we sat at the kitchen table, wasting no time before diving in.

"Mmm," Hassani groaned, leaning back in his chair, eyes closed in satisfaction. "Damn, that's good."

I giggled, forking another bite of pasta into my mouth. "It is."

Like I said, it felt good having him home before night fell. Cooking, joking. Just being.

I wanted to hold onto this moment, to pretend things were as simple as they had always been. But deep down, I knew better. Something was different. Something I wasn't saying. Something he wasn't saying, either.

I pushed the thought aside.

Tonight is good. Keep it that way, I thought to myself.

But then, Hassani's phone vibrated against the table, the screen lighting up between us.

I wasn't even trying to look, but my eyes landed on it anyway.

Harper.

My stomach knotted.

I wanted to ignore the feeling, to pretend I was overreacting. But lately, it felt like she was everywhere. And I wasn't sure if I was imagining it or if I needed to be paying more attention.

Unlike before, this time her message showed right on the lock screen. I didn't even have to snoop.

> Harper: Hope you're finally getting a second to relax. I can't stop thinking about our discussion earlier... You always have the best ideas. Made my day, thank you. It's breaking my heart that I couldn't pick your brain for a little longer...

The words blurred together after that. My stomach twisted.

I lifted my gaze to Hassani, and he was already looking at me. Not at his phone. At me. His lips parted slightly like he was about to explain, but after a pause—just a little too long—he finally said...

"She had a miscalculation in one of her interior layouts." *He reached for his red wine.* *"I walked her through adjustments. That's what she's texting about."*

"Hmph." I huffed and took a sip of my wine.

I wanted to say more.

Why now? Couldn't this have waited until work tomorrow?

But I bit my tongue.

Because it was little things like this.

Little things that would bother anyone with sense.

Little things that, if I said anything about, would make me sound ridiculous.

So I said nothing.

Instead, I reached for my glass again and gulped down another sip.

I never brought up Harper texting Hassani that night at Vernon's. Never told him I'd unlocked his phone and saw that she'd been texting him since the day they met.

I hadn't needed to.

Because after that night, she hadn't texted outside of work. At least... not to my knowledge.

This was the first time since then.

And suddenly, dinner wasn't so good anymore.

"*Aw*, these are so beautiful," Monica gushed as she and a few other teachers, including Janae, approached me from behind.

Her voice yanked me back to the present, forcing me to focus on the flowers again.

I fixed a smile onto my face and turned to them.

"From Hassani?" Monica asked.

"From Hassani." I smiled. "I have no idea how I'm getting these home. Might have to just leave them in my classroom."

"*Mm-hmm.* What he do?" Janae asked next.

I giggled nervously. "Huh?"

"They *always* do this," Janae said, nodding toward the bouquet. "Distract you with pretty things so you forget why you're mad at them."

I exhaled sharply... then forgot to inhale again.

"Janae, do not *start* with this." Monica laughed, shoving her playfully. "Always acting like Debbie Downer from *Saturday Night Live.* Y'all remember her?"

"Of course!" Kaedee chuckled. "I used to love her skits."

The ladies all laughed.

I tried to, but I couldn't get into it.

Because although Janae was jaded...

She might have been right.

And she would know.

Was I getting these flowers *just because?*

Or was this the start of another one of Hassani's unspoken apology tours?

I didn't let my face show the doubt creeping in. Instead, I forced a smile and lifted the bouquet from the desk.

"All right, y'all," I announced. "I'm about to take my garden to my class and plant it on my desk, so I can get ready for my babies. Y'all take care."

"Enjoy them, Ayla," Monica called after me. "Hassani did good."

"Thank you," I replied, as enthusiastically as I could manage.

And he *did* do good. The flowers were beautiful. Thoughtful.

But for the first time, I found myself wondering if he was doing good with *us*.

Or if we were already starting to crack.

CHAPTER 12

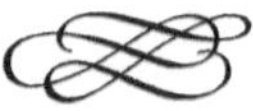

THEN – EARLY SPRING 2023... FOUR MONTHS LATER

yla

"AYLA," MY MOTHER SAID THE MOMENT SHE OPENED THE DOOR. "Beloved."

Her arms were around me before I could even say a word.

It was like she could sense that I almost didn't show up.

"Hey, Mama," I said, embracing her back.

The scent of dinner wafted through the air, meeting me at the door and damn near pulling me inside. One deep inhale, and I already knew—lasagna. My mother's lasagna. My stomach growled in response.

I'd known about this dinner for weeks, my mother reminding me every chance she got.

"Remember, I'm hosting a very special dinner at my house next Friday."

"Don't forget, beloved. Friday."

Though canceling had crossed my mind more times than I cared to admit, I knew I couldn't. Not *this* dinner.

"Is this *her?*"

The deep unfamiliar voice reached me before the man's face did.

I had to remind myself to breathe.

My mother turned toward him, and my eyes followed.

He was tall, handsome, and in great shape for a man in his early sixties. He carried himself with ease, with confidence.

"Yes, it is," my mother confirmed, pressing a hand to my cheek. Then, she reached behind her, fingers sliding into his. I watched the whole thing happen, my heart twisting.

"Ayla," she continued, "this is Warren. Warren Jameson."

"You can just call me Warren," he said quickly. "Warren is just fine."

I swallowed hard but forced a smile. "Nice to meet you, Warren."

He stepped in close to my mother, her palm resting gently on his chest.

And I watched the whole thing happen.

Forgetting, again, to breathe.

Warren was the reason I'd almost canceled.

Especially after I spent too long in the house, waiting for Hassani to show up, only to get a call from him telling me to go to my mother's without him.

"The vendor for the community center's flooring sent the wrong shipment of tiles." He sighed on the line. "I gotta stay a little later to approve an alternative."

His words sent my heart sinking, my head going light.

The idea of having to come to dinner alone—to meet my mother's new boyfriend for the first time—felt like scaling a steep mountain barefoot.

My mother had moved on.

And while I was happy for her, while I wanted this for her, something about it—something about her moving on, albeit several years later—broke me.

"So we're having dinner by the door tonight, yeah?"

Mr. Franklin's voice boomed from inside the kitchen.

I couldn't help the snort-laugh that burst out of me, my mother and Warren chuckling alongside me.

It was the exact laugh I needed.

"Ayla, you have me in this kitchen, smelling all this good cooking, waiting on you and Hassani," Mr. Franklin said as he walked closer. "Where's *mi bwoy*?"

"Working."

I tried—*really* tried—to keep the irritation out of my voice. But the way Mr. Franklin's brows furrowed told me I failed.

Still, he pulled me into a warm hug, a much-needed comfort, then kissed my cheek.

"I'm sure he won't be long," he said, reassuring me. "Come on."

Mrs. Franklin greeted me with her usual big hug in the kitchen, and just like always, warmth spread through me the second she wrapped her arms around me.

The comfort of familiarity.

After giving me a tight hug, she turned away to pull her infamous rum cake out of the oven. Soon after, we were all seated at my mother's dinner table—my former dinner table—eating and talking.

I pulled my phone from my lap while the Franklins engaged in conversation with my mother and Warren, shooting Hassani a quick text.

> Me: I'm here at my mom's. Her boyfriend is too. I don't know how possible it'll be, but I really need you to show up for me tonight, baby.

"So, a pre-K teacher," Warren said from across the table.

I quickly placed my phone flat on the table and smiled. "Yup."

"How's the teacher life?" he asked next. "I've never known a teacher personally and always wondered what it's like."

"One of the best things in the world," I replied, my smile growing more sincere as I spoke. "My students are great." I snickered. "And they keep me on my toes."

Laughter rippled across the table.

"I'm sure they're great practice," Warren added.

My gaze dropped to the way he placed his hand over my mother's. The gentleness of it. The ease.

And I smiled.

He was affectionate. Not shy about showing it.

And it was cute.

My dad had been the same way.

Always touching her. Always finding some way to be close to her whenever he was near.

"At this point," Mrs. Franklin chimed in, "I'd say Ayla's an expert on children."

I laughed, shaking my head.

"She's been rounding up the little ones for years now." Mrs. Franklin flashed a grin. "And just so you know, I already cleared out a room for my grandbaby. Just an FYI."

I pressed my lips together.

"I've done the same," my mother echoed, smiling warmly at me. "Ayla's old room too."

"I'm just waiting for the phone call," Mrs. Franklin added. "So I know what color to paint the walls."

I forced a giggle and lifted my phone off the table, hoping—praying—there was something from Hassani. A reply at least... but nothing.

I quickly typed out another message, then deleted it before I could send it.

I wasn't going to beg my husband to show up for me.

I sighed, setting my phone back on the table, gritting my teeth before exhaling the tension away.

The comments from my mom and Mrs. Franklin were innocent, yes, but they stung. The topic of babies had come up before, way back when Hassani and I started dating. But after we got married, they never brought it up again.

I had been thinking about it, though.

Ever since I met Bryant Greene and his wife, Zoe, at Hassani's work social last year, the idea had lingered in my mind. For years, I told myself we had time. That we should just enjoy each other first.

But now that I was ready...

I wasn't sure he was.

I worried that with all the work Hassani was doing, a baby would feel like nothing more than an inconvenience.

"Well," I said, lifting my glass of wine to sip. "I'd have to have my other half around a lot more before I can make that kind of announcement, y'all."

I was half joking and very serious, and I guess that was evident in my voice because instead of laughter, the table went quiet.

Mr. Franklin tilted his head, his brows furrowing again as he studied me.

Immediately noticing the shift in the room, I forced a nervous giggle. "I'm joking." I waved my hand dismissively. "It's a joke. Ha, ha? Remember those? Or do we not laugh at my jokes anymore?"

Mr. Franklin let out a low chuckle, his eyes narrowing playfully. "You telling me I need to sit my son down?"

"No," I was quick to reply. "He's good. *We're* good. I just… I just really, *really* wish he was here tonight to meet Warren."

And that part was true.

What I wouldn't give to reach beneath the table, take Hassani's hand, and squeeze it—to steady the chaos racing in my mind.

Because my mother had a boyfriend.

And she looked happy. In love, even.

It was kind of breaking my heart.

"Well, I look forward to meeting him," Warren said, nodding with a smile. "I hear he's working on a really big project."

"A major one," Mr. Franklin added, his grin stretching wide. "He's the principal architect in charge of *all* the commercial and residential structures in the new village. Greene Gardens."

Warren's face lit up. "Get out of here! He's working on that?!"

"*Mm-hmm*," Mrs. Franklin confirmed with a proud nod. "We're so proud of him."

"*So* very proud," my mother added.

They carried on talking about Greene Gardens, and I just listened.

On the outside, it was a massive accomplishment. A huge feat.

But on the inside—the inside of my marriage—it was a string of canceled plans, broken promises, and empty *"I'll make it up to you"* tours.

It didn't feel so grand from where I was sitting.

By the time we'd taken our last bites of food, I knew.

He wasn't coming.

He hadn't replied to my message either.

And I couldn't complain. Couldn't seem sad about it. Because he was working on this *huge* project that we were all so proud of him for.

I need my bed right now.

"You're leaving, Ayla?" Mrs. Franklin asked as she wrapped her arms around me.

"Yeah." I hugged her tight. "I need to go home and rest before school tomorrow. There are only a few weeks left, and I want to make sure everything's in place so I can end the school year right."

That was partly true.

The truth was, I was tired.

Tired of pretending I wasn't upset.

Tired of trying not to care.

After saying my goodbyes to Mr. Franklin as well, I joined my mother at the front door.

She smiled at me as I pushed my arms through my denim jacket. Then, with a knowing look, she asked, "So…?"

I met her gaze and nodded slowly. "He's great, Mama. Absolutely perfect for you."

"But do *you* like him?"

"I do," I answered. "I like him *a lot*."

But even as the words left my lips, I felt my chin quiver, beyond my control.

And when I tried to stop it, I felt my eyes well with tears.

My mother noticed.

Her face mirrored mine before she nodded, inhaling a deep breath. "I know, I know."

She held out her arms, and I walked right into them, hugging her tight, fighting to keep my emotions in check.

The tears weren't just sad.

They were happy too.

Happy that she was finally moving on.

And sad because she was *finally* moving on.

She held me tighter, her voice soft in my ear.

"Your daddy will always be in my heart, Ayla," she whispered. "I promise you that. I swear."

"I know," I said softly. "I love you."

"I love you too, beloved," my mother replied, pressing a gentle kiss to my cheek. "Call me when you get home, so I know you got there safely."

"I will."

As I stepped out of our hug and made my way to the car, tears brimmed in my eyes. I quickly wiped them away with the backs of my hands when I heard…

"Ayla!"

Before I even turned around, I knew who it was.

I took a steadying breath, drying my face with my denim jacket's sleeve before facing him.

Warren jogged down the steps toward me. "I know we already said our goodbyes," he said, a little out of breath. "But I wanted to thank you, away from everyone else."

I frowned slightly. "Thank *me* for what?"

"For being open to meeting me."

I blinked at him a few times, not expecting that.

He sighed, rubbing a hand down his mouth before placing both hands on his waist. "I, *uh*… I know it wasn't easy. It wasn't easy for me either."

I didn't say anything, just nodded.

"I also lost a spouse years ago," he revealed. "My wife. She passed from cancer."

My stomach tightened at the words. "I'm so sorry," I said sincerely.

"I appreciate that." He nodded. "And my condolences to *you*."

At that, I smiled, genuinely.

"My wife and I never had children," he continued. "Didn't get the chance to. But I really admire how much love you and your mother have for each other."

His eyes softened.

"She told me you were a huge part of her healing after losing your father. And without her even saying it, I know you're a priority to her. Which means you're a priority to me too. And so is your happiness… with her being with me."

My throat tightened as he went on.

"So, if you don't like me, you can say it," he added, a small, nervous chuckle following his words. "Although… it would really crush me."

I snorted a laugh. "There's nothing not to like, Warren. You're great. Perfect for my mom."

As soon as I said it, he let out the deepest breath, his head dipping slightly as he nodded. "Good. Great."

"My mom picks *really* great guys, so…" I smiled. "I wasn't expecting anything but great."

A wide grin stretched across his face, and something about it warmed my heart.

"It was really great meeting you, Warren."

I walked up to him, wrapping my arms around him in a hug. He embraced me back, strong and steady.

"Please take good care of her."

"Of course," he promised. "You have my word."

The drive home was a quiet one.

No music. No audiobook. Just the soft hum of my tires on the pavement, my windows cracked open to let in the cool night air.

I needed stillness.

To breathe.

A few miles from home, my phone rang through my car's Bluetooth.

My heart leaped, thinking it was Hassani.

I quickly glanced at the dashboard screen, but it wasn't him.

Still, it was a welcomed name. A voice I needed in that moment.

I answered with a smile. "Hey, Aunt Laurie."

A gentle laugh came through the line, underscored by the sound of seagulls crying in the background.

"Always answering on the first ring," she teased.

"You're the only person I know who's always somewhere with seagulls in the background. I always need to hear that."

She chuckled. "*Mm-hmm.*" A pause. "So, how are things?"

I exhaled. "Okay… I guess. Just leaving Mom's." I turned onto the street leading to my house. "I met her boyfriend tonight."

She gasped. "You did?!"

"Yeah." I swallowed hard. "He's *great*. You'd like him."

"Oh, *Favorite Girl*," she cooed. "I *already* do, from our phone calls. What I really wanna know is… do *you* like him?"

I hesitated. "I do."

"So why do you sound so…?" She exhaled. "I don't know. Unlike yourself."

I wanted to vent.

To tell her how things felt different now.

How Hassani was constantly away from home. How he kept canceling on me. How I wasn't sure if I was overreacting or if something was actually wrong.

But it all just sounded so stupid to say out loud.

Instead, I said, "I just wish you were here tonight."

My voice wobbled a little, surprising even me.

"I wish you were here *any* night. It's like trying to find Carmen Sandiego with you."

She hollered a laugh, and I couldn't help but laugh too.

When the humor settled, I sighed. "I *miss* you, Aunt Laurie. *A lot*. The last time I saw you was… *God*… I think summer of 2020."

"Has it really been three years already?" she mused, mostly to herself. "It couldn't have been that long ago."

I frowned. "It was."

"Well, shit." She clicked her tongue. "Guess I gotta change that now, don't I?"

I pulled into our driveway, cutting the engine. My eyes lifted to our house, its beautiful blend of wood, stone, and glass glowing under the soft porch lights.

I was staring directly at Hassani's imagination. His creation.

And for the first time…

I wasn't eager to go inside.

Because I knew I'd be going in alone.

"I know tonight wasn't easy for you," Aunt Laurie said gently. "Seeing your mama with someone new… I'm sure that was hard."

"*So* hard, Aunt Laurie." I dropped my head against the headrest, shutting my eyes. "But she looked so happy."

I swallowed. "And I swear, that was the only thing that got me through dinner tonight."

"She will *always* love your daddy, you hear me?"

I pressed my lips together, my eyes stinging.

I blinked fast, trying to keep the tears at bay.

But some emotions don't listen to reason.

"But your mama… she held out for a *long time*, Ayla."

"I know."

"She was perfectly fine never knowing love again," Aunt Laurie added. "That's how *hard* she took your father's passing."

I nodded, even though she couldn't see me. "I know."

"You know…" She sighed. "The hardest part of moving on isn't learning how to let go. It's knowing that moving forward doesn't mean you're leaving them behind."

A tear slipped down my face, and I was quick to wipe it away.

"Now, I haven't met Warren," she continued. "But I've spoken to him a few times, and he seems like he gets it. He's not trying to replace anyone. He respects the place your father still has in your mother's heart. And for that, he's all right with me."

"Me too," I whispered.

I cleared my throat a second later, forcing myself to push past the lump forming there. "Anyway, I just got home. Hassani had to work late, so… it's just gonna be me tonight."

Aunt Laurie sighed softly. "Call me if you need to talk some more, okay?"

I nodded again. "I will."

As soon as I ended the call, I slumped against my seat's headrest, fixing my eyes on the house in front of me.

Tears blurred my vision, making the once-crisp edges of our home waver like a mirage.

And then, just like that… I was crying. *Really* crying.

I couldn't even tell if it was because life as I knew it was shifting—watching my mother find love again—or if it was because I felt like I was being left behind.

By her.

By *Hassani.*

~

HASSANI
Hours Later…

I TURNED THE STEERING WHEEL AND GAVE THE CAR A LITTLE MORE GAS as I rolled up to our house.

Tonight had been *hell.*

Between the stress of working late and the growing pressure to keep the Greene Gardens Project on schedule, I was teetering on the edge. And this was only the first few phases of the project.

That was *not* a good sign.

I pulled into the driveway and noticed Ayla's car parked.

I figured she'd already be inside, but as I pulled up beside her car, expecting to see the house lights dimmed, I was surprised to find her still sitting in her car behind the wheel.

I shifted into park, peering through the glass, and the look she shot me made me jerk my head back.

I was ready to lower my window and say something, but before I could, Ayla shoved her driver's side door open, stepped out, and slammed it behind her.

Didn't say a word.

Didn't even glance my way.

Just stormed toward the house, walked up the stone path, and…

SLAM.

The door shut behind her with enough force to shake the frame.

I exhaled through my nose, shutting my eyes.

Fuck.

I was *not* in the mood for this.

Not tonight.

I ran a hand down my mouth, willing the tension in my body to ease as I grabbed my laptop bag and stepped out of the car.

I tried to leave the office early. Ayla had been reminding me about this dinner at her mother's for weeks. She said she mentioned it even earlier than that, but honestly? I couldn't remember.

Things had been chaotic. The project was at a critical stage, and keeping everything on track meant long hours.

But I did *try* to leave.

I even told my team earlier in the day that I had to go, but then…

"The vendor sent the wrong tiles for the community center flooring," Harper informed me, dropping a folder onto my desk.

I let out a slow breath, already feeling the headache forming behind my eyes.

"I really think this can wait," I grumbled, already reaching for my bag. "I need to get out of here."

"You have to approve the alternative," Harper insisted, nudging the papers toward me. "You need to review the swatches now."

I clenched my jaw.

"Damn," I groaned.

"Ayla will understand," Harper added casually, giving me one of those looks. "She has to. She knows how huge your role is here. It trumps a dinner. No matter how important she thinks it is."

I inhaled sharply.

"No one truly understands the weight of this project like you and I do," she went on, a small smirk tugging at the corner of her mouth. "But they will when they see what we create together."

At the time, I agreed with her.

But standing here now feeling the weight of Ayla's anger in the silence of our house... I wasn't so sure.

I stepped inside, shutting the door behind me. The air in the house felt thick, like it had absorbed all the tension from earlier and refused to let it go.

The lights were on, most of them. I could hear movement in the kitchen.

I exhaled slowly before making my way toward her.

"How was the dinner?" I asked, stepping into the kitchen.

Ayla didn't flinch.

Didn't acknowledge me.

Didn't even pause what she was doing, pulling dishes from the dishwasher, stacking them in the cabinet with slow, precise movements.

I sighed, setting my laptop bag down on the counter like I did every night.

"I'm *sorry* I missed it," I started, keeping my voice calm. "Approving the alternative flooring took longer than I expected."

Nothing.

Not even a glance.

Ayla just *kept going,* stacking dish after dish like she *had* to keep moving or she'd snap.

I clenched my jaw.

She was *mad mad...* again.

And I wasn't sure if I had the energy to deal with it.

Ayla shook her head as she closed the dishwasher, her movements stiff and clipped.

I exhaled through my nose, trying to keep my patience in check. It had already been a long day. One problem after another at work, each one demanding my attention. My mind was spent. The last thing I wanted was to come home and find another problem waiting for me here.

And yet... here we were.

The pressure of this project was getting to me. No one understood the weight I was carrying, the responsibility on my shoulders. I had to make sure everything stayed on track. Bryant trusted me to get it done. And I trusted myself too—or at least, I used to.

Lately, I wasn't feeling as sure.

And the one person who always kept me grounded? The one person who could talk me off the ledge?

She was standing right in front of me, refusing to say a damn word.

"Are you gonna talk to me tonight?" I asked, closing the space between us. "'Cause, Ayla, I really don't have the energy for this silent treatment shit. Not tonight."

"Oh," she said, finally turning to face me. "You don't want the silent treatment tonight. That's good, Hassani. That's real good. It's nice that *you* know what *you* want."

I exhaled sharply, my patience thinning. "Man, what is your deal, Ayla? What's up?"

"I don't think you understand how much I needed you at my mother's house tonight," she said, her voice thick with hurt that hit me square in the chest. "*That's* what's up."

"I *had* to work," I shot back. "What the fuck? You think I wanted to work late? You think I wanted to get home at this hour?"

"I *told you* about this dinner for weeks, Hassani!" she shouted. "Weeks! And you *still* bailed on me when I *needed* you the most."

"I *had* to *work*, Ayla!" I shouted back.

She scoffed, rolling her eyes so hard I thought she might tip over from the force of it.

I clenched my jaw, forcing myself to look away, to breathe through the frustration.

"Sometimes…" I groaned, shaking my head, "I don't think you understand how big this project is, A."

Her expression went flat.

Then she shook her head. "I needed you tonight, Hassani."

"Ayla, it was *just* a fucking dinner, baby," I argued, throwing up my hands. "And like Harper said—"

She scoffed. Loudly.

The moment Harper's name left my mouth, Ayla's entire face twisted into something terrible.

"Harper?" she snapped, her voice laced with disbelief. *"Harper said? Has she officially made it into my house* now?"

I frowned, completely thrown. "What?"

She just *stared* at me.

Her chest rising and falling, her eyes glassy with unshed tears.

And just like that, the fight left me.

I hated seeing her like this.

Even if I thought she was being dramatic as hell, I *hated* it.

I stepped toward her, reaching out, but she moved fast.

"No," she whispered, shaking her head. *"Uh-uh."*

My brows furrowed. "A—"

She blinked.

A tear slipped down her cheek.

"Baby, what's *wrong?"* I whispered. "Talk to me."

She didn't answer.

She just turned, and stormed out of the kitchen.

I reached for her, instinctively grabbing for her arm, but she slapped my hand away.

Didn't stop.

Didn't look at me.

Just kept going.

I let out a sharp grunt, pressing my hands flat against the kitchen island to ground myself.

To come home after a day like today, only to walk into *this?*

A mess. A fucking mindfuck.

I clenched my jaw, forcing myself to leave it alone.

I made my way upstairs, expecting to find her in our room, but when I stepped inside… nothing.

The room was empty.

I should've gone after her. Should've pushed. But I couldn't. Not tonight.

Instead, I walked into the bathroom and turned the shower on.

I barely touched the cold nozzle, letting the heat bite at my skin.

It's like I said, the day started fine, but then Harper dropped that shit about the flooring on my desk, and suddenly it was all hands on deck. I was grateful we caught the mistake before it turned into a real problem, but not at the expense of my home.

Not at the expense of *this*.

By the time I was done showering, drying off, and going through my nighttime routine, I stepped back into our bedroom, half-hoping to find Ayla there.

But it was still empty.

I sucked my teeth and climbed into bed, muttering, "Man, whatever."

I pulled open the side table drawer and grabbed my sketchbook, needing something to settle my mind.

A balcony overlooking the water.

That's what I was working on.

I tilted my pencil, shading in the soft curtains I imagined billowing in the breeze, but my focus kept slipping.

I leaned my head back, letting my eyes drift up toward the skylight. Then I turned my head—just once—to glance at Ayla's side of the bed.

Still empty.

I sighed and grabbed my phone off the nightstand.

It's like I said—I was exhausted. Up at 4 a.m. In the office by 6. Running on fumes. I needed to set my alarm and turn in.

I thumbed in my passcode, swiping toward my alarm clock app, and froze.

There was a new text.

One I hadn't even noticed. I'd been so caught up with everything at work that by the time I finally wrapped up, I just grabbed my shit and walked out—didn't check my phone, didn't think twice.

I'd considered calling Ayla on my way out, but figured it'd be better to just talk to her at home.

But now, sitting there, I saw it…

The text I missed. Unread. Just waiting.

From Ayla.

A sick feeling settled in my stomach as I clicked in.

Ayla: I'm here at my mom's. Her boyfriend is too. I don't know how possible it'll be, but I really need for you to show up for me tonight, baby.

I stared.

The words swam on the screen.

Then my stomach dropped.

I sucked in a breath through my teeth, my hand covering my mouth.

"Oh, shit."

That was tonight? I thought it was just dinner with our parents.

My chest tightened.

"Fuck."

It completely slipped my mind that tonight was the night Ayla's mother, Sonia, was introducing her boyfriend to Ayla and my parents.

Ayla had mentioned for months that her mother had been dating again. She said she was okay with it—over and over—but I knew her. I *knew* that meeting him would make it real in a way Ayla wasn't ready for.

It made sense that her mother's boyfriend would be there. A family dinner. A serious relationship. *Of course*, he would be there.

But I forgot.

And I forgot how big this was for Ayla.

How big of a deal it would be for Ayla to sit at that table, watching her mother with another man—when all she had ever known was her parents together.

Tonight must've been so damn hard for her. And I wasn't there. I didn't even check my phone until that moment in bed. I was too focused on getting home once I was done with work.

"Shit," I said under my breath.

A pang shot straight through my chest.

"I wasn't there. Fuck."

I threw off the covers and bolted out of bed, taking quick strides to the bedroom door. I moved from room to room, searching for her. When I reached the stairs, I took them two at a time, heading straight for the guest bedroom.

The door was closed, but I didn't hesitate. I turned the knob, pushing it open.

The sound of Ayla's muffled sobs hit me like a punch to the gut.

She was crying into the pillows.

And my heart shattered.

So many times, my father had told me, *Be there for Ayla. In whatever way you know how to be, be there for her.*

And I *had* been.

I was there for her in high school when she called me at one in the morning, three in the morning, when she couldn't sleep because she was thinking about her father. When she barely spoke, just cried, and all I could do was sit on the other end of the line and listen.

I was there when she came back to school after September 11th and broke down at her locker—every night after, she was convinced her dad would walk through the front door any second. I didn't know what to say back then. Didn't know how to fix it.

But I was there.

And that was enough.

But tonight?

Tonight, I *wasn't* there.

And it wrecked me.

It wrecked her.

"*Aw*, baby, damn," I whispered, my throat tight, my chest aching, eyes watering. "Baby."

She cried harder.

I kissed my teeth, blinking back my own tears. "Come here, baby. Come here."

I didn't wait for permission. I scooped her into my arms, holding her close, feeling her fists ball into my shirt as she buried her face against me.

Her sobs broke me all over again.

"Fuck," I intoned quietly against her hair, pressing my lips to the top of her head. "I'm *so* sorry. I forgot tonight was the night, baby. I forgot."

She didn't say anything. Just nodded against me, holding on tighter like she wasn't trying to let go.

I sat at the edge of the guest room bed, adjusting my hold on her before standing up again.

Still cradling her against my chest, I carried her out of the room, up the stairs, taking them one at a time, slow and steady.

She wasn't heavy, but damn if my heart didn't feel like it was carrying everything at once.

I fought back my own tears because that's how it always was.

Whenever Ayla cried, I felt it.

Every time.

I climbed into bed, keeping her close. I held her.

Until her sobs faded into soft sighs.

Until her body relaxed against mine.

Until she finally fell asleep.

But me?

I didn't sleep at all.

I stared through the skylight for hours, lost in thoughts of her sitting at that dinner table alone, going through one of the biggest shifts in her life… without me by her side.

And as much as work mattered, as much as I had told myself I couldn't afford to drop the ball on the Greene Gardens Project…

I had dropped the ball on *her*.

And that?

That was something I wasn't sure how to fix.

CHAPTER 13

THEN – EARLY SUMMER 2023... TWO MONTHS LATER

*H*assani

I RAN A HAND DOWN MY FACE SLOWLY AND SIGHED INSTEAD OF grunted. My eyes were heavy as hell, and my pulse kept ticking higher the longer I stared at my computer screen.

The hour was after 8 p.m... or maybe 9 p.m. I honestly couldn't tell anymore. It didn't really matter—not with this new issue sitting on my desk.

Last-minute revisions had me parked at my desk, stress settling in like an unwanted guest, yet again.

"Can I get you more coffee?" Harper asked, hovering near me. She leaned against my desk, hands pressed into the surface as she studied the blueprint of the residential layout I'd created—the one she'd found a flaw in just minutes before I was set to head home.

We were in Phase 3 of the Greene Gardens Project, preparing the first neighborhoods, commercial spaces, and parks for occupancy. Project managers were waiting for the go-ahead to schedule launch events—public unveilings, ribbon-cutting ceremonies, all marking the milestone of welcoming the first residents.

And now, *this*.

"No coffee." I sat up in my chair, dragging in a deep breath. "Let me just…" I exhaled hard. "Let me get back to this."

Minutes before I was ready to leave, Harper had walked through my office door with urgent steps, saying she'd discovered a flaw. A flow issue, as she called it.

Her concern? The open-concept townhouses from Phase 1.

She claimed that, in some areas, the interior spaces felt too enclosed. That the natural light didn't move through the units the way it should. Her solution? Wider entryways and larger interior windows to improve the visual connection between rooms.

At first, I wasn't convinced.

"Does that really need to be altered, though?" I asked, frowning as I studied the blueprints on my screen. "The open-concept looks fine to me, Harper."

"Well," she smiled, "that's why you're the architect, and I'm the interior designer."

And just like that, I'd been stuck at my desk ever since, searching for the flaw.

I scanned the plans. Ran simulations. Cross-checked light distribution in the 3D renderings.

I still didn't see it.

But Harper *was* the interior designer. This *was* her specialty. And if she was this convinced, I had to at least consider that she was seeing something I wasn't.

Another deep breath left me as I reached for my sketchbook. Not my personal one. The one I kept specifically for the project. I loosened my tie, unbuttoned the first two buttons on my dress shirt, and rolled my sleeves up to my forearms. Then, flipping to a fresh page, I picked up my pencil.

I needed to rework this. Figure it out.

As I started sketching, Harper stayed planted by my side, watching. I glanced up briefly, catching her staring at me.

"You don't have to stick around for this part, Harper," I said, my focus back on my work. "You can head home."

"It's fine," she replied easily. "I enjoy your company. And I want to be a part of all aspects of this project, so when history is made, I can say I was right there with the genius that is Hassani."

I huffed. "*Hmph.*" Didn't feel like a genius right now.

My pencil moved in careful strokes as I sketched a concept for wider interior windows.

"I still can't figure out what *the genius* likes to eat, though," she added.

I lifted my eyes to her. "What?"

She smiled wider. "For most of the nights you've stayed late, when I ordered in? You never eat."

I just looked at her.

"I've tried Chinese, Indian… *heck*, even Italian. And everyone *loves* Italian, right?" She giggled. "But still, nothing. You don't even take a bite."

I smirked slightly. "Those are fine. I just don't like thinking about food when I'm dealing with a crisis, you know?"

I leaned back, stroking my beard as I examined the sketch, shifting my gaze between the blueprints on my screen and the design I was drawing by hand.

Something still wasn't clicking.

I shook my head, exhaling.

I still don't see what's wrong with the blueprint.

"Well, what do you like to eat?" Harper asked, her tone light. "What makes Hassani go, *yum?*"

I let out a scoffing laugh, finally turning my attention to her.

It wasn't lost on me that Harper was attracted to me. She didn't exactly keep it a secret either. Harper was a beautiful woman, and she knew it. And while Ayla had made it clear she didn't like her—probably for that very reason—I felt like I had it handled.

Harper and I worked together on a massive project, and keeping our working relationship functional was a priority. We needed to get the job done and get it done right. Calling out her forwardness, making it an issue, had the potential to create unnecessary tension—tension that could impact the work. So, I convinced myself it was easier, more logical, to let her flirty ways fly. To ignore it.

Women like Harper weren't new to me. I'd dealt with plenty before. And in my mind, she was harmless.

Because at the end of the day, *I* was in control.

And there was no amount of beauty or flirting that could change that.

"I like simple things, I guess," I replied, already shifting my focus back to my work.

"Like?"

"Surf and turf's the one thing I know I can never go wrong with," I said, sketching as I spoke. "My wife and I love the surf and turf at Vernon's Prime & Seafood in Lower Manhattan. It's near the Freedom Tower."

I smiled to myself as I thought about how much Ayla loved their bread pudding. Watching her eat it was one of my favorite things. She was such a vocal eater when she really enjoyed something.

"She orders it every time," I added. "That and their bread pudding. The dessert is her favorite."

"We should go there then."

That got my attention.

My gaze lifted to hers, and I blinked once.

"I could use something to eat, and so could you," Harper continued. "Plus, you could grab *Ayla,*" she stressed her name, "that bread pudding you mentioned. I'm sure she'd be happy to have it when you get home."

I looked away, considering that.

Bringing home the dessert would soften the blow of another late night at the office.

Things *had* been… *off* between Ayla and me for months. Missing that dinner at her mother's house—the one where her mom introduced her boyfriend—was a serious blow. To both of us.

And even though Ayla told me she forgave me, I couldn't shake the feeling that things had changed.

We spoke less on the phone. Spent less time together.

Most nights, by the time I got home, she was already asleep. And on weekends? She was either running errands, visiting her mom, or off doing something solo—mall trips, coffee runs.

She was distant.

And I'd been trying to figure out how to fix that. Maybe the bread pudding could be a start.

"So, what do you say?" Harper nudged. "We can head out now, which means you'll get home earlier. Then, we can pick this back up tomorrow."

At that moment, anything besides staring at these blueprints felt like a good idea.

So… I agreed.

It didn't seem like a big deal.

It was only after Harper and I pulled up to Vernon's that I felt uneasy.

The feeling hit me the moment I stepped out of the car, reached for the restaurant's front door, and held it open for her.

Because I'd only ever done that for Ayla whenever *we* visited Vernon's.

This place had been our spot since my parents first brought us here years ago. Ayla fell in love with it that night, and from then on, it became the restaurant we always came back to.

And people here knew us.

I suddenly realized how this might look.

I hadn't thought about it when Harper suggested it.

Hadn't thought about it during the car ride over.

Hadn't thought about it when I found parking out front.

But now?

Now, it was *all* I could think about.

We stepped inside, and I instinctively held my breath as we approached a group of people who crowded the podium.

Please don't be here. Please don't be here.

The small group parted for Harper and I, and as luck would have it, Miranda, the usual hostess, wasn't at the stand.

Instead, a male host greeted us.

I let out a breath of relief.

And then immediately frowned.

Why the hell am I relieved? I'm not doing anything wrong... right?

"Good evening," the host said, looking between us. "Do you two have a reservation?"

"Nope," Harper giggled. "We're walk-ins."

My eyes scanned the restaurant, taking in the intimate booths, the dim lighting, the couples leaning close over their meals.

None of it helped the uneasy feeling creeping up my spine.

"No worries," the host said. "We have a few open tables. I can seat you now."

"Oh," I cut in, shaking my head. "We don't need a table."

I turned to Harper.

"You're just picking up food, right?"

"Well," she pivoted, facing me fully. "We *could* just eat *here*."

"Oh, nah." I chuckled nervously, trying to keep my tone light. "I'm not eating. I just came to grab the bread pudding and head home."

Harper let out a soft laugh, unfazed. Then she glanced back at the host before refocusing on me.

"Well, look," she said smoothly, "let's take a seat. I'll order my food, you can order *your* dessert, and by the time it's ready, you can head out. No biggie."

I blinked.

The host chimed in. "Sounds like a solid plan. Our kitchen's fully staffed tonight, so you won't have to wait long, sir."

I shrugged. "Okay. That works then."

Deep down, it didn't feel that way. But I was already here. Once I got the bread pudding, I'd head home.

Harper chose one of the green leather booths when the host asked if she had a preference.

That was somewhat reassuring. I'd never sat at the booths in Vernon's with Ayla. Always at the center table.

Our center table.

A table we always reserved ahead of time.

Still, as I slid into the booth across from Harper, an unease settled in my chest.

I don't know if it was because this was Ayla's favorite restaurant and she wasn't here.

Or maybe it was the dim lighting. The soft jazz. The intimacy of the booths, things I'd never really noticed before tonight.

Because from an outsider's perspective?

It definitely looked like I was on a date.

"Surf and turf," Harper said, scanning the menu. "That's what you like, right?"

I shifted my focus to her. "Yup. One of the best."

"Good evening, you two," our server greeted as he stepped to the table. "I'm Jalen, your server for the night. Would you like to start with drinks?"

"Hey, Jalen," I spoke first. "I'm just here to order the bread pudding. Can you have it packed to-go once you take her order?"

"Of course." He nodded. Then, turning to Harper, "And for you?"

As Harper gave her order, my gaze drifted, scanning the restaurant once more.

That feeling rolled through me again. The one I couldn't quite place.

But I knew one thing for sure.

I didn't like it.

Harper laughed softly. "You're serious about getting out of here, huh?"

I turned my focus back to her. "Yeah. Just trying to get home to my wife."

"Ayla," Harper corrected smoothly.

I didn't respond.

She gave a light chuckle. "You always say *your wife* like everyone at the office hasn't met her." She scoffed next. "*We've* met her."

I licked my lips but said nothing.

It wasn't the first time Harper had said something like that. I always chalked it up to mild jealousy.

Like I said, I knew women like Harper. I knew how to navigate them.

No need to argue. No need to address.

"You and Ayla have been together forever, huh?"

I smiled. "We still have forever more to go, but yeah, we've been together a while."

"Do you ever miss being single?"

I frowned.

"You know, the freedom of it?"

I pulled my lips into a slight shrug. "I don't think I understand what you mean. I still have freedom."

She bit at her bottom lip, lashes fluttering. "Good to know."

That?

Now, *that* was concerning.

A good enough reason for me to flag Jalen down and check on my order. But just as I shifted my focus away from Harper to search for him, I saw something that made my stomach drop.

More like *someone…*

My dad.

Stepping into the restaurant.

My entire body tensed.

I don't know why I had that reaction.

I wasn't doing anything wrong.

But the moment I saw him, all I could think about was Ayla.

And before I could sink a little lower into my seat, his gaze locked onto mine.

Shit.

He saw me the exact moment I saw him.

And instinctively, I wanted to hide.

That alone should have been my answer.

The fact that my gut reaction was to duck, to disappear—*that* should've told me everything.

Because *this?*

Sitting here with Harper?

Was *not* as innocent as I thought it was.

The way the booth was positioned in the restaurant, you could see straight through the oversized windows to the Freedom Tower.

You could also see everyone who walked through the front door.

That's how I saw my dad so quickly.

And that's how he saw *me*.

He stopped a few feet inside, scanning the booth.

His eyes moved between me and Harper, back and forth, slow and deliberate.

Then he blinked hard.

But still—he started toward us.

I sat up, forcing a smile.

Turning to face the outside of the booth, I scooted forward.

"Dad," I greeted, standing to extend my hand.

"Hassani," he returned, gripping my hand and pulling me into a brief hug. "Wasn't expecting to see you here."

I chuckled, a little too nervously. "I… *umm…*"

Before I could even finish the sentence…

"Your *dad*?!" Harper's voice cut in, bright and excited. "Wow! What a pleasure to meet you."

She was already rising to lean in for a hug, but my father took a subtle step back.

Instead, he extended his hand.

"Oh." Harper giggled. "Right."

She shook his hand instead. "I'm Harper. I work with Hassani on the Greene Gardens Project."

My father's gaze shifted to me.

Then back to Harper.

Then back to me.

He smiled, but I could see the wheels turning. "Pleasure to meet you, Harper."

"You're Jamaican," she noted, her expression lighting up. "I know that accent anywhere! My best friend's parents are Jamaican."

Then she turned toward me, lightly tapping my chest.

"Hassani, you never told me your dad was Jamaican."

I barely registered the words.

Because my father's eyes?

Were already moving swiftly between me and Harper again.

And suddenly?

This looked *really* bad.

"I'm just here to pick up the bread pudding for Ayla," I explained quickly. "Then I'm heading out."

"*Hmph.*" My father's response was short. Weighted.

"You should join *us*," Harper invited.

I briefly closed my eyes, silently wishing she'd just shut the fuck up.

"There's plenty of room," she added, gesturing toward the booth.

My father didn't even hesitate. "*Aw*, you're too kind," he said smoothly. "Nah, man, I came to pick up dinner and dessert for Hassani's mother."

Then… he clapped a heavy hand onto my shoulder.

Gripped it firmly.

Locked eyes with me.

"I'll be back at your table in a few minutes, though," he said to Harper before shifting his attention to me. "I'll be back."

Now, look… I'm a grown-ass man, right?

Late thirties. A few years from forty.

But no matter how old I get, *that* look? The one my father *just* gave me?

That shit still put the fear of God in my chest.

That firm, wordless stare. The one only I would recognize.

Because I've been seeing it since I was a toddler getting into mischief in my playroom.

That stare was *no* joke.

And it spoke volumes. Loudly.

Fuck.

"I can't *believe* your dad is here," Harper mused as I slid back into my seat.

I didn't respond—not because I couldn't believe it, but because I could. I just couldn't believe that out of all the things I should've been worried about, it was the prospect of running into my father.

Vernon's was his and my mother's spot. They've been dining here for decades. Ayla and I only started coming after joining them for dinner one night, and we'd been hooked ever since. So, of course he'd be here —of all fucking nights. Shit.

"He looks more like your brother," she continued, giggling. "Just with brown eyes instead of your hazel-green ones."

I barely heard her.

Because my father was now standing at the takeout counter.

And when he turned to look at me again?

He was still giving me that look.

"Your father's *very* handsome," Harper added, a slow smile pulling at her lips. "Gives me a little insight into how good you'll look when you're older."

My stomach clenched.

I forced a smile.

Then?

My father was on his way back.

"Harper," he said as he returned to our table, a Vernon's takeout bag in one hand.

Harper's smile stretched.

But my father didn't return it.

"I hate to do this to you, young lady," he continued, tone pleasant, but weighted. "But I've been trying to get a little of Hassani's time for weeks now. And you all have been keeping him busy."

Harper let out a soft giggle. "Oh, I'm sorry."

"No apologies, please." My father's smile widened, but there was no humor behind it. "I'm sure what you all are doing is wonderful work."

His eyes slid to me then returned on her.

"But I do need to steal him from you tonight."

The glance he gave me was quick. But I felt it.

A warning.

A command.

A finality.

"Oh." Harper's smile wavered.

Then she turned to me, gesturing toward the table. "Aren't you waiting for Ayla's dessert, Hassani?"

"Yeah." My voice felt rough. "I already ordered it. Just waiting for it to come out."

"Why don't you let Harper enjoy that dessert?"

My father's voice was casual.

Too casual.

His attention shifted back to Harper. "You're gonna love it. I promise."

He smiled, big.

"It's warm and buttery. Has a creamy mascarpone cheese that'll stay on your mind for days." He laughed, holding up the takeout bag. "Hassani's mother loves it *so much*, she sent me here at this late hour to get it."

Harper's grin faltered.

But she nodded. "Okay then."

Without missing a beat, my father reached into his back jean pocket, pulled out his wallet, and placed a $100 bill on the table.

"Everything is on me," he told her smoothly.

"Oh!" Harper let out a nervous laugh. "You don't have to—"

"I insist."

His tone was polite.

But final.

"It's the least I can do for interrupting and taking Hassani with me."

I saw it instantly.

The way Harper's smile dropped just a little.

The way she forced herself to nod.

"Okay. I guess… yes. Thank you."

My father's focus returned to me. "Let's go."

I barely got out a "See you later" to Harper before I was following my father out of the restaurant.

The moment the restaurant's doors shut behind us, I let out the breath I didn't even know I was holding.

"Where are you parked?" he asked.

I gestured toward my car a few feet away.

"Good." He pulled out his Range Rover's key fob and unlocked the SUV in front of us. "Follow me to Long Island. I need to drop this food off to your mother."

I nodded and did exactly as he said.

The whole drive to Long Island was strange.

My father didn't call me. Didn't text.

Didn't do anything except drive ahead of me.

And the entire way there, my thoughts raced.

That pause at the door when he first saw me sitting across from Harper?

That look?

That wasn't *just* surprise.

That was something *else*.

And I was starting to realize exactly what it was.

We reached my childhood home in under an hour.

By then, it was already ten at night.

I pulled into the driveway behind his Range and watched as my father stepped out, takeout bag in hand.

He gestured for me to stay put before disappearing inside.

Less than ten minutes later, he stepped back outside.

Then he headed straight for my car.

I rolled the window down when he was within feet.

"We're going to the Green Room."

"The Green Room?" I glanced at the dashboard clock. "Come on, Dad, not now. It's almost eleven. I gotta get home, get to bed, and be up for work in the morning."

"I'm aware." His voice was steady. "I won't keep you long."

Unbothered.

Then he gestured at his Range Rover before walking to it.

"Drive behind me."

And so... I backed out of the driveway so he could too, with no choice but to do as he said.

Again.

A few miles later, I was pulling into a parking spot at The Green Room, one of the local billiards in Long Island.

I'd only been here twice with my dad.

He had a billiard table in his man cave, so coming here was usually just a way to get out of the house. The Green Room was where he hung with his friends… and had talks with me he didn't want to have at home, where my mother might be within earshot.

And the second I saw him disappear inside without waiting for me, I knew this wasn't about pool. It *never* was at The Green Room.

The scent of liquor and faint nicotine greeted me as I stepped inside.

The Green Room was an old-school billiard hall.

A spot where regulars came to unwind, talk shit, and play the game.

This was where my father brought me to have the birds and the bees conversation when I was thirteen. I got caught by a teacher making out with a girl in my junior high school's stairwell and they were quick to phone my parents about it.

That talk my dad had with me at The Green Room, wasn't G-rated at all.

This was also where he brought me when I failed my first major exam years later in high school.

And now?

Here we were again.

At eleven at night.

After he'd just caught me at Vernon's with Harper.

I opened my mouth to start explaining, to tell him exactly what happened. But before I could get a single word out? He told me…

"Rack up."

The instruction was short. Firm.

He was giving me a chance to talk.

But it would be on his terms.

So, I pulled the rack toward me.

Arranged the balls.

And the silence?

That shit was kicking my ass.

"Aight, Dad," I said after a long moment, exhaling sharply once I was done racking up the balls. "Your silence is driving me crazy, for real."

"*Hmph.*"

That's all he said.

"I know what this is about." I leaned against the table, cue in hand. "And I promise you. What you saw tonight? It's not what you think."

He stood at the opposite end of the table, quietly chalking his cue stick as he watched me.

Not blinking. Not reacting.

Just watching.

"I was only there to get Ayla's dessert," I continued, my voice firmer now.

"*Hmm.*" His gaze didn't waver. "And when you brought the dessert home to your wife?" His accent thickened as he spoke. "And she asked you why you were there and who you were with…?"

He tilted his head slightly.

"Would you have left out the fact that you went to her favorite restaurant… *with* your co-worker?"

My stomach twisted.

Because the answer?

Was obvious.

I hadn't even thought that far.

"Break," he said through his teeth.

The single word cut through the air, instructing me to take the first shot.

I licked my lips, stepped forward, and got into position.

Angled the tip of my cue stick.

Steadied my bridge hand, just like he taught me.

Aimed for the apex of the white ball.

Took my shot… and missed everything.

Fuck.

Without a word, my father stepped up next.

Leaning forward, he lined up his shot, barely taking a second to adjust.

Then…

He sank a ball.

Effortlessly.

"You know," he said casually, still focused on the table, "I like to give people the benefit of the doubt… but you're making that real damn hard, son."

I hate losing.

Always have.

It's something my father actually *loved* about me.

He fostered my competitive nature as a kid.

Fed it. Encouraged its growth.

It's the reason I even went after the Greene Gardens Project. The reason I dared to negotiate my compensation—and got exactly what I asked for.

Even when I wasn't sure I could actually get it.

"I don't like what I saw tonight."

He didn't look up as he spoke.

Just studied the table.

"You're playing a dangerous game with your life, son. You know that?"

I wrinkled my brows. "What are you talking about? How?"

He took his next shot. Sank nothing this time.

Then lifted his eyes to me.

"I wasn't doing anything wrong," I said quickly, my grip tightening on my cue stick. "It's like I told you, I was just picking up dessert for Ayla."

The dim lighting.

The old-school billiard tables.

The neon sign near us buzzing softly.

All of it felt so damn heavy now.

Like he wasn't just preparing for a game… he was preparing to whoop my ass.

Not physically.

But whoop my ass in a way that would stick with me for the rest of my damn life. I could just *feel* it.

"If I were Ayla's father," my dad said finally, voice low, steady, "and I walked into Vernon's and saw you sitting across from that woman?"

His gaze sharpened.

"The first thing I'd think? Would not be *'Oh, my son-in-law was just picking up dessert for my daughter.'*"

He arched a brow.

"Do you think Ayla would see it that way, Hassani?" He asked. "That you weren't doing *anything* wrong?"

"Dad, I was—"

"Your go."

The cut-off was swift.

I clenched my jaw.

Shoulders sagging in frustration.

But I did as told.

Got into position.

Held my cue stick steady.

Lined up another shot.

Struck the white ball…

And missed. Again.

"Fuck!" I barked before kissing my teeth.

My father chuckled at my reaction.

Then he circled the table with calm precision.

"You know what I don't get, son?" he mused, chalking his cue stick.

He glanced at me.

"You got a damn *good* woman at home."

His stare hardened.

"And yet? You're out here entertaining someone who ain't your wife."

My pulse ticked faster.

I clenched my teeth.

It was bad enough I was losing this game, which I absolutely hated.

But now?

Now he was accusing me of something I didn't even do.

"But you know…" My father laughed to himself, shaking his head. "You always did *love* admirers."

He leaned against the pool table, rolling the cue stick in his palm.

"The girls used to flock to you—from the time you were building blocks in kindergarten to the days you were running track in high school and college." He smirked. "But I let it be."

His eyes shifted up to mine.

"Because you were young. And I knew you didn't need to be concerned with settling down with any of these *likkle* girls."

His smirk faded.

"And that's why I told you *hell no* when you said you were interested in Ayla."

My jaw clenched.

I looked away, shaking my head.

I *hated* when he reminded me of that.

When he made me go against what I wanted.

What I *finally* have now.

He nodded to himself, ignoring my reaction.

"Because I knew that girl was a good girl," he continued. "And although I knew my son was a good guy…?" His voice dipped lower and he lifted his gaze. "You were *nowhere* near ready to keep a girl like her smiling all the time."

A sharp laugh.

"No, son. It would've taken just one girl with sweet-smelling perfume to turn your head so fast—"

He snapped his fingers.

"—it would've spun off like a bottle cap."

"Dad." I exhaled sharply.

I met his gaze, squaring my shoulders.

"You know I wouldn't cheat on Ayla, right?"

His eyes narrowed.

A heavy, wordless glare.

I gritted my teeth.

"You know *that*, right?"

My father finally spoke.

"What I *know*…"

He leaned over the table, lined up his cue stick. Took his shot. Pocketed a solid ball. Then straightened up again.

"…is that tonight?" His voice was calm. "You looked like a man who could be mistaken for someone else's husband."

"What?!" The bass in my voice came harder than expected, echoing around us.

"Yes." He walked around the table, lining up another shot. "You say you'd never cheat—"

Another swift strike. Another ball sunk.

"—then why put yourself in a position for it to happen?"

I guffawed. "You're overreacting right now."

"No." He finally looked up at me. "*You're* just lying to yourself."

A beat.

"And worse…" His expression darkened. "You're lying to your *wife*."

My fists curled at my sides.

"I would *never* cheat on Ayla," I repeated, teeth gritted. "*Never*. I'd have to die first."

"Then stop putting yourself in positions where you have to go back on your fucking word," he roared.

I took a breath.

Stepped back.

My chest was rising and falling now.

Everything around us muted.

All I could hear was my father's words, bouncing off the walls of my head.

He sucked his teeth loudly then leaned over the table again.

Another shot. Another ball sunk.

I exhaled. Loudly.

Annoyed.

Frustrated.

Defeated.

"I know what it's like, *yuh* know," he finally spoke again.

He lined up another shot.

"Before I started working at the bakery in Long Island City? You *know* where I was working." He glanced up at me. "You think I don't know about the women who like to get too friendly at work?"

I opened my mouth. "Dad—"

"I knew them," he cut me off. "*Plenty* of them. I'm your father, aren't I?"

He took his shot.

"But I ain't never put myself in situations that would make your mother suspicious at a work event."

Another ball rolled—but didn't sink.

"Didn't create situations where my female co-workers would even *think* I saw them as *anything* more than what they were. Co-workers."

His eyes flicked up.

"Because no matter how much control you *think* you have?"

He tapped his cue stick twice against the table.

"A woman has ten times more than you and *always* will."

I swallowed hard.

I wanted to argue.

Say that his experience wasn't mine.

That Harper wasn't even a factor like that.

But fuck…

It didn't feel that way anymore.

And I hated that my father could see it before I could.

"Let me be very clear when I say these next few words to you, *bwoy.*"

My father didn't look at me.

Just circled the table.

Like a shark.

"When I talk?"

He finally stopped.

Lifted his gaze.

"I mean every word I say. Because I say that shit with conviction, you listening?"

My throat felt tight.

I didn't move.

Didn't blink.

Didn't breathe.

"So when I said, on your wedding day, that Ayla was officially my daughter on paper?"

He tilted his head.

"But she had always been my daughter before then?"

His gaze pinned me in place.

"I wasn't talking for show."

He lifted his cue stick and pointed it directly at me.

"*Yuh* hearing me?"

I swallowed. Hard.

"Because she became my daughter when her father didn't come home on September 11, 2001. You gettin' it?"

The room felt thicker.

My lungs felt tighter.

I could hear my father's inhales and exhales now.

And I knew…

So could he.

He didn't move for a long moment.

Then…

His shoulders lifted.

A sharp exhale.

"So."

He finally looked away.

Studied the table.

A few solid balls left.

A whole lot of striped ones.

Evidence that I was having my ass handed to me.

In this game.

And in life.

"Ayla ain't *just* your wife, Hassani."

He bent over the table again.

Angled his cue stick.

Lined up his final shot.

"And while I may not have known her father Aden long before he started working under me in that North Tower..."

A brief pause.

A deep inhale.

"I made a promise to myself after that September 11th night."

He lowered his voice.

"The night I saw Aden's wife cry until she passed out from exhaustion on her living room couch."

His grip on his cue stick tightened.

"I swore *that night* I'd *always* protect his daughter..."

A beat.

"The way I know *he* would have."

Then, before he took the final shot...

He froze.

Glanced up at me one last time.

"Ayla is my *one* and *only* daughter, Hassani."

His voice was low.

"And I will never, *ever* accept a new one."

Then...

The last ball dropped.

And I closed my eyes.

Tightly.

Because if his goal was to make me feel like shit, to feel the full weight of his disappointment?

He had achieved it.

With flying colors.

"You lost this game." My father stood to his full height, locking eyes with me. "Don't fuck everything up and lose your wife, too."

He pointed at me.

"You lost the game—"

His voice dropped.

"Do *not* lose your wife."

I stared at him, throat tight.

Then my gaze dropped to the table.

Empty.

Just like my stomach.

And in that moment, I realized my dad was right.

I wasn't blind.

Harper was beautiful. She was into me. Clearly.

I saw it.

But I never let her attention cloud my judgment.

I was in control. *Always.*

Women had always been drawn to me—but I knew how to handle that.

Didn't I?

Agreeing to go to Vernon's, though? A bad call.

But it was innocent… right?

Right?

Or had I been wrong all along?

THE DRIVE HOME WAS TORTURE.

Even after my father pulled me into a hug, told me he loved me till his dying breath, his final words wouldn't stop playing.

"You lost the game… Don't fuck everything up and lose your wife, too."

The idea of losing Ayla?

Never crossed my mind.

Not once.

Not even on the worst days.

I still remember that night. Standing outside her hotel room in D.C. in the early hours of my wedding day, the one I had with my ex-fiancée, Sienna.

I begged Ayla to admit it.

To say what I'd known for years.

That she loved me.

That she had always loved me.

I waited. And waited.

And when she finally said it, I knew.

Forever.

Me and Ayla.

That was the plan.

That was the whole damn point of getting married in the first place.

So why did I feel like everything was falling apart?

The Greene Gardens Project was supposed to be the final piece.

The thing that would set us up for life.

Money was handled.

Our love was unshakable.

I thought that was all we needed.

But now?

Shit.

Now, I wasn't sure anything was enough.

The constant delays at work.

The flaws I should've seen before creating them.

The pressure of Bryant's expectations weighing me down.

I was starting to feel like I wasn't the guy who should be leading this project.

And I hated it.

I pulled into our driveway.

Dragged my tired ass up the paved walkway.

Stopped a few feet from the door.

Looked up.

And for the first time, my house, the one I designed, the one I built, didn't feel like home.

I slid my key into the lock.

Stepped inside.

Darkness.

Expected.

I was home late as hell,

And I hadn't even called.

Again.

I made a mental note… fix this, Hassani.

Make it up to Ayla.

Somehow.

But for now, I just needed our bed.

I was done.

I moved down the corridor.

Turned toward the kitchen for some water.

Flicked on the light and nearly jumped out of my skin.

"Oh, shit!"

Ayla was sitting at the table.

Silent.

Still.

Eyes locked on me.

My hand flew to my chest.

"Baby." I chuckled, trying to shake it off. "Damn. I ain't even know you were in here."

Nothing.

No reaction.

No smile back.

Nothing.

And slowly, the nervous laughter left my lips.

My chest tightened.

I could feel it.

Something was wrong.

"Baby…" I said softly. "Why you just sitting there all quiet?"

Still no words.

Just those sad, tired eyes staring straight through me.

And in that moment, I realized… she was done.

I swallowed.

Hard.

Tried to read her expression.

Tried to understand how we got here.

"Ayla… why are you still up—"

"Where were you?"

Her voice was low.

Weighted.

Angry.

My jaw tightened.

My throat closed.

I opened my mouth to say something, but nothing came out.

Nothing came out, because if I told her I was in Long Island with my dad getting my ass handed to me, I'd have to tell her why. She knew all the stories about The Green Room. She knew my dad only brought me there whenever he needed to humble me, bring me down to size, as he put it. And if I told her he brought me there because he found me at Vernon's with Harper... I just knew I wouldn't know peace that night.

A sharp, bitter scoff left her lips. "Were you out with Harper, Hassani?"

Fuck.

I shut my eyes.

Hard.

So much for leaving that part out.

"You lost the game... don't lose your wife."

My father's voice slammed right into me.

Like a brick to the chest.

"Ayla—"

"Yes or no."

She cut me off.

Voice sharp.

Clipped.

Unforgiving.

Her eyes?

Dark.

Cold.

There was no running from this.

No deflecting.

No fixing it with sex this time.

I *had* to answer.

Yes or no.

I wasn't going to lie.

I'd lied to other women.

But Ayla *wasn't* other women.

So… I told her.

"I *was*, but then my—"

"God." She exhaled sharply. "Hassani, I can't do this shit anymore."

I held my breath.

Didn't let it go.

"I can't do this, and I don't want to."

"Ayla—"

"Every fucking night…" she cut me off. Her voice was shaking. Her hands were shaking. "… since you started this project, Hassani… has been hell for me."

I shut my eyes.

Dropped my tense shoulders.

Because shit…

Since I started this project, it's been hell for me *too*.

"This woman you're working with… *hmph*." Ayla laughed bitterly then inhaled a breath. No humor. Just *pain*.

She damn near growled.

"She is up to something. And I'm *tired* of telling you about her."

Her voice cracked.

"Tired of you making excuses. Tired of you making me feel crazy. And yet, here you are, walking into this house, at this hour, telling me you were out with her."

I shook my head. Held up a hand.

"Nah, man, you didn't let me finish—"

"Were you or were you not out with her, Hassani?"

Her voice was sharp as glass.

I nodded. "I was, but not for—"

"I want…"

Her voice hitched.

Like she couldn't breathe.

Like the words were stuck in her throat.

"A," I stepped forward. Reached for her. "Baby, I—"

"I want a divorce."

The words hung in the air.

Thick. Heavy. Final.

And I swear, I felt my heart crack inside my chest. Cracked so hard I had to step back to keep my balance. Grabbed at the space over my heart a second later.

"You lost this game… don't lose your wife."

Fuck.

My knees buckled.

I had to force myself to stay on my feet.

"Ayla." I took a step forward but stopped when she held up a hand.

She stood next.

Turned away.

"A. Boogie," I whispered.

Whispered because I couldn't find my voice.

Was this shit happening?

Because it felt like a really bad fucking nightmare.

She kept walking.

Even as I reached for her hand.

She slapped it away.

My pulse hammered.

My breath came shallow.

The air was too thin to inhale.

"Fuck, Ayla, come on, *don't do* this right now."

She stopped.

Just for a second.

Then turned.

And her eyes gutted me.

"I've been losing you for months, Hassani." She blinked fast. Her bottom lip quivered. "But tonight?" She shook her head. "You lost *me.*"

"Ayla, please."

But she was gone.

Into the guest bedroom.

Door slamming shut behind her.

I stood there.

Hand on my head.
Jaw damn near on the floor.
This was *so* fucking bad.
And what's worse…
I felt like there was nothing I could do about it.

PART IV
THE RENOVATION

The process of rebuilding and restoring. Choosing each other again, even after the cracks...

CHAPTER 14

NOW - EARLY SUMMER 2023... PRESENT DAY

*H*assani

I PULLED INTO THE PARKING LOT OF THE SHOPPING STRIP IN LONG Island City, Queens.

It was early, but Island Rise Bakery was already buzzing with life—people coming in and out, some balancing boxes of baked goods in their hands, others lingering outside to chat before heading to work.

I smiled. My parents' bakery. My second home. My first job.

From the time I was a baby, my parents brought me here, back when the business was just starting out. My dad always says it was my mom's idea. Her way of investing instead of spending his tax refund on new furniture. She'd been baking since she was a kid, and she knew she could make a living doing it. And she was right.

Now, the bakery was a Long Island City staple—a bright yellow-and-green awning stretched over the entrance, proudly displaying *Island Rise Bakery* in bold script. I didn't even have to step inside to take in the scent of fresh spice buns, patties, and warm hard dough bread.

Normally, I'd appreciate the sight, the smell, the familiarity of it all. But today?

I didn't want to be here. Not for *this*.

Hours earlier, I saw Ayla for the first time since she told me she wanted a divorce. Two days. That's how long she'd been locking me out—sleeping in the guest room, avoiding conversation. This morning was the first time we'd touched, and even though we'd hooked up in the kitchen...

Something was off.

I knew it. She knew it. And I still couldn't make sense of it.

With a deep sigh, I stared up at the bakery's awning before stepping out of my car. I wasn't here for the food, or even to check in on my mom.

I was here for my father.

After 9/11, when most of his colleagues never made it home, my dad never went back to work anywhere else. He'd grieved in his own way, pouring himself into the bakery alongside my mother. He never left. And I never forgot.

That day changed everything for both of us.

One of the colleagues he lost was Ayla's father.

And the little girl that colleague left behind? The one who used to call my house at one in the morning just to cry into the phone?

She became mine.

I shook my head, forcing myself back to the present. I didn't have time to get lost in the past. I had to be in Manhattan in an hour. I was already late. But at that moment, nothing mattered except getting the advice I came here for.

I pushed open the glass door, immediately met with the warm, sweet aroma of baking bread and fresh patties.

"Morning, Hassani!" Mrs. Douglas, one of the bakery's regulars, greeted from the counter.

The other patrons present also greeted me in waves.

I lifted my hand in a wave. "Mornin', y'all."

The moment my mother spotted me from behind the register, her face lit up. She moved from behind the counter, wiping her hands on her apron before pulling me into a hug that made me bend my knees just to fit.

"What a sweet surprise," she smiled brightly, stepping back to scan me head to toe—a habit she's never grown out of. "But *bwoy*... you look run down."

I snorted a laugh. "Thanks, Ma."

"Nah, man, I'm serious," she said, hazel-green eyes narrowing with concern. "You look tired."

I exhaled. "I really am."

She studied me for a second longer, then tapped my shoulder. "You're working too hard, Hassani." Then, tilting her head slightly to see around me, she asked, "Where's my daughter?"

The mention of Ayla twisted something inside me, but I kept my expression neutral.

"She's home, resting," I said, scratching the back of my head. "I'm heading into the city soon, but I need to talk to Dad real quick."

"He's back there," she said, nodding toward the kitchen. "Go see him, and I'll have some fresh spice buns waiting when you get back. Don't forget to carry some home to Ayla."

"Aight." I forced a smile. "Sounds good, Ma."

She gave me that mom-look, the one that meant she wasn't buying it. "You sure you're all right?"

Not in the least.

"I'm good, Ma. I'm good." I pointed over her shoulder. "I'm gonna go talk to Dad."

"Go 'head." She squeezed my arm once before turning back to the counter.

I pushed through the kitchen doors.

Inside, the air was thick with the scent of fresh pastries and flour, the ovens humming quietly in the background. My father was pulling a large baking sheet of golden-brown patties from one of the commercial racks when he glanced up, doing a double take when he saw me.

His brows lifted. "Mornin', son."

I stopped just inside the doorway. "Mornin', Dad."

My dad had always been in great shape, but ever since he started working full-time at the bakery—lifting trays, kneading dough, moving sacks of flour—he'd bulked up even more. Early sixties, but he could pass for forty easy.

He set the tray of patties down on the steel counter, dusting his hands as he turned to face me.

"What's going on?" he asked. "Shouldn't you be at work?"

I let out a slow breath through my nose.

Immediately, his shoulders lost height. His whole stance shifted.

"What happened?"

I swallowed. "Ayla said she wants a divorce."

His chest caved in slightly as he gripped the metal counter for support. He squeezed his eyes shut, shaking his head before turning away.

I ran a hand down my beard. "The night I came back from the billiard hall with you, she was waiting in the kitchen... wanted to know where I was."

"*Mm-hmm,*" he muttered, already knowing where this was going.

"And, yeah..." I scratched the back of my head. "I told her... I was with Harper."

My father sucked his teeth so loudly it echoed. "Hassani!"

"She asked if I was with her," I defended, stepping deeper into the kitchen. "I didn't want to lie."

"She ask *yuh*, and *yuh* just hand her *di* answer?" he sneered, shaking his head. "*Mi nah* tell *yuh fi* fabricate *nuttin'*, but Hassani... *yuh* don't know when *fi* be a smart man and just omit?"

"She didn't give me room to. She didn't even let me explain! She just stormed off, locked herself in the guest room, and she's been sleeping there for two damn nights—"

"*Shh, shh!*" My father waved a hand through the air, shutting me up instantly. "*Bwoy, yuh nuh* have no sense?! *Yuh* a tell me too much."

I clenched my jaw and stopped talking.

Whenever my father got pissed, Patois, as always, jumped in and out of the chat. That's how I knew he was really mad.

He took a deep audible breath to settle himself, raising a hand before continuing.

"Your marriage is *your* marriage," he said, calmer, fixing me with a look. "Venting to the wrong people, even family..." He held up a finger. "Won't fix things. *Overstand?*"

I nodded.

"Fixing your marriage," he continued, pointing directly at me, "should be your focus. Not telling me how bad it is."

He gestured toward the back of the kitchen. "Come. I don't want your mother overhearing any of this."

I followed him past the ovens, the scent of warm coco bread lingering in the air. Soon, the other bakers would be here, starting on the next round of pastries.

But right now, this talk? *This* was urgent.

My father turned to face me, crossing his arms. "Your first mistake?" He held up a single finger. "Letting her sleep in another room."

I blinked. "What?"

"You should've *never* let her sleep in another bed," he said firmly. "*Never.*" He swiped a hand through the air. "That was your *first* mistake."

"Okay...?"

"Your second mistake? Was going to sleep angry," he added. "So, make sure *yuh* following me." He held up his hand and used his fingers to count off. "You never go to sleep angry, and you damn sure don't sleep in separate rooms when you're angry. You hearing me?"

"I hear you," I mumbled, nodding.

When it came to relationships, my father understood what made them work. Whether it was friendships, family, or his marriage to my mother, he just knew how to keep them intact.

It's probably why Ayla's father respected him enough to invite him over for dinner at their brand-new house, all those years ago. A silent way of saying, *"You're like family now."*

I exhaled. "So what do I do?"

His face scrunched up. "Excuse me?"

I frowned. "Tell me what to do."

"No." He shook his head. "I will not *tell you* what to do, Hassani."

I blinked hard. "Dad—"

"Dad what?!" He laughed, and I wasn't even close to finding this shit funny.

"This is *your* marriage," he pressed, jabbing a finger into my chest. "*Yours*. You understand it better than you think. Better than me, I tell you that. You know what it will take to change Ayla's mind."

"I already *tried* that this morning," I grumbled, referring to our random ass hook up in our kitchen. "Didn't work."

"Good." He nodded. "Now you know what doesn't work. Now try something else. And if *that* doesn't work? Try something else. Keep *trying* until you find what works."

I exhaled sharply, running a hand over my head.

"Let's say I tell you what to do," my father continued. "Let's say I give you the magic answer, and it works. What happens next time, *hmm?*"

I turned to face him, brows furrowed.

"You'll come back to me again? And again?" He scoffed. "And again *and* again?" He sucked his teeth. "Look *yah, bwoy. Mi nah yuh* marriage 8-ball, Hassani."

I dropped my head to my chest, letting it hang there.

"Lift *yuh* head, *bwoy!*"

I snapped up immediately, swallowing back the feeling of defeat.

"Because you know you'll have another falling out with Ayla, right?" His lips curled into a smirk. "This isn't going to be the last time you two butt heads."

I ground my teeth together. "She told me she wants a divorce, Dad." My voice cracked slightly as I pressed my hands together. "A divorce."

My father sucked his teeth. "She don't want no divorce."

"She *said* she did."

"Because she's *pissed*," he said, like it was obvious. "You were out with another woman after work hours, *bwoy*. What did you expect? Applause?"

I clenched my jaw. He was right, but damn.

"You think Ayla's gonna celebrate that shit?" he pressed. "She's mad. That's why she said it."

I let out a frustrated groan, rubbing both hands down my face.

The worst part?

As much as I wanted to fight what he was saying, I couldn't. Because deep down… I already knew it was true.

Everything was too much.

I had to be at work soon—probably late again—and I'd have to stay even later to fix the design flaw I'd been struggling with for days. I hadn't really spoken to my wife since she told me she wanted out of our marriage. I felt like I was failing at everything.

I had driven all the way to Long Island City to get advice from my father, and he wasn't even giving it.

"I can't tell you what to do," he repeated. "But I can tell you this—fight for your forever."

I locked eyes with him.

"Fight for your wife the way you fight for this damn project. I see you sacrificing everything to make sure it's running well—"

"Even the project is driving me half-crazy, Dad," I mumbled. "For real, man. Shit."

My dad stopped and stared at me for a few beats. Then he closed the space between us and took me by the back of my head. He leaned his forehead against mine and that was all I needed to release the tension in my shoulders. My dad gave me a few seconds before lifting his head to press a kiss to my forehead. He patted my shoulders twice then stepped back.

I took a deep breath, trying to inhale courage.

"You're experiencing a shift, and that's okay," he assured me. "But while you're killing yourself over Greene Gardens, make sure you're tending to your own garden." His voice deepened. "You must protect your marriage, Hassani. You *must*. That's the only way you'll keep it. There's no other way, son."

I swallowed hard, letting his words sink in.

He was right.

I had been pouring all my time and energy into work—into making sure this project was successful—but I had forgotten balance. I promised myself I would balance. I promised Ayla.

I nodded, my voice hoarse. "Aight." I cleared my throat. "Aight."

And just like that, the advice I was looking for was right there in my father's last few words.

You must protect your marriage, Hassani. You must. That's the only way you'll keep it.

Tonight, I was going home to my wife.

Tonight, I was fixing this.

I PUSHED THE SIDE BUTTON ON MY PHONE, LIGHTING UP THE SCREEN.

I sighed.

Kissed my teeth.

Then dropped my head back between my shoulders.

Though I was late getting into the office, I wasn't late enough to justify still being here at 8 p.m.

This damn design flaw had me stuck.

Again.

I'd been staring at the blueprints since morning, honestly, since Harper pointed it out days ago, but something about it just wasn't adding up.

I leaned back in my chair, rubbing my eyes. My brain was a split battlefield—half of it still stuck on my father's words earlier, the other half stuck on these goddamn blueprints.

I turned toward my computer screen, narrowing my eyes at the design, searching for the flaw.

Still couldn't see it.

The anger built in me like a slow fire.

Harper said there was an issue. She claimed the interior spaces were too enclosed. That the natural light flow was off.

But I was having a hard time believing that.

I had designed this meticulously. Measured every curve, every angle, every single detail.

Something about having to fix this didn't feel right.

"Hey, Hassani," Harper's voice cut in as she pushed open my office door.

I exhaled sharply. Didn't even bother looking at her.

"What's up, Harper?" I muttered, my eyes still fixed on the screen.

She strolled in, taking a seat across from my desk.

"You're such a dedicated man," she said softly.

I kissed my teeth, finally looking up. "That's what they pay me for."

I pulled my sketchbook closer, flipping to the same page I'd been stuck on all damn day.

"Although," I said low, pencil already moving, "I've been struggling to find this flow issue you said was here."

I glanced up, only briefly, before returning to my sketch.

Harper giggled. Nervous.

"I...*umm*... I have to be honest about something."

I barely looked up. "Okay...?"

She exhaled heavily, like a weight had been lifted off her chest.

"There *isn't* a flow issue."

I stopped mid-stroke.

The pencil hovered over the page.

I lifted my head, fully focusing on her now. "What?"

Harper pressed her lips together, then exhaled again. "There's no *real* problem with the light flow through the townhouses."

I jerked my head back, feeling my jaw slack slightly.

She gave a small, hesitant laugh.

"I just..." She leaned in closer, her voice dropping. "I just wanted more time with you."

A cold wave crashed into me.

Hard.

What the fuck did she just say?

I blinked, slowly, deliberately. "I'm sorry?"

The air shifted.

Like I'd misheard her. Like the universe was giving me one last chance to pretend I didn't hear what she just said.

She swallowed, then pressed a hand to her chest. "I *never* do this, Hassani. I swear I don't."

She placed a delicate hand on my desk next.

"This is my career," she whispered. "I'm a respected designer. I've worked too hard to get here."

Then she lifted her big, wide eyes to mine. Breathless. In awe.

She sighed, shaking her head. "You're just... *so* different."

And that's when it hit me.

Is she telling me she lied?

I straightened, hands tightening into slow fists.

"Harper," I said, voice controlled, measured. Sharp. "What are you saying to me right now?"

She licked her lips. Didn't even hesitate.

"I lied about the design flaw," she admitted. "What you created was perfect. There was never anything wrong with it."

I exhaled, forcing all the air out of me. There was some relief in knowing what I created was *perfect*. I knew the design was solid, even after putting myself through hell trying to find the flaw she swore was there. But as much as that gave me relief, it also left me confused as hell.

"I've intentionally been creating delays to spend more time with you."

Something in me recoiled.

"What?" I whispered.

Harper leaned forward, voice low. "The urgent model home adjustments. The wrong flooring situation. The design revisions..." She took a deep breath. "You didn't have to stay late for any of those things."

My pulse slammed into my ears.

The urgent model adjustments? That's why I missed Ayla's work mixer.

The wrong flooring? That's why I missed the dinner where Ayla met her mother's boyfriend for the first time.

The design flaw? That's why I stayed late the night Harper suggested we go to Vernon's. The night I ran into my father. The night I ended up in The Green Room getting my ass handed to me. And, most devastatingly, the night I came home to a fed-up Ayla who told me she wanted a divorce.

Harper had lied. About *all* of it.

The flow issue. The accessibility concerns. The layout revisions.

Every delay was a fucking lie.

"You wasted *my* time," I said, voice low. My eyes lifted to hers, steady. Controlled. Lethal. "You wasted the *team's* time. Harper…"

I dropped my head, inhaled deep, trying to rein myself in.

"Do you know how much money you may have cost this project?"

Harper didn't even flinch. She squeezed her eyes shut, then opened them again. Serene. Unbothered.

"I don't care about any of that."

My breath halted in my chest.

She doesn't care?

"You *don't* care?" I repeated slowly.

"No." She shook her head, like she was clarifying something simple. "I see those things as means to an end."

"Pardon me?"

She sighed. "I'm not used to wanting someone as much as I want *you*, Hassani."

My head snapped back so fast, my neck cracked.

"I've been with successful men before. *Plenty*," she added. "But *none* of them—not even one—is like *you*."

I clenched my jaw. "I'm *married*, Harper. Married."

"I know." She was quick with it. "And… I don't care."

She scooted to the edge of her seat, bold now. Confident.

"Hassani." She sighed. "You are too extraordinary to belong to just one woman. Let's be real here."

She tucked a loose wave of hair behind her ear.

"I'm not trying to replace Ayla," she said, her voice soft. "I just want a little space in the world you've already built."

I stared.

"No one has to know." She shook her head, almost pleading. "I promise, I won't say a thing."

My eyes collapsed closed.

How could I be so fucking stupid?

Believing Harper was simply attracted to me was one thing.

But her creating fake problems to keep me late? Causing me to stress out unnecessarily over this project? Costing me time—precious time—away from Ayla?

Time I could have spent nurturing my marriage?

Now that shit was unforgivable.

My pulse pounded, hot and violent, thudding in my temples.

Harper wasn't just playing games with work.

She was playing games with my fucking life.

And worst of all?

Ayla—my wife, my friend, my entire goddamn world—had been right about Harper all along.

And I didn't listen.

I exhaled sharply, then locked eyes with Harper.

"You never asked me about Ayla."

Her brows furrowed.

"And now, I see why." A humorless laugh left my chest.

"If you'd taken the time to ask me about her—instead of plotting against her—you'd know she's a phenomenal woman."

I leaned forward, voice steady.

"A woman who has been through hell and back—but never let it change her for the worse."

A pause.

"A woman who doesn't look anything like what she's been through."

Harper stilled.

"You would have known that I've known Ayla since we were fourteen years old. That we started as just friends. *Only* friends."

I swallowed hard. My chest burned.

"And our bond—our love—only grew stronger after she lost her father on September 11th, when he didn't make it home from his job in the North Tower."

Harper gasped. Loud. Eyes wide.

"Yeah." I gritted my teeth to keep my chin from quivering.

"It's a pain she still feels today." My voice dropped, rough around the edges. "A pain I wish I could take from her—*every* fucking day, Harper."

My jaw locked.

"A pain I have been helping her heal from since we were kids."

I forced myself to breathe.

"A pain she tries to hide from the world, but with me?" I clenched my fists. "She lets it all go. Because she trusts me, Harper."

I leaned in just slightly.

"She trusts me with her life... *and* her heart... Harper."

Harper swallowed hard.

"Ayla is the strongest person I know," I continued, voice breaking just slightly. "But even though she's the strongest..." I shook my head. "I'll be damned if I *ever* add to her pain in *any* way."

I straightened, then exhaled.

"And what you're suggesting?" I lifted my chin. "That would bring my wife *a lot* of pain, and me *a lot* of shame."

I let my words hang between us.

Shit.

I shook my head, chuckling darkly. "You've already done that, Harper."

Harper's lips parted, but no sound came out.

"But I can't blame you." I said with a wry smile. "*I* allowed it. *I* allowed all of it."

My voice dropped lower.

"Damn."

I ran a heavy hand down my beard, staring past Harper, lost in every mistake I'd made.

Every bullshit late night.

Every call I didn't return.

Every moment I put work above my wife.

All because of *her*.

"You're upset right now," Harper said, voice too calm. "I get it. Completely."

She leaned back, crossing her legs.

And then?

She had the audacity to smirk.

"But trust me, Hassani," she whispered. "You won't regret what we can have, too." She fixed her gaze on mine. Certain. Unshaken. "I'll see to it."

I scoffed, closing my eyes tight. It took everything in me to swallow back the quiet rage building in my chest, locking up my muscles, making it hard to breathe.

I inhaled a sharp breath, opened my eyes, and zeroed in on Harper.

"Nah, I *definitely* would regret it." I nodded. "Because I love my wife, Harper. *So* damn much that just you suggesting it is enough to make me lose it—let alone actually doing it."

I watched as her chest caved in a little at that.

"I waited, and waited, and waited for *years* to make her my wife," I added, voice hoarse.

"Ayla is my one and only. And I have no interest in sharing myself with you—or anyone else—when I have *her*."

I leaned in slightly. Voice low. Steady. Unshakable.

"Are we clear, Harper? Because it's very important that we are crystal fucking clear on that shit."

She just blinked.

I exhaled sharply, lowering my attention to my sketchbook. Then my eyes drifted to the blueprints on my screen. Realization hit me like a punch to the gut.

I never had to stay late.

I didn't have to be here right now.

Harper sabotaged my work.

And probably my marriage.

But what killed me? What truly gutted me?

I let her do it.

I let it *all* happen.

"I need to go," I murmured, mostly to myself.

I pushed up from my desk, shoving my laptop into my bag and tucking my sketchbook under my arm.

"Harper." My voice was thick, heavy. I sniffed back the heat in my nose, blinking fast against the sting in my eyes.

I don't even know why I want to cry.

"I can't trust you here with my things, and I need to lock my office door when I go. So…" I gestured at the door. "Please, leave."

She parted her lips like she wanted to say something.

But instead, she nodded.

She walked to the door, then paused—turned slightly.

I turned and gave her my back.

Because what the fuck just happened here?

THE ENTIRE DRIVE HOME, I WAS IN SHAMBLES.

I played back every bullshit late night.

Every moment of self-doubt.

Every second of imposter syndrome creeping in because of delays I never should've had in the first place.

Time. Energy. Stress. All of it… wasted.

And I couldn't lie to myself. I knew *why* this happened.

I never stopped her.

I ignored the signs, believing it was harmless. That *she* was harmless.

But my father was right.

I'd been lying to myself.

When I pulled into the driveway and stepped out of the car, I let out a breath.

But it didn't help.

I unlocked the front door and stepped inside. Darkness.

All the lights were off.

Except one.

The guest room.

I stared at the faint glow spilling into the hallway, my father's words echoing in my mind.

"Never let her sleep in another bed."

But I didn't go to her.

I couldn't.

I needed a moment. To think.

To process.

To figure out how the hell I was supposed to fix something that never should've been broken in the first place.

Ayla told me. She *told* me, and I told her she had *nothing* to worry about.

She trusted me.

And I let her down.

Upstairs in the master bedroom, I changed into my basketball shorts, heart still hammering.

My chest was tight. My muscles tense.

There was no way I was sleeping like this.

So I took the stairs back down.

Kept going.

Straight to the basement.

Ayla and I had turned it into a half-library, half-gym.

She had her books.

I had the treadmill, the stationary bike, the step machine.

I went straight for the treadmill.

Jumped on.

No warmup. No stretch.

Just ran.

Fast. Hard.

Like I could outrun the rage choking me from the inside out.

Like I could leave behind the self-loathing scraping my ribs raw.

Like I could erase the mistakes.

But the mistakes ran faster.

I was a solid twenty minutes in when I realized I wasn't breathing at tempo.

I wasn't just sweating.

I was burning.

Inside. Out.

Harper lied.

She played me.

I thought I was in control.

But I was *being* controlled.

I cranked the speed up higher.

Faster.

Harder.

I pushed myself to the absolute limit, until my legs gave out beneath me.

I barely caught the treadmill's railing in time, hauling myself off the speeding belt. My feet landed on the outer frame, knees shaking, breath ragged.

I hit the stop button.

The treadmill slowed to a halt.

But my pulse didn't.

I took a step, then collapsed.

Straight to my knees.

And I couldn't fight it anymore.

The tears came full force.

I pressed my palms against the cool floor, body rocking as my chest heaved.

Silent wails—the kind that gut you from the inside out—echoed around me.

I balled my fists, lifted them, ready to punch the floor.

But at the last second, I didn't.

Instead, I spread my fingers against the hardwood.

Steadied myself.

And I gave in.

I let myself cry...

Cry about letting Ayla down.

Cry about doubting myself.

I cried about questioning my own abilities to the point of being led to the slaughter.

And I cried about being so fucking blind.

Harper may have cost me my job.

A career I bled for.

But worse—so much fucking worse…

She may have cost me Ayla, too.

And that?

That hurt the most.

"Every night, since you started this project, has been hell for me."

Ayla's words. Words I could agree with but only understood from my point of view at the time…

They came roaring back with a vengeance.

Because I get it now, A. Boogie. I fucking get it.

But was I too late?

CHAPTER 15

yla

THE RAIN OUTSIDE PELTED AGAINST THE GLASS, CREATING A SOFT rhythm as it fell against the skylights. Aside from the melody of raindrops, the house was quiet… too quiet.

It was another day of me not speaking with Hassani. Another day of finding random things to do to keep my mind off him, and the beef we had.

Or, rather, the beef *I* had with him.

It took everything in me not to unlock the door for him that first night he arrived home after our fight—the night after I told him I wanted a divorce. The morning after I said those words, I made sure to leave the house early, before he could get up. I didn't even have anywhere to go. I just got in my car, drove to the nearby mall, and sat in the parking lot until it opened.

Petty as all hell, but I wanted to prove a point.

For once, I felt like I had *some* power over a situation that just seemed to be getting worse.

I *understood* that the Greene Gardens Project was huge for Hassani. I'd been mindful of being a supportive wife. But somewhere along the way, I lost myself. Every decision I'd made ever since he took on this project had revolved around *his* schedule. Even our annual summer trip. There wasn't one. I didn't want to plan a getaway that would pull him away from work, even though I *really* wanted to go somewhere. Last year, we had to settle for a staycation in the city. And this year? I didn't even bother planning anything. I knew Hassani wouldn't have the time.

As shown by his *many* late arrivals home lately.

This morning would have been another one of those days where I left the house at dawn, but the steady rain kept me inside. I figured I wouldn't be a punk about it and avoid my husband.

Even though yesterday morning was random as hell.

Having sex in the kitchen after not speaking to each other for a full day? Wild. But I missed him. *A lot.* I just hated feeling like I wasn't being heard.

I woke up early today, but he had already left. I didn't even hear him come home last night. The dinner I made still sat in the fridge. Untouched.

Did he even come home?

Was he with Harper again?

I shook my head, trying to push the thought away. Because I knew Hassani wasn't cheating. I *knew* he wouldn't.

He got a lot of attention from women, that part was true. And maybe another man would take advantage of that. But that wasn't Hassani's style.

I used to watch him in relationships. Single, he was a flirt. But in a relationship—at least the ones I remembered him being in, back in high school and college—he was a one-woman man. By choice. Loyalty was encoded in his DNA.

But still... *anyone* could give in to temptation just once. Even the most resilient monogamist.

I just couldn't understand how and why he kept underestimating Harper.

Granted, I'd only met her once. I hadn't been to Hassani's office in Bryant Greene's building, and I hadn't cared to. But that *one* time I met her was enough.

That woman was bad news.

Hassani walking into the house after 2 a.m., confirming my worst fears that he'd been out with her? Proved he didn't see what I saw.

Why did it feel like I was the only one who could see so clearly that Harper was a problem?

I had just finished cleaning the stovetop when my phone chimed. Thinking it might be Hassani, and deciding I would answer if it was him, I grabbed my device only to see another one of my favorite people calling.

"Hey, Carmen Sandiego," I answered, sliding onto the stool at the kitchen island.

Aunt Laurie hollered a laugh, which made me laugh too.

"Oh, don't you start that, Favorite Girl," she teased.

I giggled some more. "What's going on?"

"Nothing much," she replied. "I'm just here, sitting on a beach in the Maldives, sipping a little wine and watching what is possibly one of the most iconic sunsets I've ever seen in my life."

I smiled, resting my chin in my hand. "Yeah, that really sounds like *nothing much*, Aunt Laurie."

She laughed, making me smile even harder. "How about you?"

What I wouldn't give to just be honest. To tell her how lonely I was feeling. How much I missed my husband, who had been working non-stop. To admit there was a co-worker who didn't respect boundaries —who I knew was trying to be more than just his colleague.

Instead, I said, "Just finished cleaning. I'm listening to the morning rain while taking a little breather to talk with you."

"And I am so honored, Favorite Girl."

I nodded. "The honor is all mine."

"You know," she started, "I'm dating someone new."

I lifted my head. "Oh?"

"Good man," she added. "A little younger."

I arched a brow. "How young?"

"He's legal."

I snorted a laugh.

"He doesn't speak much English," she said. "Met him in Ghana a couple of months back. Exchanged numbers. And I recently returned one of his phone calls before a flight to Thailand."

I smiled as I listened, loving the escape into Aunt Laurie's world for a little while.

After her divorce, when she returned to her jet-setting life—this time, more for leisure than work—I knew she would be fine. *This* was the Aunt Laurie I remembered. The world traveler who practically lived out of her suitcase and loved every moment of it.

I was glad I at least got to dabble in that lifestyle long enough to know it wasn't for me.

"I'm shocked you're in a relationship again," I told her.

She laughed. "If I can barely call it that, Favorite Girl. He doesn't talk much, but we understand each other better than most people who do."

"Interesting." I tilted my head. "How?"

"You don't always need words to know when someone loves you," she said softly. "Sometimes… it's just the way they show up."

I blinked at that.

"My lover shows up in his own way, and always in ways that benefit me. Like now." She snickered. "He's getting me another glass of wine at the beach bar. Got me this glass of wine the first time, and I didn't even have to tell him what kind I wanted. He knew from watching what I order. Remembering it without me reminding him."

"That doesn't need language, huh?" I mused.

"Exactly."

I shook my head, smiling. "I'm just so happy for you. I remember when you said you'd *never* date again."

"And I also told you I'd always be open to love, even after every-thing that happened."

"You did."

"Because I realized I was wrong," she admitted. "You can't plan for life, Favorite Girl. You just gotta live it."

I frowned, circling my fingertip against the island's surface. "What if you did plan for it, and it's not going according to plan? What if… what if it's *way* harder than you thought it would be, and you're not sure how long you can deal with it?"

I want a divorce.

The words echoed back at me, sharper than I remembered them, making me flinch.

Had I really said that?

Had I really meant it?

I *did* say it and I *did* mean it… but not really.

I told Hassani I wanted a divorce and, yes, I meant it… but I didn't really *want* a divorce.

I *wanted* my husband to hear me.

I wanted him to figure out how to be successful, not just at work, but with us, too.

We were doing so well before that damn project. And while I understood that the only constant is change, I wanted us back. The *us* before Greene Gardens.

Aunt Laurie was quiet for a moment, and in that silence, I could hear the soft crashing of waves in her background.

What I wouldn't give to be on a beach right now.

"You don't throw away something valuable just because it gets hard," Aunt Laurie finally said. "You fix it, if it's worth it."

She paused before adding, "And, Favorite Girl, if you planned for it —as brilliant as you are—I'd put my life on it, and bet every dollar I have, that it's worth fixing."

I tucked my lips into my mouth, rubbing them together.

"Do you want to talk about it?"

"No." I shook my head. "I'd much rather hear more about the Maldives and this new boy toy you got."

"Ha!" She laughed. "I do *not* have a boy toy."

"*Mm-hmm.*" I smirked. "You so got a boy toy, Aunt Laurie."

After another few minutes on the phone, Aunt Laurie cut the call short to tend to her *lover*, as she called him.

I left the kitchen and made my way to the master bedroom.

I had been putting off decluttering my side of the walk-in closet for years. Every time I walked into the back area to grab a pair of shoes or swap out clothes for the season, I'd glance at the stacked boxes in the corner and say, "This summer, I'm going to handle that."

But this summer? I meant it.

I got down on the closet's carpeted floor and began pulling the cardboard boxes toward me.

For years, I'd been searching for a poetry book I lost somewhere in the house. It wasn't on any of the shelves Hassani installed, so I figured if it was anywhere, it had to be in one of these boxes. That was part of my incentive to finally declutter.

I unpacked one box, then reached for another, pulling it out of the corner, when I spotted something unexpected.

My old camera.

The one my dad gave me when I was a teenager.

And sitting right beside it was the newer camera I purchased shortly after Hassani and I started dating.

My heart stuttered at the sight of them.

The newer camera was the one I'd taken on our wedding and honeymoon trips to Jamaica and Saint Lucia.

The older one… I hadn't used in years. The last film I developed from it captured my time in Egypt.

I palmed it, feeling a dull ache press into my chest from the weight of it in my hands.

I used to *love* this 35mm film camera like it had a heartbeat.

And to me… it did.

Slowly, I ran my thumb over its casing, angling it toward the light so it bounced off the lens.

I set the camera beside me and leaned forward for my other camera. A simple point-and-shoot digital one with a standard LCD screen.

I immediately powered it on, skimming through the photos stored inside.

As I flipped through them, a smile stretched across my lips, unstoppable.

There were shots of me on my wedding day.

Shots of Hassani and I on our honeymoon.

God, we looked *so* happy.

Like, truly happy.

Lost in our own world.

I clicked through more photos—one of him by the pool, sketchbook in hand, of course.

I snickered, shaking my head. Not much has changed. The sketchbook was still a huge part of our life.

More images appeared...

The villa we stayed in.

The beach, in Saint Lucia, we visited every single day.

Plates of food from every restaurant we tried.

Then... clips of us kicking up sand as we ran along the beach, laughing—completely and utterly carefree.

I even stumbled upon photos of *me* that I had no idea Hassani had taken.

Candids.

Photos where I wasn't posing.

Ones where I wasn't even looking at the camera.

A warmth blossomed in my chest, spreading through me.

The rain outside pounded against the skylights, dulling the daylight into gray, but inside?

Inside, I felt sunny.

These pictures—*our* pictures—brought back my mother-in-law's words from our wedding day.

"Marriage will bring you moments of joy so bright they'll take your breath away, but it will also test you... And in those times, remember this: You are stronger together than you could ever be alone. Keep reaching for each other, no matter what. That's how you'll build a love that lasts a lifetime."

I sighed, a deep pang pressing into my chest.

Back then, I had nodded, letting those words wash over me like warm sunlight.

But now? Staring at these pictures? I wasn't so sure.

Had we already stopped reaching for each other?

I turned the dial on my camera and reclined back on the carpet.

I aimed the lens at the closet ceiling and pressed down on the shutter button, listening to one of my favorite sounds in the world.

Click.

The soft hiss of the shutter was invigorating, like the sound of a soda bottle opening.

God, I missed this.

Laying there, camera in hand, I realized it had been *years* since I had last really picked one up.

Before Hassani and I got married, you couldn't see me without a camera.

It was always Ayla and her camera.

I turned onto my side, running my thumb along the camera's body.

"Dad always said I had an eye for it..." I whispered to myself, lifting the lens to eye level.

I aimed at the racks of clothing on Hassani's side of the closet and pressed the shutter button.

Click.

The way the soft shadows played against the walls made the shot look like something out of an editorial spread.

"*Hmph.*" I smiled. "Maybe I *still* have the eye."

I sat up, pushing off the floor, and left the closet, snapping photos of anything and everything along the way.

By the fifth shot, my mind was racing with all the things I could capture while the daylight still lingered.

It was raining, yes, but the clouds cast these deep, moody colors across the sky.

And the skylights made everything look incredible with the way light poured in from above.

"Gosh, that's beautiful." I sighed, analyzing the shot I had just taken of the raindrops streaking across the skylight in our living room.

I lifted my gaze and twisted my lips to one side.

"I wonder..."

I took long strides toward the kitchen next, going straight to our coffee bar.

Despite hating the D-Slam sculpture, I had left it exactly where Hassani put it.

I figured… he loves it, so I can learn to love it, too.

With my camera in hand, I took a few steps back, angling the lens toward the melting coffee cup sculpture.

I positioned it just right, letting the soft skylight glow cascade over the surface, then…

Click.

I peeked down at the LCD screen.

Cringed.

Then snorted a laugh.

"Nope," I said under my breath, shaking my head. "You are *still* ugly as fuck, *chile*. Damn."

That snort turned into a full-blown laugh.

I immediately turned the camera on myself, holding it out at an angle…

Click.

It had been too long since I had taken a picture of me.

When my face appeared on the LCD screen, all I could do was exhale in amazement.

There was nothing glamorous about me that day.

No makeup. My headscarf still wrapped around my hair.

Just a tee and shorts.

But I looked…

Beautiful.

Not because of what I had on or *didn't* have on.

I looked beautiful… because I looked happy.

I lowered the camera and held it close to my heart.

"Reunited, and it feels *so* good," I said tenderly, smiling.

Then I turned on the arches of my feet and sprinted toward the bedroom.

I *had* to tell Hassani.

I had to call him.

I had found my camera.

The skylights—the ones I told him his sketch of the house needed when we were teenagers—were absolutely perfect for it.

I had to tell him what a genius he was.

I had just reached the bedroom when I stopped, deciding…

He's likely busy working. I'll text him instead.

Me: I found my old camera today. The skylights make every shot look unreal. I love your brain so much, baby.

I stared at the message for a long moment.

My finger hovered over the send button…

But I didn't press it.

I removed my finger.

Then I deleted the message altogether, closing out the text app.

Because…

I wasn't ready.

Not yet.

We weren't cool.

Hadn't slept in the same bed for three nights.

I had said I wanted a divorce…

And even though I hadn't meant it, he didn't know that.

And honestly?

I wasn't ready to forgive him.

Not yet.

I shook the thoughts free, dropping my phone back onto the bed.

I focused down on my camera and sighed.

Today was about me, anyway.

I ran my thumb along the camera's body, a smile curling at my lips.

"What else can I photograph?" I whispered to myself, already eager for the next shot.

CHAPTER 16

$\mathcal{H}$assani

The rain outside tapped against the glass, leaving behind streaks of water against the tall floor-to-ceiling windows. It was heavier moments ago but becoming lighter, hinting the weather would clear up soon. I sat back in my seat, inhaling a deep breath as I rolled my head around my neck, trying to shake off the tension.

I was tired… both physically and emotionally.

I'd been sleeping like shit for days now. Tossing, turning, barely catching two hours of rest before the morning hit.

I thought I wouldn't know what a bed felt like without Ayla in it, but I'd found out three damn times already. And I *hated* every second of it.

That morning, I dragged myself out of bed, feeling like a shell of myself. I was exhausted, frustrated, but most of all?

I was ashamed.

I didn't go to the guest room to talk to Ayla the night before. I wanted to. But I was too defeated, too embarrassed, too damn disappointed in myself for letting Harper outplay me. My father had been right. I'd been lying to myself.

So, instead?

I showered when I was done with the treadmill in the basement.

I laid in bed, staring at the ceiling and through the skylight.

And by 4 a.m., I knew exactly what I needed to do.

I left the house early, calling Bryant's assistant, Chelsea, on the drive to Manhattan, asking if he had any availability. I figured he wouldn't. Bryant Greene was a billionaire. His schedule stayed booked.

But when his assistant called me back five minutes later to tell me she'd squeezed me in for an early meeting?

I took it.

I didn't want to have this meeting.

But I needed to.

"Hassani."

I turned at the sound of Bryant's voice as he stepped into his office.

I pushed my hands into the armrests of the chair, preparing to stand, but he held up a hand.

"Please, don't get up."

His office was huge—a penthouse-level workspace with views of the Manhattan skyline. It was the kind of office that screamed power.

Bryant walked in, reaching for the button on his suit jacket as he studied me. "How are you?"

I exhaled. Forced a nod. "Better this morning."

His brows furrowed. He held up a hand, pressing it to the lapel of his designer suit. "You're not quitting... are you?"

His voice was half-joking, but I caught the tension in it.

"Because if I need to schedule a session with my therapist, let me know now."

I let out a low chuckle. "No, Bryant. I'm not quitting. Wouldn't dream of it."

He laughed lowly, visibly relieved as he exhaled. "Okay, good. Because when my principal architect calls for a last-minute meeting, it's usually *not* a good sign."

Bryant shrugged off his jacket and placed it on the nearby coat rack before stepping behind his desk.

He didn't sit down right away.

"So… what's going on?"

I sighed, clenching my jaw.

Pissed that I even had to do this.

"It's Harper, Bryant."

A flicker of wariness crossed his face as he finally took a seat in his chair. "What about her?"

"She's been pulling some shit that's slowed down the project." I shook my head, jaw tight. "Some of the issues were real, but she was holding them back just to make them urgent later. Other issues? Completely unnecessary. And when I say unnecessary, I mean I had no business staying late on recent nights to fix them."

Bryant sat up straight, his focus sharpening. "Explain."

I leaned forward, resting my elbows on my knees.

"She sabotaged work just so she could spend time with me."

His brows shot up.

"Remember the last-minute revisions on the model home layout?" I continued. "The *open concept space* she flagged as a concern?"

"I do."

"She *knew* about the issue two weeks before she brought it up, then sat on it like it was nothing. I wouldn't have even known if I didn't go digging through the email archives this morning. If she'd flagged it earlier, we wouldn't have had to push back finalizing the investor pitch by two days."

His jaw tightened. "So she just… sat on it? To keep you here late?"

"Exactly." I nodded. "And I bought into it at the time because it seemed legit. Just like I bought into her next *urgent* issue with the community center's flooring."

I jabbed my fingertips into the desk.

"She claimed we needed to review swatches because the original supplier messed up the order. Sounded important. But she already had a second vendor lined up with an *exact* match. She could've handled it over email. Instead, she insisted I stay late to approve a whole new batch in person."

Bryant's expression was stone-cold now.

He clenched his jaw. "How much time did that cost us, Hassani?"

"Not much," I replied. "Not in the grand scheme of things. We're still on schedule for launch."

"No delays?"

"None." I swallowed hard. "I've gone over everything before our meeting and can confirm that. The project is still on track to hit all the targets… it's my home that's taken a hit."

I shook my head. "Look, I don't want to bring my personal life into this—"

"Hassani." Bryant interjected, voice firm. "Your personal life is part of this project's success. If work is affecting it, your personal life will affect work too. Everything's cyclical."

I exhaled slowly. "Okay, then…" I licked my lips, collecting my thoughts. "Every issue Harper has brought up? Every night I stayed late to handle them? It was always at the *worst* times." My jaw clenched. "Times when I needed to be there for my wife."

I ran my tongue over my teeth, shaking my head.

"This last issue—this design flaw that didn't even exist—I spent *days* Bryant, trying to redo a layout for one of the residential units. Harper claimed the design didn't 'flow well with the natural lighting.'"

I released a sharp breath.

"But Bryant, there was *nothing* wrong with it. She knew I had already double-checked everything. I was racking my brain, doubting myself, because I knew the design was solid. I'm intentional like that."

Bryant gave a slow nod. "You're *very* intentional, Hassani. It's why I insisted on hiring you."

"Yeah, well." I scoffed. "I still spent hours—too much company time and resources—going over blueprints that didn't need fixing."

Bryant dragged a hand down his mouth. "Jesus."

"I don't want this getting messy," I continued, forcing myself to stay calm. "But I *can't* work with her anymore. She's made this project unnecessarily stressful and difficult. And now? She's made things even more uncomfortable… after propositioning me to cheat on my wife."

Bryant's head snapped up.

"Yeah," I confirmed, nodding. "And she was *very* clear that an affair was what she was aiming for. It was her motivation for sabotaging the project."

Bryant let out a scoffing laugh, rubbing the inner corners of his eyes.

"While all the other things she's done are surprising…" He sighed. "I wish I could say the same for *this*."

I frowned. "What do you mean?"

Bryant tilted his head. "Harper has a tendency to aim a little too high, if you know what I mean."

My brows furrowed. "She's done this before?"

"Never to this extent but, yes. She's done this before. The…" He gestured vaguely. "Propositioning, as you politely put it."

A knot formed in my stomach.

"Another employee mentioned she did this with him, too." I exhaled, referring to Levi. "Are you saying there are more besides him and I?"

"Yes." Bryant's jaw ticked. "Me."

I jerked my head back. "You? For real?!"

So this wasn't just about me.

This wasn't a one-time lapse in judgment on Harper's part.

She had a pattern. A strategy.

Levi had hinted at something similar, but I had been so damn convinced I had control. That I could manage the situation.

But in reality?

I was just another pawn in her game.

And the worst part?

I *let her* play me.

All those nights I told Ayla there was nothing to worry about… that she was overthinking?

I was wrong.

I should have listened to her. I should have trusted her instincts. Instead, I let Harper string me along like a fool… and now?

I was paying the price.

Bryant's gaze shifted toward the glass door of his office.

Without a word, he pushed himself out of his seat, heading toward it.

"Harper was a recommended hire." He pushed the heavy glass door closed, securing it. "This was two years ago, one of the first projects I was hands-on with in a long time. She was the interior designer for the project."

I sat up, listening.

"She *tried* with me." He exhaled. "And failed miserably." He shook his head. "Beyond being happily married, I don't sleep with my employees. It's undisciplined, trite, and severely bad for business. And…" His voice softened. "I just love my wife."

My chest tightened.

"I love my wife too," I echoed, my voice rough. "Which is why all of this is so fucked up." I scrubbed a hand down my face. "Pardon me."

"It's fine." Bryant shook his head. "It's more than fine. But listen…" He sat back down, his gaze serious. "I can't fix anything outside this office in your personal life. But I *can* reassign Harper. Just like I did when she tried to cross boundaries with me."

I frowned. "Why not just cut her loose?"

Bryant met my gaze.

"I mean…" I cleared my throat. "Respectfully, I don't want to be the reason someone gets fired. But if she's done this before with you, and someone else here told me she did the same thing to him… why not just let her go?"

Bryant exhaled, shaking his head.

"Because Harper is calculated, and that makes her dangerous." He chuckled bitterly. "She's the kind of woman who wouldn't hesitate to flip the script."

My frown deepened.

"It's one thing if she only sabotaged the project. If that was the case, firing her would be a no-brainer. But the moment you bring in the affair proposition? That's where things get messy."

I clenched my jaw.

"She can easily flip this on you, Hassani." Bryant's voice was firm. "She could run straight to HR, claim *you* propositioned *her*, and start screaming discrimination."

My stomach sank.

"If I fire her immediately after she invites you to have an affair? She can claim sexual harassment. And you better believe she'd be loud about it." Bryant shook his head. "And I am *not* trying to tie up my firm with lawyer fees. Not on this project."

I sucked in a deep breath, gripping my knees.

"I want everything clean with Greene Gardens."

"Yeah." I leaned back in my seat. "I wouldn't put any of that past her."

Bryant nodded. "That's why I've been playing the long game with her. Reassigning her every time she steps out of line. Keeping distance. She's a liability waiting to happen, but I need her to do something concrete. Something that gives me grounds to fire her without it blowing back on me."

I gritted my teeth. "She just gave you something. Intentionally delaying a project as big as Greene Gardens? That's concrete. It's totally unprofessional."

"It's absolutely unprofessional, but it isn't concrete." Bryant shook his head. "It's not enough. If I fire her outright, she'll spin it, Hassani. She'll say it's retaliation. Maybe claim you came on to her. She'll say whatever the hell she needs to say to protect herself. And trust me, you don't want to be in the middle of that. You already said she's caused problems in your marriage. Allegations of sexual harassment will *not* help. Even if they're bogus. You *can't* un-ring that bell."

I dropped my head back, exhaling hard.

"A man like myself knows *all* the tactics." Bryant chuckled grimly. "I've seen it used on people I know, and it's enough to make me *very* protective of anything with my name on it."

I shook my head.

I didn't want Harper to get fired, but it wasn't right that she could pull this shit again without any real consequence. No one else should have to go through what I was going through.

But Bryant was right.

If Harper was slick enough to manufacture issues on a major project, then she was smart enough to weaponize any situation.

"I'll reassign her to a project I'm heading in Boston." Bryant nodded. "She'll be faced with a decision that'll be a win-win for us. Either she takes the transfer, and we never have to deal with her again… or she quits." He gestured with his hands. "Either way, she's out of our hair."

I nodded, then dropped my head into my hands.

"Hassani, you've done an excellent job on this project," Bryant continued. "I'm blown away by how much you've accomplished in just a year. And while I appreciate the hard work, you look like you could use some rest. A lot of it."

I lifted my head to meet his eyes.

"Because you look like hell, man."

I exhaled, rolling my shoulders back.

"I don't think you've taken a day off since we started Phase 1. Have you?"

"I haven't." I shrugged. "I've made time around it, though."

"That's not enough." Bryant pressed his hand into the table. "I need my principal architect refreshed. I need you looking at blueprints with fresh eyes, not severely tired hazel-green ones that are red-rimmed. While I love the headway we've made, I don't want your home to be the sacrifice, either."

He scoffed, shaking his head. "And I'm a totally different man telling you that."

I focused on him.

Bryant leaned back, hands clasped. "Work was my life before Zoe. It was my pulse. This office has an en suite with a shower stall. That sofa behind you?" He pointed, and I glanced over my shoulder. "Doubles as a very comfortable bed. There were nights I didn't even make it home. That all changed when I met Zoe… quite randomly, I might add." He laughed. "Hassani, I spent every waking moment in this office. It was practically my home."

"And Zoe changed that?" I asked.

"In a major way." His smile softened. "She made me realize I wasn't actually living."

"That's amazing." I smiled. "Not the not living part. The other part, obviously."

Bryant chuckled. "I've learned that your career is important, but the foundation of any great man is the home he builds. It makes no sense to spend all your time building an empire if you have no one to share it with."

I nodded slowly, letting his words sink in. "You're right."

"To circle back," he continued, "Harper's actions haven't caused *any* major delays, correct?"

"None," I assured him. "Despite the setbacks, the project is still on schedule for the launch date."

Bryant tapped the table. "Then take the rest of today off… and tomorrow too."

I blinked. "What?"

"Go home. Get your head right. Relax." He leaned forward. "If you need longer, take a week or two after that. You've earned it, Hassani. Seriously."

Two weeks away from work sounded great.

Ayla and I didn't take our annual summer trip last year because of the project. We had to settle for a staycation in the city over a weekend. And this year we hadn't even started planning a trip… because of me.

"Okay." I nodded. "Let's start with today and tomorrow off. I'll see how that goes."

"Sounds good." Bryant clapped his hands once. "I'll have Chelsea send out an email letting the team know you're out for the rest of today and tomorrow."

"Thanks, Bryant."

"*No*, thank *you*." He smiled. "You're my dream architect."

I laughed.

"I'm serious, man." He nodded. "You get the vision in ways no one else could have. You remind me of a dear good friend of mine. Lennox. May he rest." Bryant inhaled a deep breath. "I say all that to say... I'm looking to have a very, *very* long partnership with you, Hassani."

"As am I." My smile was genuine. "This has been my dream job, and you've been my dream partner—despite the nonsense as of late."

Bryant smirked. "Consider that handled."

He gestured toward the office door.

"Now go. Enjoy the rest of your day off... and tomorrow."

After wrapping up my meeting with Bryant, I left the building and got back into my car, hitting the road, but not for home.

An hour later, I pulled off the interstate and made my way past the newly installed village sign.

My lips curled into a small, tired smile as I drove along the freshly paved wet roads, glimpsing the sidewalks, the parks, and the first completed neighborhoods.

The rain had stopped, leaving behind puddles and a shimmer of dew on trees and partially built homes.

Even with only the builders present, their machinery humming in the air as they worked, the place already felt alive.

The scent of wood, dust, and progress filled my lungs.

Damn, it felt good seeing the vision come to life.

This all started from a doodle in my sketchbook.

I'd visited the area when we broke ground but hadn't been back since. Returning now felt necessary.

I drove past the parks, the lakefront boardwalk, and a newly developed biking trail, caution tape still wrapped around it.

The houses under construction gave a glimpse of what the village would soon become.

I had a front-row seat to history.

I pulled up to a section of land facing the lake, put the car in park, and just sat there, staring out in front of me.

When I first landed this job and learned about the custom home lot program, I didn't hesitate to sign up.

When I got the green light, I purchased the land by the lake, envisioning a summer home modeled after the villa Ayla and I stayed in during our honeymoon in Saint Lucia.

For months, I'd been sketching, refining ideas, planning to surprise her.

A dream retreat, right here in New York. A place where we could escape every summer.

I unhooked my seatbelt, grabbed my sketchbook off the passenger seat, and stepped out of my car.

The bottoms of my sneakers pressed into uneven dirt and scattered rocks as I made my way toward the land that was supposed to be ours.

I kneeled, laid the sketchbook down on the damp soil, and flattened my palm against the earth.

Feeling the weight of everything settle into my bones.

What if I'd already lost her?

My chest ached at the thought.

I closed my eyes, pressed my hand deeper into the soil, and prayed.

I'd never really prayed before, but kneeling there—in that moment —it just felt like the right thing to do.

"Dear God," I whispered. "*Please*, let me fix this. Let me heal things with Ayla in time for us to enjoy this place together. *Please.*"

I stayed there, eyes closed, feeling the cool wind sweep across my face, feeling my eyes burn with unshed tears, and hoping God would answer me.

By the time I returned home that night, it was after 8 p.m.

I'd spent hours in Greene Gardens, walking the village, feeling the energy of something great coming to life.

Bryant was right. We'd made serious headway.

Sitting in an office, reviewing project timelines, wasn't the same as seeing the progress with my own eyes.

The parks were complete. The homes were rising. Business spaces were forming.

It felt real.

It felt damn good.

But none of it mattered if I didn't have Ayla.

After a quick shower, I pulled on some sweats and made my way down the stairs, toward the guest bedroom.

For the first time in days, I felt clear-headed.

Last night, I couldn't face her. I was too ashamed, too drained, too disgusted with myself for letting Harper outsmart me.

The night before that, she locked the door.

Tonight?

If she locked the door again, I'd do whatever it took to get her to open it.

To open her heart to me again.

Because I wasn't giving up.

Not now.

Not ever.

The guest room's door opened with ease, and I exhaled with relief.

Ayla was in bed, facing away, but I knew she wasn't asleep. Not yet.

She turned onto her back as soon as I stepped inside, her eyes meeting mine in the dim light.

I didn't say anything. I just climbed into bed beside her, lifting the summer down and pulling it over me.

This bed was smaller than ours. A queen-sized mattress in the guest room that was never meant for me. With my tall frame and long limbs, it didn't fit. But Ayla was here, and so, I would be too.

I laid my head against the pillow, locking eyes with her as she shifted to face me. Her expression softened as she studied me, her gaze searching my face. Taking me in. Reading me like she always did.

Then, without a word, her hand came up to my face. I closed my eyes at the warmth of her touch, pressing into her palm.

A moment later, she wrapped her arm around me, pulling me into her.

And *God*, I needed it.

I let go. Just for a second. Let myself sink into her embrace, breathing her in, feeling her against me, her warmth, her heartbeat.

I held her tighter. Buried my face in her shoulder, inhaling the scent of her skin. I kissed her there.

Once.

Then twice.

Soft, lingering kisses trailing up toward her lips.

She moaned the second we kissed, and that sound? That sound did something to me. Like always.

Our lips parted, tongues brushing, searching. Slow, deep strokes as we got lost in each other again.

I pulled back first, needing to breathe, but barely able to let her go.

"I haven't been able to sleep without you," I whispered against her lips.

"Me neither," she admitted.

"Let's not do that anymore," I said, cradling her face in my hands. "Please, let's not do that ever again."

She nodded, and I kissed her again. Deeper this time. More.

We moaned into each other's mouths, the kiss turning heated, turning desperate, turning into something... more. Because it always did.

I twisted her onto her side, positioning myself behind her.

She gasped, and I groaned as I slid inside, my hand immediately moving to her clit.

"Hassani..." she whispered, her voice breaking into a moan. "Oooh, baby..."

"Yeah, baby," I whispered back, my lips brushing the back of her ear. "I've missed you."

She turned her head, eyes locking with mine. "I've missed you more."

I kissed her again, swallowing her moans as I rocked into her, her walls gripping me in a way that made me forget everything else.

She twisted in my arms, pushed me onto my back, and straddled me.

Slowly, she lowered herself onto me, taking me in inch by inch, stretching around me.

My head pressed back into the pillow as her heat surrounded me, my hands finding her waist. Holding her steady. Helping her move.

She rode me slow, deep, dragging out the moment, her moans falling in time with every roll of her hips.

Our eyes stayed locked, the connection between us unbreakable. She fought to keep her gaze on mine, but I felt the second the pleasure took her under.

Her eyes fluttered shut. Her head tipped back.

"*Mmm*," I moaned, gripping her waist tighter, guiding her. Sliding my hand up to cup her breast as I matched her pace with slow, intentional upstrokes.

The air thickened between us.

The rhythm built.

I sat up, chest to chest with her, then turned, pinning her beneath me.

She gasped as I pushed deeper, her legs wrapping tight around me, heels pressing into my back.

Her nails dragged along my skin, hands searching, gripping.

This was home.

She was my home. My escape. My peace. My everything.

And in this moment, I knew... there was no way she could leave me.

"*Oooh*, Hassani," she whimpered. "Oh, God, I'm coming again."

And so was I.

I grabbed her wrists, pinning them above her head, locking our bodies together, making her *feel* me.

I slowed my strokes, dragging it out, savoring the moment, memorizing her.

Because nothing else in this world mattered more than this.

Than her.

"Yes," I groaned, my voice syncing with each deep stroke. "Yes, Ayla. Come on, baby... Come on..."

She exhaled a long, shaky breath, and I felt her unravel beneath me.

That sound. That feeling. It sent a pulse through me, and suddenly, I couldn't hold back anymore.

My movements shifted from controlled to instinctive. Nothing calculated. Nothing measured. Just us.

I chased that feeling with her. Let it consume me. Let it take over.

My breath caught. My teeth clenched. My toes dug into the mattress as I drove deeper, staying longer in the greatest place on earth—right here, inside her.

And then, release.

A tremor ripped through me, taking me under an undulating wave of pleasure. With her.

By the time I remembered to breathe, I'd collapsed on top of her, pressing my face into her skin, inhaling her instead of air.

Her arms wrapped around me, tight, like she felt it too.

Like she needed this just as badly.

"Don't leave me," I whispered against her, my voice hoarse, raw. "Please, baby, don't leave me."

Tears filled her eyes as she whispered back, "I won't. I won't."

I kissed them away. Every single one.

"Come upstairs, A. Please," I begged, balancing on my forearms so I could see her. So she could see me. "Come to bed with me. I need you there. Badly."

She nodded, her fingertips brushing tenderly against my face. "Okay."

PART V
THE FOREVER HOME

A place built to last. Peace, permanence, and loving without fear...

CHAPTER 17

yla

THE HUM OF THE WAITING ROOM TV AT MY OB-GYN'S OFFICE FILLED the space, the muffled voices of a daytime talk show blending into the background noise. I sat near the receptionist's desk, flipping through a For The Culture magazine I'd grabbed off the table, though I wasn't really reading. Just passing the time.

My eyes drifted to the stack of magazines beside me again. One caught my attention. Mommy Digest.

I hesitated. Then, before I could overthink it, I exchanged one magazine for the other, the glossy cover now resting in my lap.

I'd been coming to this OB-GYN since college, every summer, like clockwork. Same doctor. Same routine. Same annual conversation about renewing my birth control prescription.

But this year? This year felt different.

I ran my fingertips over the cover of the pregnancy magazine, my thoughts drifting back to two nights ago.

To Hassani.

To the way he held me.

To the way he whispered, *"Let's not do that anymore."*

The nurse called out another patient's name, breaking my trance. I glanced down at the page I'd absentmindedly flipped open. It was an ad. A mother cradling her newborn, smiling down at them like they were her entire world.

My stomach tightened.

Was that something I wanted?

I exhaled, shifting in my seat.

Distracted again, my mind drifted back to two nights ago—to Hassani and what he said to me right before I fell asleep.

"You falling asleep on me, A. Boogie?" he asked, pressing his hand to my cheek.

I smiled, my eyes heavy. I was definitely falling asleep. I'd missed this bed so much that the moment I laid down, sleep wasn't far behind.

Sleeping in the guest room didn't feel good. Every night, I went to sleep with our disagreement on my mind and woke up thinking about it the next day. It was torture, but it was the only thing I felt I could control.

"I want us to go to couples' counseling," Hassani whispered. "If that's okay with you."

I blinked in response, my eyelids growing heavier.

"I think we need it," he nodded, running his hand along my face. "I think it would be good for us."

The appointment was set for tomorrow, and I was both anxious and intrigued.

With Hassani home the entire next day, we spent time searching for marriage counselors. I wanted someone married, someone older. To me, that was the next best thing to a husband or wife on their deathbed—people literally fulfilling the 'til death do us part' promise —because they were the only ones I felt were truly qualified to give marriage advice to people they didn't know.

This doctor though, the one we found? She seemed like she knew her stuff. We'd see how that went.

A few feet away, a pregnant woman eased into a chair, sighing as she settled in. She placed a protective hand over her belly, absently rubbing it while scrolling through her phone.

She looked beautiful. The kind of radiant you see in maternity billboards—soft, glowing, at peace.

Something inside me squeezed.

I stared too long. I knew I did.

When she lifted her gaze, my cheeks heated. I quickly looked away. Too late…

Our eyes met for the briefest second before she returned to her device's screen, unfazed.

Still, I found myself stealing another glance.

What would it be like, to watch my belly grow rounder, fuller?

I couldn't picture it. Not really. But I knew it could happen.

Just… not for me… yet.

At least, that's what I'd always told myself.

I'd always loved babies, but having one? It had never been at the forefront of my mind. I'd been content with life as it was. Hassani and me. Our routines. Our travels. The dreams we built together.

But once…

Once, I thought about it. *Really* thought about it after Hassani made mention of it.

"I hope our children have your eyes."

Hassani's voice had been low, warm, filled with a kind of certainty I wasn't expecting.

We were lying in bed, both of us wide awake in the middle of the night. He'd just moved back to New York from D.C., his new apartment only a short walk from mine. It was my first time spending the night there, and we'd been talking about everything and nothing.

I smiled into the dark. "Really?"

He reached over, tracing his fingers along my cheek. "Mm-hmm."

I scoffed. "You're the one with the world-famous eyes. Are you kidding me?"

Hassani chuckled, pulling me closer, his arm looping around my waist.

"Your eyes," he murmured, "are like the rarest crystal balls, though. Every time I look into them, I see my future."

He paused, pressing his forehead against mine.

"And it's so bright, A. So damn beautiful."

Hassani and I had talked about having kids a long time ago, but lately? It hadn't come up.

And if I was being honest, I wasn't sure if I wanted to be the one to bring it up. Not now. Not with him in the middle of this *massive* project... even if the project wasn't set to wrap up for another five years.

Would I be handling pregnancy alone? Would I be raising a baby alone while Hassani was buried in work?

I swallowed hard.

"Ayla."

The nurse called my name, her gaze locking onto mine. She only had to say my first name—I'd been coming here for years.

"We're ready for you."

In the exam room, the nurse took my vitals, ran through the usual intake questions, then handed me the paper gown.

Routine.

Just like every summer.

I changed, then perched on the exam table, drumming my fingers on my thighs as nerves I hadn't even noticed crept in.

Why was I nervous?

Nothing was different this year... right?

The door pushed open.

"Ayla," Dr. Lenora Whitfield greeted, stepping in with her warm, knowing smile. "Welcome back."

I giggled. "Good to feel welcomed in my second home."

"You look great."

I exhaled. "Well, at least I look it."

She laughed. "How are things?"

"School's out, so one less thing to stress about. That's a win." I shrugged. "What about you?"

"I get to see my favorite patient for her annual check-up." She quirked a smile. "So I'm fabulous."

I playfully rolled my eyes. "I know you say that to everyone, Dr.

Whitfield."

She gasped, pressing a hand to her hip. "I do not!"

I grinned.

Dr. Whitfield was in her early sixties, a highly respected Black OB-GYN with decades of experience. When I first came to her office, I'd researched everything—her credentials, her reviews, how long she'd been practicing. I even grilled her during our first appointment.

I didn't want a rotating door of doctors.

I wanted just *one*.

Someone who knew me, who could follow my journey for years to come.

And I found that in her.

The appointment moved along in familiar rhythm.

She asked the routine questions about my health, cycle, any concerns. I had none. Everything was fine.

Until we reached the part I'd been dreading.

The part that had never made me nervous before.

Dr. Whitfield smiled knowingly.

"So..." she teased. "Are we renewing your birth control prescription today?"

I bit my lip, fingers curling around the edge of the exam table.

I didn't answer.

Not right away.

She tapped my knee playfully, breaking the tension I didn't realize had settled in.

"Ayla," she mused, "every year I ask you about babies, and *every year* you tell me..." She pitched her voice high, mimicking me. "Not yet, Dr. Whitfield."

I hollered a laugh. "I *do not* sound like that!"

"I'm just saying." She smirked. "I think you like making me wait."

I shrugged. "Well... this year *might* be different."

Her eyebrows shot up.

I lifted a hand. "I'll take the prescription renewal, though."

Her expression softened.

I didn't want to renew it.

But *now* wasn't the right time.

I wasn't going to tell her that, though.

Because then I'd have to say the rest of it.

That Hassani was drowning in work. That I was afraid of getting in the way. That despite sharing a bed again, things weren't magically fixed. That bringing a baby into this mess felt… reckless.

I wasn't ready to say any of that out loud… especially not to my doctor, who definitely didn't need to know all that.

Dr. Whitfield studied me. Really studied me.

"Are you sure?" she asked gently.

I held her stare.

"Ayla, you're in excellent health." She tapped my knee again. "Your body is healthy now, but waiting too long…" she hesitated. "It increases the risks."

I nodded. "I know."

We'd had this conversation every year since my thirtieth birthday.

I could feel my eyes welling and, in that moment, couldn't understand why.

She handed me a tissue before I even realized I needed one.

I blinked fast.

Damn it.

I forced a laugh. "I don't even know why I'm crying."

She smiled. "Look. Whatever's on your heart, figure it out with that good husband of yours." She winked. "But don't let fear—or your idea of the perfect timing—make the choice for you. Because there's never a perfect time, Ayla. There's just the right time for *you*."

I smiled back, dabbing at my eyes.

"I'm going to send in your refill to your pharmacy and, as always, I'll give you a paper copy," Dr. Whitfield informed, tapping my knee one last time before giving it a gentle squeeze.

THE THICK SUMMER HEAT AND THE CONSTANT HONKING OF HORNS

greeted me the moment I stepped onto the streets of Manhattan after my appointment.

I inhaled sharply, closed my eyes for a beat.

Just breathe.

I needed to get behind closed doors before the sting in my eyes turned into full-blown tears.

I didn't even know why I wanted to cry.

Maybe because I wanted something so bad now, but felt like I couldn't have it.

Maybe because deep down, I already knew… if I even picked up the pills this time, I was going to take them.

A sharp horn blast snapped me out of my thoughts.

My head jerked up just in time to see the pharmacy I always went to for refills.

I exhaled slowly.

My fingers tightened around the crisp paper copy of my refill.

Just go in.

Just pick it up.

But my feet wouldn't move.

My hand loosened. The printout crinkled as I shoved it into the back pocket of my cutoffs.

My breath hitched.

The weight of the moment pressing tight against my ribs.

I'll get it later…

Or maybe I won't.

I turned toward my car, blinking hard.

Don't cry.

Not here.

Not now.

Why are you even crying right now, Ayla?!

I swiped my hands over my damp cheeks, whispering to myself, "Quit trippin'. This is *not* that big of a deal."

But even as I said it…

I wasn't sure if I was right.

CHAPTER 18

ASSANI

THE SOFT HUM OF CONVERSATION AND THE OCCASIONAL SCRATCH OF Dr. Aldridge's pen filled the cozy office. The space felt warm, inviting, not at all clinical, which was exactly what I needed.

"Welcome back," Dr. Aldridge greeted us with a smile that was both sharp and kind. "How are you two feeling today?"

I glanced at Ayla.

She did the same.

"Well… *I'm* good," I answered, pressing a hand to my chest then focusing on Ayla once more.

Ayla giggled. "And I'm good too."

Dr. Aldridge's smile widened. "Great. Last session, we focused on why you're here—communication struggles, expectations, and what you both want to get out of counseling."

I nodded.

The first session had been pretty laid-back. Things between Ayla and me had gotten better in some ways since then, but there were still cracks we hadn't filled. And if I was being honest? I didn't trust myself not to say the wrong thing these days.

That's why I was here, again. Why *we* were here.

"Today," Dr. Aldridge continued, "I'd like to go a little deeper. This is your second session, and I want to make sure you're getting the most out of it."

"Sounds good to me," Ayla said, throwing a glance my way.

"Same."

Dr. Aldridge studied us for a beat before asking, "How do you both feel about being back here today?"

I glanced at Ayla.

Ayla glanced at me.

The doctor's smile tilted. "Do you always look to each other to make decisions?"

I blinked, shifting in my seat.

"I… just didn't want to cut her off," I admitted.

Ayla chuckled. "Same. I've never done therapy before, so I don't know the etiquette."

I snorted. "Can you imagine if therapy etiquette was a thing?"

"I bet there's a book about it somewhere." Ayla quirked a brow and grinned. "Probably a bestseller."

I shrugged. "I feel like you'd buy something like that."

"Oh, you *know* I would." She smirked, leaning in and wrapping her hands around my biceps. "Especially if it's a series. Then I'd steal more space on your bookshelves to house them."

She stuck her tongue out teasingly, then laughed, burying her face in my arm.

"Laughing, but I know you're *so* serious." I smirked. "You little shelf bandit."

Ayla laughed even harder against me. Her laughter was always so contagious, that light, sweet sound I hadn't heard enough of lately. I found myself chuckling along with her, tension melting away.

When I looked back at Dr. Aldridge, her smile had shifted—something knowing, something warm.

"Oh, damn, I'm sorry." I shook my head and exhaled a laugh. "What was your question again?"

She set her pen down. "Not important. Not after what just happened."

Ayla and I exchanged a look.

"*What* just happened?" I asked, frowning.

Dr. Aldridge's eyes bounced between us before she leaned forward slightly. "I don't think we talked about how you two met."

Ayla's lips twitched, eyes flicking to me.

I licked my lips, a slow grin pulling at my mouth.

Damn. That was a good memory.

"So, let's do it now… how did you two first meet?" Dr. Aldridge asked, interest gleaming in her gaze.

"In my parents' kitchen," Ayla started. "Hassani showed up with his parents for dinner. My dad had just started working at a firm where Hassani's father was his boss, and my dad wanted to make a good impression."

I snickered. "It felt like something straight out of a sitcom."

Ayla giggled. "Right?! My parents made me dress up in my Easter Sunday outfit. Meanwhile, Hassani showed up in a tee, jeans, and sneakers. I was *so* annoyed by that."

Dr. Aldridge laughed.

"Well," she asked next, "was it love at first sight?"

"Yes," Ayla answered immediately.

My head jerked toward her. "Wh—what?"

She pressed her lips together, clearly holding back a smile.

"Oh, nah." I turned fully to her. "You can't just drop that and go silent."

I gestured at Dr. Aldridge. "Please tell her she can't do that, Doc."

Dr. Aldridge chuckled. "How about you, Hassani?"

I tore my gaze from Ayla, grinning as I nodded my head.

"Definitely love at first sight. *Definitely.*"

Ayla's smile spread, slow and sweet, her dimples showing.

"I actually pestered my dad a few times in high school about asking Ayla out. I was more direct with him our freshman year, straight-up telling him I wanted her to be my girlfriend. But after that, I started asking more roundabout questions, hoping he'd changed his stance. It was always a no, though."

Ayla's eyes widened. "Really?! No way."

"Yup." I nodded, watching her reaction.

Ayla's jaw dropped. "You never told me that."

I smirked. "You never told me it was love at first sight."

"So it seems like you two didn't date when you first met?"

"Nah." I shook my head, turning back to Dr. Aldridge. "We became friends and stayed friends straight through high school and college. But when I was finally ready to make things more than just friendship, Ayla didn't want that… even though she was my first."

Dr. Aldridge's brows arched. "Your first?"

I nodded. "My first love, my first intimate partner."

"Same," Ayla echoed. "For both."

"It was her idea, actually." I gestured at Ayla with my thumb. "Changed my life completely."

Dr. Aldridge's smile could probably be spotted from the opposite skyscraper. "So you were *friends* first?"

I nodded. "Yup."

"My dad passed away in 9/11," Ayla said next.

Dr. Aldridge pressed a hand to her chest. "Oh… my condolences."

"Thank you," Ayla replied. "Hassani became a really good support system and still is."

Dr. Aldridge leaned in. "So you two said you were only friends from high school to college. How did we get here as Mr. and Mrs. Hassani Franklin?"

"Well…" Ayla snickered. "He sent me an invitation to his wedding… to a different woman."

Dr. Aldridge's gaze flicked to me, her expression making it clear she had questions. I pressed my lips together to keep from laughing.

"Hassani?"

"It's true." I moved my head up and down. "I was engaged to a woman I started dating in the last few weeks of college. We were together for five years, and marrying her just seemed like the right thing to do. So, I asked her to marry me, and she rewarded me by cheating with the man I made my best man."

"Oh." Dr. Aldridge dropped her eyes to her notebook. "Okay."

"It was a blessing in disguise," I noted. "Something I only realized when my ex-fiancée confessed she'd slept with my childhood friend."

"I want to revisit this in a separate session," Dr. Aldridge said, eyes sharp with interest. "But what stands out to me the most is that you two were friends first. *Only* friends, right?"

"Yup." I nodded.

And that time in my life? Absolute torture. I didn't say that out loud, because I'm lucky it's just a memory now and not a regret. But damn, wanting Ayla and pretending I didn't back then? That was the hardest part. I loved being her friend—she was an *amazing* friend—but I wanted more the moment I met her in her parents' kitchen.

"You were friends before you were lovers. That's a gift," Dr. Aldridge said. "Not everyone has that foundation to return to. So let's rebuild from there."

Ayla and I glanced at each other. I smiled, and she did too.

"In our first session..." Dr. Aldridge looked at me. "Hassani, you said you wanted to fix things but didn't know how." Then she turned to Ayla. "And, Ayla, *you* admitted to being tired of feeling unheard."

I looked at Ayla again. Without thinking, I turned my palm up, and following my cue, she placed her hand in mine.

Dr. Aldridge smiled, lowering her eyes to her notebook. "How did you settle your disputes when you were only friends?"

I tilted my head toward the ceiling, then lowered my gaze to the coffee table in front of us. It had tissues, notebooks, and water bottles on its surface, but I wasn't really seeing them. I was digging through my memory, trying to recall a single argument we'd had back then.

I came up with nothing.

"We didn't have disputes as friends," Ayla said.

"Yeah," I agreed. "I can't think of a single argument we had as friends."

"And married?" Dr. Aldridge asked. "How do you settle disagreements now?"

I made a face—one of those half-shrugs with my mouth.

"Sex," Ayla and I said at the exact same time, our voices amplified from how in sync we were.

Ayla snorted, and I did too before we both burst into laughter.

Dr. Aldridge chuckled. "Well, okay. You two have a healthy sex life. That's very good."

I nodded proudly.

"But sometimes, sex isn't a fix. It can actually make things worse when communication is what's really needed."

I tilted my head to the side.

"You need to trust each other emotionally before relying on intimacy to smooth things over," she continued. "Ayla mentioned being tired of feeling unheard. There's no amount of sex that will fix that." She sighed dramatically, then smirked. "Unfortunately."

I arched a brow. "Are you sure?"

Ayla giggled, and Dr. Aldridge smirked.

"*Yes*, I'm sure, Hassani." She leaned in slightly. "I'm going to suggest something that may seem difficult at first, but I'm confident it will work for you two given your history."

"Okay…?" Ayla voiced hesitantly.

"I'm going to suggest that you go through a period of abstinence to help rebuild your emotional connection."

"Abstinence?" Ayla repeated.

"Excu—" I stopped, inhaled deeply, then exhaled. "I'm sorry… what?"

Ayla blew air through her pursed lips. "Abstinence. *Hmmm*."

Dr. Aldridge chuckled at our synchronized disbelief. "I know, I know—it sounds extreme, but hear me out."

I'd rather not!

I side-eyed Ayla, who looked just as stunned as I felt.

"Abstinence will allow you to refocus your connection outside of physical intimacy. You two clearly have a *very* passionate relationship," she said, amusement in her tone. "That's great. But *passion* can't be the only thing holding you together."

I sucked my teeth. "I mean…"

Ayla elbowed me lightly.

I smirked.

Dr. Aldridge held up a hand to cut off my comeback before I could make it. "Sex is important, yes. But emotional intimacy? That's what truly sustains a marriage."

I sighed, running a hand over my beard. "So, what exactly are you suggesting?"

She folded her hands in her lap. "No sex for at least two weeks."

Ayla's eyes shot wide. "Two, what?"

I damn near choked. "Two *entire* weeks?"

Dr. Aldridge laughed. "Yes, two weeks. It's a temporary reset. The goal is to rebuild your foundation through communication, quality time, and emotional connection. I want you two to focus on intimacy in other ways. Holding hands. Eye contact. Thoughtful gestures. Having conversations that don't end in..." She waved a hand. "... bed."

Ayla and I stared at each other.

No sex for two weeks?

I tapped my fingers against my thigh, then dragged my palm over my mouth. I had no words.

Ayla, still blinking like she was processing, finally asked, "And... after the two weeks?"

"Then..." Dr. Aldridge smiled. "Back to your regularly scheduled programming."

Ayla and I laughed.

"And we'll evaluate after." Dr. Aldridge smiled. "You two say you didn't have disputes as friends, and while marriage and friendship go hand in hand, they aren't the same. That said, I think you'd benefit from revisiting that foundation."

I sat back in my seat, letting that settle.

"This abstinence isn't about punishment," she continued. "It's about shifting your focus. Relying less on physical intimacy to smooth things over and more on real communication. You need to remember how to be *just* friends again—even if only for a little while."

"I like it," Ayla said immediately, tightening her arm around mine.

"If it'll help, then cool." She smiled up at me. "I loved being just your friend."

I exhaled. "I know. I did too." Then I shot her a pointed look. "But I *really* love being your husband… especially at night after a *long ass* day."

Ayla giggled.

"Like, I *love* to *husband* all over you. And a lot. *Every* night."

She playfully smacked my arm. "Hassani!"

That made me laugh.

"But I'll do it." I kissed her forehead, my lips lingering a little longer. "*Whatever* it takes."

Half an hour later, our session was winding down, when Dr. Aldridge asked a question that caught me off guard.

"If you could say anything to each other, knowing you wouldn't be judged, what would it be?"

I glanced at Ayla, who was already looking at me.

The answer was easy. I'd felt it ever since she said she wanted a divorce. And if we were here to be honest, then I had to say it.

"I feel like I'm failing you."

Ayla released a shaky breath, her face softening into a frown. "You're not failing me at all, Hassani."

"But I feel that." I nodded. "I felt that when you told me you wanted out."

"I didn't mean it." She shook her head quickly. "I was *pissed*. Saying it was the only way I felt in control of something I had no control over. But I didn't mean it." Her lips quirked up slightly. "No take-backs, right?"

I nodded, my throat too tight to speak.

Dr. Aldridge turned to Ayla. "And you? No judgment."

Ayla closed her eyes for a moment, exhaled, then opened them— meeting mine head-on.

"I want a baby… like, very much."

My whole body tensed. I blinked hard, sure I misheard her.

"You do?"

Ayla nodded.

I sat up straight, my heartbeat hammering. I had purposely never brought it up, not wanting to be that guy pressuring her. I figured she'd tell me when she was ready. But she'd been holding this in? Why?

"I didn't know that," I spoke in a low voice, then turned to Dr. Aldridge. "I didn't know that."

Ayla's voice softened. "I was afraid to bring it up because I didn't want to disrupt your work on the project."

"What?" I whispered. "My work?! Ayla. Nah, baby. Come on." I pressed a hand to my chest. "You wouldn't have disrupted anything." My voice cracked as I exhaled. "A baby? You want a baby? Why wouldn't you tell me that?"

I sagged my shoulders, trying to catch my breath.

How long had she been thinking about this? How many times had she stopped herself from saying it out loud? My wife—my best friend —felt like she had to keep something this big from me?

"A?" I shook my head. "You should've told me. 'Cause *I* want babies too. I've just been waiting on *you*. I didn't want to pressure you. I wouldn't be the one carrying life. I wanted to leave that choice to you."

Dr. Aldridge leaned forward. "See? You both love each other deeply, but you've been making decisions out of fear instead of trust. It's like trying to cook in a pitch-black kitchen—it doesn't work." She smiled gently. "But we're going to work on that."

At the end of our session, Dr. Aldridge left us with a plan: rebuild our friendship, prioritize our passions, communicate openly about fears, and—unfortunately—abstain from sex until we could do all of the above.

"Demonstrate emotional intimacy, trust, and communication outside of physical connection," she'd explained. "Signs of this will be openly expressing concerns and feeling safe to do so, addressing your issues instead of avoiding conflict, and not using physical affection as a shortcut to smoothing things over."

Dr. Aldridge smiled. "And, of course, having fun. Genuine fun. Without feeling like intimacy is the *only* way to reconnect." She leaned forward. "Finally, you'll break the abstinence rule when you both mutually agree you're ready. Not just one of you trying to make the other happy. It should feel earned, not a Band-Aid over something unresolved."

I glanced at Ayla, who flashed me a small smile.

"What we uncovered today was good—great, even," Dr. Aldridge continued. "But what you'll uncover on this journey will be even better. When you check these key signs and realize you're hitting all the marks, you'll see this isn't just a rule to follow. It's a tool to help rebuild what's already there between you two."

"You were right about Harper," I told Ayla.

We were lying in bed, hours after our session. I'd finished work early just so I wouldn't be late for our appointment with Dr. Aldridge. I was serious about fixing things with my wife. And so far, things were going well.

"Right about what?"

Ayla was curled up in one of my old tees—one she'd borrowed and never given back—her legs tucked close to me. It was almost midnight, and I had to be up early for the office tomorrow, but I wasn't ready to sleep.

I traced my fingers along her thigh—a compromise, since touching more than this was officially off-limits.

"That I needed to be careful with her." I exhaled, shifting on my side. "I knew she was attracted to me—"

"Who isn't?" Ayla smiled, shrugging playfully.

I twisted my lips in an exaggerated expression, making her giggle.

"Oh, please." She reached out, tracing her fingers along my jaw, then tapped my nose. "You know you're 90s fine."

I scoffed, but before I could reply, I sighed. "She took it too far, though."

Ayla's smile faltered slightly. "*That's*... not surprising." She hesitated, then added, "I, *um*, I went through your phone and saw some of her messages to you."

I raised my brows.

"That night you took me to Vernon's?" she continued. "After missing my work mixer? When you left the table to wash your hands?"

I nodded slowly, already knowing where this was going.

"She texted while you were gone." Ayla exhaled. "I unlocked your phone and read it. And once I saw that, I saw all the other ones." Her voice softened. "I knew she was inappropriate. But I *also* knew I had no right to snoop." She bit her lip. "I'm sorry."

I closed my eyes briefly, then opened them. "Nah. *I'm* sorry. I *hate* that you felt you had to do that."

She smiled, a little sad. "Not more than me."

"But…" I sighed. "You weren't wrong either." I took a deep breath. "I haven't brought it up in counseling yet because I wanted to tell you first."

Ayla's smile disappeared completely.

"She propositioned me."

Her whole body stiffened. "Propositioned?"

I licked my lips. "Promise you won't get mad."

She stared at me for a long second. "No."

I snorted. "No?"

"*Uh-uh.*" She shook her head. "Hell *no.* What did she do? It must've been bad if you didn't bring it up in counseling. Did she try something with you?"

"She wanted to have an affair."

Ayla scoffed sharply, pressing her tongue into her cheek. "That fucking bitch."

"And while *that* was crazy," I added, "the other shit she did? Was worse."

Ayla lifted her head slightly. "Other shit? Like what?"

"She made up problems to keep me late at the office."

Ayla blinked hard. I could see her mind working, piecing it together.

"She delayed telling me about real issues until they became urgent.

And then she straight-up invented problems that weren't problems at all."

Ayla sat up slightly, her fingers—which had been idly tracing my forearm—going completely still.

"She wasted my time. She wasted my team's time. She kept me from being home. With you."

Ayla shook her head, staring past me. Her jaw tightened.

"...I mean... I knew she was a problem, but damn, Hassani..." She exhaled, her shoulders rising and falling sharply. She pressed a hand to her forehead, looking away for a beat. When she turned back, her eyes were wide. Searching.

"She really did that?" she whispered. "Messed with your work just to keep you late there with her?"

I nodded, hating the confirmation. Hating that I let it happen. Hating even more that I waited this long to tell Ayla because I was still processing it myself. That—and because I was too embarrassed to admit I was wrong about Harper.

Ayla grunted, sitting up completely. "I *told* you about her."

"You did, baby." I swallowed hard. "You did."

Ayla kissed her teeth and shook her head, her frustration mounting.

"So what?" she demanded. "You're supposed to just keep working with her? Like nothing happened? Because her actions weren't just unprofessional, Hassani. They were evil."

"*Very.*" I nodded. "And no, I'm not working with her anymore. Bryant is reassigning her to another project—out of state."

Ayla exhaled, rolling her shoulders back. "I mean... I guess that's *okay*, but damn." Her gaze softened. "How are you feeling about it? Are *you* okay?"

I huffed, rubbing my face. "It was scary, honestly. I could've lost my job. I didn't think she'd take things that far. You warned me, and I didn't listen. I thought I had it all under control... I was wrong."

Ayla shook her head with a knowing smirk. "Oh, I knew you had *nothing* under control and I also knew Harper was insane the minute I met her."

I arched a brow. "Yeah?"

"*Mm-hmm.*" She folded her arms. "Because anyone who says a D-Slam sculpture is *must-have art*? That person is crazy. They *need* a full psych evaluation—like, yesterday."

I kissed my teeth. "A, be serious for a second."

"Shit, I *am!*"

"A!"

Ayla bit her lip, trying to fight back her smile.

I exhaled. "She was the reason I wasn't there that night for your mother's dinner."

Ayla held her breath. I caught the flicker of something in her eyes—something she was trying to push back.

"The flooring issue..." I ran a hand down my lips. "I didn't have to stay late for that."

Ayla shut her eyes and shook her head.

"It was my fault."

"It's fine."

"It's not." I reached out, cradling the side of her face, brushing my thumb along her cheek. "It's *not* fine. I fucked up. I'm sorry."

Ayla didn't look away. "You *did* fuck up," she admitted. "I won't lie to you—you *fucked* up *so* bad, Hassani. But..." She exhaled, her voice softening. "There are worse things you could've done. So... it happened." She shrugged. "And, yeah—it felt like a gut punch and a hit to the chest at the same time."

Her jaw tightened slightly. "I cried *so hard* that night, baby..." She rolled her eyes, keeping the welling tears in. "I hadn't cried so hard in so long... but, it is what it is now, Hassani."

I scanned her face, searching for any lingering resentment. But all I saw was acceptance.

"...But for real?" Ayla added, narrowing her eyes. "If I see her ass in the street, I don't know if I'll be able to keep it cute. For her sake, I hope I can."

I grinned, leaning in. "Why, Mrs. Franklin... is that the Brooklyn coming out?"

She laughed, her head tilting back in ease, and I couldn't help but join in.

Once she'd sobered, she ran her fingertips over my chest. "No more *not* listening to me when I tell you stuff, okay? *Especially* about people. Okay?"

"Okay. No more." I resumed absently stroking her leg, my fingers gliding along her skin. "I promise on everything I won't ever do that again."

Ayla's lips curled into a sly grin. Her eyes gradually drifting down to my hand. "You're gonna make this abstinence thing really hard, huh?"

I groaned, sliding my hand down to her lower back, pulling her flush against me. "Dr. Aldridge isn't here though…" My lips brushed her ear. "She doesn't have to know."

Ayla busted out laughing, swatting my chest. "You better stop, Hassani! Be good—for me. For us."

I sighed dramatically against her ear, then buried my face in the pillow with a growl.

That made Ayla laugh even harder.

I had no idea how we were going to do this. If she was still in the guest bedroom, maybe I'd survive. But right here next to me? In our bed? Yeah. She was killing me softly.

"I'm serious about following her advice, Hassani."

I grunted into the pillow once more.

"Hey." She swatted my chest again. "This was *your* idea to see this woman."

"I didn't think she was gonna cockblock, A."

Ayla giggled. "She's not cockblocking. She's helping. And so far? I think it's working. It's only been two sessions, and we've already talked about things we never talked about before. Freely."

"Yeah," I remarked low. "Like *you* wanting a baby."

Ayla held my gaze. She pressed a hand to my chest, and I exhaled.

A baby.

I had so much to make up for. So much I didn't even realize I'd been missing. And now—this?

I wanted to give Ayla everything. Always. But this? This I needed to sit with. Shift my focus.

Because how the hell did I not see it? How did I not know?

Why didn't I ask?

I swallowed, rubbing my temple. "I'm gonna need some time to forgive myself for that one, A. Boogie. Because how did I *not* know that?"

Ayla pressed her lips together and sighed.

The fact that she put her wants on hold for me… That would need to be a real conversation. And when we had it? I had to make damn sure it was at the right time.

She nudged me. "You remember when I used to call your phone in the middle of the night in high school?"

I smiled immediately. "How could I forget?" I chuckled. "My phone would ring at the craziest hours, and I'd have to snatch it up before my dad knocked on my door to ask…" I dropped my voice and deepened the accent, "*Who inna di bloodclaat ah phone yuh dis hour?!*"

Ayla snorted, then burst into laughter. "But you always answered."

"I *always* answered." I nodded. "Because I knew you needed me… and I really liked being needed by you, baby."

Her eyes watered. She pressed her bottom lip between her teeth like she was trying to hold back the weight of that moment.

"Transparent moment," she murmured.

I focused on her. "Yeah?"

"Since we're supposed to be communicating openly or whatever…"

I smirked. "Or whatever."

She exhaled. "I was really bummed last year when we didn't take our annual trip. And… I'm kind of bummed that we won't be doing anything again this year."

I nodded slowly. "Then we gotta fix that."

She arched a brow. "How?"

I ran my fingertip along her delicate jawline, then pinched her chin. "When I went to Bryant to tell him about Harper, he told me I could take two weeks off."

Ayla leaned back slightly, studying me.

"I just need to give him and the office a few days' notice."

Her face lit up with a smile. "Okay!"

"I was thinking about it on our drive back from Dr. Aldridge's. After hearing her talk about everything we need to focus on this week..." I smiled. "I was thinking... a road trip."

"A road trip?!"

"*Mm-hmm.*" I licked my lips, sliding my hands down to pull her closer by the curve of her ass. "You, me, and nothing but the open road. In an RV."

She scrunched up her face. "An RV?!"

"Yeah."

"Like... camping and stuff?"

"Something like that."

She rolled her eyes away, sighing dramatically.

"Oh, don't do that." I squeezed her ass, smirking. "You know I'm gonna make it dope. Come on now."

Ayla fought back a smile. "I know."

"You still trust me, right?"

Her eyes snapped to mine. She was nodding before I even finished my question. "I never stopped."

"So *trust* this will be dope. You down?"

A road trip was something I'd been wanting to do for a while. With two weeks to ourselves, this felt like the perfect chance, not just to escape, but to reconnect. With my wife. With my friend... and to kill time while abstaining.

"Okay!" She squealed. "Let's do it! Where are we going?"

"It's a surprise."

Her face lit up even more, and damn, I wanted so bad to lean in, kiss her, roll her under me and sink into her warmth. But that damn rule...

I still wasn't sure how this "friends first" thing was supposed to fix everything. How the hell was I supposed to be just friends with my wife again?

But the way Ayla was smiling right now? That glow? I hadn't seen that in over a year. Too long.

Maybe Dr. Aldridge *did* know what she was talking about. Because this? This was the most excited I'd seen Ayla in a minute… and damn, it looked so good on her.

I took her hand and interlocked our fingers, lifting it to my lips to kiss the back of her hand. Then I gently pulled her closer, and she melted against me, settling against my biceps.

We hugged for a while, her fingers tracing slow circles against my back.

I lowered my lips to her forehead, leaving a simple kiss there.

And for the first time in a long time… I felt at home again.

CHAPTER 19

yla

"Oh my God," I held my hands out in front of me, wiggling my fingers. "I have no more heart in my chest because it has completely melted away. Give me my baby!"

The soft coos from my friend Sunni's daughter, Amara, sounded like my favorite melody as Sunni handed her to me. She was five months old and so damn chunky.

"I could eat you," I said, burying my nose in her tiny neck.

"*Uh-uh*, don't eat my baby."

I giggled, holding Amara close to my heart and giving her a sweet hug. "Little princess, I would've been completely heartbroken if I didn't get to see you before my trip."

I inhaled Amara's scent again, sighing at the soft, powdery sweetness.

"She smells *so* good." I pressed my lips to her chubby cheek. "You smell amazing, girl. What you got on?"

Sunni laughed. "Here," she said, tossing a burp cloth over my shoulder. "Cover yourself with this because Amara can go from cute to *eww* real fast."

I shook my head. "I'm sure your spit-up smells like roses. Don't it? Freshly picked too, huh, girl?"

"Tell me you're an auntie without telling me you're an auntie." Sunni kissed her teeth. "Because only y'all would say some silly stuff like that."

I bounced Amara in my arms, completely lost in her gummy smile and big, bright eyes. "Baby girl… you hear something?"

Sunni let out a laugh, her face lifting to the ceiling. "Not y'all got me feeling like the third wheel in my own house."

It was one of those soft, sun-baked July days when I stopped by Sunni's house in Jersey to visit her and my goddaughter, Amara.

Sunni had been a stay-at-home mom since she found out she was pregnant last year—but the "stay-at-home" part barely applied to her. She and Amara were always out and about, especially during the summer. I was just glad my girl made time for me to see my goddaughter before I left for my trip.

"The last time I saw you," I said to Amara, "you were a little, itty-bitty one-week-old newborn."

"You see her all the time via FaceTime," Sunni reminded me.

I brought Amara closer, pressing another kiss against her cheek. "I can't kiss her like this via FaceTime."

Amara giggled and kicked her little legs as if she understood me.

Amara was sitting on my lap when she grabbed my finger and held onto it. Something about that made my chest tighten with longing.

God, I wanted this.

We were sitting in Amara's playroom. I had been at Sunni's for the past hour, but I needed to be back upstate New York before a certain time to rest up. The next day was the first day of Hassani and my road trip.

I was both excited and nervous about it. I had never been in an RV in my life.

When Amara woke up from her nap, Sunni and I moved from the

solarium to the playroom, and that's where we stayed as I held Amara in my arms.

Sunni's home had transformed after she got pregnant with Amara. The space went from neat and stylish to warm and inviting—filled with all the little signs of her happy family life. I had always loved coming here, but today, being surrounded by baby toys and family photos, it felt… different.

It felt bittersweet.

I couldn't help but feel torn between my love for my girl's family and my own struggles.

Was I waiting too long?

"Getting back to what we were talking about in the solarium before Amara got up," Sunni said, pulling me from my thoughts. "I'm proud of Hassani. I think he handled himself well with that woman."

I shrugged a shoulder and smiled down at Amara.

I had told Sunni about the situation with Harper. She had already heard me mention Harper once before, so she was familiar.

"I hate that he didn't listen," I admitted. "But I'm happy he handled himself well, too."

Sunni kissed her teeth. "Women like that make marriage harder than it has to be."

"And I don't get it," I added. "How do you have the audacity to do something like that? Like… how does that happen? How does the brain allow such a decision to be made?"

"She was probably looking for validation." Sunni shook her head. "Nothing boosts an insecure woman's fragile ego like breaking something in seconds that took years to build—and, of course, something *she* didn't build herself. Makes them feel like a real winner."

I exhaled a scoffing laugh.

"My Nana, may she rest in peace, used to compare marriage to owning a blown glass gallery."

I blinked. "A blown glass gallery?"

"*Mmm-hmm.*" Sunni nodded. "She used to tell me that marriage is like spending hours and hours creating a one-of-a-kind, handcrafted glass piece. And she said I should watch out for people standing outside my gallery with steel bats, trying to get in—knowing damn well neither they nor that bat belong there."

"*Hmph.*"

"Trying to explain to the person with the bat why they don't belong in the gallery with that bat is pointless," Sunni continued, adjusting herself in her seat. "Because they know better. They already know they're not supposed to be there. They just got bad intentions and get some satisfaction from making you uneasy and as miserable as them. It gives them great delight to see you worried over something that matters to you and that they think they can't create themselves." She shook her head. "So, Nana *always* said that's what security is for— which, of course, was a double entendre.

"She said if my security is in place and knows their role, which is to protect and secure..." Sunni tapped my knee."... security being Josiah, of course." She winked, referring to her husband. "Then we're good, and people with steel bats won't be able to get in. But if security just thinks that people with steel bats *just want to look around* and ain't gonna do anything—which, in real life, is like going out for a late-night drink or taking a call in the middle of the night—then my fine glass piece will always be in jeopardy, no matter how long it took or how hard I worked to make it."

I nodded, absorbing that.

"So, I don't worry about these women with steel bats standing outside my glass gallery." Sunni shook her head. "My alliance is with my husband. He knows what's at stake, and he knows his job. No good can ever come from worrying about other women anyway. Just move out the way and let karma do what she do, too. Because the ill-intentioned can rationalize not taking vows or respecting someone else's marriage all they want—but karma is a mirror. It doesn't judge, only reflects energy. And in time, it gives everyone exactly what they deserve and what they've earned... for better or for worse."

"I feel you," I said, nodding in agreement. And even though I knew my trust in Hassani was the most important factor, I still couldn't shake the uneasiness deep down.

Women finding Hassani attractive was one thing, but offering to be mistresses and actively trying to sabotage his career just so they could be around him? That was a whole different beast.

"We're going on a road trip tomorrow," I told Sunni as I positioned Amara over my shoulder, rocking her gently.

"You and the wannabe mistress?"

I kissed my teeth and whipped my head toward Sunni. "Sunni. Too soon."

She giggled. "I'm sorry. You and Hassani, right?"

"Yes, Hassani and I, smart ass."

Sunni's giggles turned into a bellyful laugh, which got a laugh out of me too.

"It's a trip to reconnect."

"I'm excited for you."

Just then, Amara started to fuss in my arms.

"I think she's hungry." Sunni unhooked the top of her nursing bra. "Hand her over."

I pressed another kiss to Amara's soft cheek before gently passing her back to her mama. As soon as Sunni got her in her arms, she cradled her daughter and guided her to her breast.

I smiled, watching them—a simple, beautiful moment of motherhood. They looked like a painting.

Sunni glanced up at me. "Maybe Aunt Ayla and Uncle Hassani can make a baby on this trip so you can have someone to play with."

I laughed, brushing it off, but deep down?

I wouldn't mind if that happened.

I spent another hour with my girl and her baby before kissing them both goodbye and heading out. I promised to visit them one more time before the school year started once I was back from my trip.

As I drove back to Upstate New York, my mind kept circling back to babies.

I hadn't picked up my prescription since my appointment a couple of weeks ago.

I kept telling myself I would... but some part of me really didn't want to get them.

But I also didn't like keeping that from Hassani.

I reasoned that when I got home tonight, I'd tell him. Let him know I stopped taking them when my last pack ran out.

I PULLED INTO THE DRIVEWAY AND NOTICED ALL THE LIGHTS WERE ON inside.

When I stepped through the door, I saw our bags packed by the front entrance.

We were really doing this.

By tomorrow morning, Hassani and I would be on the road, in an RV… an RV that I hadn't seen yet.

He promised me it would be like a hotel on wheels. I still wasn't convinced, but I was curious to see if he was right.

I walked into the kitchen and found Hassani sitting at the island, his head bowed as he feathered the tip of his pencil across a page in his sketchbook.

He lifted his head and smiled. "Back in time for us to make dinner, huh?"

"You know it." I twisted my lips to one side. "What are you working on?"

"A little something-something," he said, adding a few more strokes before closing the book. "I'll share very soon. You ready to get started?"

I hesitated.

I wanted to tell him about the prescription right then.

I hadn't done anything wrong—technically, we had already discussed babies. He wanted them. That was a relief.

But did he mean right now?

"What's up?" he asked, lowering his head slightly to meet my gaze. "Why does it feel like you're trying to solve a calculus problem over there?"

I giggled. "What?"

"You always wear that look when you're doing math." He licked his lips. "It's sexy."

I rolled my eyes.

"That's one of the reasons I loved when you tutored me in high school and college."

I bit back a smile.

"Probably why I loved failing math so much too."

I hollered a laugh, quickly discarding any thoughts about telling him about the prescription.

An hour later, we had wound down, moments away from going to sleep.

We were going on an adventure tomorrow.

That night probably would've been a good time to bring up the whole baby thing, but after I got in my head, I decided against it. We were back in a good place, and things were still delicate. It just didn't feel like the right time to suggest another shift for us.

As Hassani showered in the en suite, I waited in bed, scrolling through my phone.

Our new thing—though it wasn't really new to us—was cuddling. A substitute for what we really loved doing, since we couldn't make love right now.

I skimmed through different posts from people I knew, but stopped on one from my high school friend Chloe.

She was announcing her pregnancy. Her first.

A pang of jealousy hit me, twisting the muscles in my stomach.

I almost hated myself for wondering…

Will that ever be me?

I clicked out of my phone the moment Hassani emerged from the en suite.

He was wearing nothing but boxers.

Boxers that did very little to hide the imprint of his dick.

"Distracted?" he teased as he climbed into bed.

I sly grin spread across my face.

Hassani pulled me into him, and I nestled comfortably in his arms, my back pressed against his chest.

"I love you, baby," he whispered in my ear before pressing a soft kiss there.

"I love you too."

I wanted to say more. Maybe tell him about Chloe, then ease into everything else: the pills, the baby. But instead, I just stayed there, wrapped in his arms, letting the warmth of his body speak louder than the words I couldn't bring myself to say.

I didn't want to ruin a good thing by adding something new... not yet, at least.

CHAPTER 20

yla

"Wow." I climbed the RV's stairs, glancing behind me for only a second. "That was so much fun."

Hassani smiled as he trailed up behind me.

The entire trip had been fun—an experience I never knew I needed.

I dropped myself onto the plush leather seating, kicking my feet up and smiling to myself.

I had totally underestimated how dope it was to live on the road.

Hassani gestured at the microwave. "I'll pop some popcorn, and we'll watch a movie on the flatscreen?"

I nodded. "Sounds good."

It was Day 7 of our road trip, and honestly, I never thought I'd even make it past Day 1.

The night before we left, I wasn't looking forward to it at all. All of that changed the second I stepped outside our house the next day.

Because parked in our driveway was a luxury RV—glossy white and silver, tinted windows, sleek as hell.

My jaw hit the floor.

Earlier that morning, Hassani had kissed me on the forehead and whispered, "Go back to sleep, baby. I'll be back in a couple of hours."

I'd stayed in bed longer than I should have, dreading this trip, convinced this RV would be some dusty, cramped thing from the 1980s.

But when I finally stepped outside and saw it?

I should've known better.

Because my man was behind getting it.

"This is insane," I said, walking up to it.

The RV was wide and long, but not too long—almost the size of a small box truck.

"Baby," I said, watching as Hassani pulled my bag off my shoulder. "You sure you can drive this thing?"

"I got it here, didn't I?"

"I know, but..." My eyes scanned the exterior. "Damn."

But the inside?

Blew. Me. Away.

Hassani wasn't lying when he said it would be like a hotel on wheels.

Plush leather seating. A massive, curved TV. Stainless steel appliances. Elegant stone countertops.

There was even a kitchen island in the middle.

I ran my hand over the white marble surface as I moved through the space, shaking my head in disbelief.

The private sleeping area had a queen-size bed and a built-in closet— perfect for storing our clothes.

But what really sold me?

The bathroom.

"Okay!" I hollered, pushing the door open.

Full glass-enclosed shower with marble accents. Sleek sink and toilet.

This was not the RV I had pictured.

I turned to Hassani, grinning so hard my cheeks hurt.

He smirked. "So?"

I ran up and jumped into his arms. "I love you."

He hollered a laugh and tightened his grip on me.

"I thought you were gonna have me out here roughing it."

"Aw, come on now." He leaned in and kissed me. *"I wouldn't do that. Not when I'm planning to make this the best trip ever."*

And it had been.

Seven days on the road, and it hadn't felt like it.

Every day, we moved from one city to the next.

Our first stop was The Catskill Mountains. We parked near a waterfall, grilled dinner over an open flame, roasted marshmallows, and I captured every moment on my camera.

The next day, we drove two and a half hours to Lake George and stayed in a lakeside lodge. The lodge was cabin-style, with a private dock overlooking the lake.

I watched one of the most beautiful sunsets of my life.

Later that night, we soaked in the hot tub, steam rising into the evening air as the lake stretched out before us.

We only stayed for a day, but before we left, Hassani had a surprise planned—a couples' massage he'd booked ahead of time.

That next afternoon, he was brave enough to try pineapple pizza for the first time.

Hassani stared down at the six-inch personal pizza in front of him.

We were at a quaint little café, tucked away in a small town straight out of a postcard.

The kind of place that looked exactly like the logo on a camping gear brand—rustic, charming, smelled like heaven.

It was a beautiful day, not too hot, so we sat outside at a wooden table, ready to eat.

I knew I was ready.

I lifted my slice of pineapple and ham pizza and took a bite—my eyes widening, then closing as the sweet and savory mix lit up my taste buds.

I glanced at Hassani and couldn't help but giggle.

"What are you waiting for?" I asked, my mouth still full.

Hassani had told me he'd try my favorite pizza, something he'd avoided his entire life.

He wanted to see why I loved it so much.

He leaned forward... and smelled it.

I laughed even harder. "It's good, baby."

"I can't believe you're about to have me eat this right now."

"You don't hate pineapples anymore."

"I don't."

"It's like your favorite fruit now."

He winked. "Thanks to you."

I smiled. "Okay, so then dig in."

Hassani inhaled an audible deep breath.

"You are so dramatic." I leaned forward and picked up a slice from his plate. "Say ah."

He licked his lips and leaned forward, opening his mouth just enough for me to slide the point of the pizza slice in. He bit down, pulled off a tiny piece, then started chewing.

At first, hesitant.

But after a second of chewing, he looked up at me and blinked hard.

I smirked. "I know."

"Yo," he started. He grabbed the slice from my hand, brought it to his mouth again, and took an even bigger bite. His eyes widened after that one. "Yoooo!"

"See?"

"This is actually really good, baby!"

"Mm-hmm." I hummed, stuffing the rest of my pizza into my mouth. "Told you."

"It's like..." He took another bite and moaned. "I can't even—"

"Describe it?" I grinned. "I know. And I love that it's impossible to put a name to it. It's like a mystery party in my mouth."

I sighed, staring down at the rest of my pizza adoringly. "I can't believe I've gone this long without having you."

"You used to always get this when you'd tutor me when we went to Garvey," Hassani recalled.

"Every time."

We stared at each other for a moment, his hazel-green eyes catching the light of the afternoon sun.

Something about the way he looked at me made me blush.

"*I love you, baby,*" Hassani said.

"*I love you.*"

That night, when we returned to the lodge, we laid in bed, talking until we fell asleep… Hassani holding me close.

Days three and four were just as adventurous.

Before heading south, we hiked in Lake Placid, surrounded by the breathtaking Adirondack Mountains. Then, we drove down to Virginia and woke up to a view of the Blue Ridge Mountains.

The night before that morning view, though?

Something about the sounds of nature surrounding us did something to us.

Something *really* good.

Too good… because it challenged the hell out of that damn abstinence rule, Dr. Aldridge had us agree to uphold.

"*Oh, my God.*" *Hassani groaned.* "*I swear I can smell your pussy through your shorts, baby.*"

I flashed a teasing grin. "*You want me to get up?*"

"*I want to fuck you,*" *he growled.*

I gasped.

"*I'm sorry, but shit, I really do, A.*"

We'd been good. Keeping busy, distracting ourselves. But at that moment?

I had to agree with him. I wanted him, too.

His hand slid down my hip, fingertips sinking into my flesh as he palmed my ass.

"*If we do it and we don't come…*" *He smirked.* "*It might not count.*"

"*Hassani.*"

"*She ain't here, man,*" *he said, referring to our therapist.* "*Come on. We're married. Sex when you're married is encouraged.*"

I laughed.

"*If there's any rule we're breaking, it's the rule for being married and not having sex. My man God can't be happy right now.*"

"*Hassani.*"

He groaned then licked his lips. "*Even the way you're saying my name is making my dick hard.*"

Lifting the summer blanket, he said, "*See?*"

I glanced down at his hard-on, tenting his boxers, damn near slipping out of the slit.

I bit the side of my bottom lip. "We could..." I lifted my eyes to him again, "... touch ourselves."

"Touch ourselves?" His brow arched. "What do you mean?"

"I can touch myself, and you can touch yourself."

"You mean like... masturbate?" He blinked. "Together?"

I shrugged. "Yeah."

A slow grin formed on his lips before he licked them slow as hell. "Aight."

I smiled too, moving closer and pressing my lips to his.

He moaned the moment our mouths collided.

My hand slid down between us, slipping behind the seat of my panties.

I exhaled. So did he.

"Is your hand where it needs to be?" he whispered.

"Mm-hmm."

He moaned, shifting closer. "Mine is too."

I found my clit and started circling it. Really slow.

Hassani captured my lips again, his tongue sliding into my mouth, caressing mine with each hot, open-mouthed kiss.

The more we kissed, the firmer I pressed against my pink ball.

Heat rose between us.

Our movements shook the queen-sized bed inside the RV's private room.

I inhaled his heavy breaths. He inhaled mine.

Our moans synced.

I broke the kiss just for a second to glance down between us.

My stomach clenched at the sight of him—his hand wrapped tight around his erection, stroking up and down.

I swore my fingers moved even faster at that.

I looked up into his hungry, half-lidded eyes.

Jaw clenched.

Breath uneven.

Then, he smirked.

I giggled but quickly got back to it, closing my eyes and locking the vision I'd just seen into place.

A few moments of circling and moaning, and I was right there... ready.

I opened my eyes to Hassani, thinking he was too.

But he wasn't.

He was watching me. Completely.

I slowed my pace, panting now. "Why'd you stop?"

"'Cause you're so damn beautiful," he whispered, breathing hard. "Keep going."

I laughed softly. "We're supposed to be doing it together."

I wanna watch you," he said, placing his hand on my wrist. "Keep going. Don't stop."

And since I was right there, teetering on the edge, I kept going, my eyes fluttering open, then closed again, until I let go.

A small, quick wave of delight coursed through me, not lasting long but leaving a heavy pulse in its wake.

When I opened my eyes, Hassani's bottom lip was trapped between his teeth.

As I caught my breath, he took my hand, brought it to his lips, and guided my fingers into his mouth.

His eyes fell closed as he sucked them slow, deep.

My jaw dropped.

I nearly screamed.

"Mmm," he moaned, sliding my fingers out of his mouth. His eyes locked on mine. "Nothing tastes better than you."

I smiled, watching him through low lids. "Your turn now."

We kept true to the rule that night.

But God, was it getting harder.

Day 7, our final day, was in Charleston, South Carolina.

Hassani hadn't mentioned it, but I was sure we'd be driving back to New York after tonight. And honestly? I was looking forward to the return trip.

Before returning to the RV, Hassani built a small campfire outside.

He told me he learned how to do it online, and honestly, I was impressed every time he built one.

He was very much about this RV life.

And, I guess I was too now.

Although, there was no way I was dealing with dump stations like Hassani had to before we headed to Charleston.

We were somewhere between Tennessee and South Carolina when Hassani announced…

"We gotta stop at this dump station."

I blinked. "What's a dump station?"

"Exactly what it sounds like." He turned the steering wheel, guiding the RV off to the right. "A place we gotta dump shit."

"Shit like what?"

He glanced at me. "Shit."

I winced. "Ewww."

"We're literally about to dump our shit, baby." He chuckled as he parked.

I contorted my face and gagged.

He snorted, then broke into a laugh.

Reaching for me, he pressed a kiss to my forehead. "I would never ask the passenger princess to do such labor."

He unhooked his seatbelt. "I got it. Make us some coffee in the meantime."

Now, that I could do.

I waited in the RV and watched from the panoramic windows.

Besides the luxury amenities, my favorite thing about the RV was the windows.

They were large, sweeping, letting us experience stunning views of mountains as we drove.

And right now?

They were giving me a clear view of my husband, saving the day handling the dirty work.

I stepped down the RV stairs and stopped at a comfortable distance—far enough so I wouldn't smell anything—then lifted my mug to sip my coffee.

Hassani was hooking up a long hose to the bottom of the RV.

"I design luxury homes for a living," he mumbled to himself as he adjusted his rubber gloves, "yet here I am, dealing with actual shit. My God."

I snorted. "You okay over there, Mr. Franklin? Need a hug, baby?"

"Nah, baby," he replied. "But I might need therapy after this."

I laughed. "I mean... we are in therapy. You should bring this up next session. I'm sure Dr. Aldridge would love to hear how we bonded over this."

"Bonded?" He twisted his lips, giving me the universal yeah right expression. "I'm over here hooking up hoses to places where my wife and I dropped shit off—literally."

I gagged. "Hassani!"

"And she's standing over there, sipping coffee and laughing while I risk my life."

I sipped my coffee on cue. "Baby, risking your life is a stretch."

He laughed as he turned back to the hose, opening the valve.

"What now?"

He smiled. "We let it do its thing."

"Is it okay to do this here?"

"It is," he replied, pulling off his gloves as he walked back to me. "This site was made for this—I mapped it out before we even got here."

Hassani stood in front of me, looking as good as ever, even handling one of the nastiest tasks I'd ever seen him handle.

And somehow, I thought it was so damn sexy.

He caught my look.

"Oh, I know that look." He smirked, tossing his gloves over his shoulder.

I stood on the arches of my feet and pressed my lips to his.

Hassani wrapped his arms around my waist, pulling me close.

"I don't know what it is, but seeing you be about this camp life is so damn sexy."

"Yeah?"

"Mm-hmm." I wrapped my free arm around his neck. "Very much so."

He pecked my lips.

"Thanks for handling this, because I don't even want to know what would happen if we had a plumbing situation in this RV."

"I would never let my woman deal with something like that."

I smiled up at him.

"See, this is when I'd scoop you up, take you into that private room up there, and do everything to you except let you rest..." Hassani shrugged. "Which... we could still do, because she ain't here."

I tossed my head back in a laugh.

We didn't do it that night.

Hadn't done it at all during this trip.

Aside from that one moment, Hassani and I had been good. Intentional. This trip was about reconnecting, and we had.

And honestly?

I almost didn't want to go home tomorrow.

It was our final night on the road, with just one more day left of the abstinence rule Dr. Aldridge had made us promise to follow. Tonight, we were just chilling in the RV.

Most of the trip, we'd slept on the road, except for two nights—nights one and two—when we stayed under a roof at a lakeside lodge and then later a romantic boutique Inn.

The RV was perfect, definitely a hotel on wheels.

I was so glad I trusted Hassani on this.

The movie for the night was *Strictly Business*.

I'd never seen it, but Hassani had—many times—and he swore I'd love it.

After a quick shower and twisting my hair into chunky twists, I joined him in front of the flatscreen. We had a giant bowl of popcorn between us as we sat across from each other on the plush couch.

We'd popped three bags to make sure we had enough.

The RV was parked in a quiet, forested area inside an RV park.

The peace, the quiet, the stillness?

That was what I'd miss the most.

I tossed a kernel at Hassani between scenes, and every time, he caught it.

Which, of course, made me laugh.

I held my smile, locking eyes with him.

"What?" he asked.

I shook my head. "Nothing. This just reminds me of when we used to hang out in my room, just chillin' and eating popcorn."

He smiled too, nodding. "The last time we did this was weeks before graduation—when you were tutoring me for my final exam in that apartment you shared with Sunni."

"The night we hooked up," I added. "*Mm-hmm*."

"*Hmph*." His smile gradually faded. "That night was everything to me. I was so damn happy to be back inside you."

I snorted.

He smirked. "You laugh but I'm serious."

The movie was still playing, but it was just background noise now.

Because nothing else was as interesting as just talking with him.

"There was a moment where I felt like it was surreal," he added.

"I know." I nodded. "I didn't think we'd *ever* do *that* again after prom night."

"Me neither."

For a moment, we got quiet.

Then, I asked, "Do you ever think of *her* and what y'all could've had if you forgave her?"

He turned his focus fully on me.

"Sienna." I shrugged. "I mean… you two *were* engaged. She wasn't *just* your girlfriend, so I'm sure—"

"Nah, I don't think of her in that way," he said, shaking his head. "Because the whole time I was with her, I was thinking about you. And now that I have you? I can't even imagine anyone else. On God, baby."

I tossed a piece of popcorn into my mouth.

"Sometimes she crosses my mind, though," he admitted. "But never in a *what if* way. Never in a *what if I hadn't found out about her and Marcus* way, either. More like in a '*whew*, that was a close one' kind of way."

I snickered then tucked my lips into my mouth. "Sometimes I wonder… if you would've still married her—if you hadn't found out about Marcus."

Hassani nodded slowly. "I would have."

My stomach tightened.

"Then I would've regretted it." He exhaled. "And been miserable, because she wasn't *the one* but I would have kept forcing her to be."

His eyes softened.

"You were *always* the one, A. Boogie."

I couldn't help smiling.

"All this talk about Sienna…" he mused. "And that night we hooked up before graduation—it just reminded me of something you shared with me back then."

I arched a brow.

"Your greatest fear," he said. "With falling in love."

My brows stayed lifted. "My greatest fear?"

I had changed so much since college.

Sometimes, I didn't even recognize myself.

I liked me back then.

But I loved me now.

"You told me you didn't want to fall in love because you were afraid of losing yourself in it."

"Oh." I blinked hard. "Wow." I jerked my head back. "You remembered that? What I told you?"

"I remember *every* personal thing you tell me, A." He nodded. "And *that*? What you said? It was hard to forget."

I laughed softly. "I didn't *even* remember that, and *I* said it."

Hassani's expression turned serious.

"You lived that fear, Ayla."

I stilled.

The dialogue from the movie filled the silence.

Hassani sighed, looking away. "You lost yourself in my dream… and I was so caught up, I didn't see it until now."

I reared my head back.

That realization settled in.

Because I hadn't seen it that way before.

But I did now.

"You gave up parts of yourself in our marriage."

His eyes flicked to my camera.

"Photography."

Then, they moved to my hands.

"Wanting a baby."

We held each other's gaze.

"Why did you do that?" Hassani's light eyes darted between mine. "Why did you keep wanting a baby from me? You never said *anything*?"

I released a weighted exhale. "You worked really *hard* to get this project, Hassani—"

"Nah, man."

Hassani closed the space between us, moving off the couch and onto his knees in front of me.

And just like that, my eyes started to water.

Tears welled beneath my lower lids.

Because I knew.

I knew exactly why I kept this from him.

Hassani had just made me realize something huge.

The very thing that kept me from serious romantic relationships in the past—the fear of losing myself, the way my mother had when my father died... the way Aunt Laurie had when she found out her husband was living a double life.

In a different form, that was the life I was living, too.

Keeping my desires hidden.

Holding my own heart hostage.

"I just thought it wasn't the right time," I told him. "It wasn't a big deal at first. I haven't felt this way the *whole* time. I promise. The baby fever just... slammed right into me that night at Bryant's Greene Garden's event."

Hassani watched me closely.

"It wasn't even him and his wife that made me want it," I continued. "It was just... *seeing* what was possible."

"You should've *told* me that, though," Hassani spoke softly, his hand running up my thigh. "You should've said something. I would've figured it out. *We* would've figured it out."

His touch was warm. Reassuring.

"Don't do that again, aight?"

I nodded.

"If I can't make the mistake of not listening to you about people and situations ever again," he added, "then you can't keep things to yourself like that, okay?"

"Okay," I echoed.

"No matter how big or small you think it is…" Hassani pressed his hand to the side of my face. "Tell me."

"Okay, then…" I swallowed, steadying myself. "I stopped taking my pills."

Hassani's brows wrinkled.

I'd been holding this in since my OB-GYN appointment, but right now?

This felt like the right time to say it.

"I got the prescription to refill my birth control, but I haven't picked it up… and I don't want to."

His reaction was instant.

"Good." He winked. "Don't pick it up."

Then, softly, he pinched my chin.

"We don't need them anymore, anyway." His smile bloomed, and so did mine. "'Cause you know… we got babies to make. Lots and lots of babies."

I laughed as his thumb brushed my cheek.

"Man, see?" He kissed his teeth. "This would've been a dope ass story to tell our kids."

I squinted, confused.

"How their big sister or brother was made in a hotel on wheels, but *noooo*." He playfully rolled his eyes. "'We gotta listen to Dr. Aldridge,' Ayla says. 'It'll be good,' she says."

I burst out laughing.

"Unless… you know…" he mused, his voice low and tempting.

His eyes flicked toward the private room.

Then, his brows jumped.

I laughed even harder.

We didn't have sex that night.

Instead, we finished the movie—this time with me curled up in Hassani's arms—before falling asleep and him carrying me to bed.

The next morning, I woke to the gentle movement of the RV.

I blinked my eyes open and stretched my arm to my right, feeling the bed was empty beside me.

Frowning, I sat up, my gaze drifting forward.

Through the window, I watched as trees rushed by.

We were moving.

I got out of bed, padding across the wood floors, struggling to keep my balance as I made my way to the front of the RV.

And there, behind the wheel sat Hassani.

Hands gripping the steering wheel, focus locked on the road.

"What's going on?" I rasped, my voice still thick with sleep.

He peeked over his shoulder, grinning. "Good morning, sleepyhead."

I plopped down in the passenger seat, hooking my seatbelt.

"Good morning to you too," I muttered, rubbing my face.

Then, I frowned.

"Shouldn't you be a sleepyhead too? Where are we going?"

Hassani smirked. "We need to drop off the RV at its partner location."

"Drop off the RV?"

"Yeah."

I stared at him. "We're not driving back to New York?"

His smirk widened. "We are *not* driving back to New York."

I leaned forward, narrowing my eyes. "Hassani, what is going on?"

He laughed.

"It's a surprise."

He glanced at me. "Just go back there, do what you do in the bathroom, and be ready to go when we drop off the RV."

I didn't move. Still suspicious.

"You trust me, right?" he asked, shooting me a quick glance before refocusing on the road.

"Of course."

"Then go on and do what I said. Let me maintain the surprise, woman." He shot another look my way. "Go."

I snickered as I unhooked my seatbelt and headed to the bathroom.

I went through my routine, and at the end of it, gathered my chunky twists—the ones I twisted yesterday before the movie—into a messy bun.

Rinsing my face with cool water and showering in the RV's shower stall.

By the time I was done, I heard the RV's reverse beeper, signaling Hassani was backing up.

Stepping out of the bathroom, I watched him unbuckle and rise from his seat.

"You ready?" he asked.

I smirked. "Ready for what… I don't know."

Hassani just grinned.

I was so confused as Hassani and I made our way to the RV rental office, handing over the RV keys.

"We got everything off the RV, right?" he asked.

"Yeah," I confirmed. "I double-checked before stepping out."

"Aight, cool."

He pulled out his phone, tapping away.

I squinted. "You're driving me crazy with the suspense, baby."

We stood in the lot, surrounded by other luxury RVs—each one just as beautiful as the one we'd spent the past week in, calling it home.

Hassani tucked his phone into his back pocket.

"Car will be here in ten minutes," he informed me. "You wanna wait inside?"

I gave him a pointed look.

"*I wanna…*" I said, mimicking his voice dramatically.

Hassani burst out laughing.

"…know what the *hell* is going on."

He wrapped an arm around my shoulders, pulling me in. "I'm flying you out."

My brows shot up. "Wait, what?"

"Remember when I told you Bryant said I could take two weeks off?"

"*Uh-huh.*"

"Well," he started, "we just spent the first week on a road trip… now we're gonna spend the next week somewhere *very* familiar."

I gasped so hard my ears rang. "What?! Where?!"

Hassani just grinned. "Somewhere *very* familiar."

I clutched my chest. "Oh my God, Hassani! Just tell me where we're going."

He tucked his lips into his mouth and shook his head. All I could do was laugh.

Last year, we hadn't gone on our annual summer trip.

This year, I worried it would be the same.

But now...

First, he took me on a road trip. And now we were flying out to... somewhere familiar?!

I was beside myself.

Where on earth was this *somewhere familiar*?

For the next few minutes, as we waited for our black car, I peppered him with questions.

"Is it somewhere warm?"

"Of course."

"By a beach?"

"*Definitely* by a beach." He smirked. "That's why I told you to pack swimsuits."

My stomach fluttered. "I totally forgot about that! I thought it was a little weird when you told me to pack swimsuits for a road trip, but I just rolled with it."

I'd been dreaming about stretching out under the sun and letting my skin glow.

Ever since I found my camera and saw the honeymoon photos, the urge to be a beach bunny had only grown stronger.

The black car pulled up in front of us.

"Come on." Hassani took my hand. "We have a flight to catch."

The ride to the airport was short.

It wasn't until we stepped out of the car that I realized something.

"Wait..." I looked around. "We're in Florida?"

Hassani chuckled. "Yup."

I blinked. "When did we get to *Florida*?!"

He smirked, shutting the car door after thanking the driver.

"Where we parked the RV last night was in a town that borders

Florida," he explained. "I drove a little through the night so we could make this flight."

My heart melted.

I knew I couldn't love this man any more than I already did… but then he went and did things like *this*.

"Baby," I whispered, still in awe. "I can't believe we're flying out somewhere, and I have no idea where we're going. But I'm *so* stoked!"

He hooked an arm around my neck and pressed a kiss to my forehead. "Anything for you."

Taking my hand, he said, "Let's get checked in and grab our tickets before we miss the flight."

We made our way to the check-in desk, then approached the flight board.

Hassani leaned down, his lips brushing my ear.

"Our flight number is DL421," he murmured. "Tell me where we're going."

I squinted up at the departure board, scanning for the number.

Then my eyes grew like saucers.

ST. LUCIA.

I gasped.

Then, even harder.

I turned and jumped into Hassani's arms.

He caught me, laughing, as I covered his face in kisses.

People around us chuckled softly, watching our public display of joy.

"I love you."

Hassani pecked my lips once. "I love you."

My feet hit the ground as we grabbed our tickets.

As we approached TSA, I looked up at him, still in disbelief. "Saint Lucia, baby?"

He winked. "Saint Lucia, baby."

The airport buzzed with its usual chaos.

Flight announcements echoing.

Travelers rushing to gates.

But inside, I felt light.

Like I was floating.

I was in a dream, living and loving every second of it.

Hassani and I grabbed our things after making it through TSA. He draped an arm over my shoulder as we headed to our gate, me talking a mile a minute, still riding the high of finding out Saint Lucia was our destination—completely unaware he'd slid my passport into his carry-on days ago before we left for our road trip.

Somewhere in the background noise, I heard a laugh.

A *very* familiar laugh—one I could pick out in even the loudest of places, including an airport.

I stopped walking immediately and froze.

My head turned toward the sound, my brows furrowing.

Hassani frowned. "What's up?"

I heard it again.

And this time, I knew exactly who it belonged to.

My Aunt Laurie.

Standing at a coffee kiosk, laughing that signature, infectious laugh of hers.

The one that always reminded me of Jackée Harry's.

"Oh my God... is *that* Aunt Laurie?!"

Hassani whipped his head around, following my gaze.

"That *is* her." I inhaled a deep breath, cupped my hands around my mouth, and yelled, "Aunt Laurie!"

She turned her head, her long, sleek hair whipping through the air.

Her eyes widened, and that gigantic, pageant-winning grin she always had—the one that reminded me of Whitney Houston's signature smile—took over her face.

I didn't even think.

I took off running.

Aunt Laurie did the same, meeting me halfway, and when we finally collided, she wrapped her arms so tight around me I could barely breathe.

"Favorite Girl!" she shrieked. "What the fuck?!"

I hollered a laugh, stepping back to take her in.

My eyes scanned her, from her perfectly styled hair to the flowy, low-cut sundress she wore so effortlessly.

My aunt, in her late fifties, looked amazing—not a day over forty.

"You look *fabulous*."

"And you look *gorgeous*. My goodness, you sex kitten," She ran a hand down my twists, then over my shoulders. Her eyes narrowed playfully. "Your hips got rounder, ass fatter… and my goodness, these boobs are looking so full with your sexy self. Look at my girl!"

I leaned my head back in a laugh. "What the hell are you doing here?"

"I should be asking *you* that." She giggled. "I'm in my natural habitat. Are you kidding *me*? You're technically trespassing."

I pinched her and she laughed.

"I knew the only way I'd see you was if I sprouted wings and flew alongside whatever plane you're always escaping on."

She hollered a laugh, pulling me back in for another tight hug.

This time, it was longer, warmer.

I squeezed her back. "I missed you *so* much."

"And I missed you *more*."

Behind me, I heard Hassani chuckle.

"Hey, Aunt Laurie," he greeted. "Random seeing you here."

She turned, patted his chest, and pulled him into a hug—one that forced him to bend his knees just to meet her height.

"Random ain't even the word." She grinned, her eyes bouncing between us. "You two look phenomenal. Where are you off to?"

"Saint Lucia." I lit up. "Hassani surprised me with it *literally* minutes ago."

Aunt Laurie's smile stretched even wider. She held up her hand and gave Hassani a high five. "My Favorite *Guy*."

I snickered. "And you? Where are you headed?"

She batted her lashes. "France. Cannes."

Just then, a young man approached.

Instinctively, I stepped aside, assuming he was just passing by…

But to my surprise, he stopped beside Aunt Laurie.

"Oh, perfect!" She turned and pressed a hand to his chest. "This is Kofi," she introduced. "My boyfriend… and my *lover.*"

I blinked. Hard.

But I still managed to smile.

I extended my hand. "Hi."

"Hello." His deep, rich skin stood out against the crisp white shirt he wore. His face was young. "Kofi."

I nodded and smiled. "Nice to meet you, Kofi." Then I turned back to my aunt.

"He doesn't speak much English," she explained. "But I've been teaching him… and he's been teaching me his."

Aunt Laurie looked so happy.

Vibrant.

Whatever Kofi was doing, it was working.

"That's great." I smiled, squeezing her hands. "I'm so happy you're dating again and have a boyfriend… emphasis on *boy.*"

"Aht!" She smacked my hand.

"How old is he?"

"Thirty."

I folded my lips into my mouth, struggling to hold back my smile. "Aunt Laurie!"

She giggled.

"Has Mom seen him yet?"

"Not yet. But soon."

"Make sure when you bring him to New York, I'm there. Because I *gotta* see her face when she meets him." I smirked. "I would really hate to miss it."

She slapped my arm, while Hassani extended his hand to Kofi.

"Pleasure to meet you," Hassani said.

Kofi just smiled, accepted Hassani's hand while offering a polite nod.

"Anyway," Aunt Laurie said, "we have a flight to catch."

"And so do we," Hassani added.

I pulled her in for another hug, pressing a big kiss to her cheek. "I love you."

"And I love you." She kissed my cheek in return. "I'll see you very soon."

"I'll be waiting."

One last squeeze, then I stepped back, focusing on Kofi.

"It was great meeting you."

He pressed his hands together, bowing softly.

He did the same to Hassani.

"Nice meeting you," Hassani said to Kofi, then extended an arm to Aunt Laurie who gave him a big hug. "You two have a safe flight."

Aunt Laurie patted Hassani's chest again then she winked at me. "And you two do the same."

"Enjoy, Aunt Laurie," I teased.

"Oh, Favorite Girl." She smirked. "I always do."

I giggled, shifting my gaze to her boyfriend and smiling. "Bye, Kofi."

I stood there, watching as my aunt and her young, beautiful boyfriend disappeared into the crowd.

A deep chuckle rumbled beside me. Hassani draped an arm over my shoulder.

"One of these days," he mused, "we're gonna have to capture her in a mason jar and spin the cap on real tight so she can't escape this time."

I laughed, pressing into his side, wrapping my arms around him.

"Nah," I said in an undertone, watching Aunt Laurie and her boyfriend fade into the distance. "Getting older has taught me Aunt Laurie is a wildflower—you can't capture her. You just admire her… then let her go, and miss her terribly after."

I inhaled a deep breath, letting my words settle in my heart, knowing I'd see her soon… just like she said.

Hassani squeezed my hand. "Come on," he said, guiding us toward our gate.

～

MY SPIRITS WERE ALREADY SOARING AFTER THE ROAD TRIP AND Hassani's surprise flight, but when we deplaned and followed a driver in a crisp black suit holding a sign with our last name, I felt like I was floating.

The entire drive to the villa, I had my head practically out the window, soaking up all the sights I was so happy to see again.

When the villa from our honeymoon came into view, my heart stopped.

As soon as the driver pulled up to the grand entrance, I was hit with a rush of memories.

Everything felt the same.

Stepping out of the black car.

Walking through the arched doorway.

The sprawling living room, the romantic bedroom, the daybed outside by the infinity pool.

I pressed a hand to my chest and sighed, taking it all in.

"I thought the only way I'd see this place again was in my dreams."

Hassani came up behind me, wrapping his arms around my waist, bending his knees to kiss my neck… lingering there.

The last time we were here, we'd woken up on that daybed by the pool, wrapped up in each other, watching the sunrise. I had no idea what life would hold for us when we left, but I knew one thing—as long as I had Hassani, I would be fine.

We popped a bottle of champagne and sank into the plush seating inside, our laughter filling the space as we recounted all the hilarious moments from the road trip.

"We *have* to do it again," I said between sips, my face glowing from the warmth of the champagne.

"Already planning it." Hassani winked.

As the sun dipped lower, we made our way to the beach, basking in the soft, golden light of our first evening back in Saint Lucia.

According to Hassani's itinerary, the next few days would be packed—scuba diving, dining on the beach, a sunset cruise.

But tonight, we just wanted good food and an early night.

By the time we returned to the villa, I was ready to collapse into bed.

That was… until Hassani pulled out a small bottle of oil.

"Can I give you a massage?"

I turned, midway through pulling off my sundress, prepared to toss it over a chair for later retrieval.

"A massage?"

Hassani held up a sleek glass bottle of edible massage oil.

I burst into laughter.

"Where did you get that from?"

He smirked. "I had it delivered to the villa before we arrived."

My lips parted.

It was *the* oil.

The same chocolate-coconut blend we first received in a honeymoon gift basket from the resort where our villa was.

The one he used to wake me up before sexing me senseless.

The one I used on *him* before our final sunrise session on our last day.

It tasted like melted chocolate and coconuts.

It felt like sin.

And now, it was back… so were we.

"'Cause what kind of trip would this be if we didn't have this on hand?"

I wrapped my arms around his waist, shaking my head. "Not one I'd want to be on."

He licked his lips. "So? Can I give you that massage?"

Of course, I said yes.

After a steamy shower, I lay face down on the villa's luxurious bed, my bare skin cooling against the crisp sheets.

Hassani warmed the oil between his hands, then rubbed it on my back.

His strong hands smoothed it into my skin, gliding down my spine, his thumbs digging gently into my lower back.

And I couldn't keep in how good his hands felt on me.

"You sound *so* good," he spoke under his breath, his voice husky.

"*You* feel good," I whispered.

His palms swept over my ass, moving lower, massaging my thighs.

Then…

His fingers grazed my slit.

A deep moan spilled from my lips, my face burying into the pillow.

And right then, I knew.

Our two-week rule expired that morning, and I was hoping we would celebrate it when I woke up. Instead, I woke up to a moving RV with Hassani behind the wheel.

One of the key signs Dr. Aldridge had told us to look for before reintroducing intimacy was were we both ready? Which I definitely was.

Lying there, I mentally checked off every single thing she told us to watch for.

Emotional safety? Check.

Open communication? Check.

Feeling like best friends again? Check.

Physical affection that didn't just lead to sex? Check. Check. Check.

And now?

Even if we hadn't hit every mark, there was no way I could hold out any longer.

We were in Saint Lucia.

I was horny.

And I was *done* denying myself.

I turned onto my back.

Hassani's smirk stretched into a slow, knowing smile.

"What are you doing?" he asked.

I held his gaze, my breath catching.

Because this wasn't just lust.

This wasn't just hunger.

This was safety.

This was trust.

This was healing.

And we'd earned every bit of it.

I grabbed his hard dick through his linen pants, using my hold to pull him closer.

"Our two weeks are up."

"Is it?" He smirked. "Wow, I had *no* idea. It's not like… I've been counting down every minute of every day and conveniently planning this trip just in time for *that*… or anything."

I gasped. "What?!"

He licked his lips. "What, *what*?"

I giggled. "Aside from that, you big ol' sneak…"

He laughed.

"We've done everything Dr. Aldridge told us to do," I said, shifting onto my knees and rising until I was eye-level with him on the bed. "Everything… except mutually agreeing we're ready."

His hazel-green eyes darkened.

He licked his lips. "Aight?"

I traced my finger along his collarbone, watching the way his chest rose and fell under my touch.

"I feel we're healing," I whispered. "Do you?"

"I do."

No hesitation. No doubt. Just truth.

I lowered my hands to the waistband of his boxers, hooking my fingers there and pushing them down.

"Are you ready to reintroduce—"

Before I could finish my sentence, his mouth crashed into mine, swallowing my laughter as it melted into a moan when our bodies hit the soft mattress.

His hips angled against mine, the thick weight of him pressing right where I ached the most.

I braced myself, inhaling sharply, my breath catching at the first push inside.

Deep. Full.

A perfect, homecoming stretch.

"I'm more than ready," he exhaled against my lips as he sank into me. "And for real, A?" He groaned against me. "We've *earned* this, baby."

"*Mm-hmm,*" I moaned.

We moved slow and sure, his hand finding mine, fingers interlocking, grounding us.

I clung to his shoulders, my bottom lip folding into my mouth, trapping a smile between moans.

God, I'd missed him.

Not just physically, but emotionally.

And damn, that was a good-ass combination.

His lips found my neck, lingering there as he set a rhythm we could get lost in.

A few strokes in, he paused, balancing on his forearms to look down at me.

His gaze searched mine, his fingers tracing my jawline.

"I can't believe how close I came to losing this," he admitted, voice thick with emotion. "Losing you."

I shook my head, pressing my fingertips to his lips, and he kissed them. "You *never* could."

His body shuddered.

With a low, gravelly groan, he resumed his deep, steady thrusts, drawing a sigh of pleasure from me with each push forward.

"*God*, I love you," I breathed.

He kissed his way from my neck to my lips, whispering against my mouth, "I love you more, baby."

Our movements synced, a slow, sensual dance—one we knew by heart.

And just like that, we were back.

Back here in Saint Lucia.

Back home in each other.

Back to us.

CHAPTER 21

$\mathscr{H}$assani

"Oh, wow." Ayla exhaled beside me. "*Wow.*"

I snickered to myself, turning the steering wheel as I guided my car to the left.

That was all she'd been saying since we passed the *Welcome to Greene Gardens* sign.

"Whoa." She sighed again. "That's a whole park."

I smiled, nodding. "A *whole* park."

"And this is like... a real road." She craned her neck, eyes peering through the passenger window. "And those are sidewalks."

I grinned. "A road and sidewalks."

She nudged me. "Shut up."

I laughed with her. "What? I'm just saying—you're amazed by my roads, sidewalks, and parks."

"And houses, and businesses." She gestured outside. "And, and, and..."

I hollered a laugh.

We'd landed only three hours ago from Saint Lucia. After dropping off our bags at home, I told Ayla I wanted to show her something.

We were still riding the high from our trip—the memories fresh, the energy light. Which made this the perfect time to drive out to Greene Gardens.

She shook her head, her cloud of defined coils shifting with the motion. "I wasn't expecting this."

"What were you expecting?"

"Vast land," she replied, turning to face me. "Maybe two or three houses here and there. Dirt roads. Honestly, open spaces."

I listened proudly, watching as her eyes shifted from one structure to the next.

"This is almost complete." She turned back to the window, taking it all in. "*My* man did this."

"Well… I helped *design* it, with my team."

"No, *you* did this." She laid a hand on my arm, her fingers stroking my forearm. "I feel like I'm about to cry because we are literally driving through your doodle. We're inside your vision. We're in another one of your dreams again. This time on wheels."

I peeked over at her just in time to see her eyes welling up.

Taking her hand, I brought it to my lips, kissing it gently.

"Now I see why you were working so hard in that office of yours." She sighed. "An office *I've* never seen."

I glanced at her, surprised. "That can't be. You've been to the office."

She shook her head. "I haven't. I didn't bother visiting because I figured you were working so hard on *this*." She gestured outside. "And it's not like you invited me or anything…"

Damn.

I scratched the side of my head. "I'm sorry about that, A. Boogie."

"It's okay."

"No, we *gotta* change that before you head back to school in August."

Like every school year, Ayla was set to return to Park Avenue Prep to set up her classroom, plan her curriculum, and attend staff orientation before the new term started in September.

"Hassani, you don't have to do that."

I took her hand again, kissing her knuckles. "I *want* to. Very much."

Peeking over at her, I caught her smiling.

"The team would love to see you," I added.

"All except *one*, I'm sure."

"Well, *that one* I'm pretty sure you're talking about? She's not there anymore."

Her brows lifted.

"Her office was cleared out before I left for our trip. She's gone."

"*Hmph.*"

I knew that while our road trip and island getaway had brought us closer, it would still take time for Ayla to fully move past the Harper situation.

But we'd get there.

Suddenly, Ayla gasped. "*Ooh*, that lake is gorgeous! It's so scenic, like a painting in a museum."

I slowed the car, pulling over a few feet from the shoreline.

"I'm glad you like it."

She smiled softly.

"Because you're gonna be seeing a lot of it."

Her brows furrowed. "What?"

I gestured with my head. "Come with me."

Grabbing my sketchbook from the side compartment, I stepped out of the car and made my way around to help her out.

I focused on her bejeweled sandals, realizing I probably should have told her to wear sneakers since the dirt might get into them as we walked closer to the lake.

As we made our way toward the water, I could feel her eyes drifting between me and our surroundings.

All of the custom lots had already been sold. I was one of the first —if not *the* first—to secure mine.

And I knew exactly which one I wanted from the moment I first toured Greene Gardens.

It was *this* lake.

The first time I saw it, I knew.

It fit the vision I'd been creating since 2017.

I led Ayla towards the grassy area near the water.

"This view is amazing," she said softly. "It's mad tranquil."

I snorted. "Tranquil?"

"Yeah," she whispered this time. "*Very* peaceful."

"It's *ours*."

"Huh?" She whipped her head in my direction so fast. "The *lake* is *ours*?"

I laughed. "Nah, baby, not the lake." I turned her to look at the land behind it. "This lot is ours."

Ayla stood there for a moment, staring. "To do what with?"

I opened my sketchbook and flipped through a few pages until I landed on the sketch of the villa I'd been working on for years.

"To do *this*." I held the sketchbook out in front of us.

"Oh my God," she whispered at first. "Oh my God!" She said louder this time. "Is that the villa in Saint Lucia?"

She looked up at me, then back at the book, taking it out of my hand. "Did you sketch the entire villa, Hassani?!"

"I did."

"Hassani!" She pressed a hand to her mouth. "This looks exactly like it. You drew it *exactly* like it."

"Because we're gonna build it." I pointed out in front of us at the land. "Exactly like it. Right *here*."

Her hand flew back to her mouth again. "What?!"

Ayla gasped and reached for the sketchbook, her fingers trembling slightly as she flipped through the pages. "Hassani..." Her voice was barely a whisper, her eyes darting between the sketches and the land in front of her. "You... you've been planning this?"

I just nodded, my eyes locked on her watering ones.

"I've been working on it for a while," I told her. "Us going back to Saint Lucia was for us to reconnect and for me to sketch the parts of the villa I was unable to remember from memory."

Ayla glanced at the land again, then at the lake.

I turned her by her shoulders and held up the sketchbook.

"We'll put the infinity pool right here," I explained, pointing ahead of us. "The wraparound balcony…" I turned her again. "Over there."

She brought the sketchbook closer to her, her beautiful fingers leafing through the pages as I held it. "All these pages are sketches for the villa?"

"All of them in this part of the sketchbook," I explained. "The ones in the other section are for home improvement projects for our house."

She stopped leafing and rested on one of them.

"Wow," she whispered. "I remember standing right *here*."

Ayla touched the sketched outline of the infinity pool, her fingertips tracing the lines like she was memorizing them.

"On our last night in Saint Lucia during our honeymoon, we stood by the pool, and I told you…" She exhaled, blinking rapidly. "I told you I never wanted to leave."

I kissed her forehead. "So, I made sure we'd never have to again."

She parted her lips. "This entire time…" Ayla shook her head. "All this time, I thought you were working when you were sketching in this book."

"I was," I replied, wrapping my arm around her waist and bringing her closer to me. "On my most important work. *This*."

Ayla blinked, and tears streamed down her face. I wiped them away, and she took a breath.

"This book." I held it up beside us. "This isn't work for *work*. This book is *only* for things that only we can enjoy, baby. Only us. *Just* us."

Ayla closed her eyes and moved in even closer. She balanced herself on the arches of her feet to press her lips to mine. "My God, you're amazing," she said on my lips.

"Like attracts like," I said back, pecking her twice. "Because baby you're amazing, too."

My hand was in hers as I walked us to the land where the villa would sit.

"We start building in a month," I told her. "We are standing right now in our forever summer home."

"Ayla wrapped her arms around me again, tighter this time, pressing her face to my chest as I closed my eyes."

We had been lost, but we had found our way back.

Here, on this land we'd one day call our second home, I realized—we weren't just healing.

We were building something new.

Something stronger.

Something that would cement our forever.

EPILOGUE

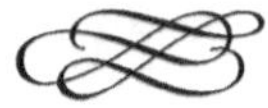

ONE YEAR LATER – EARLY SUMMER 2024

*H*assani

I STOOD AT THE BACK PATIO DOOR, STARING OUT AT THE LAKE IN FRONT of me. The water lay still, but the trees standing tall in the distance swayed with the gentle breeze. The infinity pool sparkled ahead, and I just knew Ayla would flip when she saw how much it resembled the one in Saint Lucia.

Ding-dong!

The doorbell ringing pulled me from my thoughts. I turned on my Jordans and headed for the door. When I pulled it open, two movers stood on the other side. Behind them, another mover was lifting the gate at the back of the truck.

"Hassani Franklin?" one of the movers asked.

"That's me." I smiled. "How y'all doing today?"

"Good, good." The mover nodded. "I'm Tony, and I'll be handling the move today with my guys. Are you ready for us?" He smiled next. "We've got all the furniture for the rooms ready to unload and set up."

"Music to my ears, man." I stepped back, opening the front door wider. "Go for it."

It was move-in day for the summer villa—the one that had once existed only as a vision and as unfinished sketches in my sketchbook.

"We'll start with the living room," Tony said, directing the other movers on where to place the couch for Ayla's and my living room set. "Do you have an idea of how you want things arranged?"

"I've got something better." I reached for my sketchbook, which was lying nearby, flipping it open to the page with the living room layout Ayla and I had worked on together. "This is *exactly* where everything should go."

Tony's blue eyes widened as he glanced at the sketch, then back at me. "Did you draw *this?*"

I nodded. "I did. I've been sketching this for a really long time."

"*Damn.* You an artist or something?"

"An architect," I replied proudly. "I designed the properties in this neighborhood—including the one we're standing in right now."

His jaw dropped. "Get out of here!"

"Hey, Tony," one of the other movers called behind him. He and another mover held part of the sectional Ayla and I ordered. "Where we putting this, boss?"

Tony shook his head, snapping out of his awe, then chuckled. "*Uh...*" He glanced at the sketch again before turning to the mover. "Right here."

His reaction was one I'd grown used to since the start of Ayla's and my summer home project. I had been here for every step of the build, checking in on the progress daily after work and spending weekends with Ayla overseeing details when she was off from school.

I watched as the movers carried in our furniture, setting the pieces down—the side tables in the living room, our king-sized bed in the master bedroom. Then, I stepped outside onto the patio, letting them do their thing.

So much had changed in a year.

A year ago, I didn't know if I'd ever get the chance to build this villa, let alone stand on its patio. My mind drifted back to the day I came here, when this spot was nothing but dirt and rocks. I had prayed on this very soil, asking for the chance to make my wife happy again, to live the life we had always dreamed of.

I smiled, pressing my hand against the patio railing, my eyes following the gentle ripples on the lake. The tranquil waters, as Ayla called them.

And in that moment, I realized something.

God had answered every single one of my prayers.

Even my wish for a baby... the one I had whispered in a new prayer the moment Ayla told me she wanted one.

I rubbed my hands together absentmindedly, wringing them a little before pressing a hand to my chest, a nervous tick I'd developed lately.

Ayla was pregnant.

And while I was excited as hell, I was nervous, too.

I wanted this. God knew I wanted *this*. But more than anything, I wanted to be a great father. I had one, and my life had been blessed exponentially because of how great my dad is. I wanted to be that for my son, too.

I had cried that January morning when Ayla's pregnancy test came back positive. Cried even harder when the doctor confirmed we were having a boy months later. And while I was thrilled, I couldn't shake the fear of the unknown.

The only thing that kept me from worrying too much was Ayla.

She was made to be a mother.

She had always loved children—babysitting as a side hustle back in high school, being the kind of teacher her preschoolers adored. I *knew* she would excel at it.

But me?

I had designed homes. Built entire communities. But I had no blueprint for fatherhood.

What if I messed this up?

I knew figuring it all out would be an adventure. But I looked forward to embarking on that adventure with Ayla. Plus, there wasn't a single day that went by when she didn't reassure me how amazing of a father I would be.

And whenever I thought about her confidence in me, my anxiety always faded.

She had always been supportive, even as I worked toward becoming the principal architect of the Greene Gardens Project.

Speaking of which, things had been running smoothly at work since Harper was long gone.

Issues were minimal, and whenever one did pop up, resolving it was never stressful. My team was excellent, and we were far ahead of schedule.

Harper didn't quit like Bryant had hoped, but she was out of our hair like he promised. I rarely thought about her anymore. She was just a name in my past, where she belonged.

Greene Gardens was now open to new residents and business owners. There was still plenty of work left to do, but so far, everything looked beautiful.

It was exactly what I had envisioned with my team. What I had envisioned *myself*.

I turned to look inside the house through the patio's glass doors, my heart swelling with excitement.

The movers were placing brand-new furniture exactly where it belonged, Tony glancing down at my sketchbook and pointing out placements based on what Ayla and I had mapped out.

Life was unfolding exactly how I had imagined.

The only thing missing in this house was my wife. My friend. My Ayla.

My eyes moved around the exterior of our summer home, taking it all in. I had nailed every detail, making it look like an exact replica of the villa she loved so much.

She had one week left in the school year. After that, she'd be on summer break, free to spend *all* her time here—or as much as she wanted

I let my eyes drift over the property again, imagining it full. A home alive with love, laughter, and more than just Ayla and our son.

Because I wanted a big family.

And I knew Ayla did, too.

I wanted to give her everything she had ever dreamed of.

She deserved it. *We* deserved it.

And now, *finally*, we had it.

∽

AYLA

I AIMED MY CAMERA, ADJUSTING THE FOCUS BEFORE PRESSING THE shutter button.

A warm breeze lifted the hem of my summer dress, brushing against my knee as I relaxed on the patio lounge.

It was my first late afternoon at our summer home.

Ever since touring the property on the day the movers arrived, I had been counting down the days until the school year ended.

I ran a hand over my growing belly and smiled.

Our baby boy was in there, nice and comfy.

At my last doctor's appointment, Dr. Whitfield had joked that this time last year, she had said a little prayer for Hassani and me to give her a baby to deliver this year.

She'd get her wish this October.

I glanced down at the LCD screen on my camera, admiring the shot I had just taken.

Then, lifting the camera again, I adjusted the focus and waited for the blur to settle before pressing the shutter button once more.

Last year, at this time, I was telling Hassani I wanted a divorce.

A divorce.

I shook my head, inhaling deeply.

The thought flashed in my mind, intrusive, like an unwelcome guest trying to ruin a perfect moment.

Then, Harper's name crept in, threatening to stir emotions I didn't want to entertain.

But before I could spiral, I closed my eyes and followed my therapist's advice.

"I acknowledge this memory, I accept that it happened, and I send it away with love," I whispered.

The weight of it lifted, slowly at first, then all at once.

When I opened my eyes, I was met with the breathtaking view before me.

Serenity.

Love.

When Hassani first brought me here, I couldn't believe my eyes.

I couldn't *believe* that ever since we had returned from our honeymoon in 2017, he had been quietly sketching his own version of the Saint Lucia villa we had stayed in.

It seemed neither of us had wanted to forget our time there.

And instead of wishing and hoping to return, we now had it.

Our summer home—a perfect replica of the Saint Lucian villa, complete with an infinity pool that offered the illusion of it spilling into the lake.

Lifting my camera again, I moved it around, searching for my next shot.

Incorporating photography lessons into my preschool curriculum this past school year had been one of the best decisions I had made.

My babies at school had loved it.

Every morning, as soon as their little feet stepped into my classroom, they would ask if we could start taking pictures.

I already missed them.

School had only just let out, but I was already making mental notes to include photography in my curriculum again next year—right before I left for maternity leave.

I was *so* excited to be a mother.

Sunni had already put together a gift registry for me and was planning my baby shower.

She told me to leave it *all* to her.

I wouldn't.

But I loved knowing she was there for me, like always.

She had been one of the people who had encouraged me not to be afraid of love.

And I was so grateful to have such a solid sisterhood with her.

I watched as the clouds shifted over the water, a soft, lazy dance against the sky.

Then, in a whisper, I spoke into the quiet.

"Life is good."

And with that, I pressed the shutter button.

I caught sight of Hassani as he stepped out of the house and walked over to one of the lounge chairs, sinking into it with a sigh.

Smirking, I lifted my camera, aimed it at him, and pressed the shutter button.

He playfully struck a model pose, making me laugh.

I thought back to when we were just teenagers at Garvey High in Long Island—how I used to photograph him while he trained for his track meets, just because.

And now, here I was, photographing him again. Only this time, as my husband, while carrying his firstborn.

Life.

So damn beautiful.

"Would you just act natural?" I teased.

"I *am*." He winked. "Just make sure you get me from the perfect angle." He smiled, lowering his gaze to his sketchbook.

I inhaled a slow breath and let it out. My bottom lip quivered— until a soft smile eased it into place.

"My dad used to say something similar," I murmured, loud enough for Hassani to hear. "*Make sure you capture me at the perfect angle.*"

He smiled knowingly. "Great minds, huh?"

I nodded, echoing softly, "Great minds, indeed."

Because this man had designed a summer home just for us—one of our forever homes—and now, we would be spending the entire summer in it.

The soft scratch of his pencil against the page filled the air, a familiar and comforting sound.

I smiled as he worked, knowing that whatever he was sketching would become my new favorite thing.

"Let me guess," I mused. "You're sketching something new for the villa?"

He smirked but didn't answer right away. Instead, he lifted the sketchbook, tilting it just enough for me to see.

My breath caught.

It was a drawing... of me.

Sitting right here on the patio lounge chair, my round belly peeking out beneath my sundress.

Emotion swelled in my chest.

How silly I had been to assume he was *always* working when he was sketching in his book.

I remembered those first months of marriage, when we had just moved into our home and he'd spend hours sketching little projects for the house.

But once he started the Greene Gardens Project, I had figured the sketchbook became solely for work for *that* project.

I was *so* wrong.

Hassani has *always* been about us.

About his love for me.

About our future.

It was foolish to have *ever* thought otherwise.

Things had been so good since we returned from Saint Lucia.

And life got even better when we found out in January that we were expecting.

I was five months along now, and every day, I fell more and more in love with the life we were creating.

Hassani set his sketchbook down a moment later and made his way over to me.

When he arrived, he kneeled in front of me, pressing a gentle kiss against my belly.

I ran my fingers along the back of his head as he rested there, whispering something to our baby boy.

A second later... our baby kicked.

Hassani and I gasped at the same time.

His eyes shot up to mine, wide as ever.

"Did he just—?"

"Kick?!" I nodded quickly. *"Yes!"*

His entire face lit up with pure joy, and my heart melted on the spot.

"Has he ever done that before?" he asked, his voice filled with awe.

I smiled through my tears. "No. This is the first time."

Hassani let out a breathless laugh, his hand still resting over my belly.

"But from that kick," I mused, "I can already tell he's gonna make good use of those legs… just like his dad."

He chuckled. "And he's gonna be just as mathematically accurate as his mother—'cause he got me *good* just now."

I giggled, wiping at my eyes.

"You know how I always bring up how I used to call you in the middle of the night back in high school?" I asked.

Hassani grinned, his thumb tracing soft circles over my belly.

"Mm-hmm," he said. "And every time you bring it up, I remember how every time I saw your name on my phone, I knew I wasn't getting any sleep that night."

I smiled, brushing my fingers over his hand. "I think our son is going to be like me."

He arched a brow. "What, you mean calling me at 2 a.m.?"

"No." I laughed. "Keeping us up at all hours. You *do* know babies do that, right?"

Hassani groaned dramatically, shaking his head.

"See? I knew you two were gonna team up on me," he joked.

I radiated with joy, loving how light things felt between us now. How easily we could laugh again.

Then, he leaned in, pressing his lips against my forehead, and whispered, "And I can't wait. For every single moment of it."

My chest tightened with love as he cupped my face, bringing his lips down to mine in a deep, slow kiss.

Taking his time.

Savoring.

Loving.

"I love you, A. Boogie," he whispered against my lips.

I smiled, my heart bursting. "I love you, too, baby. So much."

He pulled away just enough to smirk.

"Come on," he said, standing up and holding his hand out for me to take. "It's time for you two to eat... and me too."

I laughed, letting him gently pull me to my feet.

As he led me inside, he pressed a soft kiss to my cheek.

I glanced back at my camera, sitting on the lounge chair, and smiled—excited to see what memories I could capture this summer.

Memories I would one day show to our son.

For now, I simply followed Hassani—the man of my dreams—into the home he created for us.

Our home.

Our summer dreams.

Life was so, so good. And I was beyond grateful it was all mine.

Mine... and mine only.

THE END.

AUTHOR'S NOTE

Dear reader,

Thank you for reading *My Only*. What a journey, right? If that prologue stole your breath… mission accomplished. 😂

I know seeing Ayla and Hassani on the brink of divorce may have shocked you. After their blissful ending in *My First, My Last*, this felt jolting. But their story isn't just "happily ever after"—it's about the work, the challenges, and the love it takes to hold onto that happily ever after.

That's why I anchored us in the wedding and honeymoon scenes—to show clearly what they were fighting to save. I wanted you deeply invested before Harper Royce tore into their world. She was the kind of antagonist authors dread to create because she was a pain and my daily push to return to the keyboard and write their survival story. Harper tested them… and me.

The building of Greene Gardens mirrors this. Hassani literally builds a village, all while needing one to help rebuild his marriage. Themes, symbols, spirals—they're everywhere, and you may catch something new with each read. I hope you do—this story is meant to be journeyed again.

It's been my joy to not only update these two but to give them a conclusion that feels as satisfying as the bold beginning of something new.

If this is your first BK book, welcome to my tribe. You're a Brookelynite now! If you're here from past reads, thank you for a decade of riding with me. 2025 marks ten years of this adventure, and I'm blessed by your support.

See you at the end of the next book!

Love,

Brookelyn (BK)

ACKNOWLEDGMENTS

First, thank you to my husband, my rock and fiercest supporter. You believe in me more than I sometimes believe in myself. Love you, babe!

To my two children, who adapt when Mom disappears into her writing zone: your understanding taught me time management, and you remind me every day I can do this. Thank you.

To my readers—those who email, DM, and comment—you're always in my thoughts as I write. I love your honesty and your strict energy at times. You know me well enough to know what awaits you on the page… and I wouldn't have it any other way.

Finally, a shout-out to me: I want to thank myself for sticking with this journey for ten whole consistent years. Still learning, still passionate, still excited for every new book.

Here's to many more adventures together. Thank you!

DELETED SCENES

Want more Ayla and Hassani?

If you're not ready to say goodbye just yet, I've got a special gift just for you. ♥

More to Love is an exclusive collection of deleted scenes—sweet, steamy, and full of heart—created especially for readers who wanted just a little more of these two.

You'll get instant access to *More to Love* when you join my mailing list. As a subscriber, you'll also be the first to hear about new releases, exclusive content, and behind-the-scenes extras.

Type this link in your browser to download for free (https://BookHip.com/SCTWATZ)

Because some love stories deserve more pages.

BOOK CLUB QUESTIONS

1. Before this story, how did your perception of Ayla and Hassani shift from *My First, My Last*? How did *My Only* deepen or complicate your feelings toward each character?

2. What did you think of their two-week "abstinence reset" in counseling? Did you find it effective in rebuilding their emotional connection? Why or why not?

3. Hassani's profession—and the architectural themes—play a central role. How do the "blueprint," "framework," "fault line," "renovation," and "forever home" section headings reflect their relationship journey?

4. How did the creation of Greene Gardens mirror the support system Ayla and Hassani needed? What's the role of a "village" in their journey toward healing?

5. How did Harper Royce's presence challenge the couple? Did you find her actions climactic or undercutting to the story's core themes?

6. The Franklins and Ayla's mother brought warmth, humor, and advice. Which parental moments stood out to you most, and how did those moments reinforce the theme of community?

7. From Hassani's whispered prayer on the land they would eventually build their summer home in Greene Gardens to moments at the altar, how did spirituality or faith contribute to the emotional texture of *My Only*?

8. The narrative emphasizes that they were first friends before lovers. How did their friendship save them—or put them to the test—as they transitioned into marriage?

9. What lessons about communication, commitment, or compromise did you take from Ayla and Hassani's marriage counseling scenes? Have you seen these reflected in your own relationships?

10. If you could step into their world for just one scene—whether it's the wedding, the honeymoon, the reset, or the pregnancy reveal— which moment would you choose, and why?

CHARACTER CAMEOS

Characters who appeared in My Only listed in no particular order. Find links to all titles via this link: (https://bit.ly/3QdG4c6)

Bryant Greene
Greed

Zoe Greene (neé Stewart)
Greed

Levi Weston
Cali & Lee

Calese Weston (neé Monroe)
Cali & Lee

ABOUT THE AUTHOR

Brookelyn Mosley is a captivating voice in the world of black romance literature. With a gift for weaving heartfelt narratives and steamy encounters, she invites readers on journeys of love, passion, and self-discovery. Through her compelling storytelling, Brookelyn celebrates the beauty of black love and explores the complexities of relationships with authenticity and depth. With over 40+ titles, her stories resonate with true-blue readers, touching hearts and inspiring conversations about love, identity, and resilience.

Connect With Me Online!

Facebook: http://facebook.com/brookelynmosley
Facebook Reading Group: Brookelynites Book Lounge
Instagram: @Brookelynmosley
My Website: BrookelynMosley.com
My Readers Website: BKBookLounge.com
My Mailing List: https://brookelynmosley.com/bk-insiders-club/

www.ingramcontent.com/pod-product-compliance
Lightning Source LLC
Chambersburg PA
CBHW031206310726
48969CB00001B/234